I0682123

PALLADIUM

BY EDDI SASENIC

First published in 2010 by Teulon Media Company
West Hill House, 6 Swains Lane,
London N6 6QS United Kingdom

© Copyright Teulon Media Company 2010

All rights reserved
ISBN: 0-9566-7820-3
ISBN-13: 978-0-9566-7820-1

The moral right of the author has been asserted.

EXCEPT WHERE ACTUAL HISTORICAL EVENTS AND
MARKET EVENTS ARE BEING DESCRIBED FOR THE
STORYLINE OF THIS NOVEL ALL SITUATIONS IN THIS
PUBLICATION ARE FICTICIOUS. THIS IS A WORK OF
FICTION AND ALL CHARACTERS IN THIS NOVEL ARE
FICTICIOUS, ANY SIMILARITY BETWEEN THEM AND
ANY INDIVIDUALS ALIVE OR DECEASED IS PURELY
COINCIDENTAL.

No part of this publication in any form including electronic
formats may be reproduced, stored in any retrieval system, or
transmitted in any form or by any means without the prior
permission in writing of the publisher, nor may it be circulated
in any binding, cover or form other than in which it is published
and without a similar condition including this condition being
imposed upon the subsequent purchaser. No part of this work
may be produced without the publisher's consent.

Front cover design by Marmalade World London

Over the last six days Baa and I had paid Enselma 80,000 dollars cash for the mud and even before the slender canoe bore her upstream he'd slipped away. Not an irresponsible man, Baa is just one of those annoyingly intuitive bastards who knows, really knows, when somehow things will work out. Slim guided him up a shallow creek to a bank where animals risked predation to lick a clay that contained something their bodies needed. Telling himself that every poison and every antidote, every disease and every remedy thrives within the jungle Baa tasted some before continuing farther into the green gloom. Eventually they reached a clearing where the teak-skinned man waited. Slim went off to fish.

The shaman, seemingly in beautifully modulated English, perhaps said but certainly conveyed to Baa that by focusing upon and performing rituals for an entity it could come into existence and have influence in our world. "Tell me something I didn't know," Baa said as he gifted him a polished greenstone.

The shaman morphed into an elderly seventeenth century European who said, "You really do imagine things are fixed points..." Baa felt this uncomfortable truth slither across the back of his neck; the shaman placed a small, comatose frog onto the palm of his right hand "... so perhaps you better see for yourself." Baa licked the back of the tiny amphibian then followed the shaman along a broad jungle path paved with massive slabs of stone.

They journeyed for a long time but Baa did not grow tired - something he thought might be to do with the clay. He was pretty certain the frog's secretions were hallucinogenic, yet he felt no effect. The path had now risen above the jungle and for the first time he noticed that the oddly shaped slabs underfoot did not butt together but overlapped. Later, when the trees were so far below them that he couldn't make them out other than as a solid green mass, he noticed that the path's edges curved downwards. Supposing this was to drain rainwater away, he wondered at the ingenuity of the path's builders and, still looking down, remarked on this to the shaman. Receiving no reply he looked for his companion and saw he was a good hundred yards ahead. Baa started to call out to the man to wait but the words died on his lips as he marveled at the millions of stars that surrounded him. The path was not just off the ground it was off the planet and leading him far out into space; below the earth was a blue, green and white glowing sphere and to the right was a full yellow-gray moon. Dizzy, he stumbled and could have slid and fallen from the path had not the shaman returned and caught his arm. "Come and you will see," he said as he led Baa onward into a vastness where they passed the sun.

The path broadened and then dropped. "We must take special care just here," cautioned the shaman as he led Baa down an incline to a flattish area where there were two small caves. Standing with their backs to these, he saw that there was a seam across the path a meter or so ahead of them after which it continued but was much narrower and darker. Remaining on the wide part, they sat down in front of the caves, and the shaman produced some dried fruit from a little skin bag tied to his belt; chewing on his portion of the fruit, Baa imagined the narrow part of the path was moving very slowly toward him but sliding beneath the seam. He mentioned this to the shaman and asked if the dried fruit was causing this illusion. "It is hardly an illusion," the shaman replied. "Now stand — for we will go back." Baa got to his feet, turned and started to follow the shaman up the incline; it was harder to clamber up than it had been to descend, and he sought to get a handhold between two ridged pieces of vertical stone and haul himself up. The stones moved, sliding soundlessly open to reveal an enormous yellow eye. Like a rabbit, Baa was paralyzed as the eye looked at, into and through him. After a while the stones slid back and the eye was hidden once more.

The shaman helped him up to where the path was level and broad again "Not many get to see that."

"Does...does it live there?" Baa asked. But the shaman only laughed. In fact he cackled and continued to do so until they were getting back into the jungle.

At the clearing they drank some water and a weary Baa suddenly realized that the eye was the pathway and the pathway was the eye. He turned and said, "The whole thing is a huge snake isn't it?"

"Of course," replied the shaman. Baa had another sudden realization but, before he could speak, he found himself in the river. It was now dark red and flowing with primal urgency. Something just beneath its surface bore him onward and he'd barely time to marvel at strange Dali-esque banks and overhangs before a white, foggy mucus enfolded him in an embrace of tepid death.

Back at the general store cum bar cum hotel that served as our base, I'd called Baa's satphone and discovered it was switched off. Cursing, I looked out through the doorway at the surrounding jungle where the vibrant perfumes of new life were, as ever, counterpointed with the stench of decomposition. Both Raphael, the pilot, and Socrates routinely referred to that great oxygenating lung of the planet as inferno verde – green hell.

From Raphael I learned his air taxi had burst some bit of its engine. Baa and I had hired the little plane for a week and used it to ferry mud out and dollars in every day. The local connection of a London agency had recommended the unlikely named Socrates and his son as our muscle and that connection's wish to protect their reputation ensured that those mens' loyalty was dependable, if unrelated to sufficient smarts or sobriety to relax me. Beer not coffee was their breakfast drink. Baa could be gone for days and in remote northern Amazonia, up toward the border with Venezuela, that delay would ensure at least an attempted robbery.

Calling Manaus, I booked another plane on a credit card to move me and the accumulated last of the mud into town. The price I'd had to pay to get an aged Learjet - yes they really sent a Lear - down on the seriously crap airstrip had eaten some of our profit but the deal was, all things considered, easy money. The grey-brown alluvial from local streams averaged 93.6 percent gold and was simple to refine: it would fetch over half a million 1999 U.S. dollars. The hundred or so grams of tiny yellow grains that Enselma's indigenous workforce had painstakingly separated out and she'd been paid extra for would be dropped back into it.

At Manaus airport, the local agent handed over the laptop satchel he'd had in his safe while the Lear's flight attendant carried my small, worn Globetrotter case into the terminal; it weighed less than twelve kilos. I upgraded from business to first class and checked that case through to London. The dried alluvial inside my smart laptop satchel weighed twenty-seven kilos and there was another nineteen kilos in my briefcase, but flying first you rarely get bothered about hand baggage weights. It wasn't bulky. On previous trips we'd always carried our bounty of dried sediment as hand baggage for the noble metals, especially gold, are so dense they occupy very little space. Had you thirteen metric tons of pure gold it would measure less than a cubic meter; however I was just one person and forty six kilos weighs forty six kilos; I cursed Baa's selfishness. I phoned a London freight agency with my flight details and arranged that they'd have someone to meet me on arrival at Heathrow to clear the alluvial with customs. I thanked them, went through the gate, and cursed Baa some more while struggling up the aircraft steps.

As the Boeing climbed through equatorial humidity I enjoyed my first glass of wine in a week then fell asleep with the strap of my locked satchel looped through the briefcase handle and wrapped around my wrist.

Waking hours later, the armrest's little LED screen told me we sped through the northern tropical night six miles above the Atlantic. That first class was almost free of fellow travelers encouraged broad nocturnal thoughts. Thousands of miles to the left lay the eastern United States where Vida now lived with new husband and an ever-increasing number of their children. Our three years of marriage had occurred by default and, although the split hadn't been without pain, each of us had been blessed with a lack of bitterness. Half the globe away to the right was my not-seen-for-more-than-a-dozen-years father and thousands of kilometers directly behind my similarly unseen, no-longer-missed mother lived in Argentina. Had all this wreckage damaged me? Quite probably, but I'd no intention of dwelling on it as I'd a life to get on with. I'd deal with such considerations little by little - a nest egg of disappointments to mull over in my old age perhaps. The pretty stewardess served what proved to be a very good meal during which I wondered about geographical symmetries of relationships.

●　●　●

Refining the alluvial gold was taking a few days in London and Baa called to say he was returning but would need to recuperate at home from his recent inner-space travels. The next afternoon my phone's caller ID displayed FatG.

George, who is no longer fat, says a Russian with platinum can't reach Baa. I feel something somewhere jar — know what I mean? That odd sensation, neither pleasant nor unpleasant but noticeable. George is a broker, and he only handled material once it was processed into market-acceptable form, so I supposed he was looking to get a deal together. In answer to my questions he tells me, "Rick I've got nothing on the guy. He only really talks with Baa but suddenly can't reach him."

I was due a little revenge "Got a number for Ivan?" I wrote it down then phoned Baa on his bedside line. "How are you feeling today sunshine?"

"Like a train hit me."

"That's the spirit — write this down." I gave him the number. "Some Russian's been phoning FG for you. I'm resting, so can't help I'm afraid?"

"You're in a very vindictive mood today, Dorothy. What's the guy want?"

"You apparently — you still speak Russian, don't you?"

"I'll not know 'til I try," Baa said and hung up.

Perhaps it was hiring that Lear with a card or some earlier extravagance I'd deemed vital that got me on a list that got me invited to a showcasing. Not my usual stroll in the woods, but Baa was taking care of business so why not?

The venue on Park Lane was a gathering of the self-possessed. Serious movers, theater and concert backers, sports entrepreneurs, wealth managers, savvy folk, media faces, and others who rarely flew commercial.

The invitation had been logo free, which suggested the promoters would be looking for sponsors as well as investors. I'd a gut feeling that cash was funding the canapés and champagne, that actual banknotes had moved, and that all sorts of contact lists had been rented to generate a turnout large enough to ensure the cash evaporation could be accounted for on a cost plus percentage fee basis.

I suggested as much to the very bright, very connected Robbi Level who'd appeared air kissing in my general direction "Who cares, darling. This thing is a waste of time but the food's always good here." Robbi, who spoke at rather than to people, was not my cup of tea. She was a face who put money into shows and complex systems of block-bought tickets and profited by being smart and in touch with other people who speculated in similar ways. Not at all ugly and with a gym-slim figure she remained totally resistible for, somewhere at some time, femininity had locked itself in an iron castle and, seemingly, atrophied.

She'd once got me, along with her pubescent son, to a first night and at the after-show party asked my view on the couple of hours we'd just sat through. My opinion that it was poorly contrived rubbish the brain dead might get off on delighted her for she too thought it would make money.

When her son had asked her if she didn't think theater was a medium that should promote art that might enrich humanity, she'd snapped back that "One could as easily ask the same about daytime television and just how naive would that be?" He'd retorted that babies starved but some people tried to do something about it and her reaction had been to ask me "What am I going to do with him — he's not of this world?" I'd told her I thought he had a point about art. Intent on the last word she'd explained she could not see any point of either art or humanity if it didn't benefit her. Our paths hadn't crossed until now.

Recognizing Bobbi as a player, a pr person condensed before us asking, "Are you folk all okay here?" Pointedly ignored by Bobbi the pr started to cling and to lose him she ran her memory for my file and announced I needed to know if art had a point. Pr favored me with a glance reserved for the terminally stupid and quickly magicked a lovely woman to give me a press release. She was very self-assured and I liked her looks so used lots of eye contact when asking if she worked full time for these people.

"No — and you, are you some sort of investor?" Her voice was rich and mid-Atlantic.

"Someone thought I might be. You ?"

"I'm an actress — show-casings are opportunities." She smiled at us both but Bobbi had already left, only her body remained. One of its hands waved across the room, the mouth lisped a farewell and then the whole ensemble swam away, pr fish in attendance.

"Well, thespian, you're very beautiful," She tried not to appear pleased, so I went on. "But can you really act?" Her slightest of slight frowns was instant. "Don't child — you'll crease the merchandise." I made as if to smooth her brow with my thumb: her grin forgives, ice breaks, and Ellie assures me she can act. I learn that her path includes an apartment a couple of streets away from my home and that she'd had the questionable wit to not not get involved with a married player from LA. It seemed the man only rarely showed. In no way did she come across as a woman in love but did seem to be in a sort of conditional awe of the guy. The obvious take was that a fathering thing pressed her buttons but that didn't ring quite true. On no basis other than a feeling, I supposed he might be finding her a tough call.

Her flirting was subtle and smart, very together without any ball-breaking animus, and she was teasing. "You've an annoying ability to make a girl open up, what's…" when an announcement interrupted. It apologized for a short delay to the appearance of the Wasting Knights and someone said something obvious about wasting last night. Nearby the owner of spectacular if unlikely breasts emitted a neighing laugh. Glancing at her watch Ellie said, "This delay's a nuisance."

"Why?"

"Because I've a date."

"That's a pity." I told her and meant it. "Tell me about the band, Ellie."

"The hook's in the name."

"Right."

"How's your history, Mick?"

"It's Rick," I said too quickly and knew she'd read that as insecurity. "And Rick's knowledge of history is shallow," I fronted it out.

"Strange — I'd figured you as the curious type." She looked right into my eyes when she spoke, and I like that from a person.

"You did, did you?" Those eyes were actually beautiful. "History is usually the victors' lies," I replied, and taking fresh glasses of champagne from a waiter's tray, I passed one to her. "I guess you've touched a nerve somewhere though." That admission worked, and there was warmth in her smile.

"The briefing I got says the name means," she faux-yawned and waved her sheaf of press releases. "that the Templar Knights' treasure is being wasted. You don't really know about them do you?"

"Do," I huffed. "Lads on horses who went to Jerusalem — I buy books at airports, lovely to look at."

The compliment absorbed effortlessly, she asks, "And the Romans?"

"Made their kids conjugate verbs so they grew up to be complete bastards — built very straight roads though."

"My, but we are the frequent flier!" Her smile was inward and ancient, that smile of a woman who knows with certainty that the man is trying. "I'll give you the bones. Three hundred years after Jesus the Roman Empire was going down the tubes, fragmenting. An emperor called Constantine decided belief in the old Roman gods was no longer tenable: hyphenating their gods' names with the gods of the empire's subject peoples wasn't keeping the business glued together anymore. Gnosticism, coming out of the east like the dawn, was an enormous threat." The timbre of her voice had a curiously alluring gravitas. "As you'll know, the Roman Empire hijacked and adapted Christianity to suit its needs. Put simply, it imposed a monotheism it called Roman Catholicism on its subject peoples. The Roman imperial wealth machine would continue as it had before but now billed as a holy empire."

I'd always felt that religions prevented people finding what they called God. I asked, "You mean Rome just rebranded — it stayed in the business of power and taxes but with a new religion implanted to help its core business survive?"

"Very good," she smiled again "Now fast forward seven centuries during which time Islam occurs and spreads. In the west, the Iberian Peninsula is occupied by the Moors. The Roman Catholic Church's area of influence in the east is continually evaporating, and Rome needed an enterprise to focus energy and effort to its remaining European power-base. It also needed to give Islam a slap to demonstrate it had clout, hence the crusades. The Roman church induced knights to raise armies, travel to the eastern end of the Mediterranean, and fight bloody battles."

"A heavy call to make on already comfortable, privileged men."

"Correct; and so they offered heavy rewards. Crusaders would definitely gain entry to heaven in the next life and perhaps gain a hundred tons of gold in this one. That was the gold the Romans had missed when they'd sacked the temple in Jerusalem."

Pretty sure they didn't have tons as a unit of weight in twelfth-century Europe, I said, "Nice figure — how were they so sure of the quantity?"

"Since burning the library at Alexandria, they had a near monopoly on information as well as literacy in the west. Monks read every piece of paper, every papyrus, every scroll, every tablet, every holy book, every record they got hold of and they read the accounts of the gold that Israel had amassed and what Israel had done with it. They read the Roman accounts of what they had taken," she sipped some champagne. "Allowing for sticky fingers, the equivalent of about a hundred tons was unaccounted for and every indication pointed to it having been buried beneath the Temple. An easy sell for the church, so the knights lead men off on crusades. In the event Rome got what it wanted but more than it anticipated." Handing her sheaf of press releases to a hovering waitress, she said, "Would you make sure these go out with the drinks please? Bruno knows all about it." She turned back to me, "Ancient Egypt's echoes were still loud back then, its knowledge available to those with the wit to uncover it and that knowledge underlies more than was then or is now generally realized. It didn't correspond with the view of heaven and earth that Rome was peddling."

This woman's energy was waking me up. I said "Okay, Europe was a place stinking of shit and death — the moldy bread's hallucinogenic, people are mostly illiterate and not very conscious so supernatural powers are objectively real to them. Religion is what saves them from drowning in that chaos. The church is the religion, the big power in Europe." She nodded in response. "So when a lot of battle-experienced, heavily armed guys with serious wealth and some new smarts return it's a big threat to the status quo. Right ?"

"There you go, slick." She sipped her champagne slowly before adding, "A threat taken so seriously that accommodations were reached. The knights stayed out of Rome, kept their knowledge to themselves, and paid for some cathedrals. In return the Roman Catholic Church prevailed upon local monarchs to tolerate and allow them to live tax free. Knights settled in Paris and London, building their temples and setting themselves up in a forerunner of the banking business, although usury was not strictly legal for them."

"Knights replacing serfs with debtors," I drained my own glass. "Lot less hands on."

"Just think loans-business. Time passes and here in London King Edward First literally ransacks their treasury, taking half of it, and then in 1307 Philip, king of what was then France, organized arrests, murders, trials and subsequent executions. He wanted their wealth and he was nervous about their clout. The Roman Catholic Church would have had to have concurred. Most of the Templar Order perished one Friday the thirteenth, but many fled from France to Scotland and Portugal and…"

"And here in London?" I interrupted

"On this isle of pragmatism the accommodations were adapted, and the Templars survived whilst those still alive over in France probably hid within other sects. The implication in the band's name is that the core knowledge of the Templars, the Egyptian, is being wasted." She stepped close and tapped the press release I still held. "And there's the rub." She used that curiously old-fashioned phrase. "I think the idea, which doesn't seem all that bright from the commercial point of view," she'd lent closer and husked this into my ear. I felt the warmth of her breath and her perfume was slight enough to enhance not drown her skin's own scent, "is that nowadays with Napoleon long gone and the beliefs behind the French and American revolutions diffused and diluted, the groups that spun off from the Templars are wasting because they're not evolving."

"You're a bit glam for a theologian," I said. "Have others told you that?"

"This is hardly theology – but I am nice to look at, aren't I?"

Using the pretext of moving her out the way of other champagne swillers and spillers, I put my hands on her arms and turned her so that my body shielded her from the crowd and asked, "So the backers of this band…" Young Pr reappeared now doing fluffy-bunny earnestness squared and claiming Ellie's attributes were needed to deflect or otherwise deal with a situation elsewhere. As they moved away Ellie grabbed my wrist and pulled me along too. I did not resist.

We arrived at one of the vast room's side tables where two large men stood and a trim lady sat: I noticed the woman wore a slim gold neck chain with a small crucifix. They'd had that table arranged entirely for their comfort to the exclusion of others' convenience.

This trio had presence. Both men exuded an aura of joylessness, and the one speaking employed the persona and bearing of Important Man Who Does Not Tolerate Fools. "…even by today's standards this exploitation of the young is crass." A silvery Pr elder was trying for soothing noises as the speaker turned and, ignoring Ellie, addressed me "Do you suppose disrupting harmonies that took centuries to establish is wise or even smart?"

Not liking his manner, I thought to shake his cage so asked, "Are you guys from a local church or something?"

His blood pressure increase affected the air. Silvery Pr started to speak, "These gentlemen and lady are…"

I interrupted, "But surely the Church of England is just a sort of property company these days isn't it?"

Large man guffawed — you couldn't call it a laugh, and Trim said, "We are nothing to do with that church." I fancied she suspected I was toying.

"Ah, so you must be the catholic lot." I looked directly into the eyes of the first large man. "Same line of work — religion's just there to stop the young men taking what the old men have."

His glare more than contempt now he said, "You really have no idea..." I sensed Trim lady was also about to say something but his imperiousness had got to me so I persisted, "The Wasting Knights ... could that be wasting like in murdered by this church of yours limbering up for the Inquisitions?" I was just winging it, of course, but even if they were going to react Pr elder again spoke before they could.

"No, no killing the Cathars was years, oops silly moi..."

Ellie smoothly stepped in: actually she smoothly sat, half on the edge of their table. "Perhaps it's just a bit of gentle irony," she offered.

"Nobody does irony anymore," snapped Trim. Then to me she said, "You're nothing to do with this band are you?"

"There's no fooling you." I smiled my friendliest insincere smile.

Ellie gave them an inclusive look and said, "You know, perhaps the band thing is a way of saying the enantidromia has stalled." The two men seemed to freeze, then the so-far silent of them placed a chair in a very definite way at the table for her. Simultaneously he produced a waiter who poured a fresh glass of champagne and laid a plate with a selection of canapés before her along with a napkin.

I may not have known that, in her context, by enantidromia she broadly meant good arising from bad but I did realize that this trio had weight. I also knew now I was seriously turned on by Ellie. Wouldn't you be? She is beautiful to look at — she's got face and she's no fool; plus there's a naughtyness about her.

In counterpoint to the there-ness of her physical presence, her last statement seemed inflated. It had the discomforting edge of a subject on an entirely different level from the day-to- day and it caused a vague unease. Forces stirred. She was still talking with the trio and I felt the conversation was heating when younger Pr, who intuition advised was as old as time, leaned in close to me to say, "I wouldn't worry about discomforting edges, in essence the show has to go on." A slight shrug appealed for worldly understanding.

Shaken I managed to say "That's a nice shrug you've got there."

"Why thank you," younger pr said, looking genuinely pleased. Then with voice lowered, "The lady and the man who spoke to you are from the church and the other gentleman isn't."

If that information contained a hint it was lost on me. Ellie was continuing, "You know that the Empire went on slaughtering those who didn't accept the dogma. Over the centuries so many were butchered, tortured, exiled, or burnt alive in the name of the Empire's version of Christianity — would you figure millions ?" she sighed. "But… like omelets and the Scots and the Native Americans…it's the human way."

On the far side of the room a mike rustled and someone announced that the Wasting Knights were about to showcase a couple of instrumentals and the first was entitled Skit Song. There were now enough people to make the stage set difficult to see other than the huge skull and crossbones laser-projected on the far wall just above and behind the band. Noise precluded conversation for the next fifteen minutes. Ellie had stood up to look and I'd sunk onto her chair to snack some canapés and look at her. This pert girl's tight trousers told me she was going commando, refreshing for I'd long tired of thongs. My mind wandered down the ever intriguing road and I felt Trim Woman looking at me.

"Can you see alright from down here?" she deadpanned.

"Perfectly," I assured to be rewarded by a flicker of something across those hard eyes. So her blood moved.

The unremarkable band noise finished, applause rippled and churchman said to Ellie, "Young lady, you very well know that all peoples have been abused and enslaved at some time in their histories. I doubt you're one of the deluded sentimentalists who think in absolutes, yet you're implying others are somehow right and the Roman Catholic Church is wrong?" Erotic images had dissolved as I refocused on the here and now.

"Not at all," she replied. "I've no idea how right or wrong others are. Perhaps the empire's uphill struggle from Maozia to not executing Galileo was so exhausting its own evolution stalled. Dis-education is still encouraged; evil pedophile priests who force their penises into childrens' bodies are protected." She shuddered. "That doesn't make you shudder too?" She put down her barely touched glass of champagne then asked, "How's that for exploiting the young!" You could hear their brains changing gear as she charged on. "So, leave aside what the self-deluding claim are just individual failings and remember incineration — not that many generations ago thinking, moral people were burned alive by the Roman church as an example to others." She was glaring at them now. "Tell me, do you suppose burning alive is more painful than crucifixion?" Nobody answered her. "Quite. Well they burnt their enemies because to crucify them might have proved a little too…your not done thing …" she nodded toward Trim Woman who colored a mite, "ironic."

But this Ellie is something I thought as Fat George's office vibrated my phone. They asked if I wanted to sell the now refined alluvial gold as the market was looking weak, holding his call, I reached Baa's bedside and relayed the message, adding I thought we should sell half. Baa thought change was coming for gold but not yet so agreed and I switched back to the broker who acknowledged the order. Clearing, I noticed Ellie's changed tone, she seemed to have switched from hardball and I didn't understand the context of what she was saying.

"...don't know, but I might suppose they think the whole Gnostic message is wasted — did you notice their first number was called Skit Song ?" There was that sort of extended aaah sound one expects from Japanese corporate groups. "You could easily suppose their message is that the accommodations have become diseased."

Not-from-the-church man smiled as a snake might if it could and said, "How could anyone really think that, look at the progress that's been made. Any fool knows civilization is not free — there are costs."

"Impoverishing the human spirit hardly makes for civilized people — it brings madness. Civilization is not simply command and control — if you make people live in two dimensions you evolve flat people, you know." Ellie smiled sweetly at him.

In response he arranged his features to convey a mask of stern reasonableness. "Young lady, on balance, the accommodations served most and the fact is that outside of Catholicism gods eat the people, and within Catholicism the people eat God."

Trim woman smiled at Ellie, "The Mass my dear…and you know matters of this world are gray — mixtures of dark and light. As for burning people, well, perhaps resurrection after incineration is too complex." This apparently bizarre remark actually lifted the mood a little. I'd missed things again!

Ellie's mouth smiled back at Trim and said, "I don't buy that, but to cut to the chase because," she glanced at her watch. "I've got a date to get to, despite assassinations some of the knowledge was, as you're well aware, passed down to others. Too many of whom have become rather less worthwhile." With that she bid us farewell and left before I got my wits together. Hurrying out into Park Lane I saw her taxi pulling away and there wasn't another empty cab around. Wildish ideas of flagging down a car and paying the driver to follow rushed into my head but no - her taxi was held in traffic fifty yards away. I ran. As I reached it and banged on the window, the traffic moved, and the driver thinking 'tasty bird- bloke - aggro' accelerated, but she'd seen me and told him to stop. I puffed to where the cab was now halted on the other side of the intersection and climbed inside. "You'll have to be a bit quicker than that Mick," she said.

"Fuck," I panted looking into her eyes. "Wrong cab."

Her date was a drink in a Hill Street hotel, with an Australian woman who was something called a Line Producer.

Resident in LA and passing through en route to a shoot somewhere Balkan, her partner back home had contact or clout or something useful to Ellie; now she traveled with insurers of production costs, accountants and others whose functions I wouldn't have immediately associated with movie production. I asked one of them about this and she laughed, "I guess it can seem like we outnumber production people - like war y'know, in the old days an army was nearly all fighting soldiers but today there's about forty backup personnel for each fighter — it's more efficient."

The movie people unanimously declined my insincere suggestion of a meal together saying their body clocks were screwed and that they just wanted to crash before continuing eastward early the next day…blah…blah. I left with Ellie and walked round into Curzon Street, up to Park Lane and on through the pleasantly warm spring evening and a pedestrian subway into Hyde Park.

"I liked the line about religions stopping young men stealing what the old men have," she said, slipping her arm into mine.

"Airport shopping can really broaden," I told her.

"Yes, people take stuff then say God-given laws prevent others taking it from them — perhaps there's no other way," she spoke as if to herself.

"About every society's done it. Exactly who were those nasties?" I asked.

"Not sure—I thought you'd figured them."

"Only for being the enemy," I told her as two horses trotted past, one of the riders was smoking a huge cigar. "Won't the showcasing people mind you just leaving?"

"No, they're lucky to get me and they know it. Also I was there for a bit longer than I was booked for."

"They pay well?"

"So-so, the agent takes twenty percent."

"You seem very knowledgeable. History's your thing?" I asked.

"No, I just read the background notes and ad libed."

"Really? You had me thinking you cared about that stuff." Early summer's evening sun was now low enough to make me screw up my eyes as we continued westward.

"What would be the point of caring? You alluded to history being bullshit and that would make religious history even more crap, I suppose. Then again, what would be the point of getting involved? You're going to die one day anyway," she said, producing dark glasses from her bag and put them on.

Still squinting I said, "Somehow I don't think you're quite that cynical…or ungodly, but you really handled those people well — your agent should charge more next time."

"Mmm." She looked thoughtful, "But Rick, those guys were kind of creepy, weren't they?"

"What?"

"Creepy," she repeated.

"No, the other bit." We'd paralleled Knightsbridge and reached the park's West Carriage Road. I turned us south toward Exhibition Road.

"What other bit?" she asked.

"You said 'But Rick.'"

"So?"

"So, you got my name right."

Smiling, she leaned closer and squeezed my arm. It felt good that arm squeezing did and I told her so as I flagged down a cab to take us to where it was early enough to get proper pastas at an outside table without reservations. As the evening's humidity increased a distant storm threatened rain and I was enjoying being with her. That she was so at ease with her natural sensuality made her doubly attractive and, whilst I figured she'd never lacked for admirers, I wondered if she knew herself as well as she supposed.

"Seriously you really do seem clued up on religion — as a teenager were you ravaged by nuns at a convent school?"

"What?" a slight pause of the fork as it transferred a morsel of vongole to her mouth. "Lesbian nuns?" Her very direct look conveyed mild shock.

"Yes."

"Lesbian nuns ! Why, Rick," she said as her eyes widened and she leaned forward. "Do you mean sort of severe yet darkly attractive lesbian nuns —eyeliner and high-heels kind of thing?"

"Yes," I spoke through a mouthful of food. "Exactly th…"

"Dream on." A very long cool stare, but I'm getting a distinct feeling that we're connecting. "Actually, it was Shakespeare."

"Shakespeare ravaged you?"

"Um…yes, so many times with his sonnets. But I didn't mean that – I was at stage school reading Midsummer Night's Dream." Ignoring the wine she replenished her glass of mineral water. Why hadn't I done that for her? Because I was a touch disorientated — she was just too sure of herself.

"When do we get to the nuns?" I asked.

"Not now, it'd upset your digestion. Oh I'm sorry — it's wrong to tease." Fuck it, she was being patronizing "Look, I promise you that I never went to a convent school, so there never were," her smile was not unsympathetic, "severe yet darkly attractive lesbian nuns touching me… and the other teenage girls…" Her eyes were sparkling with mockery as they looked right into mine. "Sorry, I can see that's a big disappointment, Rick, but it is the truth." she sipped some water. "The nearest to that sort of thing was once when some Japanese schoolgirls on an exchange visit had to share our dorm because their coach had broken down" I'd stopped eating. "They were really were quite adventurous actually…oh, don't gawp—it's so unattractive." I could only laugh as she did. "Poor, poor men — you don't acknowledge the goddess so she has you so easily…"

"Truce?" I pled.

Again she laughed, "But of course."

"Sucker." Even I didn't believe me and she had the grace to make a wry grin before going on.

"I was actually reading Dream to do Titania" I thought of the metal titanium and must have looked blank for she explained "Midsummer Night's Dream - Titania the Fairy Queen! She's speaking with Oberon, the Fairy King, about their responsibility toward humans and she says, "We are their parents and originals and…" this Ellie was, as I may have mentioned, very sensual. She was really enjoying her pasta. "I didn't quite get that so I asked a drama teacher who I think also didn't quite know but said it meant archetypes. When pushed, he didn't seem too clear on what they were either. Anyway I looked up archetype, it's a Greek word, and I came across a reference to Jung — you know who I mean?"

"Psychothingy geezer — like Freud." I signaled for another bottle of mineral water.

"Kind of — a different dimension to Freud — but I found this dream of Jung's. In it he's in the center of an Italianesque city and a Crusader Knight from centuries earlier walks through the crowds of townspeople, but they don't see him. He's invisible to them, but he walks right up to Jung." She'd finished her vongole and now used her fork to take pasta from my plate "Umm, yours tastes so good, Rick."

Some truce. "Lucky clams." I stared at her mouth.

If it's possible to snort seductively, and I mean to exhale air sharply through the nose in an alluring way, she managed it "The point about all this is that I'm not sure even Jung at that time appreciated the full significance of that knight"

"You mean that he was a Templar?"

"Well he knew that the knight was a crusader and connected him with the Grail but I'm not sure he saw the knight as a bearer of the knowledge of ancient Egypt and Babylon recovered from entombment in Jerusalem. He was bringing it to Jung who was in this Italianesque town that had resulted from the Roman Empire."

I suddenly understood what people meant when they say dreams' images are symbolic and literal all at the same time. "You're saying the town was Italian because we all live in a present that is conditioned and caused by what happened in the time of ancient Rome?" Mouth full again she nodded and I continued, "What did the knight say to him?"

"Nothing. The visor was down and being down meant Jung didn't recognize him, didn't see his face, didn't see his eyes and could not hear what he had to say."

"When did your Jung guy have this dream?"

"First half of the nineteen hundreds I guess."

"I know nothing about this stuff," I said, and she regarded me neutrally. "But maybe you should check out the Lord Mayor's gaff Mansion House — that's City of London — it has something in it called the Egyptian Hall although it doesn't look very Egyptian."

"Well, well, well, you're not just cute to look at are you?" She wasn't as impressed as I'd hoped. "It's the room's proportions that are Egyptian, and it's not a place I'd care to check out — there's more to the City than you'd probably dream."

"Now I'm getting bored. Let's just talk about me — so how cute would you say I am?" I asked.

"Like between one and ten?" she leaned back and surveyed me.

"Yeah."

"One…maybe one and a half."

"So okay for a gargoyle like you then?"

"On a bad day perhaps…"

"Like today?" Please relax. I'm sure I'd kept anxiety from my voice, expression and body language - well, fairly sure I had.

She, of course, didn't answer that but walking around to her flat, we put numbers and addresses into each other's phones. Her right breast was against the back of my upper left arm, and I felt myself getting very turned on — hyperaware of that wonderful breastfullness brushing the back of my upper arm. I didn't remark on it. I figured that if I commented it would stop. Why chance the exotic contact, that marvelous paradox of soft-firmness and firm-softness, being removed. Senor Optimistico had started shuffling about below, but after those pretty lips brushed my cheek and sighed a thank-you for dinner, her front door closed. I rapped upon it and it was immediately reopened; smiling she said, "Hi! It's Rick, isn't it?"

"I thought you really ought to know that if you'd played your cards right you could have probably snogged me a bit."

"I was rather afraid of that."

"There's no need to be fearful—these are my very own teeth, and they get brushed every day."

"Huh." She does a long look "But do you floss them?" I was enjoying her again, I looked down at the floor and shuffled my feet, "Well…do you floss them, Rick?"

Still looking down, I mumbled, "Not every day."

"I didn't quite hear that."

"Not every day."

"Aha!" she camped. "I thought not!"

"If you've some floss, I could do them now!"

"I bet," she laughed. "I wonder if I could trust a dinner with you."

"Trust! Me use knife and also fork— me no animal."

She gave me another long look. "It's not you I'm concerned about," she said levelly. I'm lost for words; we just stand there looking at each other until she says, "I'll call you soon," and closes the door.

Not just lost for words—I'm lost for thoughts.

Ignoring the dead weight of disappointment compounded with confusion, I and my inner-child and my inner wounded hero and inner unknowns ambled the few hundred yards through the evening's increasing humidity to my own door. With a beer from the fridge, stripped and, bedroom windows wide open, I sat on the garden chair I kept in my wet room as water cascaded over me. I'd thought I'd got her but hadn't— yes, I was pissed off about that. But tomorrow, I told the child and the hero and the unknowns, is another day!

I'd better very quickly tell you about the over-mortgaged house that had sort of fallen into my lap two years earlier. It's terraced and not really big, so I'd gutted it and made each whole floor into a room—the basement, a kitchen-diner that lead up to a small patio; the ground floor, a living room that leads down to that patio; the first floor, my bedroom and wet room; and the loft I'd converted into another bedroom and, during an oriental moment, installed a semi-sunken bath beneath the roof light. It had all cost much too much, but then things do, don't they?

Cold beer inside and hot water outside pleases and confounds; this combined with those lingering feelings of rejection that had been so keen to blossom into cloying, dark self-pity meant it was a moment or two before I became aware of the phone ringing. It displays her just entered name. "Hello, Ellie."

"Rick, there's a dead man in my flat."

"What?"

"Just kidding—it's the sort of thing people say in novels."

"You mean we're not in a novel? This is real?"

"I guess," she sighed

"Why shucks, woman, you're drunk or crazy or both—what's my role in this novel by the way?"

"You might be the good guy, but I do feel that's unlikely."

"I could get a white hat," I tell her.

"I'm glad we met today. I enjoyed being with you."

"Then I'm definitely not the good guy."

She laughed. "Good point. Look tomorrow evening I've got to go to a screening at six, would you like to come and have dinner afterward— my treat" I paused too long, "Oh dear, the boy's fainted," she said.

"Ellie, I'd like to, but you've got to know I don't put out just for a meal."

"Oh, come on, don't give me a hard time Rick," she pleaded. "How can you be so spiteful?"

"Try wearing me down gradually—you know, sort of playing to my needs and boyish fantasies," I told her.

"Do you mean fantasies about boys or pubescent erotic fantasies or I suppose both are possible—are you bi—actually how old are you?"

"Pubescent erotic stuff sounds interesting…" I paused, but she didn't reply "Don't think I'm bi…" She still said nothing. "Is the movie likely to be any good?"

"Doubt it. I figure you for late thirties."

"Swop?"

"Twenty-eight,"she said

"Soon to be forty," I answered

"I am sorry. I'll speak louder from now on—I'll text you tomorrow's details; by the way, we have to go dressed as carrots."

"I figured that but what's a text?"

"Your nurse will explain—big kiss." She hung up.

You might suppose she'd rung me too quickly, and I might agree with you had I not been so pleased that she had.

We started seeing each other casually. An easy familiarity between us as we avoided emotional hooks; she because she was, at least theoretically, so involved with Mr. LA Married, and me because…well, I just knew with Ellie what you saw was only a fraction of what you would actually get—the baggage was unguessable. It would just not be a good idea.

I learned that she'd got into comparative theology when she'd become a Buddhist and Mr. LA "He's a very clever guy, you know" encouraged her, explaining that "beliefs were on the move—things will happen soon."

• • •

Two weeks later, Baa and I picked up a connecting flight from Lisbon toward Manaus. I'd better tell you that Baa was not poor, maybe seven million 1999 GBP net I would guess, which was a lot of money then. With a house in London and a villa in Spain, he was British by birth but also somehow legally resident in both Angola and Guatemala. I think I mentioned before that he's very intuitive, but it's actually a bit more than that. Later when a tad wiser, I'd come to understand that he had, by an apparent whim of nature, more conscious access to information registering in his back brain—the old reptilian bit that sits there within our skulls apparently not doing much. "You're not going to go retarded hippy on me again are you?" I asked.

"No way of knowing, old son."

"Aside from the inconvenience to me and the dosh those sort of stunts cost, does it ever occur to you that you're risking your life?" I knew him, and he knew me, which meant we both knew the question was not entirely serious.

His response did not surprise, "You're just not made to hang with action heroes are you? Did I never tell you I'm the kind of guy who only feels alive when there's risk—being in danger of not being?"

"Did I never tell you what a sad cunt you're becoming?" I said.

A clever oddball with a capacity for ruthlessness, he was some ten years older than me, and as far as I was concerned he was an honorable man. We co-owned a smelting unit that was a convenience to facilitate other business rather than a profit center in itself, and we handled most matters on a deal-by-deal basis. So far the understandings outnumbered the misunderstandings between us — more workable than their marriage somebody had commented. The deals we'd shared together were usually profitable. A couple of fuck-ups excepted, the worst we'd ever done was to break even. In milieus of nerve and front, Baa shone, his affable persona concealing big balls.

As a young man, unblessed with great good looks or particular physique or wealth, the big boys hadn't taken his calls when he was getting started in business. Then he'd beaten off all, and it was huge, competition to bed a supermodel icon whose legs finished only slightly below her armpits.

Painfully beautiful to regard, this creature was about permanently enveloped in that mist of narcissism and ersatz regality so worshipped by the media. She was an exotic planet who mostly orbited herself. Rich and powerful alphas, their larynx's and lungs constricted by contemplation of the image of a goddess, queued behind their penises ever anxious to shower her with earthly treasures along with their semen: she was their dream trophy. Powerful women longed to melt for her in order that they might savor a moment's control.

Punter planets are attracted to where stars have been so rarely did she have to part with any of the millions she earned each year for restaurants, airlines, car manufacturers, clothes designers and hotels were only too delighted to have their products and premises graced by her presence.

Also rarely was she actually a deux with a man for they were not quite her thing.

Sensing this at a shiny people gallery event, Baa contrived conversation with her by uttering names of those he didn't actually know in a not unamusing way so he could let slip that he was an hermaphrodite. This misinformation of course intrigued. His supermodel target focused on him intently and he went on with her to a party where the vision spent close-up time murmuring with him on the ramifications of dual, as distinct from bi, sexuality. You see Baa didn't look gay, or anything else for that matter. Baa looked totally neutral; he's got a vibe but visually he's a blank canvas. It was thus that he could and did use his intuition and exploit a natural showmanship to paint himself as he wanted to be seen.

Although supermo was no fool Baa played her like a violin and, of course, she took him to bed. As the lift rose to her penthouse, he'd asked if she'd ever made love to a hermaphrodite before and breathed an inward sigh of relief when she said she'd not. She also confessed overexcitement and that she liked his smell; Baa was already in the bed when seventy-four inches of neo-divinity stalked naked from its bathroom "But we are in such a delicious rush, my darling." She slid beneath the single sheet "I'm so pleased, Baa, I…" Her hand briefly caressed his throbbing cock, paused for confused thought on his scrotum, and now sought a vagina. "Now you bitch-bastard, where's this pretty clitty you've teased me about." She pulled back the cover, dragged her long hair across his torso and briefly amid her confusion licked the top of his penis before exploring further with eyes and tongue.

"Later baby later," pleading in his voice as he sought to turn them both so he could enter her.

"Heh! It's not there!" she shouted. There had then been a brief but intensely awkward pause. "You don't have one!"

"Don't be hurtful, I do," he protested. "It takes a bit of finding…you've got to be gentle with me." He caressed her clitoris, discovered it was very, very wet, and so without delay, exploited that opportunity. This led very quickly to the first of several orgasms. Seriously amused by Baa having got her by having the balls to say he did not exactly have balls, supermo made a great fuss of him for a couple of months before moving on. He hadn't cared when she left because as he explained, "You could hardly love a narcissist unless you're a masochist — also some of that girl's toys were fearsome." Baa was instantly in great demand. All the beautiful girls who weren't quite as beautiful as supermo wanted to have what she'd had, and if truth is told, wanted to be had by what had had her. Getting Baa's sperm was like redemption for them and giving it away, as young men are hormonally driven to do, cheered and invigorated him no end.

Our Baa fucked the planet, and his stock in Boy-world became stratospheric as rumor and reality fed off each other; his calls always got taken.

Drinks, meal and movie done, we still had hours over the Atlantic and he talked about the growing demand for palladium, which is a metal in the platinum group, and his belief that its price would rise. Baa said a report saying part of the Norilsk mines in Siberia were being updated was, in his view, the precursor to a tightening of that metal's supply. It seemed Norilsk was the largest source of the world's palladium. Whether the mines were as rumored or whether this was part of a chess game was, he figured, secondary to what market perceptions would do to the price. Palladium, you see, is in the catalytic converter of every car, tiny amounts are in mobile phones and computers, and if you've any crowned teeth or bridges in your mouth, they may also contain some palladium in alloy form. It's also utilized in the nuclear industry and years earlier two scientists, Pons and Fleischman, had astounded the world with their claims of using it in achieving energy by cold fusion. Apart from the Russians, another big source of supply is the Republic of South Africa, but as that nation allegedly even cooperated with the Soviets when Russia was the USSR on matters mining, it seemed a reasonable bet they'd be along for the ride if something was going on. North American mines also produced it steadily, but the large Norilsk production was crucial to the world's supply-demand balance. I asked about above ground stocks of the metal in Russia and Baa explained these were not only unknown but a Russian state secret.

It looked like it might be a punt and we exchanged information about how the metal physically got from supplier to consumer. I could feel Baa was, if not being sparing with facts, certainly holding something back. "Yes young Skywalker," he confessed and told me he'd been working to put an extraordinary deal together through Fat George's contact. He said he'd be willing to put up all the capital and I asked him why he needed me. "Rick, what I'm talking about here could be huge. It's most probably legal, but it is edgy — very much unknown territory. I'll be dealing with strangers and you know how it is." He meant not just that precious metals were commodities with prices constantly changing but were prone to theft, pilfering and substitution. He and I could go separately to the Amazon and buy alluvial gold because we each knew what it was, how to test it, how to get it refined and what it was worth; each of us had sufficient funds and contacts to exploit the situation as individuals but it made more sense to work together. If this new deal he had was that edgy he'd have use for an extra head; two heads are rather more than twice one head.

"You want to fuck me with this?"

"Natch, you're the fall guy."

If I said he'd got me very interested it would be no small understatement.

Later as the movie finished he removed his earphones and said, "My nose tells me we'll make landfall soon."

"You mean your watch, mighty one!"

"Probiscus." He tapped his. "I smell Brazil."

"Oh yeah, what smell is that then?"

"Fecundity."

I had a window seat and raising the blind saw the south Atlantic six miles below us now bore the tan stain that said we were well within four hundred miles of where the planet's most massive river washes its mud into the ocean.

At Manaus, Socrates and his son were waiting with the pilot of a block-booked air taxi. "I misread the guy's name" said Baa referring to their breath, "it's not Socrates it's 50 crates." We flew out above the rainforest, but our easy-bucks days there were over if not for ever certainly for a while. Within forty-eight hours we were to discover a cartel that 'handled security' in African unregulated diamond mining was now expanding far into the Amazon basin; they'd blown in Inselma's ear and she was considering the advantages of doing her business with them. Casual brutality and murder was just day-to-day life for such people: they would be arriving sometime soon with helpers. These alluvial gold sources in remote tributaries were going to be taxed and controlled. It was probably our fault for having paid Inselma out in hundreds that would have found their way back toward the city, raising eyebrows along the way.

Neither Baa's nor my first inclination was to stay on for we would have had to hire murderers, without such we would die and with them the business would become all but profitless unless one of us took up permanent residence there. In case you've not witnessed it, let me explain that violent death can be a surprisingly casual occurrence: the more sensitive amongst the living know to leave the scene quickly for a released by violence psyche can bring harm. How? Why? Later, later.

Just then, standing in the humidity by a tributary of Rio Negra itself a tributary of the mighty Amazon, we silently considered the situation and what it would require to continue in business there. Not only did our souls recoil, but we each felt there were better things to do, there were easier ways to make money. I did wonder what we might have done if there weren't other ways to make money — if that alluvial gold was our only option, how might our souls have fared at our own hands? We humans are such adaptable folk.

We bought around eighteen kilos of mud quickly and left Socrates and son there as decoys with the air taxi while we flew on a local eight-seater amphibious plane to Manaus. From there we went southeastward via Brazilia and Belo Horizonte to Rio de Janeiro.

Waiting around for delayed flights was made bearable at Rio's Galileo Airport by the prerecorded flight announcements featuring the sexiest voice in the world. Baa was remarking on it and voices in general, when a petite but muscular German transvestite suggested we listen to old Marlena Dietrich material. Tv introduced herself as Angelina Folly en route to Chicago and as the flight delays continued we fell into casual conversation: an abundance of complimentary drinks over-relaxed us. After an elderly man and woman had gravitated to our group Angelina shrieked "O mine darling, zis is so gorgeous! From where did you get it?" She craned forward to better see the woman's gold pendant.

It was a gold skull with crossed bones beneath it "Your wife makes a very pretty pirate," Baa told the man who seemed to take some sort of offence.

"Easy tiger," his wife soothed him. "This gentleman's only being pleasant." Then she turned to Baa and said, "Excuse my husband. He's touchy about some things. It's not a pirate symbol — it's a pre-Columbian design I found in Peru."

"Sorry, no offence was intended," Baa spoke levelly to the husband. "It's just that it's what you'd see on a pirate flag — at least according to Hollywood."

"It's me who should apologize," the man said and offered his hand to Baa and then to me and then rather uncertainly to Angelina. He introduced himself and his wife explaining they collected pre-Columbian art.

"Strange, the last time I saw that design was when a band was playing and somebody was saying they were some sort of ironic statement to do with the Knights Templar." You, of course, know that it sometimes helps to be vague and sound a bit confused because then people are more likely to give fuller explanations.

"It's about certain some of the Templars got to North America during the fourteenth century," the man volunteered.

"Well before Columbus then?" asked Baa, picking up on my vibe.

"Very much before, and I believe they got to Central and South America too." We all must have looked blank for he continued, "that could explain the skull and crossed-bones design in Peru …and also why the Spanish were welcomed as foretold demigods arriving from the east with beards on their pale faces." Nobody said anything and I was thinking about the Celts and Scandinavians who'd also reached North America long before Columbus. Then had come the Spanish — mass murdering in the name of the prince of peace. The Spanish had done much the same in the central and southern Americas as had the Roman Empire in western Europe — ancient cultures had been decimated. "The skull and crossbones was a Templar symbol — one of their flags. The crossed bones perhaps making an X for the Archangel Michael and the skull for Golgotha," the man said as if this explained everything.

"Or," said Baa, "that their worship of life beyond death included sacrifice — most belief systems do or did."

I kept my own counsel. You could see it, of course; even a single individual with old-world knowledge would have impressed ancestors of the Aztecs up north in Mexico and the Incas over to the west in Peru immensely. It seemed likely the knights, not people who feared death, could have been honored guests and would have speculated to their hosts that eventually more Europeans would arrive from the east. Maybe they'd thought of establishing their order in this new world. The Catholic priests traveling with the Spanish seemed to have particularly sanctioned — perhaps even encouraged the slaughter. Had their church known something I wondered — given them a covert mission of death? So long ago, it was just idle speculation yet... Just then the flight was called and I readied myself for the long ride back to London. From my window seat, I glanced out at the one million two hundred thousand kilos of concrete and stone that are the 36 meter high statue representing Christ the Redeemer; from 730 meters up it overlooks part of the city's coastal strip, the ancient prohibition against the making of images long ignored. Redeeming what and who, I wondered.

I'd made half a dozen visits to Rio and each time the city was bigger. Like Brazil's power and influence, it continually grew, and I wondered about this country whose very name had existed three thousand year's earlier in Celtic myth as Hybrazil, the western land of the fairies.

As on previous trips we carried our bounty of dried sediment as hand baggage, on this return to Europe we had, unfortunately, only mud containing eighteen kilos of 93.6 percent pure gold — around 200,000 U.S. dollars then.

The flight from Rio was direct to London and an hour before arrival I nudged slumbering Baa to tell him I smelt Europe. "And it smells of what Obiwan ?" he asked.

"Hypocrisy."

From Heathrow, one of his cabs took us to a safe deposit in a small street between Belgrave Square and Buckingham Palace. He wanted to talk more about the palladium deal; his way of organizing things would have blanked out Amazonia and now be focused entirely on palladium. "Baa, I'm too shagged to think straight just now."

"I'll e-mail. Ring when you've read it." He'd also wanted to go on for a meal, but I hadn't been up for that either — I was too tired, jet-lagged and drained. I left him and his driver outside my house, rehydrated with Vitel, showered, peed and slept the sleep of the exhausted. I awoke still on messed-up body time; it felt good to be in my own bed but not good to be in it alone: I'm not talking sex here — I'm talking loneliness. One reason my marriage had been brief was that I'd never been able to crack finding a balanced relationship. Like you, I need companionship yet I can only handle as much as I need —and no more. Too much and something within starts to suffocate and beckons subtle sabotage; too little and I feel like I'm feeling now in the London summertime 3:00 A.M.-ish predawn. Hidden things are usually concealed from us by darkness, but this particular something seems hidden by light - not a simple situation. Over the years it's wounded a few for whom I'd cared. That hadn't made me feel good. I texted Ellie telling her I was back and the woman inside who demands relationship smiled and let me drop back into sleep's balmy caress.

Sunlight. Phone bleeping. "'Lo," I croak.

"So you're in London sleazoid?" Ellie husks.

"Umm"

"That's good – you can drive me out to tennis today"

She often played tennis in a leafy, miles away place and as I pictured her jumping around in girly tennis things, loins stirred. Brain cautioned for my car was long parked outside and in my street you do not vacate a residents parking space if you can avoid doing so. I wheedled. "You think I'm just a toy, don't you? I need rest, attention, consideration…"

"Oh my poor darling, I'd no idea…."

"Jog to tennis, it'll loosen your muscles. I'll send a cab to pick you up when you've finished and the driver will have an envelope for you."

"Oh, I bet it's emeralds you sweet, sweet man! You can be so thoughtful."

"Foolish woman. The envelope will contain instructions."

"Oh…you want me to do stuff to the driver…hardly droll," She sniffed.

My erection was now getting serious. "Are you already dressed for tennis?"

"Yes."

"Are you wearing one of those little, short, white pleated skirts?"

"Why, yes! Yes, I am," she lied beautifully.

"Well, I'm here asleep in my bed, and my street door is open."

"Is that wise?"

"A girl off to tennis might notice an open door and enter the house…"

"Aha, like Goldilocks…will there be porridge? You really do know how to excite…"

"Please don't interrupt — just what is about your generation?" I sighed to impose my extra decade. "She'd find that her panties under that tiny, pleated, white skirt were starting to be a nuisance, to bother her — curiously restrictive, perhaps riding up. She'd slip them off but then remember the open door! She realizes that anybody in the street could have seen her do that. Any passing man with coarse hands could have stepped into the house and touched her!"

"Eergh! You're so revolting sometimes!" disdain in her voice. "Are his fingers rough?"

"Ingrained with filth — he's sordid and brutish."

"Oh, no. Then what might she do?" Ellie asked, failing to maintain disinterest in her tone.

"Having barely avoided being handled by this coarse stranger, she'd tiptoe upstairs and look around. Meanwhile her little pussycat started to meow and extend its claws and she'd think 'Oh fuck — not now, pussycat! I've no time — I'm going to be late for tennis.' Then she'd notice there was a guy asleep in the room and that sort of turned her on…"

"Oh dear, a court booked, an itch, and now a man — what could she do?"

"Wantonness would seize her and she'd go to the bed and s…"

"Rick, what a slut this girl is!" she sounded pained.

"And you know what the sleeping guy would do?" The line stayed silent save for her breathing. "He'd…"

"Look you're sick, and I can't waste a whole bloody day on the phone." She hung up and, with an erection to be proud of, I went downstairs unlocked, opened and left ajar my front door. Did I tell you she lived barely five hundred yards away?

Back in bed time moved too, too slowly before the door closed and feet moved on the stairs. Through loosely closed eyes I watched — there really was a tiny, pleated, white skirt atop her long, slim legs. It rode up revealing pert nakedness as she clambered onto the bed and straddled me. Oh, but she smelled so good! Her body's scent enfrenzied neurotransmitters or whatevers, and suddenly all I wanted was to possess and consume beauty, to touch and probe her everywhere with my tongue. She'd pushed down the duvet and was slowly licking my cock. I wanted to get her entire being into my mouth, and I was desperately trying not to come, to delay it all, and so rolled over and twisting around entered her. She moaned and, as one of her fingers exerted a tiny, perfect pressure on the aureole of my anus, I came whilst she did.

Now lying next to me, she looked deeply into my eyes and sighed, "Mmm, wrong house."

Yeah, Ellie was okay. Mercifully far from perfect. Her dope habit annoyed me — I don't like the smell of it around me all the time. Her weakness was human; a constant need to take the edge off the ugliness she insisted on being aware of. Perhaps she was just too bright to endure some streak of goodness that ran through her; perhaps a wounding she'd never reconciled?

Contented, I was unable to carp when, sitting on my chest using my forehead as a ledge, she manufactured a large spliff. Alight, she pulled one of my arms around her to snuggle down next to me. I made a negative grunt as the joint was held to my lips so she kissed smoke into my mouth a lot. Slim fingers caressed my scrotum, but I was so relaxed that I just lay there as I continued to do a moment or two later when a glowing piece of riz fell on to my chest. Contemplating the brief pin-prick of pain I let it burn out. She finished smoking, turned, and licked the burnt spot then traced a saliva trail down across my stomach. Her mouth was slow and wonderful, so draining that I found myself utterly released from all desire, and for quite some while my mind wandered free. "This knowledge your geezers brought back from Jerusalem — what was it?" I asked.

"I knew you'd ask me that one day."

"Don't play," I yawned. "Just tell me — please."

"Pretty please," she whispered into my ear.

"Pretty please." A pleasant nap enticed from within.

"Knowledge." Her breath was so warm.

"About what?" I yawned again.

"How to get a lamp with a genie inside it out of a cave." She was softly kissing my eyelids.

"That…" I began to ask as consciousness melted and I fell into the wonderful sleep of satiation.

Had I not I would have seen her hand touch my forehead and then her fingers caress my face before trailing across the lids of my closed eyes. I would have heard her whisper, "Perhaps also the secret name of Ra that gave Isis power over him."

This relationship with Ellie, I kidded myself, bordered on the ideal because we got on sexually and socially whilst neither of us wanted to complicate things with emotions and all the grown-up stuff. I suppose I was figuring that her situation with LA man meant she wasn't looking for children or other complications, but there was something else. It was as if we were in a house with a lot of rooms and one of them was locked — no it wasn't the cellar nor the attic — it was just a room. It was a very large room though.

You are wise and know that Nature only tolerates harmonies that are productive, usually new life and sometimes art. Even then you get the feeling her toleration is at best temporary.

Nature's law is *BE*.

She is absolute in her Law and for life to *BE* tension is needed and thus is never very far away. So being fun and an uncomplicated pleasure Ellie was destined to leave, but I'd never have guessed the manner of her going.

Sometime that afternoon jeans appeared from inside her tennis bag and we went to Soho and ate above a pub. I remember we talked about a notion that the Inquisition, the Gestapo, the Taliban and others were manifestations of the same reoccurring energy. As we were leaving, Ellie's looks attracted clumsy but not ungentlemanly attentions from affable but not entirely coherent Tweedledum and Tweedledee inebriates. Each wore a grubby linen jacket with unmatched trousers and each bore that amalgam of arrogance and tragedy found in a certain type of English drinker. They were arguing as they emerged on the street from the pub's ground floor bar "You're up yourself — your addled concept of socialism requires small-brained people to be protected by law against big brains and sooner or later some cunt would want to surgically..."

"...man's mad," said the other.

"...man's blind," said the first.

They ambled along in our wake as we headed for a drink at CC. As others have remarked, Soho is a place where you run into people and in that club was a man I'd not seen for nearly two decades. He was busy surrounding massive gins.

I'd always liked Dave. His heart was good and at the chilling, austere English public school where we'd boarded, we'd shared confidences.

His father had been killed in a war. He didn't remember his father for he'd been a baby then.

Later when his mother had told him of their loss, he would lie in his bed and miss the father he couldn't remember. He would wonder where you went when you were dead and what was it like being dead. He tried to imagine being dead; laid very still, slowing his breathing, tried not to be, tried to imagine nothing. It was very black. The spirits of life, of matter, had plucked young Dave back from the edge that is The Edge. Just briefly, for a moment he'd glimpsed something. Years passed, and his English mother, unable to find solace in Georgia, moved them from Atlanta back to England and Dave got boarded at the school in the remote countryside where he learned to play, and play well, the electric guitar. Perhaps we'd got on because whilst he'd had only one parent, I'd had only two half parents. My father in some Middle Eastern oil field compound, with a mail-order bride half his age, and my mother in Argentina, with a third husband, and none of them exactly pining for the confused, awkward adolescent they had to tolerate from time to time.

An undercurrent of some kind of awareness had run through our schoolboy clique unremarked and undiscussed for amongst the casual brutalities of our boys' school world it was almost an embarrassment. Youth takes evolutionary impetus for granted.

Whilst Dave and Ellie chattered, I recalled our group sitting in the sun idly watching other boys wander the adjacent school playing field that contained a cricket pitch. Someone had suggested trying to influence minds. We picked out a lone walking boy and concentrated, willing him to scratch his left ear. At that age nothing much rivaled the hormonal screaming of our bodies and so it was with only mild surprise that we noted our experiment succeeded. We tried with other boys and still it worked more often than not. We switched to willing the scratching of the right knee by yet other boys and that also seemed to work . Someone said we should try it on girls and this prompted imaginative suggestions. Heterosexual experiments would have to wait for ours was a boys–only school. Then the bright idea that we should try to make boys collide and fight occurred. This suggestion was taken up with relish in order to transmute aroused libidos' energy. Dave heard a voice deep within him say "No," so he blocked our efforts to start others fighting until we grew bored with failure and turned our attention to other matters.

Soho afternoons don't so much mellow as surrender into evenings, and Dave continued ginning and spoke of his traumas that required anaesthetizing. These included having been recently dumped by his long-term girlfriend. "She said I was too indefinite whatever that's supposed to mean," he confided. I caught a strange look — the glint of feminine unreason — in Ellie's eyes. Pleasures unexpected are always the more enjoyable for being so and seeing Dave was so good I'd barely registered how she'd instantly warmed to him, or the nurturing look about her as she contrived to fill his field of vision. It's quite pointless to argue with the female need to nurture.

Yes of course there was more to it; somewhere within I sensed a slight but significant feeling of relief. I could have grandly told myself it was the lifting of accumulated heroically self-imposed obligations toward the feminine — or even the dispersal by life's wind of the seeds of that sweet-sour fruit. But I was neither that drunk nor that far up my own backside, so acknowledged the discomforting truth. I was sort of relieved because I was finding myself increasingly liking her far too much and I'd no confidence in Mr Need not escaping from his cupboard and running amok. Okay, so I'm mildly fucked up.

Whilst I mused on this, Dave's tales of woe continued. In that very morning's early hours exiting a club I'd best not name, he'd been grabbed and flung into a doorway. The streets were all but deserted, and only a fool or an angel would have intervened with a couple of lads who seemed distinctly official. They'd pocketed his charlie and his cash, punched him firmly in the solar plexus and cautioned him. Apparently less concerned about his not buying from a franchised dealer than about his selling on his less-cut stuff to fellow band members, they seemed to be acting on a complaint from one of the club's bouncers.

Years back, sometime just after we'd left school, I'd gotten into a real fuck-up situation. It was serious, and I was badly down. Nobody else I knew then would have gotten involved, but Dave's volunteered help had been immediate and given simply and naturally — it was unqualified humanity.

Ellie was to subsequently move him into her flat whilst making an exit from our small world of casual intimacy. My ego took it well because the Soul whispered to it in the secret language about a world of other things. There was still a sexual edge though. Tomorrow would be another day, but, never the indiscriminate hunter automatically fucking anything attractive, it wasn't, or hadn't been, usual for me for me to jump straight into bed with a stranger. The most surprising thing about the whole matter of Ellie was how unsurprising it all was.

"Probably all for the best dickhead," I told dozing penis as we lay alone in bed the following morning. It was to turn out that I was at least partially right for quite rapidly Dave's self-respect and demeanor were to improve and a lot less charlie was to get used.

After opening windows, I made coffee, ran a bath and looked at my e-mail, discovering a few genuine messages, including a biggie from Baa hidden amongst the spam. I printed Baa's and took it up to the top floor. Hot steam softened hard copy pages and pages about the transmutation of elements. I didn't really know much about transmutation then and, in case you don't, I'll give you the bones of it. Things are, or are composed of, elements. Oxygen and nitrogen in the air you're breathing, sodium and chlorine in salt, hydrogen and helium in the Sun, aluminium in planes, the carbon in paper and the eyes with which you read this and so on. All are very different elements, yet each and all are actually made out just the same three types of identical stuff. Bear with me, don't nit-pick; I want to keep it simple so think buildings. Imagine a long row of buildings constructed out of the same three materials — cement, sand and brick — but each building has a different shape and a different function. Given a supply of those three materials, you could build a cottage or a palace or a dry dock or a water tower or a shopping mall or a factory and so on. Just as each building is composed of these same three materials, so atoms of every element other than hydrogen are composed of three things — neutrons, protons and electrons. The protons and neutrons together make up a nucleus that is sort of orbited by the electrons. Like the buildings, what an element is just depends on how much of which materials are put where. Only regular hydrogen is different; it's made out of just two bits of the stuff — one proton and one electron - as a concrete slab can be composed just of just sand and cement. Different from regular hydrogen are its isotopes; so far two, deuterium and tritium, have been found, and they are almost like separate elements: certainly they're not quite hydrogen because they do have neutrons, and this makes them likely candidates for any process of transmutation. You could think of them as a special premixed cement that combines chemically with the bricks in a wall by reacting with them.

But of course, electrons, protons and neutrons are basic stuff with which you could build all the elements and then with those build a power station, a whale, a diamond ring, a microchip, a tree, gasoline, a space station, a virus, scissors, a pair of shoes, a suit, paint, a planet, an ant, a CD, or anything else, including a person. This fact is something we so take for granted that it's hardly reflected upon but bear with me a tad longer here. An atom of gold consists of seventy-nine protons and one hundred and eighteen neutrons and seventy-nine electrons, whilst copper has just twenty-nine protons and thirty-five neutrons and twenty-nine electrons. So to change copper into gold you'll have to persuade each atom of copper to accept another fifty electrons; that shouldn't be too difficult, but you've also got to get the nucleus to accept another fifty protons and eighty-three neutrons — if you can remove them from somewhere else or somehow create them. Alternatively you could take an atom of mercury and remove one each of it's eighty protons and three of its one hundred and twenty-one neutrons and one of its eighty electrons to make it an atom of gold. It's called transmutation and science has managed to do it but the drawback was that enormous amounts of energy are consumed by the process. You see protons repulse each other with stag-gering amounts of energy. If they didn't all the protons in the universe would clump together forming the nucleus of one super dense single atom. This doesn't happen because protons repel each other. But, and it's perhaps the biggest *but* there is, if some immense force does get protons to touch they glue together. Physicists call this glue the *nuclear force*.

I won't bother you, as Baa's e-mail bothered me, with a lot of details about the energy components that make up neutrons and protons; they're known as subatomic particles and generally categorized as quarks, but it seemed to me that not too much has really been established about these. They sounded sort of sexy in a scientific way, but the real thrust of his information seemed to be about the protons and neutrons and electrons that make up atoms of the different elements.

Apparently around a gigawatt of energy was needed to change a few atoms of one element into atoms of another; to rearrange protons and neutrons and electrons. A gigawatt is about the energy release of the bomb that destroyed Nagasaki which, according to the rough mental calculations I made in my bath, is about the same as switching on one billion single-bar electric fires simultaneously. The cost of all that energy has made transmu-tation of metals uneconomic; it's cheaper to just go out and dig up the ore containing the element you want. Like me, you'll have heard claims that alchemists turned lead into gold by heating, mixing and cooling various ingredients, but it's popularly supposed by psychologists and other clever folk that they were really intent on dealing with a psychic or spiritual situ-ation. They were seeking to turn the leaden baseness of their own beings into gold. That is to say, they were concerned with improving themselves. The substances worked on in their retorts were a way of focusing intent, a kind of sympathetic magic. They sought to enlighten themselves by changing the weights of substances. Mind you, I suppose there's always the possibility that by changing one's psyche one changes the environment including what's in it. Cynics would say that by changing the psyche one's perception of the environment will change. You're wise and know that the business of the cynic is to ensure that development and creativity are prevented or perverted; cynicism always endeavors to ensure that the baby is thrown out with its bathwater. My own bathwater now growing chill, I dried, dressed and went down to my car which wasn't there.

The parking bay and those adjacent to it now had a official notice fixed to it advising of its suspension to accommodate a removals truck.

An immense pantechnecon stood in the bays. "Fuck! Fuck! FUCK!" I shouted.

"Good morning," said the passing optician, schadenfreude-ickly.

"It's not good! I was parked here," I said, indicating the huge lorry occupying the suspended bays. "And now my car's gone."

"Have you looked inside the lorry?" he asked.

It's already after midday so I walk up toward the Fulham and Brompton Roads junction where steak frite, chips, green salad and a glass of cold rose hit the spot. An espresso and I phone Baa's other landline in London's leafy St John's Wood. He has one of those phone systems that follows him about all over the world; when calling him you often got a plethora of different truncated ringing tones until he picks up as likely as not on a satphone somewhere in Australia or up the Zambezi. Today it transfers only to his mobile.

"Read that e-mail?"

"Yeah."

"I'm in Dorset with the man you've to meet."

"Sheep convivial?"

"Very amusing — quite hilarious in fact. A driver will collect you tomorrow—ten okay, Rick?"

"Let's meet here? It's holiday time, and the roads will be shit." I could do without three or four hours in traffic to the west country.

"Trust me, it'll be best here."

"It'd better be eleven then — and make it a limo"

"Eleven tomorrow then." He hung up. Strangely curt conversation? No this was business. Not only was I in a restaurant where sharp folks ate, but we were both talking on mobiles. Paranoid? Not at all; just see how many firms are in the business of selling eavesdropping technology. Scanner equipment has become just another part of doing business.

The next day a sad, even by 1999 London standards, minicab was waiting outside my door; the driver's heavily accented "You take please mister" referred to his new and expensive model mobile phone showing the text message "Limos are for lap dancers you sad tart—this will take you to Battersea."

Making a mental note to exact revenge I climbed inside and got all the windows open. I'd met Baa years back and figured it was sort of destined because, although we were in much the same business, we'd only met in a bar. I'd been in Antwerp to see a diamond dealer who'd a supply of rhodium he'd prefer not sell locally. Rumor suggested it was coming off the side of some big fish's shipments that allegedly originated in the just then disintegrating Comcon, the eastern European countries of the old Communist Block. At that time Baa was already dealing with Russians and used an Antwerp freight agency to move material from there to a refiner. Having got talking and learning we'd shared business interests, we decided to eat together at a nearby restaurant. Belgium might have been a front-runner to be Europe's heart of darkness but in bizarre counterpoint the food is often world class. Each of us had concluded our respective business arrangements in Antwerp and so sought amusements. The small hours found us in a nightclub that was essentially a large private bar with a dozen hostesses — all of whom were Russian and all of whom wanted to consume vast amounts of alleged champagne, which the place sold at enormous prices. To encourage consumption this booze was sold on a bottle and blow basis — the blow jobs were administered in small side rooms. Back then, in the early 1990s, an orgasm and champagne there cost the equivalent of about eight hundred British pounds. Baa explained that several of his business sources used the place.

Apart from Baa and myself, there were seven or eight potential suckees; Baa fell into conversation with one. They spoke together in Russian whilst an elderly guy, who seemed to be the owner or manager of the place, imposed a conversation on me. Unbidden he told me he had a holiday home in Paraguay, which he liked very much because "I can get anything there."

"Hell is probably being shipwrecked on a desert island with you," I told him.

He laughed and said he liked "so much the English humor. I get BBC on my television."

Turning to Baa, I said, "This all a bit sophisticated for my taste. I'm off."

"Me, too." Shaking hands he bid goodnight to the Russian and retrieved his credit card from the barman. As we moved toward the exit he said, "Catch the guy over there with the blondes." As it happened I'd already noticed the man for he looked vaguely familiar. "Know who that is?" he asked.

"No."

"Just think NATO, mate."

I'd bought into an ailing silver recovery business with Baa and over time we started sharing deals. After a couple of years we upgraded the smelting facility at the unit. We'd lucked into the little Amazonian tributary as a new source of alluvial gold when declining rainfall revealed a single grain in the riverbed to Enselma. Both of us had known that it would only be a matter of time before it became widespread knowledge and some of the thousands of non-locals who collect alluvial arrived on the scene along with organizers of one sort or another who live off them. That rain falls from the sky on to a mountain and washes gold out from within always strikes me as sublime — you don't have to rape the planet's body to get it. The earth gifts it for you.

Arriving at the heliport I was pleased to exit the car's seedy interior.

The chopper was very okay though, of sufficient size and power to whisk as opposed to vibrate, it bore its lone passenger south and west from the heliport to a country house-style restaurant enfolded within nubile hills near the South Devon coast. I'd exchanged barely a dozen words with the pilot, a South African with attitude, but the pretty-faced waitress who greeted me at the landing pad concealed beyond some herb gardens was a joy to behold. She lead me through endless doors then out on to a terrace overlooking a small lawn that sloped gently down to a stream. Beyond the water, oak trees cast a secret daytime gloom.

I counted a total of four tables well spaced on the terrace: the other three were laid but unoccupied. "Rick, meet Pyotr." We shook hands. He was impressive in an understated way and I experienced a sense of déjà vu as I took in his late middle-aged face and slim body.

"Hi, Pyotr, you'll notice how our host inquires anxiously as to my welfare after the journey." His English was good for it took him only a moment to understand what I meant.

"Why would I not notice that he did not?" he gave the slightest of smiles.

Having ordered from a not vast menu we talked about the remarkable beach near Baa's cottage. Not golden sands but a sort of silt-like material from low, constantly eroding cliffs that give up prehistoric fossils from the Jurassic. It was the area in fact where a humble discoverer of fossilized dinosaur bones was largely responsible for the great revision of peoples' understandings of our planet's past. Hitherto accepted biblical time frames were to be gradually dropped.

Anyone who wished to could go there and dig up about as much as they could find; but Baa told us that just recently someone somewhere had woken up, and the beach had been or was about to be made a World Heritage Site. A better bit of the laissez-faire that had made England unique would disappear, although the beach might be saved. Seriously delicious lunch passed from plates to stomachs whilst two of the other tables became occupied—one by an aged rock star and his wife, both painfully besotted with their six-foot-plus, New Orleans-accented and undeniably beautiful-to-look-at guest who went by the name of Phoebe. It was about impossible not to learn her name as the musical couple suffixed and prefixed all their flatterings and adorings with it. "They've brought their own dessert," Baa observed whilst I wondered about menages-a-trois as a way of avoiding committed relationships. Something inside my glandular system found that idea interesting whilst my feelings advised I was lonelier than I cared to know. A couple of suits arrived at another table just as we each decided we'd eaten enough.

Motioning to Pretty-Face waitress, Baa stood and led us across the grass and over the stream to a sun-dappled stone table and benches beneath a massive oak. The tree had been there before the Spanish Armada had sailed along the nearby coast: its ancient roots were now visible above the ground. Like a woodland spirit our waitress reappeared bearing espressos and iced water. Insects hummed and the day felt perfect, but I wasn't there just to delight my senses. "So girls, what's all this about?"

"Pyotr says he can transmute silver into palladium very cheaply," Baa said as he extracted a cigar from a busy-looking leather case.

"What about other elements, other metals?"

"He tells me it's confined to palladium — none of the other platinum group metals and no other elements," Baa grinned. "And not gold. He says the process is restricted because of something to do with harmonics."

"And like you he's not sought counseling about this?" I was trying to provoke Pyotr into a reaction, but the man remained impassive, even contemptuous.

"He's totally serious," said Baa. "We won't go into details right now but, for the sake of this discussion, take it that I figure he can probably do it."

"The only success in that field seems to have been minute quantities of metal at the expense of colossal amounts of energy, Pyotr. What makes you think you can do it economically?" I asked. I'd decided to flash a bit of the knowledge I'd acquired from Baa's e-mail. "If you want to add a proton, you have to overcome immense electromagnetic repulsion to get an extra proton anywhere remotely close and then even more energy to get the protons to touch so the nuclear force takes over and glues them together. If you want to remove a proton from a heavy element you're talking similar energy levels, and for all I know, maybe risking an atomic explosion." I stared right into his eyes, which did not change in any way and neither did he blink. "And you think you can do this?"

"No." He lit a cigarette. "I do not *think* we can—I *know* we can. And I know I and my colleagues can because we have done it—as you will see for yourselves soon."

"Soon? When?" Baa asked.

"Soon. I have to make arrangements - and we have to reach a gentleman's agreement. No?"

"In general terms, how does this process work?" I asked.

He stubbed out the cigarette in a rough stone ashtray. "In general terms…you know an atom's protons and neutrons, are made up of quarks and leptons, which are generic terms for interacting subatomic particles. No language yet has a really adequate descriptive word as they're neither simply energy nor are they particles of matter. For the sake of simplicity, I call them, in English, *energy blobs*. In many respects they are like areas of energy and in those terms the size difference between the volume of these energy blobs and an atom is immense. A lot of popular science is published these days and it is not unknown for incorrect figures to be used, so I put it like this — the difference is around the same as the difference between the size of your little finger…" I couldn't resist glancing at my hand at that moment, and Pytotr saw, smiled, and went on. "The size of your little finger and the size of a jetliner." He lit another cigarette. "The energy blobs are interacting with each other. There is also a field of something not really yet understood —this field seems to also be energy but of a different sort. One might better say of a different order. You see, where our energy blobs are random this field is almost stable — it seems that it affects the energy blobs but is apparently not affected by them. Like a catalyst." Despite the day being warm an unaccountable shiver ran down my back.

Baa said, "He's talking about a sort of fundamental level of matter."

"Yes, I am except that of course it is not recognizable as matter at that level," Pyotr confirmed.

"When you say the energy blobs are random do you mean chaotic?" I asked.

"A small chaos can just be a piece of a large pattern." His cigarette went into the ashtray. "Down at the size level I speak of you are very close to the formation of matter and by placing an influence there transmutation can be effected."

I understood him to be claiming to be able to influence the actions of subatomic particles, what he called energy blobs, to form or attract extra neutrons and protons that would in turn attract or lose electrons. Such occurrence would effectively transmute one element into another. I wasn't going to mention isotopes of hydrogen at this stage.

Baa took out a mobile phone and pressed a button. "More coffee and water under the tree please."

"Like the butterfly in Africa flapping its wings causing a typhoon in Japan sort of thing?" I asked.

"That is not so different." He stood up pointing toward the stream. "If you throw a few stones in there now you'll alter the flow and things down stream will change a little — very little by very little by very little more changes will occur farther and farther away. Throw a stone in and maybe in time the whole planet will be different as a result. It takes time because of its size — with the minute affects are quicker!"

The apparent logic of what he said was quite impressive but then it would be if he was a conman. He would have prepared himself well to be convincing. The coffee arrived and Pyotr asked the waitress to show him to the washroom. "He sounds good, but I know this picture he's painting is a simplified version of things. Before you put any real dosh into this, we'd better get hold of a physicist to check all this stuff out."

"I know what you mean old son, but who'd you get? Somebody who might tell us it wouldn't work because he or she didn't think it would or because they thought it might and was looking to wheedle about for more data and pinch the idea for him or herself. No, I don't think so - I have a good feeling about this guy. I believe his promised demonstration could he the clincher. In any event he'll agree to payment on results."

"But if he lets us learn how it's done — that is if it's doable — how does he know we won't just go off with the idea?"

"I figure that, just like his explanation, the technique won't be that simple and he'll keep the kernel of it to himself. But there are others involved too who you'll meet."

"They're here?" I asked.

"No, abroad."

Pyotr returned from the washroom, and I asked, "Is your process very complicated?"

"Less complicated and more complicated than you might think, Rick," he gestured around where we sat. "Would you say this was a peaceful place?"

"Certainly."

"And you would be wrong. Just in this small area there are many billions of life-and-death struggles going on at this" he snaped his fingers, "moment. Bacteria, microbes, insects, even plant life compete. What we see as harmony is only the summation of continual disharmony — masses and masses of living things engaged in endless cycles of war, disease, ruthless competition, birth and death. The transmutation technology used in the silver-palladium process is fairly simple. The trick is in its application within the apparent harmony of matter—that is why you gentleman are going to see it working without having to put money up front." Bit synchronistic that, I thought wondering if he'd bugged the table. "You will not be able to steal the knowledge of how to apply the technology because it's in here," he pointed to his head.

"So what's the next move, Baa?" I asked.

"You're in?"

"I'm in for the demonstration, and then I'll decide."

"But…" Pyotr was seemed suddenly worried.

"It's okay, Pyotr. Don't be concerned. If Rick wants out after the demonstration, and I'm sold on the idea, he'll be cool. As you've doubtless noticed, he's not entirely a gentleman, but he is sort of family. He's my responsibility."

Baa signaled for the bill to be brought, signed it, and then led us around to the front of the house, where an ancient car was parked in the shade. Aboard we glided on country lanes through green hills until turning southward on a main road.

Although school holidays had started, Charmouth beach had only a scattering of people on it that day. Baa parked where a stream trickled out on to the sand. His thirty-something year-old Citroën, a DS I think, ran so perfectly I figured he must have spent a bundle on restoration. When originally produced, it was many years ahead of it's time relative to the cars made by others. Outside of France and the francophone countries, the radical design and advanced features didn't seem to gain the acceptance more conventional looking cars had. Central locking was not a feature so while he locked up I walked Pyotr out on to the beach.

"As far as I understand it" I said indicating the strange, low darkish cliffs that ran east and west along the shore from where we stood, "parts of those cliffs are very soft, sort of lightly compressed mud. The winds and the rains erode this soft material and fossils, mostly belemnites and ammonites are revealed." I gestured toward a gang of small children busy trying to dig an immense ammonite out of the ground. As I told Pyotr of these things, it was actually getting to me just how amazing this place was— those kids were digging up, or at least trying to dig up, the fossil of a creature that had lived, consumed, shat and reproduced here some 180,000,000 years ago. Pyotr seemed to be thinking deeply about this, but he said, "Tell me, Rick, how is the coast here shaped?"

I drew a simplified outline of the south coast of England from about Southampton to Plymouth in the sandy soil as Baa caught up with us. "Once a Boy Scout always, a Boy Scout, eh Rick," he said.

The rumor was that Baa had acquired his local cottage years back as part of a deal involving some iridium metal. Pyotr asked, "Did a large meteor ever land in this area?"

"Not while I've been here," Baa said and grinned. "Something's going on along there? Perhaps another Ichthyosaur's been found? That happens occasionally, shall we take a look?" He moved away and the Russian and I followed. It was about four hundred yards to the spot where a dark blue Coast Guard LandRover was parked and a small crowd of people, mostly young kids and their mothers, were gathered around something. As we hurried toward the scene, a police Range Rover hooted its way past us.

The wine if not the food was beginning to tell as we reached the site of everyone's interest. A body, it looked like a man, lay covered in wet mud at the base of the low cliff and next to him a middle-aged woman of some beauty and much-muddied but never the less elegant dress cradled his head. She looked somehow familiar, but I couldn't place her. "Right you're all to move back now please," one of the just-arrived policemen commanded as he ushered us back from the body. "MOVE BACK!" he shouted. "There's an ambulance coming through!"

"Poor sod must have fallen right down the cliff," Baa commented as we turned to stroll back. I glanced up at the mass of cliff; it was a bit higher at this part of the beach, and there did seem to have been some sort of recent landslip from about thirty feet up.

We bought ice creams from the beach shop and sat on the sand as the sun moved down, toward the town of Lyme Regis a little farther along the coast. A poor local girl named Mary Anning had started digging up dinosaur fossils in the early 1800s and selling them as curiosities to visitors. Her efforts seemed to have been motivated by more than the money that she made although it was desperately needed to keep her and her loved ones from the poorhouse. Her tenacity yielded finds that she sold and those finds contributed to the early history of life on the planet Earth being reconceptualised. Her fossils had immensely aided the work of others and this happened a mere couple of hundred years ago; before then biblical chronology concerning the history of the planet was widely accepted as fact.

Despite Hershal long ago offering proof based on the speed of light that each clear night we saw two-million-year-old starlight, there are still fundamentalists today who refuse to accept anything other than literal biblical time scales. Such people believe the universe is only a few thousand years old; that it is now only a few thousand years since creation. Mind you, I've a feeling this whole speed-of-light business is a bit suspect, perhaps a little over simplified.

At Baa's bidding, Pyotr started to tell me the story of how the transmutation process had been discovered in a house in the Ukraine.

It was WWII's victors who wrote its early histories and, as you know, they presented things in simplistic terms of good and bad, with the good winning. A mad Austrian hypnotized the German people into trying to conquer the world but was stopped by the British or the Americans or the British and their empire and commonwealth or the Russians—delete and combine as suits. You think I'm being too cynical? Let me explain that a sane, perfectly rational if not overeducated Brazilian once told me in absolute seriousness that his country had won WWII by defeating the Nazis. His point was simple—the British and the Americans and the Soviets had been fighting WWII for years, but within a few months of Brazilian troops joining the front in Italy in 1945, the war was over. I'd wondered if more 'Brazilians' returned from Europe than had arrived but hadn't remarked on it.

To generations of Russians, British and Americans the Germans were universally hated and lost the war—end of story? To many Germans it was a battle of gods to which they'd rallied.

Erwin was a German working successfully in the City of London in the 1980s. Late one chill autumn evening in a city bar, he bemoaned the margins fellow brokers in his firm shaved from him on in-house deals. "Have a go at them about it man!" the trader on the next stool had said.

"I do," Erwin replied downing more booze. "Every time, I say, look you bastard you have cheated me here..........I say this to them!"

"And ... ?" the voice asked.

"They just laugh. They laugh at me and say, pay your gas bill, Fritz"

That Germany's military killed millions and millions is nothing extraordinary in terms of warfare, but the reason that SS-controlled production-line-extermination camps starved and gassed millions of Germans, Jews, and gypsies is a reason why understanding that war's actualities is so important. Immense forces moved in those days because the Germans were trying to literally create a new world order for human beings: nothing less than an entire reorganization that would have pro-foundly affected every remaining man, woman and child on planet Earth. It was a closer run matter than you might imagine. What the Nazis termed the *inferior races* would be enslaved and managed by Germans who themselves would in turn be controlled by a caste of warrior-monks. These warrior-monks were part of the SS who would have their own nation state within continental Europe. It was to be more or less the ancient state of Burgundy resurrected and answerable to no human. The general control of the SS, and thus through them, the rest of the planet and all human endeavor would be the responsibility of their own Nazi inner core who would receive directions from the *Ubermensch*. Literally trans-lated into English as the Superman, something of its nature is obscured: *ubermensch* means over man as in that which is superior to man. Allied propaganda referred to the German *superman* to create an impression that the Germans were simply claiming racial superiority for Germans by the fact of being German Aryans. What was really being talked about was an invoked and then incarnated deity that would be *uber mensch* ,over mankind, and also over mankind's other deities. Their plan was that a god would become incarnate and all would be subject to that god. This is in fact what was seriously intended. Very heady stuff that might have all sounded a bit too fantastical had Pyotr not been telling us whilst eating an ice cream on a beach in southern England where children prized bits of prehistory out of sands over which Ichthyosaurs, Plesiosaurs, and who yet knows what other 'osaurs roamed, fought and fucked in the blink of a reptilian eyelid in planetary timescales between 200,000,000 and 65,000,000 years ago.

In pursuit of their theological aims, the Nazis proposed all sorts of things—a telling example at one time being a claim that we do not live on the surface of a sphere in space but that we live on the inside, on the rocky rim of a spherical space within an infinity of rock. Our blue sky was said to be a blue gas near the center of the spherical space and the sun, moon and stars were lights floating in that gas. This was supposedly proved scientifically to be the case and if you think it's easy to dismiss as only madness, just remember that the Roman Catholic Church used to insist that our earth was at the center of the solar system. Their so-called science proved it. Mechanical devices were built that fully functioned to explain and accurately predict the movements of the moon, the planets and the sun but with the Earth at the center. That we are capable of going to extraordinary lengths to protect ourselves individually and collectively from realities that discomfort is a sobering consideration. The real point that Pyotr was making here was that the German scientific community, which included many of the world's most brilliant scientists, was encouraged to think out of the envelope and, importantly, was funded to do so.

They were mostly orientated toward quantum physics as the ultimate reality and that orientation resulted in some unique ways of looking at things. The fact that aircraft need lots of fuel to stay in the air raised the question of how might the fuel requirement be reduced. That the fuel powers an engine directed toward overcoming gravity led to consideration of whether gravity could be switched off in the space that the aircraft occupies. Were the scientific elite of one the world's most developed nations just indulging themselves? Perhaps we'd better wait and see as the future unfolds.

"It is my turn to buy more of this excellent ice cream, I think," Pyotr announced.

Baa said he'd like another, and I said I wouldn't. Pyotr got up and went over to the beach shop.

"Do you suppose he was a Nazi or some kind of fellow traveler?" I asked

"I wouldn't have thought so for a moment," Baa said as he fished in a pocket for sunglasses. "He's hardly old enough, and if he was some sort of second-generation one he'd presumably be talking to people in Germany or South America and not to us."

"If he's on the level."

"Hear him out and then we'll talk."

The ambulance had arrived, loaded the injured body and now drove carefully back along the beach past where we sat and thence on to the road. Some children watched with naked curiosity whilst whoops and shouts from others announced some point of success in the releasing of the ammonite from its multimillion year embedment. Looking over toward the group of diggers, my glance was drawn to a mother whose eyes glowed with an inspired and inspiring light of triumph for the success of her offspring's endeavors. An eternal moment for her — a contentment a mother lives for. Pyotr returned with his purchases, sat down again, and slowly relished his ice cream - who knows what these things are actually made from these days - as he stared out to sea.

"This house in Ukraine?" I prompted. He sort of refocused on Baa and I then and continued with his story.

The Nazi's were sometimes welcomed in the countries they over-ran by people who were not necessarily Nazis or even sympathizers but who simply preferred them to the previous rulers. Such a person was the Ukrainian who sixty-odd years earlier had lived in that house. Under the Soviets he'd manage to cling to the right to occupy what had been his family's home for many generations. In the '30s, Stalin sent death squads to take food — all the food — from Ukrainian peasants in order to starve them to death and free up land for large collective farms. Figures are disputed but at least ten million died in the famine, but the houses remained. When the Germans overran Ukraine, he moved himself into a cottage on the grounds and rented the main house to the German army, which passed it over to an SS science unit that had been looting from a large laboratory complex the Soviets had operated in the area. I said I'd not known the SS had scientific aspirations, and Pyotr snorted. "They had hundreds of scientists working on all sorts of projects under the direction of a man called Kammler. Virtually all of their work was grabbed by the Allies at the end of the war, and the Allies did not share it with each other."

For various reasons the location of this property in Ukraine was well suited to the SS unit's purposes. A long section of straight, flat road near the house was widened and resurfaced enabling Me323s, then the world's largest transport aircraft, to ferry in equipment and supplies. Most of the freight came from Czechoslovakia and Poland. It was generally supposed that the Germans thought it would be safer installed beyond the range of British bombers for it was clearly important: Hitler himself visited the place and perhaps coincidentally in 1942 briefly forsook his Bavarian retreat, Eagles Lair, for another close by in Ukraine.

When the Soviets in Ukraine were routing the German army the science unit was withdrawn, sixty ordinary soldiers were pulled out of regular duties to help hurriedly load all the equipment into a waiting giant Me323 .

The owner planned to quickly move back into the main house before some re-empowered local party member grabbed it. Whilst the Germans had been unusually careful with the property they'd rented, their ex-landlord decided to trash it a little to encourage some sort of sympathy from his compatriots and discourage those same compatriots from considering the house for themselves. It was during this largely cosmetic destruction of one of the main rooms that he discovered a new brick partition had been built. It had also been decorated effectively creating a hidden recess that was so well hidden the German squaddies hurriedly clearing the building had missed it and the filing cabinets it contained. He didn't read much German nor did he understand anything of the files' pages of formulae and their construction diagrams meant nothing to him. He carefully reconcealed the recess and lived long enough both to see Communism's demise and forget about the hidden room—also long enough also to sell the house for dollars to the eager young man from Kiev. The dollars facilitated the fulfillment of a fantasy that had increasingly occupied his mind. He had gone on an extended bonkfest to Cuba never to be heard of locally again: it seems likely his death was or will be tacky.

Alexei was half Russian half Ukrainian and quite fly; a metallurgist, he'd been able to make very reasonable amounts of money telling people where to find and how to plunder valuable industrial metals from the chaotically reconfiguring infrastructure of the old USSR. Precious metals were even available from cash-strapped sections of the military: computer boards, battle-hardened communications equipment and aero-engine thermocouples. Alexei had amassed a lot of dollars and using some he'd bought the largish house and had the ownership regularized. He installed his extended family, including his sister and Ilya there. In his thirties, Alexei was the kind of scientist who'd not got around to marrying because his mind was preoccupied with more serious matters—science stuff.

His young nephews and nieces delighted in exploring the new home and kept their discovery of the hidden recess to themselves. It is, after all, just about every child's dream to have his or her own secret place. However, sooner or later rivalries will ensure that shared secrets are blown: it was thus as little Ludmila sobbing whilst gripped by anger at some sibling-imposed injustice led her mother to brother Nikita's secret.

Alexei already had a little knowledge of technical German, but once he'd started to grasp the content of some of the files he used the emerging Internet to gather details of Walter Meissner's prewar work on superconductivity and had German technical dictionaries DHL'd. He barely went out for a year.

What the Germans, and it seems before them Poles and Czechs, had been working on was some sort of new weapon system that affected local gravity. From the papers in the files he couldn't figure out quite what the weapon was but it seemed not to have been completed. What Alexei had been able to understand was that a sideeffect of testing the system had caused materials to alter—affecting gravity had affected mass. Duplicating that part of the Germans' work would take time and quite a bit of money. Having worked on an ad hoc basis with Pyotr on various deals in the past Alexei figured he could trust him and had little difficulty persuading him to become involved.

That Baa was apparently sold outweighed nearly all my skepticism about Pyotr. The technology was another matter, of course, but you never know—would a person in the 1600s have believed in microwave ovens or even mains electricity?

Pyotr said that to see the process demonstrated we would have to visit Lithuania; Baa's glance silenced my nascent objections and we agreed to meet up in Vilnius in nine days. The gentleman's agreement was way beyond loose, amounting only to an understanding that after the demonstration we'd talk about investment in manufacturing in return for exclusive distribution of the output at a rate to be agreed.

For all I knew Baa owned a piece of the place where we'd lunched for after dropping his cottage keys to a village lady, he drove us back to the restaurant, parked the car, handed Pyotr his small suitcase from the boot, and led us to the still waiting chopper. Unable to get Heathrow

landing permission the surly son of the veldt flew us into Battersea heliport. That day's chopper would have cost Baa a penny or two and I said
as much whilst we rode to my place in one of his grubby minicabs whilst
another transported Pyotr to a Holiday Inn at LHR.

"It could cost more than a few grand if we lose time fucking about,
Rick. Do you know what the price of Palladium is now?"

"No."

"Well, it's still over two hundred pounds."

What he was saying was that this metal, hitherto the poor relation
of platinum, was still reacting to high demand at two hundred pounds
per troy ounce — priced close to the level of platinum at that time. So
what, you might think; why rush? Well, the metal we're talking about is
an exchange-traded comodity, its price can change dramatically during
the space of a day. If, still a huge *if*, we were going to get a supply of palladium, the sooner we did so the better.   The evening was pleasant so we
sat out on my patio drinking beers "Baa, baby, you know I'm up for most
things, but do you think maybe this sounds a bit too unreal?"

"What you mean is that it sounds big, Rick," he replied and, fuck
him, he was right. In the dozen years the Nazis had controlled Germany,
its science had been pretty much isolated from that of the rest of the
world and had gone exploring down all sorts of avenues; it would be
asinine to suppose that those scientists got nowhere during that time. The
Nazis, like the Japanese, were working on atomic weapons during WWII,
and subsequently American and Russian rockets were largely built and
developed by the German technicians and scientists inducted at the end
of WWII by each nation. After the war an American general said, vis-
à-vis the Russians, "Our German scientists are better than their German
scientists."

"How did Rasputin find you in the first place?" I asked. He explained
that Pyotr had wanted to avoid selling to refiners because too many
questions could have been asked, but he'd known very little about
exchange-traded commodities. So he had contacted the various commodity exchanges around the world inquiring about selling platinum.
He'd not wanted to draw attention to the less traded palladium he was
actually looking to place. One exchange had faxed him a list of metal
brokers. A few months ago he'd phoned the listed firms and the one that
had seemed the most helpful was where Fat George wore a biggish hat
and it was he who'd spoken with Pyotr.

FG had realized Pytor didn't know how the business worked for he was enquiring about selling unrefined metals to an office full of commodity dealers who worked almost exclusively off screens and phones. They would have as easily dealt aluminum ingots as gold bars because they only deal in market-standardized products. Once Pyotr understood that any metal he had would have to be refined and then delivered in a market-standard form, he'd gratefully accepted FG's offer to set up a meeting with a recommended trader. This had occurred back in March, when Baa had been down at his house in Marbella where he was negotiating disentanglement from some short-term girlfriend I'd never met. Pyotr had gone to Spain and although the metal samples he'd taken with him had checked out this, of course, proved nothing. Alexei had not accompanied him he'd explained because he was unable to get a visa to enter the EU for some unspecified reason. Intrigued enough to want another meeting, Baa got Pyotr to take Alexei to Tunisia on a package holiday, gave the woman no longer in his life a generous adios check, and locked his Spanish house.

There was no visa problem in Tunisia and Baa spent a few days there with Pyotr, Alexei and his other partner, Ilya. Baa concluded that they were most likely on the level. That Baa spoke fair Russian had been a great help and a simultaneous investigation in Ukraine had checked the bones of their story. Baa's not uncomplicated mind became fascinated because Alexei, the metallurgist, was utterly convincing in his claims and explanations which meant he was either psychotic or it really worked. His brother-in-law's younger brother, Ilya, was the clincher. He'd jollied down to Tunisia with them and Baa had established some sort of rapport with the guy and believed him when he explained that he didn't know how the transmutation process worked but it did. He'd told Baa about how discovering the process had affected Alexei psychologically—so much so that even after cracking the science it was nearly a year before it occurred to him to do something about exploiting his achievement.

"This background check—what was it?" I asked.

"Used a firm of accountants with a Kiev office who thought they'd been hired to find out everything they could about a house, its owner and the adjacent land for an American health spa operator looking to showcase so it could sell franchises in that part of the world."

"And the problem this Alexei had in getting a visa for the EU?"

"Never found out definitively, but I called the local consulate and it seemed to be entirely bureaucratic because his name is like a John Smith. They'd so many John Smiths blocked it was taking months to check them all. Pyotr tells me he's now got his visa."

Baa said he would set everything up so we could meet Pyotr and the others in Vilnius in a few days for the demonstration. "I'll call you with hotel and flight details, or you sort out your own flight from wherever you are."

"Thanks but that won't do it," I told him. "If we're going for a demo we've got to analyze the metals and for that we'll have to have our own counter-samples."

"Of course."

"And acids. But if you fly in to a Baltic state with acids samples and they're found or detected at the airport there and then palladium and platinum samples are discovered some sort of bells will get rung. Who knows how far the sound will carry. If Pyotr has moved or is moving their equipment there at the same time connections could be made. Better we split any bits and pieces we need between us."

"Even better if somebody else takes the acids in for us. As long as we're sure about the purity of our samples we can use them to recalibrate Pyotr's local equipment so we won't have to lug a lot of stuff there." Baa was looking thoughtful as he got up to leave.

"Sounds good. You'll call me then?" I said and walked him out to his waiting cab.

Soon after nine the next morning he did and agreed we'd fly together direct from Heathrow on the Saturday morning as if off for hedonism in the northern sunshine. Lots of men were to be found in the Baltic States most weekends because the girls were pretty and the clubbing relatively cheap. I contacted a refinery and arranged for them to courier over to my house one pure ounce each of palladium and of platinum in the form of thin foil; we would divide this between us. I thought about Hungarian Emil.

Every morning at nine o'clock Emil would cross the border from Hungary into Rumania carrying a suitcase. Every morning the Rumanian customs guard stopped him for a customs check and always found that the suitcase was empty and without concealed compartments and that Emil's passport was in order and he'd nothing concealed about his person. So every morning the guard let him through and Emil made the return journey each evening. This went on for thirty years until one evening, as Emil was passing back across the border and the Romanian guard said his usual "See you tomorrow," Emil answered, "No, you won't" and explained that today had been his last trip and that he was retiring. The guard told Emil, who was now safely on his own side of the border, that he'd always known he was smuggling but, never catching him, had grown increasingly intrigued as to how he did it. "As you are retired now Emil, please tell me what you have been smuggling all these years!"

"Suitcases," replied Emil. The travel sickness pills might be checked, but the foil wrapper would be ignored.

The awkward items we needed there were around twenty milliliters each of different concentrated acids. These were important for test purposes and because we'd need to be absolutely sure they were pure, we couldn't rely on acquiring them locally. We also didn't want to do anything there that would look out of character for in truth we were getting into something more than a little different with people we hardly knew in a part of the world that, until relatively recently, had been within the Soviet Empire—not an entity renowned for a transparent legal system. Baa said he'd an idea to solve that problem so I'd left it to him to sort it out whilst I made the phone call to get the foils. Then at a jewelers I bought a hallmarked ornamental one ounce pure silver ingot on a neck-chain before going home; there I took a set of tiny metal numeral punches from a drawer and selected the number eight.

●   ●   ●

Lithuania is the southernmost of the three ex-Soviet Baltic States but unlike the others its capital is not a coastal port. An ancient land-locked trading center, Vilnius is where goods heading south and east from Scandinavia were traded for products coming north out of Ukraine, Turkey, Greece, the Middle East, the Caucuses and beyond. Like most nations, its history included appalling events. Baa and I got there on the Saturday morning.

Although Fat George is one of those people who have a disarming inclusiveness about him, he was, as you would very quickly sense, very much his own man. FG always worked and played hard and used to indulge in what he'd maintained was the greatest (he meant most enjoyable) of all sins—gluttony. A plastic model of Jabba the Hut had sat on his desk. Many years earlier he'd been dragged into a lap dancing bar by coked and wined clients and he'd protested that sex was a poor substitute for chocolate. Another bottle or two and he'd produced a Polaroid and asked one of his clients to take a picture of his dick. "Fuck off, perv," said the guy.

"I do for you sweetie," an Asian danseuse said and took the Polaroid camera, knelt, and snapped his member. "Ooh is nice—this turn you on, baby?" she cooed perched on his massive naked thighs and showing him the photo.

"Nah—just wanted to see what the old thing looked like these days."

But that was yesteryear; now, he was a lean, glowing bore of a forty-five-year-old. The man ran about a million miles a week

Massive weight reduction resulted from love for the muscular young man who sold paintings; they'd met at a big gun's fancy dress party which FG had attended attired in homage to some far-off Scottish ancestry. Seventeen stone of prime British lard swathed in tartan, with a dirk in his sock, got plastered and into conversation with gallery boy. The latter wore a sleeveless black-leather jerkin adorned with serious-looking pyramidal steel studs, blade-shaped strips of black leather forming a short skirt, set off with a Roman short sword. Stick-on scar across high-boned cheek and hennaed Roman numerals on serious bicep accentuated the effect and stirred something deep and hitherto unsuspected within Fat George.

A patroling bitch bade FG look at his footwear. Where butch thonged sandals might have been expected were beige trainers from the tops of which emerged the edges of white cotton socks.

Came the small hours and George had the band play whilst he serenaded his new friend with "Stop ye' Tickling Jock" rendered bizarrely with great feeling. Midway a couple of the seriously pissed tried to look up his kilt, and our legionnaire was on them like a flash, sending one into an indoor fountain and the other to the floor clutching himself. George's warbling continued and those nearby cheered him off at the end.

His house was to turn into an art gallery, and his figure into a temple of sensible eating and manic exercise. Ges cooks well, and the Roman thing has intensified. The last time I was a dinner guest, dormouse fritters were offered, and I figure they were genuine.

George was pouring some sort of super enzyme-packed glue into his fruit juice as I entered the Radisson's coffee shop; he looked up and made eye contact, so sitting myself at a table between him and the door I signaled a waitress.

Within a few minutes Fat George flicked a packet the size of a very thick business card under my newspaper and into my lap as he exited past the waitress whilst she took my order. The packet contained thin sachets of platinum and palladium metal in sponge form, weighing thirty grams. He'd probably be leaving the hotel for the airport by the time I'd finished my coffee and cake.

Neither Baa nor I had worn rings made of these metals because for our purposes the samples had to be absolutely pure and pure could not easily be made into jewelry at that time. We'd brought the metals ourselves in the form of pure foil, but as Baa had pointed out if they got mislaid somehow during our journey, we'd have a problem. Ten minutes later, Baa sat down at the next table. "Saw something familiar," I told him.

"And I've got my glasses back," he said meaning the acids brought by FG had reached him. Both of us were a bit edgy because Pyotr hadn't arranged even an approximate time for us to go to the demonstration; he'd simply asked that we be ready to go at zero notice anytime after 10:00 A.M. the next day. Under the circumstances this was not entirely unreasonable, but it did make for a bit of tension.

Leaving the hotel Baa and I strolled in the pleasant summer sunshine, "For a bit of confusion I've told him to bring a hammer and metal chisel so we can mark things," Baa said as he fumbled a cigar from its case. "If he can really do it then he can just as well do it in England as here — make a lot better sense for us."

"I agree. An industrial unit near London turning out palladium — easy distribution to anywhere."

"I think that's what Pyotr wants us to come up with. He'll probably want us to think he'd be going along with our wishes—even reluctantly. Meantime I suppose it's easier for him to bring his equipment here. We've assumed it's just a pilot setup, but we don't know how big this plant is."

"Except maybe greed is getting in the way here, Baa. This could be one big setup to rip you off," I said, emphasizing *you*. "Why do these Russians need you? There's got to be fifty thousand plus of their own people—serious people—who'd put up the money."

"Sure, but that's fifty thousand who'd rip him off, and once the Russian mob learned the process—would our guys live long and if so on what terms?"

We stood waiting at a pedestrian crossing avoiding the wheels of tricycles pedaled along the pavement by happy six-year-old democrats. "I dealt with some Russians for a while when the USSR was coming apart, Rick. Life was very brutal there under the old regime and now it's like the Wild West must have been."

I'd heard this from others. "It's in the east," I told him.

"Not only," he retorted. "You can get there if you keep going west, the world's a sphere, Mr Vasco da bloody Gama."

"Nah, rumor innit!" I gestured to where beyond Lithuania's eastern border lay Belarus and beyond that the great mass of mother Russia, a serious piece of real estate stretching all the way to the Pacific Ocean on the other side of our planet. "But is it still like that there?"

"About," Baa answered. "Possibly there's still the odd hundred billion to be made by stealing or simply assuming control of businesses, properties, and industries. It'll stay that way until the cleverest, toughest people have got so rich they decide they want to institute the rule of law to stop others stealing their wealth away from them. With that, a notion of honesty slips in through the door, kind of like the Magna Carta…"

We'd stopped and were looking into a womens' hairdressing salon from which a couple of very pretty girls were looking back at us. Baa pointed to his thinning hair and gestured to one of the girls. She smiled and shaking her head came to the shop's open doorway. Her English wasn't bad; he flirted suggesting, that if the shop only took women clients, she cut his hair privately. She said no meaning maybe, and he told her he'd pass by another time; we walked on. "Don't you love the way girls tease?" he asked.

The afternoon was growing ever hotter and we took a beer before choosing a restaurant, having some smorgasbord type of sandwiches then returning to the hotel. I figured they were police or spooks because both had been in the hotel lounge that morning when I'd had my coffee and that was now a good four hours ago. Theatrically Dressed Man had been avidly reading the previous days *International Herald Tribune* then and he was now reading the very same newspaper with, if anything, increased avidity. The *Trib*'s a paper I like, but four hours plus? There was no drink on his table perhaps indicating a slim or even no expense account. At another table, over by the wall Blonde Boy seemed to have more generous terms of employment for he was tucking into a healthy-looking salad and a Carlsberg. Lithuania is on the Baltic Sea as are Sweden, Finland,

Russia, Estonia, Latvia, Poland, Germany and Denmark; it also has land borders with Belarus and Russia—you figure out where these watchers, if they weren't internal Lithuanian security, might be from. It occurred to me that, as they were ensconced in the hotel, if Baa or I were their targets we would probably have been followed around the streets by others. If so, that was good for they would have learned nothing; just to be on the safe side we spent the next couple of hours wandering around tourist Vilnius and buying bits of bric-a-brac. We arranged to have it couriered to the landlord of a pub in Glasgow Baa could remember the name and address of—he'd once spent a best denied night there. Its landlord was, if not too worldly, certainly too world weary to be much mystified. Baa reckoned he would festoon his bar with the stuff. Around ten, the summer sky was darkening, and we went out again; the club we found in those relatively early days of westernization was not exactly sophisticated. On learning we spoke English, one doorman, who actually had a small still bleeding wound to his forehead, waved his metal detector threateningly and warned "No guns! No cameras!"

"No, no," I said and smiled reassuringly whilst very conscious that the pieces of dense metal we'd decided not to leave at the hotel could set of his device. Whilst these pieces were innocuous in themselves, that would not stop any watchers reporting the matter; after all, they'd have had little else to report on us so far and would want to justify their pay. Baa got talking with some Swedes who were also on the way into the club and a bunch of hostess-dancers clustered beyond the bouncers. The scene didn't light any fires for me, so I left him there and returned to the hotel.

I didn't call his room the next morning. Taking an early coffee I resisted nodding to Theatrically Dressed Man and went out to stroll the bright-aired Sunday morning streets. I decided to follow the steady trickle of people along a path, past miserable beggars and into a huge building. It was my first experience of what I supposed an eastern style of Catholic Church. I could not help but be impressed.

Far more than any cathedral I'd ever visited, this church overwhelmed—not only the eye but one's spirit was drawn far upward by a massive pillar into the skillfully contrived roof decorated with depictions of the surreal; or perhaps we should say real for often the psychic truths that religions retail are overwhelming and make the day to day seem like paste. Think back a few hundred years and imagine the awe and terror such images would have inspired in an illiterate, hovel-dwelling peasant. The place was magnificent; no wonder religions were such good earners.

I wandered about inside the church feeling the enrapturement of the people; particularly those wide, old women of creased skin and ruined bodies. Motherhood, deprivation, grandmotherhood, the collapse of the all-powerful communist state and their bodies' internal systems tele-graphing physical decline were all object lessons confirming humility as being a matter of commonsense. These old ladies lived their religion and looking at them the notion arose that I might be a mother in another incarnation as some sort of karmic settlement.

Pursued by that awful idea, I hurried out, back past the beggars, intending to find some worldly cheer. As I emerged back into the city street and looked around to get my bearings, a new but mud-splattered all-wheel drive halted alongside. "Get in," Baa spoke from the front pas-senger seat.

"You look like shit," I told him with as much cheerfulness as I could muster. "Demon drink have its way with you, did it?" The car's interior was filled with the soundtrack of "Casino" as we drove by an incredibly circuitous route out of the city. The driver, a man in his middle twenties, turned out to be Ilya, and his English turned out to be virtually nonexis-tent and our laborious roundabout route to be important. "Hey, hangover boy, do you have the acids."

Baa pointed at a grip on the floor, closed his eyes and napped. Ilya drove well within whatever the local speed limit was likely to be so I assumed we weren't going too far. An hour later we'd circled the entire city and were heading westward at around a hundred and fifty kilometers per hour on a dual carriage road so I changed my assumption. "Where are we going?" I asked. "How far?"

"Soon, soon." This for Ilya proved almost chatty for it was a large percentage of his English repertoire. Another two hours passed, and we were headed south past Kaunas on a smaller but evidently still main road; then we went west again but on what was little more than a track. Flattish fields and scrubland sloped in the general direction we traveled until we reached a slow moving river. Ilya drove straight into the water and then steered parallel to the bank for a few hundred yards before slowing right down and swinging out into midstream. Not at all sure about the man, his sanity, or driving abilities, I prodded the still hungover Baa awake and gestured at the water now surrounding the vehicle. He grunted something in Russian to which Ilya replied apparently to his satisfaction for he closed his eyes again. As far as I could tell the river's hidden ford was totally unmarked, but Ilya must have known it well for we soon powered up the opposite bank on to another track. Ilya's window hissed downward releasing our cool conditioned air and admitting a warm, beige-tinged atmosphere that smelt of the sort of adhesive made from old horses. Ilya waved his left arm out of the open window and inhaled deeply. "Roussiah," he exclaimed, as in Russia, isn't it great, eh!

Pretty soon we were back on a surfaced road passing the factory responsible for the glue smell. It dawned on me that we must be inside the Russian enclave that lies between Lithuania and Poland and without the required stamps and visas in our passports. Again I prodded Baa awake. "This better be good," I told him. "We could be right up it without a paddle if we're stopped." He turned to look directly into my eyes and he did look awful—his eyes were bloodshot and his skin interestingly yellow. "Don't stare. You'll make me feel like you look." I told him.

"Relax." He held a plastic supermarket bag out to me. "If we're stopped, just buy our way through." I looked inside the bag and saw it contained dollars; apparently a few thousand in tens and twenties. Baa asked me to pass him the grip, which was on the floor behind Ilya's seat, and from this he produced a large picnic thermos of coffee. This cheered and revived us all. "How come we have to sneak into this little bit of Russia—couldn't they have done their trick for us in Lithuania or back in Ukraine?"

"Logistics and cultures. Pyotr is Russian, and Ilya says he owns the place we're going to and knows people there. As you'll have noticed, it's a very soft border, so moving out and back into a new westernized Lithuania with the product is easy he claims. So all in all it's convenient."

"Product! Product! What's with the drug movie talk? Stop trying to sound like a cunt trying to sound cool, you cunt."

Bleary eyes mocked my nervousness. "Eh, gringo, jus' yo' chill yo'self… yo leetle culo i' saff, hokay." We'd been heading southward and now turned right on to another road that led through a small nondescript village after which we turned right again down a rutted track. Quite suddenly we were out of the not unpleasant early summer evening and into something different. It was as if we'd driven into a cloud of gloom. Looking around I saw no specific changes yet there was a quality of gray about the foliage. The car stopped by a distressed brick building, and I realized there was no birdsong. Joining Baa and Ilya outside the car, the shiver was involuntary. "Very nice," I said as I looked at the dilapidated building. "A place in the country." Ilya led us toward the building, which I suppose could have once been a farmhouse of some sort. It had a malign ambiance vaguely reminiscent of those nuclear power stations so thoughtfully built along the Channel coast by the French. But this was much, much odder. It was surrounded by what I can only describe as an unfocused atmosphere and had an air of being not quite normal. Sound seemed to be deadened and, although I didn't realize it immediately, there were no smells—I mean no smell of anything around this place. No, I'm not exaggerating. Not really much bigger than a small family house, the building was surrounded by a profound sense of the absence of life—a deadness.

Once inside, my sense of foreboding worsened; the ground floor ceiling had been removed and a circular metal platform of maybe four meters diameter had been installed on top of some short concrete pillars. Over this a sort of giant four-pronged tuning fork was suspended from a crane that was itself mounted on the back of a lorry.

It looked as if the far wall of the building had been demolished to enable the lorry access. Sections of brick wall were strewn on the ground and palletlike structures made of railway sleepers had been upended and fastened together where the original wall had stood. Internal walls had also been mostly removed and if, as I supposed, this had once been a farm of some sort it seemed that the animals had been kept inside this building for there were zinc feeding troughs along part of two walls. Near the crane-bearing truck there was a worse-for-wear car without rear tires; a belt drive connected its back wheels to a generator from which cables ran to the tuning-fork assembly, the platform below it and a wooden table to which various bits of adhesive tape had been affixed. There was a stillness about this equipment that touched something deep inside me and produced an anonymous primal fear. "Baa," I said in a croaky voice that surprised me. "I don't think this shit is a good idea. I have a distinct feeling we should fuck off right now."

"Don't be a sad wus. You're going to see something amazing and we might make a lot of money."

"Listen, even a hungover fuck like you must feel there's something a bit wrong here."

"Like what?" Baa gestured around. I was about to tell him rather eloquently what I was feeling when the sound of another vehicle stopped me. An SUV, just visible through the open doorway had arrived. Three men and a rather striking woman climbed out of the vehicle and joined us inside the building. Pytor introduced me to his secretary, Galena, and to Alexei, an impressively tough-looking man whose eyes shone with intelligence. The other man seemed to just be the muscle. Galena was a center-of-attention kind of girl; she had looks and a figure that when she was fifteen maybe twenty years younger would have been fairly heart stopping, and her English was good. Alexei had Ilya and the muscle bring in spectrographic analysis equipment from the SUV. He and Ilya began to set things up connecting the equipment. Essentially such analysis is done by dissolving the metals to be analyzed in an acid complex and superheating a tiny quantity of that to a plasma state: the equipment then takes a reading of the light spectrum caused by displaced electrons in the plasma and this tells you with accuracy not only which metals are present but how much of each metal is present. To dissolve palladium a mixture of concentrated hydrochloric and nitric acids is needed, dangerous stuff which now Baa added together with practiced ease from the two small aftershave bottles Fat George had brought from London. Alexei and company had of course brought their own acids, and we would use theirs at first to analyze the metal and then reset their machine and use our own. This would show us if the Russians had doctored their acid and thus if they were intending to rip us off. Setting up their state-of-the-art analysis equipment would take a little time so I walked around the interior of the building to see what was there. Galena, at the instigation of Pytor trailed after me. Life had endeavored to make her hard, almost succeeded yet somehow failed to quite complete the job. She had a broad romantic streak you saw in her eyes and her body language. Intriguingly but nevertheless sadly this seemed tempered with an opinionated bluntness that the animus often contrives . "You are rich?" she asked.

"Don't be so hard on yourself." Yes - nail right on the head, there'd been a giveaway intake of her breath. I was distracted by a piece of metal rod by my feet. I stooped and picked it up.

It appeared to be copper or a copper alloy but it had a piece of wood - machined, worked wood - fused into it. This wood was actually laminated on one of its four surfaces with the sort of plasticized coating a worktop might have; it disappeared into the copper rod's side at an angle and emerged at a different angle from the rod's end. That end was splintered but not as a metal fractures, it was splintered in exactly the way a piece of wood might yet from out of that destruction the wood and its laminate emerged in pristine condition. I looked at Galena who glanced briefly at the merged wood and metal I held. "It happens some-times," she said. For all I knew there may have been a simple technical explanation for this weird item, but there sure wasn't for the next thing I found. It was another bar of metal that changed about two thirds along its meter or so length into glass or something that looked very like glass, and where the change had occurred the head of a rat was embedded in the bar. The rat's body was still attached, and I gingerly prodded it with the toe of my shoe; it seemed soft and not decomposed. I went back to where Baa stood, and told him quietly to come and see these things. Galena had apparently done much the same to Pyotr for he joined us to look at this bizarre object. Baa seemed unfazed. "Yes, Alexei told me odd things happen sometimes during the process—sort of by-products of the energy field."

"Oh, great. How do we make sure this sort of shit doesn't happen to us—I've seen *The Fly*." I indicated the rat and noticed for the first time that its head seemed disproportionately small compared to its body.

He called Alexei, who peered at the rat and apparently said in Russian that we shouldn't worry as we'd all be well away from the equipment when the process was occurring. "Surprise, surprise," I said to myself, feeling this whole thing was, whilst evidently dangerous, still most likely some sort of trick. Another thought occurred. "I think it would be sound if we move the spectrographic equipment away from all this. For all we know *the process* as you call it could affect the readings," I said to Baa.

He spoke directly to Pytor in Russian initiating what to a non-Russian speaker sounds like an argument but is in fact fairly normal conversation. Alexei joined in and Muscle was detailed to put the SUV on level ground outside and lower the tailboard as a table on which he and Ilya placed the analytical equipment. Ilya then rejoined Alexei and fiddled around with the centerpiece before handing me a plastic carrier bag containing the steel chisel and small hammer. Muscle brought in two silver bars along with a plastic bag bearing the logo of a well-known German company and the words ACHTUNG! Cd. Cd is the chemi-cal code for the metal cadmium. Baa produced a set of bathroom scales. "From the hotel—we only need approximate weights," he responded to my expression. He weighed the silver bars at three kilos each, and the cadmium at around a kilo. He drilled and acid tested each of the bars and, to be certain that they were silver, he melted a little of each with a blowtorch; he also bagged up a few grams of drillings for later retesting. He passed both bars to me, and whilst he slit the bag of cadmium and gingerly spooned random grains into another small sample bag, I laid the bars on the ground. Taking the hammer and chisel, I punched rough roman numerals into each bar—XIII into one and XIV into the other. I took the millimeter number eight punch from my pocket and stamped tiny figure eights in several recognizable places relative to the roman numerals on each bar. I then carried the bars to Alexei who placed them along with my one ounce ingot and the bag of cadmium more or less centrally on the disc beneath the tuning fork. He was to sprinkle a little sand over the other materials and called to Baa to check it before he did. What Baa and I were concerned with was that the materials that went in were the materials that would be coming out after the alleged transmutation: as the weight of the sprinkled sand was just a few ounces, it was largely irrelevant anyway in terms of any duplicitousness. Ilya got some kind of fire-protective clothing from our vehicle and then started the car without back wheels to get the generator running. Alexei clambered off the disc, went over to the wooden table, and switched on his laptop causing LED indicators to blink on everywhere. I was very pleased to note that Baa, Galena, and Pytor all made the same sudden instinctive move to the doorway that I did. Alexei laughed and shouted in Russian for us to run and hide thus guaranteeing as soon as we were outside, we stopped and peered back in through the doorway.

Yes, the curious part of me wanted desperately to go back in and see what was happening, but just as all elements have the same building blocks, so all living creatures are made out of atoms grouped into complex molecules called deoxyribonucleic acid—that's DNA to me and you. A human, an elephant, a lizard, and a rat all have DNA, and what we come into being as just depends on which bits of it are placed where within the DNA—which geometrical arrangement is made. Less than two percent of different placing is sufficient to differentiate between men and chimpanzees. Like me, you've probably met a lot of people about whom it's difficult to believe the difference to be that vast.

What we were all in this peculiar place for was the alteration of one substance into another by some sort of science not generally understood. As a species, we are not so long out of the forest that each of us were not trying to control an inner terror of the unknown—a fear that we would somehow become altered ourselves, perhaps wind up fused into inert matter like the rat.

A horrible stomach-vibrating hum was developing and something about the four prongs of the suspended tuning fork was changing; it was as if they somehow glowed without emitting light, as if pearlized but without the warm softness of pearls—I'm sorry, but there is really no other way to properly describe it. To my amazement the lower part, that is the extremity of each prong, became translucent and then disappeared. At the same time the large floor-mounted disc turned aquamarine, changed to a kind of gray-blue, and then became impossibly bright. Shielding my eyes and looking away from it I could just make out Alexei and Ilya at their table, each wearing fireproof coveralls and helmets with dark visors. The far wall of the building disappeared to reveal what looked like an absolute void and then there was a tremendously loud bang. The mounted disc and the tuning fork prongs were back exactly as they had been and the car without rear wheels was on fire. Ilya with coolness even a teenager would respect walked over to the burning vehicle and directed foam from a large fire extinguisher at it. It was as the smoke from the fire cleared that I noticed the wall was back in position and that Galena's hand was clutching mine as I was hers. Lest my ego swell her other hand tightly held Pyotr's.

"Well fuck me!" Baa looked drained yet walked back inside the building and over to the mounted disc. Had Alexei not shouted a warning he would have clambered up on it to inspect the metal bars. Ilya came over holding a long pole with which he pushed the metals across the disc so that they fell off the other side. I quickly joined Baa there, the silver bars had dulled and were showing long hairline cracks, my ounce ingot barely recognizable; Ilya returned this time with a bucket of brackish water that he poured out on to the metals. There was a subdued hissing and a little steam. Memories of the rat still being vivid, we allowed Muscle to carry the bars to the wooden table and drill deep into them using a battery powered Makita. When they took the drillings out to the SUV I went with them. Baa remained inside and took more drillings from the bars and the distorted ingot. I watched as Alexei dissolved the drilling Muscle had taken and switched on the equipment; it was a state of the art American model and gave us a reading of 9865 parts per ten thousand of palladium, 100 parts platinum, and traces of rhodium, ruthenium, and nickel. I wasn't what you'd call a trained expert but, from the practical experience I'd had, I was unable to fault their assaying. Everything seemed perfectly above board—but then it would wouldn't it! Baa, to the surprise of the Russians, reset and recalibrated everything using the metal samples delivered by Fat George. He then dissolved the drilling he'd taken in our acids and reran the analysis; the difference was acceptable—less than two parts per ten thousand. From his pocket he took the drill bit that he'd removed from the Makita and tested this; it contained only the tiniest of platinum group metal traces, which would be accounted for by contamination from the drilling procedure. Testing the drill had seriously impressed Alexei—I don't know why—did we look like idiots? Perhaps he was just happy to recognize his own thoroughness in another. I stood next to Baa as he used the stolen scales to weigh the bars; each was now around a kilo heavier and the roman numerals were exactly where I'd put them. I checked the tiny number eights were there then used the drill to take deep drillings of the new palladium bars, bagged these samples and put them in an inside pocket.

Having just witnessed around fifteen hundred dollars worth of silver turned into around sixty thousand dollars worth of palladium within less than an hour I was all but overwhelmed by the sweetness and sourness of avarice.

On Pyotr's say so Galena produced a bottle of champagne from the drinks cooler in their SUV and some disposable cups. We toasted each other for being part of something extraordinary; another bottle appeared, and we toasted Alexei for initiating something extraordinary. Pyotr called to Muscle to join us for a drink, but he did not answer. Pyotr and Ilya went back inside the building to look for him, and then one of them yelled, and we all ran in and found what they had. Galena screamed and ran outside again. Muscle looked like a Damian Hirst. He'd been sliced from right shoulder to left knee; there was no bleeding and no sign of the 30 percent or so of him that had been cut off. His eyes were open.

Pyotr turned to us and said, "He walked through before the energy field had dissipated." Whilst the noise of Ilya gagging outside made me have to swallow my own bile I pondered the breadth of Pyotr's English vocabulary. I was not alone in having to make great efforts at bowel control; I'd never seen a sectioned human liver before. At that very moment a plane thundered very low overhead and immediately Galena came inside shouting in Russian that the plane was military and circling back.

●　　●　　●

We all left; Alexei, Pyotor and Galena with the metals in their SUV, Baa and I with Ilya. In the confused milling about to collect everything I lost the acid bottles and the remains of our metal samples but found a cd that had come from the laptop. Too bad about the acid bottles although they would have fingerprints on them the priority was to get far away as quickly as possible. It may be that the military plane had passed low overhead by chance but if not, if Alexei's extraordinary equipment had attracted it, the fact that Baa and I had entered this country illegally was something a hefty U.S. dollar immediate cash payment would possibly have regularized. However that what we had been doing whilst here was hardly illegal was a fact the authorities might choose to overlook in view of the deceased Muscle and the odd equipment. No, it was definitely time to leave.

Alexei had achieved with the power generated by a car engine the transmutation of kilos of metal previously requiring the energy equivalent of very many atomic bombs. He'd also managed some bizarre side effects. If this had attracted the military how long would it take them to get some sort of force to the site? I'd a clear mental picture of a helicopter full of troops clacking to the building at treetop height—it might be happening right now for all we knew.

Ilya managed some serious driving without lights. When we got near the river he stopped, got out, found a largish stone with which he smashed the taillights then navigated the river by moonlight. Once back in Lithuania, he put on the headlights and drove very fast. Baa and I feigned inebriation when entering into our hotel just after the early summer dawn.

"You know this is a bit too adrenal for my taste. I'm going to fuck off quickly," I told him as soon as we were in the lift.

"With you there, old son! Sort the bills, and I'll book us on the first plane out—downstairs as soon as you're ready, yeah."

Emerging from beneath fear's shadow enlivens as did that first plane's destination. Six hours later, we each seriously enjoyed tourist oysters and champagne off St. Germain, whilst dark inner clouds rolled away. A stroll over a bridge and up to Concorde enabled us to babble practical concerns and ideas.

By the time separate taxis took us from Eurostar's London terminal that evening we'd agreed the outline of the deal we'd offer Pyotr if and when we heard from him.

Oysterful I didn't sleep much that night.

August just about empties London of its indigenes, so there's only half the traffic and being conditioned to a continual urban night-time hum I felt the relative silence strange. Surfing TV channels produced no lasting diversion so I had little choice but to face the fact that a man I didn't know had lost his life whilst standing a few meters from me…how long ago was it? I checked my watch—less than thirty hours. The guy might have been a complete bastard for all I knew; he may have deserved to die but I wasn't entitled to judge him. "But in any event so what?" I told myself aloud. "Right now as I lay here people are dying and being born all over the planet. It was just the man's bad luck or destiny. It wasn't my fault and it's not my responsibility. I was just there." Still I couldn't sleep for something that I couldn't identify, couldn't bring into conscious consideration still worried at me. That bizarre setting over in Russia was something to do with whatever nagged at me now.

Eventually I got up, made some tea and put on the radio. I lay in the darkness listening to the BBC World Service until just after the early dawn when Morpheus' arms enfolded me.

Not all that refreshed and going out just after nine in anticipation of a reassuringly familiar toast and coffee at the Picasso, I saw my car was no longer in it's parking bay. The bay now had an official notice affixed to it advising of its suspension to facilitate the fitting of street furniture. Paranoia beckons. Unwilling to consider the fine to be paid and the hassle of retrieving my car I stalk off only to be confronted after less than twenty paces by the very blonde, Panda-eyed neighbor. "I saw them take your car," she tells me excitedly. "They were here before eight this morning!"

"You saw them taking it?"

"Yes!"

"This morning?"

"Yes, it was before eight!"

I take a slow breath to calm myself a little before asking, "Then why didn't you knock on my door and tell me?"

"Oh, I couldn't possibly have done that," she huffed.

"Why not?" I'm unable to keep exasperation from my tone.

"I told you—it was before eight."

"So?"

She is utterly aghast "I'd no makeup on!"

I look at her; Panda-eyes is not a stupid person by any measure but she lives on planet Panda-eyes and is only aware of the rest of us as bit players on the stage of her existence. Still, those of us living in glass houses really shouldn't throw stones—that she'd even noticed a car being removed was something of an achievement for her. Normally such events would have remained unregistered by her conscious mind for they did not directly affect her.

Even in central London there is, within limits, neighborliness, yet I cannot be furious with her for I know something of her situation.

Breakfast and skimming newspapers in Café Picasso's normally con-soling ambience did not dismiss the persistent disquiet over the events near the Baltic. They'd disturbed something deep within only slightly less than avarice had seduced me, so I was stuck in one those situations that ever plague us and hence ever impel us to decisiveness.

I needed to ground myself and logic suggested the simplest way was to focus on the stomach and eat. In essence, we are tubes for processing matter; as soon as we're born, sustenance is poured in the mouth and passes through us. It's our first addiction. We're born craving it, and that craving, along with the mysterious factor X, has resulted in our species becoming conscious along with the potential to develop addictive per-sonalities. No gain without stress as Ellie once remarked. Being social creatures the most satisfying and affirming way to eat is in company so I decided to do the whole ritual—gathering friends and feeding them with home-cooked food I'd prepared myself.

Given the fact I've always eaten out because I can't cook it wasn't the most practical idea - yet that is what, and perhaps why, I decided to do so. The decision felt good. I phoned Baa, Dave, Ellie, and a couple from France, Sy and Monica, who'd left a voicemail saying they were in London for a few days.

I'd known Sy for maybe a decade; three years ago he'd decided the Chinese factories that thundered day and night for the dollar should no longer do so for his and he sold both his business and his home. An impressive Winnebago imported from the States was loaded with Harris, the recently inoculated, microchipped and passported Cairn Terrier, together with his own bits and pieces and driven to some friend's Surrey villa. The party there wound down around 4:00 A.M., and more than a score of us waved good-bye as Sy and Harris left, both stone cold sober, to drive to Portsmouth for the morning ferry to Bilbao. From there,

Sy would Winebago across country, abandoning the chilly Atlantic for the warm sensuality of the Middle-of-the-World sea and meander about continental Europe and bits of North Africa exploring any distractions that might occur. It occurred within a year and was called Monica, a twenty-something Swiss whose rather more than ample curves remained undisguised by blood-red motorcycle leathers. Lust at first sight physically jolted old Sy to spill some of his end-of-the-day cassis on the little terrace outside a village cafe next to the Herault's clear waters in Languedoc.

Realizing Monica was a woman unlikely to lack admirers and that she was half Sy's age, Harris decided he must take the initiative to win the day. He was aware his master had been a bit lonely of late. Less than a couple of moons back, he'd been obliged to sabotage a nascent relationship with a completely unsuitable woman who'd sought to ensnare them both into her really quite agreeable home back down toward the Spanish border. Had Harris been interrogated in depth it may have emerged that his judgment was more influenced with her having two cats than any objective evaluation of her suitability vis-á-vis Sy. Dogs, as you know, are rarely if ever overburdened with the conceit of objectivity. Harris knew that left to his own devices, Sy might screw up this new opportunity royally.

Monica had raced up the Herault river valley on progressively narrower roads rejoicing, as any healthy girl might, in the 500 ccs of perfectly balanced power roaring between her legs. The odd car had given chase, but she'd outrun them just as she had the demons that troubled her at the start of each day. Now, helmet off, she'd sat outside a village cafe to drink some tea and let the day's speed induced adrenalin drain away. An undeniably handsome young dog with its head ever so slightly cocked to one side looked into her eyes pleadingly. He was irresistible and she was pleasantly surprised that when she smiled down at him he yelped joyfully and scampered over to jump into her lap. Harris of course had far too much savoir faire to lick a stranger's face but he contrived to be clumsily adorable until Sy gathered his wits together and came over. "Pardon, j'excuse mon chien," he apologized in halting French.

"Quelle accent, c'est insupportable!" thought Harris with an internal canine shrug for he was becoming something of a Francophile.

"Harris, get off the lady," Sy instructed. Harris responded by leaning forward, barring his teeth and growling. He and Sy often played at arguments when alone of an evening—Sy would tell him off and he'd growl back; Sy would then threaten all sorts of terrible things and Harris would face him out. In the doggy universe this was thrilling stuff for Sy was unquestionably the leader of their pack of two, but Harris had class and this sort of game had really toughened him up since puppyhood. Even dealers' psycho dogs sensed it and lost a bit of their in-your-face-brutishness when glanced at by this Cairn. Forcing his eyes away from Monica's cleavage— she'd unconsciously slipped the zip on her front down just enough—Sy's mind was struggling to formulate a plan. "Right," he spoke with great severity to the little dog. "I've warned you about disobedience," he said as he lifted the growling Harris. "and that's it—I've had enough. You're going and I'll be rid of you for ever you sod." He strode across the cafe's terrace and held Harris out over the flowing river.

Monica's heart missed a beat "Halt! Nein!" She was on her feet. "Stop! Do not. Please, I will take him." Even when panicked her English was good. From his position, over the fast-flowing waters, Harris gave her his best look and she reached over to try and grab him. "Please no." Sy did not move. "I will pay you."

"How much?" Sy asked while keeping Harris out of her reach and well over the water. A look of utter contempt suffused the woman's face.

"How much do you want?" she spat out the words.

"Well…" he looked thoughtful. "I guess dinner tonight would about do it." As he spoke he retracted his arms to bring Harris into a cuddle and kissed the top of his head.

Monica burst out laughing. "Oh, man! You - and you too," she scolded the delighted Harris.

Many hours later in dark Winebago world she confided, "I was never seduced by a dog before."

"That's a relief," said Sy.

Inexplicably it felt auspicious that they were in London just now, and as their schedule would take them away again in four days, I asked everybody for dinner in two days' time.

Baa called back and said Pyotr had just phoned with an outline deal and an hour later we met for sandwiches and beer in the Australian.

To Baa's surprise and now mine, Pyotr had agreed that Baa and I receive 32 percent of the net sales income of the metals produced. Baa had asked for 40 percent figuring to agree to anything over twenty-five and so was happy. He would pay out all the initial expenses for setting up plant here in the UK and all of the legal expenses and the costs of setting up the various companies we would need to create in order to obscure our activities. Baa would not pay any fees or anything up front to Pyotr or Alexei. Baa told me he figured I should get 7 percent and himself 25 percent on the basis that he was pulling me in and fronting all the money. I did a lot of laughing and put my arm round his shoulders, hugging and telling him I'd forgotten how funny he could be when he tried. We settled on sixteen percent each, with me repaying him 70 percent of the money he'd put in out of the first monies I would receive from the operation. "Or you'll probably spit in this bloody dinner you're forcing on me," he complained.

"It would rhyme," I told him.

Neither of us was sure the whole deal was not a con by the Russians that we hadn't seen through, but on the basis that it was genuine then our arrangements with each other were reasonable. Baa was not the kind of person who needed anybody to hold his hand, but this was edgy stuff. He knew that I knew there weren't many, perhaps any, other than me he could trust if it came to a crunch.

When he went on to say, "If this comes off it'll rock a few boats—it's going to need serious layering." I saw a touch of otherness about his countenance. That hard light that comes when we decide to enter unknown territory: when matters of the primitive dark forest call down the ages through our blood.

"If this comes off, it *will* rock a few boats," I agreed.

"If we were making oil I'd be crapping myself big time."

"You wouldn't touch it if we could make oil for nothing?" I asked.

"Don't be daft—but you've heard stories—run-proof nylons, tires that last half a million miles, herbal medicines…"

"What are nylons?" I asked.

"They're getting easier to find these days."

I told him I figured a Liechtenstein company should contract out the processing to another company for a fee; that the metal produced remained the property of that Liechtenstein company that would then receive the entire sales income in a Swiss bank account.

"Yeah, makes sense to keep it open between all of us on income," He went on to suggest that the operating costs being rents, supplies, shipping costs, insurance, utility bills and unavoidable taxes would be paid into the enterprise by each of us pro rata to our end share of the sales; his thinking was that this would stop anyone getting too creative with costs.

The Australian was filling up with a lunchtime crowd; he got up and I followed him outside into the, extraordinarily for London, broad and quiet street. We stood on the pavement beyond earshot of other drinkers. "You know how the Spanish company switch works?"

"No," I said

"I'll explain later. Also I'll get in touch with Icy Gee."

Icy Gee was the producer of legal entities from nowhere. Really nowhere; they were untraceable. Baa and I said good-bye; he getting into his waiting minicab, and me hailing a passing taxi to go and retrieve my removed vehicle.

The car -pound was a million miles away, every one of them made tiresome by the cabby's faux commiserations at my misfortune—I've made a bob or two ferrying pricks like you out there to get their motors back was the subtext. He'd no idea his leeriness told of his own discontent. "That's quite a little gig you've got," I told him as I counted out the exact fare. "Do you make much in tips on these runs?"

A large payment at the car-pound office and I'm driving back into central London thinking, not for the first time, that the best car in the world has to be a chauffeur-driven one. In the West End I use the Chinatown carpark at the end of Gerrard Street. The day was becoming very hot and, after crossing Shaftsbury Avenue, I pause at the French for a glass of cold white. A young General de Gaul peers from an old photo, he wears an extraordinarily disdainful look, severely pissed off at WW II's necessary Anglo- Gallic amalgam.

Refreshed, I walk a hundred yards and queue. She finds and packs the things I order to create a small but perfectly formed cusuinic bluff. Camisa's on Soho's Old Compton Street is a treasure, a retailer of the best of Italian food and thus Italians would say the best food in the world. Homemade pastas, Parma ham in slices so thin they are meltable like butter, mozzarella made in heaven, bresaola dried by the sweetest airs, carpaccio, extra virgin olive oil, basil, etc, etc. I find I'm actually looking forward to cooking the only thing I know how for my guests. I also buy a properly hung steak from a posh butcher.

The day's glorious weather delivers a London twenty-four-degree evening on my patio; wondering why I've already drunk too much wine, I conclude that I'm actually nervous about feeding others, concerned that they won't enjoy the meal.

"Fuck it! I can't worry about that sort of stuff," I tell myself and drink some more.

We start with cold white crab and avocado bought in from a deli near the barbers and then went on to my thing. Years ago a beautiful Italian girl had written it down for me. What? You really want me to tell you what she wrote - it's just a recipe? I'm reading you wrong here—no? Well, I'll do it, but in case it's a bore for you, I'll put lines around it.

A had written: extra virgin olive oil in heavy pan, so I'd bought one of those orange French things; heat the oil; slice fresh garlic and drop them into the hot oil; cold rinse sun-dried tomatoes then cut each piece into three slivers then let your body tell you *the* moment to drop the sun-drieds in with the garlics; boil water in a stainless steel saucepan with pinch of sea salt; add homemade pasta and after three minutes, start taking a strand out every half minute to test its texture. When the pasta is ready, strain it *carro mio* and then rinse with fresh boiling water; leave it in the saucepan and cover it with the lid. Drain the oil from the frying pan and tip the pan's contents into the pasta saucepan and stir. Add fresh, warmed oil to that saucepan and stir a little more. Take saucepan to table and serve contents onto plates using a big spoon so excess oil stays in saucepan. Grate on parmesan and put a few fresh basil leaves on top of each dish. ENJOY AND REMEMBER ME.

We did, and I did—she's so married now. This simple dish opened our appetites for the slices of fillet steak that gently seared under the grill and the mange-tous briefly bathing in boiling water. Yes, I know it's hardly cooking—about anyone can do it with a few adverbs, but apparently a little salt is needed in the mange-tous water, and I'd forgotten to add any. Everyone was too polite to mention it.

A couple of spoonfuls of sorbet and Ellie and Monica were pretty impressed; Sy, Dave and Baa seemed to have barely noticed what they ate but their plates were empty.

I announced I'd been up since 5:00 A.M. preparing the meal, Ellie smiled, Baa said, "Sure Doris." Only Dave and Harris had the decency to look vaguely concerned. Harris had dined royally on raw steak some-where beneath the table and Dave seemed to have taken very little nasally. I opened more of the ludicrously expensive Margaux and put another bottle of champagne in the ice bucket for Ellie who never touched other wines. She followed me into the kitchen and started opening drawers. "I know you've got candles here somewhere. Aha—this is where they hide!" She made a point off keeping her legs straight as she bent low.

"Yeah yeah, hon. It looks great." I gave her bum a slowish full-hand squeeze.

"D'you miss me at all?" She straightened up but avoided my eyes.

"As a matter of fact I do." Such a woman she visibly relaxed. "And if it was anybody but Dave things wouldn't be calm" She positively glowed. "So relax and enjoy the guilt, you beautiful shit." Now she stood on air.

At the doorway she turned back. "The perfect host should spare himself no chore in taking care of his guests, should he, Rick? I do appreciate you."

"So you should, so you should." I followed her outside.

The sky was just losing its light as she placed a couple of big altar candles in the middle of the table and others on and around the steps. I felt contentment as they flamed. Cooking and feeding people really was grounding and I decided I might do it again, but not too soon for the truth is I wasn't entirely comfortable with a part of myself that I'd discovered. This newly uncovered aspect had wanted to get the meal right, wanted my guests to enjoy it and, here's the bad bit I couldn't ignore, wanted praise.

They had not fallen to their knees saying Rick you're a bloody fantastic cook and we each deeply appreciate that you actually took care in choosing and preparing this food.

How could people be so ungrateful? I told them this and Baa said, "Sorry, I thought it was a takeaway." I wondered if women who cook for their families got wounded by lack of appreciation. Drinking a bit more too much wine I sat amongst my guests observing them rather than really being with them.

Monica was saying, "...magic to know that Shakespeare had been on the same site watching plays he'd written, maybe just written." They'd been to the Globe Theatre the previous evening. Dave asked her where else she'd been in London. "We went round the zoo, but a tiger..." she began to giggle and it became a laugh. Sy made an exasperated exhalation, a sort of sigh with attitude. This ensured our undivided attention as Monica continued "A tiger made pee-pee on Sy."

We'd all turned to look at him as he repeated the sigh and leaned back in his chair with eyes closed.

"I thought that smell was something cook-boy had done," said Baa.

"Very brave to get in the tiger's cage though,"said Dave.

Eyes still closed Sy said, "It wasn't pee."

"Aha, that sort of relationship," Ellie swallowed champagne. "You don't always know with men do you, Monica?"

Sy said, "I'm just going to sit here quietly for a bit until you've all tired of being tedious."

"Come on folks!" Baa's tone had become headmasterly. "The man's digesting his dinner! No more silly comments." He glared around the table at each of us. "Or we'll not learn what happened to him later at the monkey house—please go on with the tiger bit Monica."

"The bloody thing was marking me," said Sy. "I was looking into its eyes thinking, I can do this because it's in a cage—it's a tiger, it could take my head off with one blow from a paw. I'm looking at it directly in the eyes and it's looking directly back into my eyes. Then it turns its back and I'm just starting to think that I've out-stared a tiger when a jet of liquid shoots thirty feet out from between the bars and hits me in the chest. They've a gland that produces scent for marking their territory."

"So you're labelled,"said Dave "scary stuff - hope it's not the one that escaped today…"

"Was!" exclaimed Monica before she could think. Then, smiling, she said, "Also that finished our visit because he had to clean up—he was starting to smell like the snakes in the reptile house."

"I plan on getting a snake," Dave, accepting a cigar from Baa punctured its end with a fork before noticing everybody was awaiting some sort of amplification. "As a coat belt—they come out of the loops and trail along the ground so I'll train the snake as a belt."

"That's not such a bad idea," Baa said, as I went to the kitchen for the cheeses. When I returned he was telling Dave that the ancient Egyptians had used gorillas as child minders "…females - exploited their maternal instinct you see. The gorillas were very gentle with the kids. Clever people, the Egyptians."

"We saw an obelisk from Egypt today like those in Paris and Washington," said Monica. "But here it was by the river near a strange church."

"Did you go inside the church?" asked Ellie.

"We did," Sy answered. "in fact there was a tour guide there." He reached for the bottle and poured more wine for himself. "Always seems a bit odd to me, Temple."

Temple is that part of London where a great number of barristers have offices that are called chambers; in the midst of these is the Templar Church, which would later receive publicity in various novels, films and articles.

"There's a very odd statue outside the church—a pole at the top of which is a horse with two knights in armor riding it," Sy continued. "This guide described them as poor knights—so poor they had to share a horse. Yet if you think about it from the horse's point of view, it's strength and capacity is controlled by two armored men cooperating together to get where they want the horse to take them. For each knight it halves the cost of the horse, halves the maintenance, and about halves the hay and halves the requirement for management."

Baa spoke, "There's a stranger church just up the hill from there. But, actually the statue you saw is a good monument to the MBM." Nobody said anything, and Baa amplified, "The Mistaken Belief in Markets, that completely free competition will deliver the best deals for consumers and make the economy lean and healthy. If politicians really believed that, and it's a pretty big *if*, but if they really did, then they weren't too bright."

"So what's this statue got to do with the price of eggs?" I asked.

"It illustrates collusion—wait and see how well competition in your domestic supplies of electricity and gas works out on this tropical island. But our Sy's already fled it—why did you, by the way?"

"I'd made my money importing—China had been a real honey pot, but things change. Ever more buyers going there meant Chinese products sold here ever more competitively—it ceased being buy it for a penny, ship it here and sell it for a pound."

"You really sold stuff for a hundred times what it cost?" I asked.

He gave me a long look. "Not quite a hundred times, but the gross was enormous at first." He poured more wine into his glass. "Now everybody gets everything made in China." He sipped his wine and then continued, "That's why there's no inflation—nothing to do with prudent government here and everything to do with China. Smart schools teach kids Mandarin," he said and wagged a finger at Dave for no apparent reason.

Dave looked a little startled and I suddenly knew he'd never considered having kids and that was why his previous girlfriend had walked. "Yeah maybe, sort of, kind of... but no, the real cost of living is increasing. House prices are kicking off." He explained he had bought a cottage in Cornwall a couple of years back. He and Ellie had recently spent a few days there and a local estate agent had told him it had more than doubled in value.

"Maybe the location is good?" Monica asked.

"That's got a bit to do with it, but prices everywhere here are going up. It's the dedication of the population of the nation to copulation." he told her.

"Not really," Baa said. "The banks are deregulated and making money lending against property is a thing they do. They're pumping credit out, and so property prices everywhere increase to absorb that money."

"And when the banks run out of money?" asked Monica.

"They'll never run out of it because they're deregulated," he was trying to fish something from a pocket of his discarded jacket. "The banks learned they could do what governments do—print their own fiat money. Effectively they print their own money these days."

"But Fiat is a car—no?" Monica asked.

"Yes, but it also means *authorized*," Baa explained.

"Authorized by whom?" I asked. "I've come across that word, fiat, in the financial press and just assumed it meant bullshit."

"Of course it's bullshit. It means authorized by the organization authorizing it—it's the Catch 22 of the banking system, including the central banks."

Ellie held out her glass and I poured her champagne. "Is it that simple for a commercial bank to create its own money, Baa?"

"It's not complicated. Mr. Banker is sitting there with a pile of mortgages so he bundles them all up into what's called a bond with some great sounding name, gets it koshered by a rating agency and then sells it on."

"So what's new?" asked Sy. "Read a book called *Liars Poker*, in the 80s I think."

"What's new is that the quantity they're manufacturing has created an enormous demand for the components of the bonds—those components are mortgages."

"You mean *components* as in if you were manufacturing shoes you would need a lot of leather, Baa?" asked Dave.

"Exactly like that. The volume of mortgages needed to make lots of bonds is huge, enormous numbers of mortgages are required so they have to get enormous numbers of people to take out mortgages...." Having recovered his lighter Baa relit his cigar; he'd never have used a candle to do that because spirits hang around candles. "If someone is earning commission by getting people to borrow money but earning zilch if they repay it, then that person is going to sign up anybody. So the leather they've made lots of the shoes out of is cardboard, and when it rains the cardboard turns to slush."

"So, leaving aside all the human misery and tragedy this stuff causes, what happens when don't repay?" asked Dave.

"Well, the sellers have got their commissions and the bond manufacturers have manufactured their bonds and sold them, so they've made their dosh so they're all happy."

"Sure, they are," Dave spoke again. "But what about the owner of the cardboard shoes—the new owner of the bond?"

"The buyer of the bond has most likely taken out some sort of insurance for it based on the rating it got from the rating agency." He drained his glass. "And the insurers repeat the process—they bundle up their policies into bonds and sell those bonds on. Perhaps back to the same banks."

"It sounds like kids playing shop," said Ellie. "It sounds like it's zero-sum. It doesn't make sense."

"It does when you factor in time," said Baa. "Essentially, if I'm saying give me credit and I'll pledge this diamond as collateral, I get the credit. By the time you start to worry that this diamond may really be a polished turd, I've borrowed from somewhere else against it and paid you back—everybody's happy. It's time that makes it work, which means that in reality, it's devil take the hindmost—just got to make sure you're not the hindmost." He splashed more wine into his glass and continued, "It's going to be OPM anyway."

"OPM?" asked Monica and when Dave explained it that meant Other People's Money, she said, "So bank robbery is the banks robbing the people?"

"From the mouths of babes," Sy hugged her to him. "In the old days, thirty years or so ago, many shopkeepers loved shoplifters." He sipped his wine slowly and when nobody took the bait, he continued, "As long as shoplifting was accepted as a fact of retailing life shop owners could hype the shoplifting figures and reduce their tax bills. If an item had been shoplifted, it didn't exist in the inventory anymore, so if it hadn't really been shoplifted, it could be sold, and the cash pocketed outside of the accounts."

"Where do you go with this?" Monica asked and somehow snuggled her body even closer to his.

"That when people start shouting about how much they've lost in this or that, there might be another scenario."

"I understand about the shoplifting but not about bond losses—how would anyone benefit apart from some ersatz sympathy?" Ellie asked.

"Suppose they show losses that are tax efficient—maybe worth twenty-five cents on the dollar of the alleged lost investment, but they really got eighty cents on the dollar of the actual investment delivered back to them off shore. Then they're getting a hundred and five cents on the dollar."

"Doesn't sound at all plausible to me," said Baa, yet again relighting his cigar.

"It's not, if you repay all the investors like that," said Sy. "But suppose you just repay some of them, as in friends and facilitators, and you let the institutional investors who use OPM take the losses. The bank execs having filed past reports showing enormous paper profits will have already taken their bonuses. By then it will have got political, and the odor of expediency will quickly drown out all other smells. Business always calls the shots with the politicians in consumer societies because it's business that delivers the goods to be consumed."

"Efficient business—no part of the animal is wasted," Dave announced to the air.

"And nothing is created," said Baa. "It's just facilitates—at a huge cost: but governments lost the poker game with the banks long, long ago. Governments can't govern without the banks' agreement."

"Unless you have an authoritarian society," said Sy.

I went into the living room and loaded some more music, and then headed down to the kitchen for more wine and a box of cheroots I'd picked up in Brazil. When I went back up to the patio, Sy, to whom Monica now appeared to be literally grafted, was telling the others "... other reason I left this country is that were it an individual it would be declared mentally ill and probably incarcerated!"

Baa guffawed. "Mentally ill's a bit strong—dysfunctional maybe."

"I might still live here if it were just dysfunctional, Baa. No, I mean if it were a person this country would be sectioned as being a danger to itself and others. It would be medicated and incarcerated."

"Well, it's certainly very medicated," Dave said and puffed contentedly.

"That's not just here. Don't you suppose that all societies in every country are in some sorts of denial?" Ellie said as she ruffled Dave's hair. "People need a quota of irrationality."

"You're right," said Baa. "People have to be in denial about a lot of stuff."

"Maybe," said Dave. "In denial all sorts of pressures occur and people go a bit crazy; read Orwell's 1984 it ain't just politics baby."

Baa poured then slowly sipped a glass of water. "Look, people need societies and people need beliefs. Those two needs taken together mean a sort of group psychology prevails. People subscribe to what will create a group to which they can belong. Innate beliefs get modified, perverted perhaps, so they can conform to the group norm—truth gets buried because most people just want to get by, to feel they can manage their heads and have homes, food and children," he chuckled. "They've little time or space for truth with a big T. It's disconcerting and uncomfortable—bit hard to digest is truth." He left his chair, moving a little unsteadily over to the cushions that I'd put out on a couple of old rugs.

Removing a small box from Ellie's handbag, Dave went over to join him saying, "That's being mean spirited. I think people are essentially good, but the…" He'd started rolling a joint and Ellie went over and kissed his forehead.

"…in their better moments, darling," she interrupted. "But just now perhaps social irrationality is a compensation for IT."

"The real problem is that we're tubes," Dave finished.

"Hear, hear," I said.

"Such charmers—how do women ever resist you guys?" she sighed.

"We are girl. We're born and have stuff put in our mouths and it comes out at the other end—we're tubes that process material into energy, and we do it from the day we're born," Dave looked around but nobody commented. "You're not getting it—we are addicted to facilitating a chemical process that supports lives and egos. We have addictive personalities—that's why so much drugs of one sort or another get used. That's the physical basis for what geezer here," he put an arm round Baa's shoulders, "is saying. So I guess you could say self-development is about not being addicted because that's the only way people aren't going to be in some sort of denial."

Ellie stood up and stretched, "And yet," she looked pretty amazing in the candle-light. "without all this would we just be automata, no more than amoebas."

"Bit harsh on amoebas," I said.

"Right. Some of my best business is done with amoebas," said Baa. "However, something just occurs—wild animals don't overeat. Cats and dogs and farmed animals are likely to, but that's because they live in our world. Wild creatures don't, not even wild pigs."

"That's disturbing," Dave said as he inhaled. "I'm going to have to think about that."

As Monica was enfolded by Sy's arms so was Harris enfolded in hers. Russian dolls I thought and with a very noticeable contact-high off Dave, I also lay down on the cushions. Feeling satiated in the deepest sense, I'd eaten and drunk well and also fed others. I was physically tired just enough not to care one way or the other about anything, not even sex. It was one of those rare interludes when all the inner and outer conflicts of life don't intrude because they are in balance.

I wondered if animals were unconscious enough to feel as content as I did just then; an image of a bird appeared, and I flowed into its being. Once there, I soared away into the warm night sky, and then there below was a river. Not the Thames that flowed within a thousand steps of my door but something much larger—the Nile. I hovered effortlessly on thermals, sensing rather than seeing the myriad humans who lived in that fertile valley and understood that, collectively, they lived in a strange kind of play world. Not quite like seven-year-olds, untroubled by responsibilities, yet with food and warmth and transport provided by the sun and the river. They were close to their gods; they were respectful of their gods, but they were not always in fear of them for it seems their gods didn't demand ritual sacrifices. Thus with fearfulness placated, their questions were more honestly posed and practically answered. They'd been able to innocently wonder and to do so for thousands of years in a world more like a child's or as a child's world should be. A whole age without our harsh contrived bullshit guilt on bullshit guilt society, a world where the gods are close and magic occurred in its own naturalness.

They were no longer overwhelmed by the earlier Edenic world but neither had their consciousness yet spawned the double-edged sword of reductionism with its relentless attempt to diminsh everything to the mundane and devalue the soul to a mechanism. Reductionism was the terrible servant that had yet to arise and pervert its master. A radience reflected up from those unseen people below and it invigorated me as the spray from warm breaking waves on a beach might. I soared higher and higher into the sky and followed the river south then fancied I reached close to the source where I slipped into sleep then immediately out again.

Everybody seemed relaxed and satiated. The conversations meandered rather than flowed. "So creation or evolution, Baa?" Ellie was asking.

"It's not an either or it's both and." He paused for her to respond and when she didn't he continued, "Creation writes the software, and evolution is a part of that software. There's nothing to suppose that the software doesn't write itself more programs according to how circumstances develop. The other month I drank some secretions from a sort of ..." He was going to start talking about Brazil but apparently thought better of it.

"Why do you live here alone, Rick?" asked Monica.

Thinking the question rude, I said, "I doubt I could bear being with anybody who'd want to be with me."

"Y'know, Groucho," said Baa. "that's more than a little bit depressing."

"Disease of our times—depression." Dave's eyes were closed as he spoke. "Package holidays for depressives—fly to sad places on DespAir— huge, huge market."

"I'm going to make us some coffee," I told them.

"No, I will," Ellie got up, and I let her because I was over-relaxed enough to adjust a couple of big floor cushions and stretch out. Was Dave smoking opium I wondered as I lay back and closed my eyes. The phrase Gold of the Nile wouldn't leave my mind and I wondered if it meant Moses had taken gold with him when he left Egypt or was it gold in the sense of knowledge or perhaps both? These thoughts disappeared at Monica's yell, it's tone alarmed. I stumbled to my feet as did the others and we crowded into the house. Ellie was across the room by the open front door, "You've had a burglar," she said. "He was incredibly fast." Monica who'd gone into the house to use the lavatory looked shaken. Outside the street was empty.

The consensus was that the intruder had just been a casual thief, and I'd not closed the street door properly. Ellie had surprised him because she'd gone into the living room to reach the kitchen rather than use the patio stairs, which were cluttered with plates and empty bottles. Nothing seemed to be missing.

"Interesting though all this may be, we're all a bit bogged down in logic," Dave announced then ignored the silence whilst we each all waited for him to continue. It seemed that a long time passed for in truth it was one of those times when something has occurred or something has been said that cuts through the façade of normality, regularity and ordinariness. As if he'd suddenly noticed we each waited on him, Dave continued, "Logic has a smaller role than we care to believe." The spell was broken. It was as if a dammed up energy had been released.

The coffee came and when Sy and Monica learned I needed to be away for a week he invited me to visit them. "She yodels though." I knew they'd bought a house somewhere in France and now they told me how they also came to own a boat.

That first night they'd spent together in the Winnebago, Sy had thought he was just on to a lucky jump. Monica, that she might as well enjoy the sex she hadn't found a reason not to have with this alone man—and he was so alone he needed a woman—and well, he was kind of nice, and there was something a bit wicked about him in an interesting way, and anyway she'd be off the next day, and, and you never know - and, and, and.

However, once initial lusts had dissipated each was slightly unnerved to discover a sort of warm, easy familiarity remained; their bodies had enjoyed and were comfortable with each other. After a week they'd driven out of the Massif to Montpellier where Sy invested in a motorcycle-carrying bracket on Winnie's rear for Monica's bike.

"Why do you waste money doing that?" she demanded. "You know I'm leaving this week—I've got to be back at my work next Monday."

"Look," said Sy. "Harris will find another dumb girl on a motorbike."

"Huh? Do you think you are the only old man with a nice dog?"

She was to leave the next morning, and theirs was not a bed free of silent tears that night.

"Please unlock my bike." It was 7:00 A.M. and she'd made coffee.

"No."

"Sy, please—we've been through this. Unlock it. I have a long way to go."

"I'm not unlocking it."

"Sy, please darling—I must leave. I have my job, my apartment, and I have obligations. "She lived in Berne and worked at a marketing company there. "Please, it is not easy for me either, but I have got a long, long ride." It had to be a thousand kilometers.

"No," he said again and putting his arms around her let himself fall backward into the RV's big padded chair so that she was pulled sideways onto his lap and into his embrace. Both noticed the way that her pretty head nestled into the crook of his neck. "If you're really going to go we'll drive out to the airport and get you a plane ticket. Then I'm going to drive to this Berne of yours with your bike on the back."

Monica was less than entirely surprised at the sense of relief that flooded her heart and her soul and her body.

Swissness made her work a month's notice, and three weeks after that, they were easing down out of the Rif mountains to the edge of that ocean of sand the size of the North Atlantic. Most of their winter was spent in southern Morocco. Her breasts placated and nurtured the little boy in him whilst his solidity and sagacity fathered the traumatized child in her. How had she been traumatized? I don't know, but something tells me it was deep and it was evil.

The following spring they'd crossed the Straits of Gibraltar and driven along the Spanish coast, crossed the border into Franc, where they bought a house in Languedoc but never really moved in. The gypsy soul had more than seduced them. They took sailing lessons before buying the *Casalina*, their forty foot sailing yacht which was currently parked in a Spanish marina opposite the Balearics.

"Come down with us, we can sail over to Ibiza" said Monica "you'll really like it Rick - lots and lots of pretty girls!"

"Don't be daft woman - they're all nineteen there" said Sy

"You can be an sad arsehole "she told him "Rick is closer in years to them than you are to me old man."

"*A* sad arsehole." he corrected.

Pragmatic thinking said that were an alibi concerning the formations of the various companies ever needed it would be more convincing that I'd been away separately from Baa yet more than that it was an oddly insistent intuition that obliged me to say,"I've some stuff to take care of but I'd really like to come down in about six days, if that would suit you guys."

It did, and Sy said to phone him or the marina office as soon as I knew my travel schedule.

• • •

Despite righteous noises politicians made back then about clamping down on tax havens, offshore companies, and bank accounts, the situation had really only changed in the sense that it had become more complicated. All these clever people employed by accountancy firms are not there just to prepare ledgers.

Apart from minimizing tax liabilities, for which Baa had often said I'd better get a foreign residence established, we needed a bit more setup that would be confusing in its complexities. This had little to do with tax considerations and lots to do with obfuscating the origin of the palladium.

Pyotr would send a fax to the nice Englishman he'd met on holiday in Tunisia. The fax would explain that he wished to establish a small distribution point near a London airport for merchandise he would be exporting to Ukraine and would Baa be kind enough, for a reasonable commission, to locate such a place? Baa would fax back politely explaining he hadn't the time for such matters but giving him the name of an estate agent who handled lettings of a couple of properties he owned. Baa would call the agent and tell him to move quickly and not mess around. Pyotr would take this unit in the name of a Panamanian SA company banking in Gibraltar.

The company would have been bought off the shelf from a London company-formation agent whose charges would be paid for by Icy Gee. He would do this from the in-credit balance on the company credit card account of a dissolved Belizian limited company the ownership of which had passed through several other off-shore entities. A UK bank account would also be opened in the name of the Panama SA company and some money wired in, ostensibly from Ukraine via Gibraltar, although actually originating from Baa. Having placed capital in the UK, the Russians should be free of UK visa problems. Pyotr and Alexei would come over and set up the industrial unit ostensibly as a distribution center but actually as a covert production line. Whilst using their UK bank account to pay the rent and incidentals, they'd purchase any items and materials connected with production equipment with cash.

Meantime Baa's Spanish company switch would be set up. A second off-the-shelf Panamanian SA company with a Gibraltar bank account would be acquired via Icy Gee as would an off-the-shelf Spanish SA company with exactly the same name. The Spanish company would have an accommodation address in Madrid but transact no business. The Panamanian company would appear superficially as a Spanish company, for both are styled SA, but a Spanish company trying to avoid tax by banking in Gibraltar. This would provide an alarm bell if anybody or any authority started an investigation and send an investigator off on a tangent chasing tax that wasn't due from a company that wasn't Spanish. We figured $30,000 would take care of Icy and make the accounts look right, plus an unknown but not huge amount of cash to bankroll purchasing the equipment Alexei would need. Pyotr and Alexei could make their own arrangements for accommodation at central London service flats as understanding just how much living in London costs would help them appreciate why it was Baa and I needed a full 32 percent of whatever was received as the metals were sold. People are usually very happy to agree a deal to make money but when the money starts ariving they often start wondering why the other person is entitled any. There was a theatrical agent who always complained that his actor-clients got ninety percent of the money he made for them.

The entire sales income would be paid into a Liechtenstein company account held completely legitimately with a bank in Zurich to which we all had access to view but from which money could not be drawn in the normal way. All funds reaching that account would automatically be paid out within one working day on preset percentages to our individual accounts at the same bank: Baa reckoned the Swiss bank would take less than one half of a percent off the top to satisfy all its requirements in this matter. It also happens that Zurich is a prime trading center for platinum group metals. "You know, Baa, there's something we haven't considered here—what if somebody finds out or figures out what we're doing? They would then know we couldn't account for the supply of the metal. Then somebody or some corporation comes along with a lot of contrived paperwork and says they've supplied us the metal, and they're still owed the money for it?" He was silent for a while; his cigar forgotten in the ashtray extinguished itself.

"You're fucking right, old son. They could take us to court in Switzerland, and we could get into a situation where our only way out would be proving we'd bought the metal from somewhere else. We're going to have to have another company that we could claim is owned by the people putting the squeeze on and we're going to have to pay the sales income to ourselves in Zurich through that new company." He fiddled about relighting his cigar. "We'll have to go through all this with Pyotr and Alexei."

The next day Baa and I went out to London City airport and took a VLM flight direct to Antwerp, where the contact of Icy Gee had an office in the diamond district. Ever since a bomb went off there outside the Diamond Club in 1981, the streets of Antwerp's diamond district have been blocked off to traffic and guarded by police patrols. A cynic might suppose it made the area so secure that other types of business might be attracted there; we told Icy Gee's man exactly what we required. Baa's credit was good here but he handed over eight thousand dollars in-front-expense money. Beers and open sandwiches on the Kaiser Lei and we landed back at London City late that afternoon.

Baa was to leave for the Marbella Club, his own villa was being repainted, at the weekend but having a long previously arranged meeting Monday, I wouldn't leave until next week.

•　•　•

Yagaci Norev's jet taxied to where a chauffeur held open the door of a nondescript people carrier. A custom's officer stepped forward, his examination of the passport was briefer than his respectful salute, and within fifty seconds the vehicle was moving. Behind its dark windows, Norev gave the driver a code that was keyed into the dashboard com-puter to bring up a map with the house's position highlighted in red. The drive would take two hours.

It was a pleasant if unremarkable hillside villa surrounded, as were its neighbors, with high railings. The wrought-iron gates were open and, parking immediately in front of the villa's main door, the chauffeur buzzed the intercom and announced his employer's arrival.

A uniformed maid opened the door, a nervous-looking man stood immediately behind her. "Welcome, Yagici, welcome." he greeted the vis-itor. "Would you like…?"

"Not yet. I have a task for you," Norev spoke to the man while staring hard into the maid's eyes.

•　•　•

That Sunday Ellie, Dave and I had been snacking our way around the annual Thai food festival in Battersea Park. Dave had stopped to watch a dance troupe whilst Ellie and I wandered on.

"Surprisingly most women find a dribbling man resistible," she advised. I'd been looking at a Thai woman of I guessed around thirty-five dressed entirely in black. She was uncharacteristically tall, and her slacks and T-shirt were tight on a slender, narrow-hipped body. Lady boy ? No, definitely not. She was stunning and she was cool enough to play on her beauty without letting it play her. Do you know what I mean? Ellie did for she added, "But she is quite something, Rick. Oh dear, relax every-body—she's got a ring." I'd not noticed that and had been about to go fishing when a glowering European man appeared, took her arm and led her away remonstrating about something. As they moved off she stole a nicely posed, but only just posed, brief glance back at us.

"Clever slut," Ellie laughed.

"You fancied her too?" I asked.

"Well, if I was going to do women, she'd be high in the list."

"I knew I was right about those nuns." Images kicked my penis awake and unthinkingly I pulled her close to my side; she didn't resist. "But I wouldn't let Dave know that," I told her. "He's a bit old fashioned about some stuff, you know." I hand over coins for bottles of mineral water and pass one to her.

"Yeah, I do know. Odd for a musican. I need to talk to you about Dave," she linked an arm with mine and steered us away from the food stalls towards the open park, "actually that side of him's more childish than old -fashioned." She stopped and swung around to look right into my eyes. "I'm going to go and live in LA, which means I'm going to have to let out the flat."

To have to let out the flat could mean Ellie would be relocating on her own unilateral decision perhaps, no not perhaps, probably in contradiction to Mr LA Married's wishes. Also it didn't quite fit with my assumption about the ownership of the flat. Was she planning to make the big play for the man she possibly really loved? She was twenty-eight years old.

"Body clock?" I asked as gently as I knew how.

Another deep look. "You're not all dribbler are you? But no, the con-trary." She stopped speaking and as we walked again I gazed around the park. Lots of people—couples, families and individuals were enjoying the sunshine; there was that urban parkland blurred noise of kids, dogs, far traffic and the almost subsonic hum of human agitation.

We sat down on the grass, leaning our backs against a contented fat-leafed tree and for the umpteenth time I'm aware of the pleasure

I take in proximity of Ellie. It's a curious contentment; I fancied her physically, and I knew she felt good with me, yet each now knowing we'd about no intention of doing anything about it had led to a different sort of intimacy—a freedom to just enjoy friendship but with the frisson lurking, the not too close nagging frisson of unbanished erotic possibilities.

"Comic book hero's opponent—the Dribbler, modest apartment somewhere in Megopolis or whatever, infant teethes very slowly so developing hyperactive saliva glands, which grow ever stronger. Chastised by uncaring parents, mocked during puberty for sodden shirtfronts by peer group, morphs into an evil genius gobbing enemies to death, acquires power and riches …"

"Rick, don't take this the wrong way…" I sensed her awkwardness.

"Ellie, I understand" I smiled at her. "But I won't do it. I'm waiting for Mr and Mrs Right."

"Cretin."

"Look girl, you're seriously okay. I'm blessed knowing you and so is Dave. I know that your heart is not around here, it might be best to just say whatever it is you need to…"

She reached over and kissed me lightly on the lips. "Thanks for that. I'm concerned for Dave—he's not in love with me or anything like that, but he really needs. There's a sort of desolation deep inside. He's not… not the kind of guy who needs to be in a club or a mind-fuck sect or society, but like most people he needs to feel there's somebody around, that there's some consistency in his world."

"He's human. There's stuff he's locked away in a cupboard. When will you go?"

"A few weeks yet. There're things to sort — LA can be unforgiving."

"Well Mrs, when you go the sad sod had better stay with me for a bit." I groaned inwardly as I heard myself say this then immediately realized I just might enjoy having him around the house.

• • •

I'd an unsought for account with Baa's minicab set up and it's office promised to send a cab that didn't smell and, extraordinarily, managed to deliver on that promise. Sun shone from within the driver's tanned black skin; there was some sort of Bach choral symphony on his radio.

"Nice music," I told him. "You've been in the sun?"

"Yeah - wid me granda', couple o' weeks down Antig'a - back here I need dis music."

I figured I was stuck with some sort of happy-clappy gospeling Christian, so just said, "Yeah, well it's pleasant."

It was and naturally soon ceased to be, replaced by an earnest sounding preacher rabbiting on about some inane sentimentalized rubbish to do with being good. I didn't have to ask; he switched off the radio. Then he launched into a tirade of his own.

"Social heducation han' responsibility! Make me laugh. Dis whole country in what call denial and no religion doing nuttin' about it, eh man?"

"Halleluah! " I said. He laughed and proffered a packet of gum.

"Try splainin' man—you just try 'splaining to some Muslim up Birmingham or somewhere that when 'is daughter fuck a white boy or a black boy or even de brown boy who ain't no Muslim. You know what the fucker does? He maybe 'as 'er killed like an Honor Killing they calls it," he pronounced the *h*. "Yeah, some weird Honor, man, eh? Ain't no fuckin' honor nowhere in that man that's 'cos the guy is afraid he lose control—he's sensing 'is own dark side in the girl. Is all projection man P-R-O-J-E-C-T-I-O-N like he's projecting his own shit on to de girl, an' he so fuckin' afraid of his own shit he tries to save 'imself by killin' de girl. Like afterward he's respectable amongst all de other blind ignorant cunt's what tinks dat's alright."

"You're not wrong," I told him as we rocketed along the elevated section of the M4. A lot of my time spent London I was familiar with most Caribbean accents but his was an odd sort of amalgam - certainly not any Antiguan I'd recognize.

"'s de same sorta shit wid de paedoes—dey's raping a kid den killin' de kid 'cos they tryin' not to know what dey did. what de darkness inside dem's done—like if de kid's dead they can preten' to demself de rape never 'appen see.......is like when some hobsessed African tortures some li'l chil' 'cos dey see their own devils in de chil'. An' de social services is complicit ennit—like de auntie or what s'pposed to be looking after de chil'so they can get de Child Allowance an' de Social - takes the fucking Chil' Protection forever an' more to do absolutely nuthin' 'cos the African scares em away. Then the chil' dies and usually dey get rid of de body an' say de kid wen' back to Africa to its parents an' de Chil' Protection don't check wid de airlines or nuttin' .... but if they don't or dey fuck up an' de res'rant man don't cum around and pick up the body for de dishes..."

"Chicken dishes? " I'd been starting to think this guy was just doing the usual rant but restaurant dishes was a new one on me. "You mean people are buying human meat?"

"Man yo' be ver' surprised de stuff goin' on. Then few times de police get involved 'an all de press write it up politically correctly. An' whitey Henglish an' now even de black Henglish an' de brown Henglish puts 'is 'ead back in de sand and hopes he can move down to Spain real soon now. 'Cos dey don't want to know 'bout 'uman sacrifices down de road or in de nex' street man. An' wot 'appen to de people wha' let de torture an' de killin' go on? Nuttin' man 'cos de fool government is against any culture o' responsibility 'cos dat way no gov'ment minister got to resign de job. Man, dey should jail de gov'ment minister 'stead dey make 'im Lord – an' give de fat pension to de council people."

"Are you in training to drive a black cab?" I ask and he falls silent for a long minute then starts to laugh.

"Oh, you ha' me there man." He smiles into the mirror. If you don't know London, you won't know that black cabs, which can be any color, are the official London taxis and that, according to urban legend, their drivers have been likely to regale their passengers with political and social comment that makes rural Texas seem a pinnacle of progressive liberal thinking.

"Yeah, I did didn't I. But seriously now, tell me about the poor black kids today off the sink estates – they're also going around full of hate and malice all tooled up – they also hate themselves so much. Don't they?"

"Me too as a kid, me too. I wanted to go an' get respec' with me nine—me somehow survive all dat an' come to know what a sad li'l gig dat is." I said nothing, and he went on. "See in de school there's no discipline an' on de street the police got no power 'cos when dey had it dey misused it. So politicians done take it o' dem. So yo' a young buck roaming free but without heducation in a world dat everyday in every-way tell yo' what clothes an' cars an' women an' shit yo' should have, but don't give yo' no legal way to get it." He slipped the car from the fast lane down the airport exit slip road then continued. "He gonna do what any young 'un gonna do—he gonna take it. Den he realize it don't really taste dat good, but dere he is—soul is injure 'cos he done bad tings. So he bury the soul, hims what d'ya call peers in de same sad shit so y'all push each other to get mo' an' mo' shit an' stuff. Den he start to know he hate hisself, an' so he start to take risks doing worse stuff an' den some dude knock him down wi' his nine an' he free 'cos he dead. An as he dyin', man he come to know dat is okay—it's good 'cos he been tryin' to get dead most of his sad life."

I'd be lying if I didn't admit this had touched me: we rode along in silence for a while until I asked, "So what are you going to do about this—what are you personally going to do?"

"Pray fo' de strong man ta come an' lead," he laughed grimly. "I'se waitin' fo' de Mussolini—you'se okay man, I know dat. But I tell you bad bad times comin' cos de good people doin' nuttin den we gonna need a real bad bastard to sort de shit man."

We'd reached LHR terminal two already and were now stopped in the set down area. He released the boot and got my grip from it whilst I got out.

Taking my bag I tipped him.

"You go safe now. Via con Dios." He nodded his head to indicate a plane that was emerging from the far side of LHR's clutter of terminals and auxiliary buildings to roar into the sky. For no good reason my eyes had followed the direction in which he'd pointed; when I looked back, he and his car had gone. Only as I waited at the check-in did I realize I'd not heard his car pull away nor his door close. Or even that there'd hardly been time for him to disappear from sight whilst I'd glanced up at the airliner.

Passing through that shopping center with planes called London Heathrow Airport was uneventful as were my flights. Being August the directs were all full so I'd had to go to Madrid and wait for a local connection to the Mediterranean coast. Whilst waiting, and just in case you want to know, I'll tell you of my childhood. It was less than joyful. Like many boys, I had a mother whose character was a model of gentle ruthlessness: my conception ensured by her physical programming and my father's libido. He was in the oil business and away most of the time before their divorce—after which he was away all of the time. As far as I knew, he was now retired and lived in Hong Kong with his third wife. His first, my mother, had gone in the other direction with her number two. My childhood recollection of Argentina was his extended family's politeness tempered with disdain toward me—you could hardly term it civilized for I was only six-years-old—and the kindness of the maids. I remember playing with the children of the maids and the dwindling number of gauchos the ranch employed. I was to gain a reasonable amount of Spanish and the ability to ride seriously hard. Ahead of the game, Hector, my mother's new husband, was gradually replacing his beef production with crops and his gauchos with large machines.

After a year or so I was sent back to England to a prep school where I boarded and kept my broken heart to myself. During most school holidays I stayed in the family home of my mother's sister; they were pleasant, neutral people whose raison d'etre I never fathomed. That family—I could never think of them as my family—lived in an ostensibly civilized bit of the home counties. At every opportunity, and regardless of the weather, I would escape their house into the surrounding countryside. Although this was either industrially farmed or equally industrially enparked into what local councils like to term *leisure facilities* I discovered bits had been missed. Across chemically saturated fields near the top of a gentle rise was a sharp fold in the ground in which a couple of acres of wilderness thrived free of lurking pedophiles. I suppose I'd been about eight or nine when I discovered this place and I believe it saved my sanity. The farm owners had determined it would cost a lot to clear the wood and more to infill the fold that, when leveled would be less than one acre; this would have made it still worth doing, but a hydrologist had warned them that the spring that emerged from the middle of that folded ground was impossible to cap and would need to be enclosed in brickwork, piped, and it's existing stream rechanneled. His survey's killer get-out paragraph had been his refusal to state rerouting the watercourse would not undermine the existing cultivated hillside. A second professional opinion had confirmed the first, and thus a piece of the woodland that had come into being just after the end of the ice age remained intact. Surrounded as it was by high-yield, intensively farmed fields, only a small boy was ever likely to venture there.

Once the spring water left the wood, it picked up chemicals from the fields and stank, but inside the wood it was pure, save for natural minerals. I could have quenched my young thirsts there whenever I choose but did so only rarely and then with that unconscious natural religious respect children can have without realizing; it's a profound awe of Nature. Equally it was the conditioning of late twentieth-century packaged lifestyle—is it safe to consume something that has not been processed and marketed by man?

The wood was inhabited by small brown people who I never directly saw and never bothered; they in turn never bothered me, but one summer's day watched interestedly as I dammed the stream with fallen branches, stones and clay. The rising waters, we're talking a rise of a couple of feet only, washed away a bit of the bank and my little dam. Some insects perished and some streamside dweller's front door hole got rearranged. The small brown people found this less than entertaining and moved away from their vantage points. It was a hot day and even inside the wood, shaded by trees and undergrowth, the heat was heavy. I cupped my hands and took water to slake my thirst laid back, and fell asleep. I found myself to be walking along a wide gravel pathway. A large silver car passed and then slid to a halt; from it a man in his twenties emerged and greeted me. His face was clear and open and to my surprise I found I was as tall as him. As if having exchanged some words we parted, him getting back in the car and driving on and me continuing along the path. I awoke to see a pair of savage eyes peering at me through some foliage and instinctively I reached for a stone and stood up. The foliage shook and the eyes were gone.

A decade after first finding the wood and after years in the thrall of puberty's snake, and hence years of having forgotten it, I returned briefly before leaving to work and live in London. The wood seemed smaller and though not shorn of its magic somehow removed from it. "No it's not," one of the small brown people whispered in my ear. "You're different now." I felt a solitary tear on my cheek as I bid the place a too brisk farewell.

Somehow this experience had given me some courage and some fortitude to be myself and to not be overly bothered by communal pressures.

I'd phoned Sy the previous day to give him an arrival time and he said he'd meet me at the airport but wasn't there. His mobile was on voicemail so figuring he might be in traffic I waited. I wondered if he had a car here in Spain or whether he used the Winnebago.

When I'd been booking my tickets in London Harris was losing control of his bladder in Spain. Did I mention that Harris has toys? Well he does. He has a teddy bear and a couple of dolls and, just like a human child, he projects aspects of his own personality on to them when it suits him to. He feels ashamed of peeing on the boat so he drops one of his toys into the pool of' urine. Yes, you've got it—he's saying the doll made the mess. It was impossible to ignore that he, like many well-cared-for mutts, exhibits a level of consciousness humans don't care to concede an animal can possess. In marketing terms he was probably a CD. He's coughing a bit so Monica takes him to the vet and he's given antibiotics. The temperature at the aeropuerto is a zillion degrees and they all arrive together in a borrowed car. Sy drives at 150 kph regardless of motor-way conditions whist Monica worries about Harris, who rides next to me in the back and pisses on the seat. We're at the boat in an hour, and Monica determines by that maternalism to which there is no species bar-rier among mammals that, although Harris is on the mend, our planned sailing for Ibiza must be delayed at least until the next day.

We go to the marina's clubhouse for late lunch. Sy now lives off investments and talks of shares and commercial property. As a worrying man it's the stock market investments he likes to talk about; so much so that you might be inclined to wonder why he'd retired. Back then dot-com stocks were in vogue. I signal the waiter for another bottle of mineral water and catch Monica's eye. She starts to mouth Sy's words in sync; he sees it and we all laugh but he won't give up so easily. "Apart from shares and bonds there's property, which takes management, there's commodities; what else is there?" Slightly agitated he drains his glass.

"Tins of long-life baked beans might be a great currency," I tell them. "but then, of course, there'd immediately be supermassive twenty-four/seven global markets in baked bean futures, tin futures…"

"Gas futures…" said Monica. "I'm going back to the boat." She rose and, kissing the top of Sy's head, left us.

"You handle precious metals—is gold a smart investment?" he asked.

"Not yet…but if you've got deep pockets and big balls I figure it is. Every time its price tries to rise, there have been big sales. The British Chancelor has called gold a barbarous relic and plans to sell a lot of his gold reserves and some other central banks are also planning to sell. My guess is that central banks are manipulating the market." Our bottle of Rioja was nearly empty. "Lots of forged currency around, lots of tech-nically bad loans out from banks, and the U.S. deficit already heading beyond the stratosphere. A thing that would call it all to account is if gold was allowed to find its free market value."

"But gold is a free market—it has been for years." Sy drained the bottle into my glass whilst signaling to a waiter.

"C'mon Sy, you're too old to swallow that crap. Gold used to be pegged at thirty-five dollars an ounce to enable governments to cover their nudity. Then, back in nineteen seventy-one, it was cut free by the US and within a few years it had gone up two thousand and three hundred percent. Eight hundred bucks an ounce from thirty ! That's when the Federal Reserve and their pals would have realized there was great danger of gold upsetting their gig. Unwilling to openly reregulate, they seem to have decided on market manipulation by selling directly and indirectly to keep a lid on the price." He raised an eyebrow but said nothing, so I continued. "Think about it—when the Americans stopped pegging gold at thirty-five bucks, it rose to eight hundred. That rise demonstrated that the world's paper currencies and hence the banking system was a nonsense— like the Emperor's New Clothes. The Federal Reserve, the Bank of England, and the central banks of the other industrial countries jumped on it. Now they call themselves G seven or eight or twenty or ninety-six or whatever. I figure they let speculators move the price up and down a little—but only a little."

The waiter had delivered an opened bottle of wine and moved away but Sy caught his eye and gestured for him to return. "Why would they let the price move at all, if that's the case?" he asked

"Because they'd have to buy back what they've sold. They'll have sold to push the price down a bit, burning speculators in the process and discouraging those speculators from holding gold at that time so those speculators unload because they're sitting on losses and getting margin calls. So then the price goes down some more, the speculators are bruised, and the central banks buy back to maintain the level of their reserves. If the central banks simply sold all they had the market would then be out of their control and it could go anywhere."

Sy lent forward, splashed more wine into our glasses and said, "You know it strikes me that property has replaced gold. As more and more money is printed the price of property all over the world rises to absorb it, some places more than others but it does go up about everywhere. Even in New Zealand!"

"If you say so," I ejected an olive stone into a fist "Never been there—is there something special about the place?"

"You should—very beautiful, serious sailing. Monica and I flew down there for a couple of months. Hired a camper van—not like Winnie but adequate. North island's a bit like 1960's Bournemouth. South island's less people—a magnificent place, but property rocketing over there too, even though they've only four million people in a place around the size of the UK." The bottle of water arrived "Gracias Carlos."

"So New Zealanders all want to live in the same bit then?" I asked.

"Not at all. It's a farming nation— sheep, grapes and tourists. Its property scene is not much different from elsewhere. It's just more obvious there because the place is so empty. I don't remember the precise numbers, but the gist of it is," he poured water, "in the past, a young couple getting married, starting a home, and so on put down a deposit on their home and borrowed by way of a mortgage to pay off the balance."

I'd drunk just enough wine and the sun was not getting cooler, I sipped some of the cold water and said, "So what?"

"So between them, they would then have to, if I've remembered the numbers correctly, do about twelve hours work per week just to make the mortgage payments. The result was reasonably happy, stable, sane people, few mortgage defaults, and general widespread well-being— not serendipity but relative to the rest of the planet, pretty good. Not anymore. Today in a country with much more space than is needed to build on in places where people would like to live, the prices have rocketed so that leaving aside all the smoke and mirrors mortgage lenders and bankers love to generate, your typical couple's got to work twice as much to service their mortgage." He sipped his wine now. "Whichever way you look at it they're spending twice as much time working for the banks."

"Does an average young couple with no experience of the past situation worry about this? Do they feel more insecure and more pressured or do they just get on with their lives?" I shuffled my chair around into the shade.

"You can bet your arse they're concerned—they know they're mortgaged to the hilt and thus less secure and this stress comes through to their kids. Crimes up, drug usage is up, and there's creeping demoralization. Just who the fuck benefits from that ?" He leaned across the table to point a large, wine filled finger at me. "You should escape, get yourself a boat, old son." On balance, the basis of Sy's wealth and security and, if the truth be told, the illusion that enabled all of us back then to benefit or otherwise from a level of material mass consumption undreamt of but a couple of generations earlier was shakier than most cared to acknowledge.

An elderly, frail Swede whose feet seem to be permanently dancing stops by our table and Sy introduces us. I figure it's a neurological thing for the man's feet move in a regular rhythm of one, one, two, three. Sven wants Sy and Monica "and Rick must come too" at his villa that evening where his wife will "entertain with operatic singing." Sy's good-natured humoring of the man turns a bit panicky and he excuses us on the basis of our sea trip starting within an hour or two.

"You and Monica see much of him?" I ask after he'd moved on.

"Less than we'd like."

Sven it seemed kept a boat in the marina and had an out of town villa with Mrs Sven. The villa was more than comfortable and afforded spectacular views, but Sven spent most of his time sitting on his boat whilst his ex-porno star, and Sy said he did mean star, wife practiced singing and sex at the house. Her teachers like the gardeners and the repairmen were selected more for their physical attributes than any skill or professional ability. "It's said," Sy lowered his voice, "that our Sven has an enormous todger that fails to function these days."

"Whatever turns you on," I replied but was of course curious about this information. "Has he showed it to you and the other sailors?"

Sy can be painfully straight. "Certainly not."

"So where does this idea come from or is it the sort of stuff you boys dream about when you're out on the briny?"

He lightened. "There really is no fooling you is there, Rick? Whilst we're out there and what's called becalmed our fantasies can run amok." He knew what I wanted to know so, of course, wasn't going to volunteer it. I gave in and asked.

"So what does old Pornella look like?"

"Look like?" He studied his glass of water.

"Could you give her one?"

"Hardly, Rick. She's married."

"Cunt !"

"That's what poor old Sven is. You see she fucks about anybody who's willing and doesn't hide it from him—it's sort of driving him mad I guess, but he just tells people it's her profession and has to be accepted. He says, like priests, porn stars don't retire."

"What noblesse, eh ! Such a gent—and the once mighty todger ?"

"Monica heard about it. You know what women are like about cocks—minds like sewers." If you've ever staggered into the wrong toilet and read the cubical walls you know this. Sy continued, "Apparently his massive organ had enthralled Mrs Sven and their viewers for years. That's how they came—no pun intended—to be married. Her specialty was Oscar winning blow jobs but she blew him once too often and a vein started giving him problems. This was some years back now. He took himself off to get the blood supply re-plumbed. Some sort of valve mechanism is damaged and he can't maintain an erection. Medical ops failed to remedy this and the Mrs explains if she can't have it three or four times a day she'll explode so he agrees to the present set-up."

"Actually I'd rather not have heard about the vein, Sy." I'm feeling a tad discombobulated. "But it does sound like he loves her a lot."

Due to the Rioja inside me, and Sy now returning to droning of investments and takeover possibilities, I find myself on the threshold of a boredom trance so suggest we return to his boat where Monica is sunbathing with a rather self-important Guy who, it transpires, is Belgian. He proffered an open a box. "Aha," Sy helped himself and then turning to Monica said, "Chocolate, Belgium's raison d'etre."

"How wise you are my captain," she tells him.

• • •

Yagaci Norev lay on his stomach. Now restricted within a tight, short dress of semitransparent red plastic, the maid massaged oil onto his buttocks and legs. Her mistress lay next to him. From the other side of the room the nervous-looking man stood and watched whilst excusing the probable failure of his mission. YN listened patiently to the fullest explanation of all the circumstances before saying "Very well, if it does not occur, another attempt must be made tomorrow. You may leave us now."

An hour or so later Norev would pace the villa's garden immersed in deep thought then use his mobile to reach a powerful person on a far away tropical island.

Feeling his power, that person was to then make two calls of his own.

• • •

My sleeping accommodation is what yachties term a cabin, but sane persons would call a large cupboard. I decide to take a short nap and discover it to be after midnight when I awaken. Harris growls half-heartedly as I stumble around in the galley locating biscuits, cheese and beer. Consuming these out on deck beneath the stars is pleasant and peaceful: the water surface is disturbed by a massive conga eel as it goes about nocturnal business probably best left unconsidered, and a marina guard plods the walkway to time register his plastic card in an electronic reader near the boat. Although he doesn't see me, he does notice a slim middle-aged woman who stands completely naked in a stern several yachts away. Climbing aboard, he unzips his fly and she silently fellates him. A sigh of literal relief and he's back off along the walkway as she disappears within her craft.

Sy's stash is neither large nor well-concealed and, rolling a smoke, I'm joined on deck by Harris. His head nuzzles against my calves telling me he's on the mend. The boat rocks gently beneath a half moon that, despairing of this particular sea, refuses to give it tides—something my scant knowledge of fluid mechanics has never been quite able to comprehend.

Awaking early in the morning, I question Sy about the cost of boats and conclude that for me to feel even remotely comfortable on one an expenditure of several million dollars would be required. You already know I'm not a snob, it's simply that, however pleasing the exterior of an ocean sailing yacht viewed from a distance, the interior is seriously practical and unnervingly tidy. I figure it's this necessary neatness that had made Harris losing control of his bladder even more stressful for Sy. His boat is moored across the end of a walkway, on each side of which other yachts are moored: it's a sort of nautical avenue we pass along to reach the clubhouse. Harris pees his way down it and I'm surprised that other boat owners ignore this, inquiring only after his health. Monica tells them—they're mostly Spanish—that he is still *mal* and rather anxiously distributes chocolate oranges amongst them. As 1999 Spain produces billions of real oranges, these expensively packaged chocolate ones are probably appreciated as quite droll by the locals. Breakfast aboard having been bread and fruit, I'm anxious to consume something a little more contrived at the clubhouse.

Harris's bladder seems to be improving but M wants to be certain before sailing. Harris needs to see, or rather Monica needs Harris to see, the vet. I can't help but be impressed by the sympathy and human kindness she'd received from the people at the marina. I'm as touched by this as I am annoyed by Sy's ill-disguised fear of visiting the vet. He loves Harris but doesn't know how to make him better and doesn't want to become involved in the lottery of medical treatment. I'm annoyed because in his place I might be the same and I'd rather not recognize that particular inadequacy in myself. He's not unaware of the neurotic lip service we pay to reductionism, wishing to believe we have conquered illness and freed ourselves from those particular tyrannies of nature.

They go directly to the Clinica Animale so I sit down alone to breakfast on the club terrace and yesterday's Belgian joins me. It's an absolutely glorious day with which he is completely enthused, the tone of his greetings overflowing with morning-fresh good-to-be-alive-ness. I'm about to tell him to fuck off when I glimpse Sven coming on to the terrace peering left and right as if for somebody to talk to. Other breakfasters hurriedly bury their heads in newspapers, one man gets up and leaves still eating a croissant. Taking the table behind Guy, he sits facing toward me. Were I to stay put, the Belgian between us will continue obstructing his line of vision. This is a truly desperate situation and as such warrants desperate measures. There is nothing to be done but engage in conversation with Guy. Coming from Brussels he speaks his English with a French accent; my, hitherto unintended, camouflage is sunglasses and, as I speak French hardly at all, I augment my English with a stage-French accent. I have no idea if Guy notices this but what other breakfasters make of two men speaking together in English but both with heavy French accents I have not considered. There are five quite formally dressed Spaniards at the table across the aisle to my left and I figure I'll be able to leave undetected when they do. But they are well into a coffee and brandy—yes, brandy—conversation that looks set to run for a while. A glance around Guy reveals Sven is reading a Swedish newspaper but he has the habit of glancing round balefully every few moments. I just know he would initiate a conversation and that, because I know of his situation, he will elicit a strained sympathetic hearing from me. I will not tolerate that side of myself so early in the day which means I'd be mean spirited to an old man with a damaged dick and I certainly don't want to be that.

Yes, yes I know; I should get a hobby or something.

My attention refocuses on Guy. He asks if Sy has really left England for good to live on the boat. Telling him there is no way of knowing, I ask him what his business is and he answers that he is an importer of Chinese goods. This jangles a small bell, the volume of which increases as he goes on to ask what Sy's business had been: even allowing for the possibility that Monica had mentioned something to him the previous afternoon, Guy's question about Sy discomforts me.

"E's a drug smuggler,"I announce, not attaching any significance to the lull in the Spaniards' conversation.

"Ha, ha," says Guy. "But, seriously?"

"Yes, it's true. Zat is why ze dog is ill. I told 'im. 'Sy,' I said, 'You cannot put so much drugs in such a small dog.' But 'e would not listen, and now," I Gallic shrug. "Look, ze dog is sick."

Sven was by then in conversation with a large woman and I slipped away back toward the boat. Halfway there I run into Monica looking for me, she announces that Harris having recovered we are to set sail.

Our voyage involved a lot of untying, motoring out of the marina, playing with more ropes to get sails up and listening to Sy's instructions to Monica and me once he had pointed the boat in the right direction. He then went below for some unspecified reason. Not wishing to be in Monica's way, I was considerate enough to go up on the cabin roof and lie on some cushions to keep an eye on the mainsail. I marveled at the blueness of the sky. Before and behind us stretched a small armada of other boats, perhaps also headed for the Balearic islands, so it was unlikely we'd get lost. Thus comforted, I slipped into a pleasant reverie. I wasn't being irresponsible—I figured if you're crewing and the captain asks you to do something you just do it; if he or she doesn't then just do what you want.

It was the chopper that awoke me. The din it made was physically painful as the pilot altered his blade pitch to pace the yacht eighty meters or so to our side whilst his passengers photographed us. I found Sy on the radio shouting at the helicopter pilot to stay away because his down-draught was a threat to our sails. The pilot was not replying so Sy raised the coastguard back on the mainland and reported the chopper, after which it moved closer still. Sy became apoplectic with rage and radioed just about everybody. The island-bound fleet had all but disappeared due to the differing speeds of the various vessels, but the two that were still within visual range radioed us with moral support and assurances they were also calling the authorities to report matters. It may not seem like much to you but when you're sitting atop hundreds of meters of water perhaps three hours from land, a few tons of thoughtless and uncommunicative airborne metal triggers awareness of one's vulnerability. From his position at the radio, Sy yelled something about sails. Harris barked and Monica signed me to take in the small sail at the bow. I clambered forward to do this while she frantically wound handles to furl the mainsail. Exciting stuff I could well do without. Still the chopper paced us and still it inched closer; the insistent clatter of its engine and the pressure of the air cushion its rotors created for it to sit on was fucking disconcerting I can tell you. The pilot being clearly visible, I paused briefly in my task to give him the international hand signal for *you are a masturbator with a tiny penis* and then got on with the business of untying the ropes that held the forward sail. I think it's called a spinnaker. I must have done something un-nautical because once the first rope was released the sail flapped madly and could have taken my hand off. However, it conveniently tangled itself around some other of the million bits of bloody rope boats have. This enabled me to catch the first rope and messily tie it to the opposite rail before releasing the second rope. I then made a pig's ear of binding the thing. The mainsail furled and the little one sort of furled the boat was now upright so I was able to climb down into the back well to find Monica emerging from the interior with a flare pistol. She loaded this and went up on the roof. Hooking one arm around the mast, she aimed the flare pistol at the helicopter which was now about twenty yards out at mast height. My support of the war effort was to pick up an orange that was rolling about in the well and with my mightiest heave fling it at the intruder. It rose toward the chopper, then was flung back by the ever-expanding downdraught, smacking neatly into the mast above Monica's head. My exploding fruit caused her to flinch in the act of discharging the pistol and the unlit flare cannoned off the chopper's windscreen before igniting and failing into the sea.

That did it. The metal bird turned into a chicken, veering away sharply and heading for the horizon. "Sweine! Ich…" Monica's blood was really up and to be honest I was experiencing a more than minor frisson of adrenalin. Harris, of course, was the most thrilled of us all, jumping about, barking and wagging his tail. I gave him a congratulatory stroke while Sy hugged Monika.

About an hour or so later our bodies had calmed, the sails were reset and a bottle opened. Monica was very sporting about the orange and I asked Sy what we should do if menaced by a submarine. To my surprise he said that one of the hazards of sailing was deck-stacked containers failing off freighters and floating just under the surface of the sea; unsure whether to believe this or not, I was aware Harris had taken up position in the bow from where he scanned the sea our craft was plowing into. With the delay and drifting off course, the SATNAV system and charts told Sy we would not get to Ibiza before dawn. He and Monica would do four hours on and four hours off to get us there because I was "inexperienced."

"You mean I can't drive your tub?" I said.

His look managed to convey his opinion at having to spend twenty minutes sorting out the front sail I'd captured, but I held his eyes. A boat on the sea is not a democracy; it's a situation where only one person can be in charge. "It was only a very small sail, Cap'n," I cajoled but his will was as of iron in the matter.

We had tinned soup, ham, olives, bread, grapes, cheese and some more wine. Monica slept first and I kept Sy company as the yacht skimmed onwards into the iridescence of a warm night sea. A billion stars overhead could only delight, and they certainly filled me with awe. Pretty much pissed I took a cushion and blanket and went and lay down again on the cabin roof. The magnificence of the night sky is wondrous when seen from the dark ocean. City dwellers like me don't often get to see the sky without light pollution. Even in the Amazon the view's spoilt either by clouds or the humidity mist but out here on the sea it's breathtaking. I lay there trying to tell myself that the starlight I saw took a long time to reach me, that I was seeing the past much of it thousands of years ago, much of it a lot, lot more.

When they changed watches I made Monica and myself coffee and sandwiches. She too reveled in the sense of wonder that a star-filled night sky inspires and we nattered on to each other about how the miraculous engine of that vast universe drove the boat we were on and the bodies we were in. Harris slept at our feet and farted from time to time.

Just before dawn came that eerie, mysterious coldness that thermometers don't register, and the mass of an island became visible on the horizon. I made more coffee as a sleepy Sy joined us to organize our approach to the port and berthing. This having been achieved, I went into my little cabin and instantly crashed.

Flowing gently within a soft sea over endless oyster beds, I was neither sure nor concerned if I was me or I was seawater. Sometimes I moved quickly covering thousands of underwater miles and sometimes

I just ebbed and flowed over the same area; the oysters' shells were transparent and I saw that in some of them pearls appeared. Some grew, some withered away.

If sleeping all day is a little death, awaking in the later afternoon is an unpleasant rebirth. Confused feelings predominate: the need to pee, followed by the gradual awareness of how gray and mechanical and relentless and awful everything is. Psychologists and people in cafes who write neatly in notebooks would claim one is projecting inner shit on the world, but I find it strange that the environment lends itself so easily to these negative perceptions. There exists an uninvestigated complicity about the matter—as if reality is flat, a two dimensional actuality, with us existing in a hologram drawn from it by our consciousness or projected from it by some other intelligence. In this dark mood I wonder if it's the world as it actually is and that those sensible enough to have been awake all day in accordance with Mother Nature's main plan are the ones who are projected. They had spent the daylight hours in their heads while I had dwelt their turn out of time in that magical realm to which sleep admits us. I fled from such considerations.

Sy was pissing about with his engine.

"You'll have noticed I was awake through both Watches, Sy." He just grunted, so I continued, "So I could have manned a Watch and got us here."

He looked up and said, "It was mostly a matter of navigation."

This was not unkindly meant: I smiled and inhaled deeply. "As a matter of fact the constellation Ursa Major pointed exactly at Ibiza town last night, so I would have found this place."

For a moment I had him but, being Sy, he held my gaze and said evenly, "No. That was last week."

"Huh, the trouble with you," I shrugged, "is that you know fuck-all about astronomy; you just rely on satellite systems for navigation." I flicked an imaginary piece of fluff away into the harbor. "As a matter of fact I've been thinking of sending off a stiff letter to *Buggering Bo'suns Weekly* on that very subject."

He returned to the little engine, which was housed below the well deck. Monica emerged from the boat's interior.

"Rick's had letters published in yachting mags," she told him. "Under a nome de plume."

"Yeah—Rusty le Sextant. I've quite a following amongst real sailors, old son," I boasted.

I took Harris for a stroll around the harbor because Sy's reply was to tell us something about the engine and Monica loyally got involved with it. Concerned that young Harris should not become overexerted during what had to be his period of convalescence, and as coincidentally a cafe was at hand, I sank into a chair and ordered coffee and a bowl of water. The waiter's surly manner isn't called for so I ask him if there's a problem "No problemo" he sneers. To annoy him I amended the order to bottled mineral water with the bowl for Harris. Noble mutt, he took his cue and snarled at the man when it was brought. He drank it, though. I sat musing on whether it would be possible to train Harris to piss on people's feet when I felt a soft touch on my neck.

"'Ello, Rick."

I took the hand now lying lightly on my shoulder and squeezed it. She came around me and sat.

"But you 'ave a little dog."

"Don't say *little*—he'll be offended," but Harris was being a tart and looking at her expectantly. "You're looking very lovely." And she was. Late forty-something Isabelle passes for ten years younger not just because of her beauty but because she understood what so many women never do— posture. She carried herself so well, she'd stand out in a roomful of cute teenagers. She looked like French women have popularly been supposed to look—desirable and utterly confident in her own femininity. I adored her and she was married to Paul. Coincidentally I'd known both of them separately in London before they married.

"He's away with Merik for another two weeks or so," she replied in answer to my question.

Now, I tell you, how they came to have Merik, a gifted young man, simultaneously the most natural person you could imagine yet utterly strange, in their lives is a story in itself and one that has a discomforting ring of destiny to it. That's reason enough not to tell you just now.

"There you go, Harris." I tipped some more water into his bowl.

"Ow strange—I know another 'arris." She stroked his head. He must have located and engaged an odd spaniel gene for the way he looked at her. "But it's 'im!" she exclaimed. "Sy's 'Arris."

He affected a simpering shrug and coyly gazed away as might a canine Byron on the pull.

"Yes," I told her. "I sailed over here with him and Monica from Los somewhere or other. Lucky I was about—really, they'd probably not have made it without me."

Smiling, she kissed my cheek and I recalled Paul had bought a boat when they'd moved to America but I'd never seen it, our paths not having crossed for well over a year.

Learning I'd no plans for the evening, Isabel suggested I bring Sy, and Monica who she'd yet to meet, to a restaurant later as her guests. I said I'd ask them but she could count on me being there.

Harris and I took another stroll around the port before returning to the boat. The sun slipped below the horizon yet the air did not cool; if anything it grew warmer as the hour of enchantment came upon me. Shadows came out to play as the lights of the boats and the bars conspired to soften features. Different musics floated on the balmy air and, as chains binding consciousness to the ego lightened, I rejoiced in the sensuality of being in my body.

Our rendezvous turned out to be in a back street away from the port; an evidently popular tapas bar with a patio restaurant at the back. Sy found Isabel at the bar and called Monica and I over through the throng. Having achieved this, I was delighted to discover what I'd never known or even suspected—Isabel had a half-sister. She was just as tall but younger, lovely in a different way, and lithe. She was called Teresa and I knew immediately that she was more than a little interested in me. How? Well, I just knew in the way that one does. She wore an off-the-shoulder top and when we were introduced proffered a cheek so I planted a kiss between shoulder and neck. There was the merest pause before she pulled back. "Don't pretend to be offended," I told her as our eyes met and I knew I'd got it right.

We drank and we ate tapas, Monica was asking Isabel about how she knew me and analyzing the vague half-truths she told her. I was still very much in my body and my body very much wanted to be in Teresa— perhaps it was something to do with life afloat. After a while she leaned against me and asked how I'd known she liked her shoulders kissed and I started to feel more than alive. Separated from the others as more and more people packed into the bar we got into serious teasing until, trying to turn to order more drinks, I came face to face with a Brutal in hate mode. Our eyes met, he Esturised, "What are you lookin' at?"

"You," my wine-flavored testosterone replied wittily for he was merely human. You know what I mean—some guys are composed of superdense material, sort of eternal earth creatures boiled in malice. Yes, all right, I know, too flowery—look, I'm bowled off my feet by this girl and half cut; just how do you expect me to explain the guy? Okay, he's seriously, pointlessly nasty but he's not the troll who eats babies.

Time slowed and the atmosphere billowed to clear a small space around us as he unhurriedly placed his large hands palms downwards on my shoulders. That action showed he didn't plan to use a weapon but, fuck, he did look fit. In these situations you are supposed to attack fast and hard not dither. Despite a younger, fitter me having passed time at a mining operation in Oz I dithered. Figuring he was going for a head butt and a knee in my groin, I thought to ram the wine glass held in my right hand into his armpit then drop and go for his balls with a fist. Don't be fooled now, this sort of shit is not my forte—I'm no expert and lots can go wrong. Whatever happened I would just keep hurting him until one of us was finished. We never made a move though, for suddenly Teresa was there. She got herself between us and yelled "Fuck off faggot !" right into the guy's face.

Big hands had already whipped off my shoulders and Neanderthal features now contorted in confusion; he took a step backward. "You…I…" he began.

"He's mine, cheap face," she shouted "just piss off."

Beneath his tan, Brutal blushed to the roots. I knew if it went off I'd have to shove the girl out of the way and so probably have to take his first hit but the feeling of the entire, now conversationless, bar was very much against him and he simply couldn't carry it. Turning on his heel, he slunk out, a confused man.

A woman laughed, conversations started again and Sy appeared through the crowd. "You're a sad old tart, Rick," he handed me drinks.

Giving Teresa a glass, I told her that as she had saved my life she now owned me.

"I was thinking more in terms of very short-term hire," she replied.

"'oliday renting, sister dear?" asked Isabel, putting a piece of tapas in my mouth. "Zat might be ok"

"Exactly, Sis," Teresa sipped her drink.

Making a mental note that this girl was to get a lesson, I said, "I hope you're into S&M, groups, coke spooned up the arse, and all the rest of the stuff I do."

"Then some." She'd that capacity for looking beyond wanton.

The back patio restaurant was reigned over by Edi. "You did not bring your 'lil boyfrien?" he purred.

"Not my kind of bitch."

"Ahh que fuerca!" he exhaled with the pout equivalent of an air kiss then turned to Isabelle. "And where is Paolo?"

"I 'ave no way of knowing my darling, but we are all famished. What do you 'ave?"

He talked seafood but I was distracted by a problem between Sy and the people on the next table to do with chairs. You might suppose something about our party was attracting negative energies. Generalizations about nationalities can be as stupid as they are dangerous but the shadows wanted to come out to play and the neighboring diners were Dutch. Between ourselves we loudly discussed the Dutch as a people, concluding they were passive promoters of child pornography and pathologically tolerant in order to evade confronting their guilt as brutal colonizers of Indonesia. That the entire fucking nation needed collective psychotherapy, but then that's 1999 Europe for you. Pendulums swing though.

I'm actually only giving you the gist of our dinner conversation, which Isabel had instigated and we'd all taken up with glee. A part of me wondered if it was just a continuation of the conversation on my patio a week or so earlier.

An obsessive national comprehension of English that had resulted from fear of Wotan's Germany meant that our Low-country neighbors understood it all. They became increasingly agitated and summoned the manager. Whilst her husband or whatever he was huffed, the woman puffed, complaining to Edi that we were rude and had insulted them.

"No they ha' not! Yo' ha' no' understood," he smiled consolation. "They detest yo' an' only speak about yo' out of politeness."

With that he turned his back on them and poured wine for us before wafting away. The Dutch evaporated.

Around 2:00 A.M. princess Edi returned with a bottle of serious-looking something and held court. Others dropped by. Many in Ibiza barely get a sun tan because they keep the same hours the kids do, but I'd had enough. Conversations in languages I was able to follow had my stomach hurting from laughing and, despite having been on an alcohol drip for hours, my lust for Teresa was undiminished. Her body was constantly conspiring in the problem so I got keys from Sy and took her back to my cupboard.

Before anything could happen I needed to pee. She came to the head—that's a tiny boat lavatory by the way—and held my dick. Fortunately there was sufficient alcohol in me not to get a full erection from her warm slim hand whilst peeing, but in the confined space it was uncomfortable in a nice kind of way.

"So you're a control freak?" I asked.

"No, I just want to hold you."

She also peed, we showered—sort of—both came too quickly, fell asleep, woke up and did it again; we slept a few hours, did it again and decided to get up, didn't, did it again, then did get up.

You'll have noticed I haven't droned an at any time how beautiful her shoulders and her neck, how long and slim her legs, how flat her stomach, how graceful her breasts, how pert her bottom, how sensuous her full lips around her wide mouth, how big her ever-so-slightly almond eyes, how graceful her arms and how elegant her hands, and neither shall I. Nor will I tell you what we did to each other that first night together for in truth it was more the case that we sleepily found ourselves doing things to each other. Being so far into sensuality that one forgets one's name is a rare occurrence for me. The tiredness only added piquancy to my orgasms and I had absolutely no problem with the tiny voice of reason that told me this woman could kill me in a matter of days.

We found an early cafe and breakfasted in a trance of exhaustion and no little state of psychic shock: something unsought had occurred. I bought bread and croissants at a baker's for Sy and Monica, and, leaving them in the main cabin, walked Teresa home. Home turned out to be moored a hundred yards away and about the biggest boat in the port. Registered in somewhere I'd have trouble finding on an atlas and called *Isabella*, it could only be Paul's and, sure enough, an immaculate Isabel sat on the stern deck feeding a caged parrot. She looked like she's slept eight hours and was drinking champagne and orange juice. This style of life afloat, I felt, was altogether more me. "Bonjour, mes enfants," she welcomed us aboard. "Glasses are in ze galley, Rick."

I fetched them and after fixing drinks sank into an upholstered sort of banquette while Teresa went to clean up.

"Sy and Monica want to sail around the coast a bit with us all today, but I told them I'm not coming." Isabelle tapped her glass on mine.

"Why not?"

"Unlike you I respect my years," she replied. "I am going to 'ave a massage, a little sleep, my 'air done and an early night."

"You've changed a lot, sweetie."

"Age, cherie."

"No, I mean you've changed—you're happy with Paul?"

"More than I thought possible. At first I was frightened, Rick. You know, to be so involved—now I'm very, very content, but that's a little different to being 'appy." Isabelle was the child of a French provincial middle-class mother whose spirit drove her to escape from a suffocating 1950s bourgeois home by marrying a handsome Italian who was big on bull and short on delivery. He'd moved on whilst Isabelle was little more than a toddler and this had predisposed her to seek negative relationships with men. Whilst her mother continued to dwell within fractured dreams, Isabel got herself to Paris and worked as a showroom model for a clothes manufacturer on wages that "at least kept me slim," as she put it. After a while she found her feet with a modeling agency in the big city and her income improved. Boyfriends conformed to the ne'er-do-well pattern as an unconscious homage to her father and eventually the laws of attraction delivered Mr. Seriously Wrong into her life. His wealth was based on being a possessee of that which has had various names down the ages and is often called The Trickster. Wealth, charm, and his good looks wooed; Isabelle succumbed and married this man who could and did do deals anywhere and everywhere. As long as his invisible patron got a share of the human hopes and endeavors involved, circumstances would conspire with all manner of lies and fabrications and escapes. Realizations that all was not as she supposed dawned, causing Isabelle's wits to awake and enable her to come to gradually understand the extraordinary world she'd entered. Finding some steel within she finally overcame the negative conditioning of her negative-father-image; her spirit prevailed and she extricated herself from her husband's webs. Seven years after the marriage she'd divorced him and, because she knew where the bodies were hidden, his lawyer agreed to a large settlement in exchange for her signing a gagging agreement. She moved to London, which she then termed the least worst of all cities, and half played and half worked, not unprofitably, at being an interior decorator. In the course of this she met a lot of people none of whom meant anything special to her and thus she was able to stabilize and investigate herself. We'd met at a party and I'd liked her immediately. It was a timing thing—she'd understood without any explanation that I was a bit bruised by my divorce and I'd sensed she didn't need an affair. We were each what the other needed just then and decided to flee a winter London for a long weekend in Marrakech. After a day wandering around the still largely medieval city, we spent most of that night talking about realities we'd encountered until the man-woman time had passed. We went to bed and slept. The next morning I looked at this gorgeous woman and said, "I can't believe I didn't." Neither of us wanted romantic entanglement, both of us needed a pal. However I have a penis, and she has a need to nurture. I was given, and such is given, a sympathy fuck. And I'm never going to admit to you how much I enjoyed it; I'll say only that it really cheered me up. Because we both knew it was only a sympathy fuck, it didn't complicate our relationship and we remained friends back in London. Subsequently I'd gotten involved with one of those not quite resistible bad-news people that seem to appear during periods of rebuilding. I don't know if they're some sort of character test by the soul or a dark-side temptation or just appear as part of social-chemical action to provoke introspection. This particular bad girl was pretty bad and when Isabelle took me for lunch I moaned about my lot. "What is it you want in your life, Rick?" she asked and I told her. "Why don't you get it then?"

I started to explain about the world, my business, my situations and so on but pressing an elegant finger on to my lips she silenced me. "No, Rick, I mean what is it in you that stops you getting what you want?" I almost sneered as I explained it had nothing to do with what was *in* me. I told her—and I wince as I relate this to you—I told her what a wonderful magnificent fucking hero I was despite life's outrageous slings and arrows; again the finger pressed on my lips. "Rick, if that man there, "she nodded toward a man on a nearby table, "took out a knife and tried to stab you, you would die if you just ignore 'im not just because of 'im stabbing you, but also because of the inability of your body to deal wiz a knife." I could not have looked at my brightest for she'd continued, "Zere's not always much you can do about ze wish of ze man to stab you, but at least if you..." She sought for the words, "Acknowledge the design of ze 'uman body—your body, my dear, you will defend yourself and perhaps escape and prevail. It's not ze best example cherie, but you get ze message—non?" My contribution to our friendship was being her walker—escorting and advising. No longer the lone beautiful woman and therefore a threat, she got into a broader circle.

Although at that time I'd already known Paul for about three years, they didn't meet through me. He was a man's man and I would not have supposed his arrogant of-this-earth-ness bordering on the brutal would have interested her. How narrow my view had proved, for she was a woman who had the depth and breadth to handle him and he was so utterly real, she could safely love him.

I fell back to the present as a bathed and scented Teresa in white robe and black sunglasses appeared and contrived to stand very close to me. I watched, fascinated, as my hand slid up her leg and under the robe to cup her adorable bare bum. Oh dear, her skin felt so right! I didn't want to stop touching it. Sitting on my lap, she snuggled close into my neck.

"You stink—go and shower," she said.

"No, I always smell when in Spain—es macho."

I told of S and M's sailing plans and we decided to go along.

It was easy to understand why Sy liked yachts as we left the port and tourist beaches behind to cross some sea and anchor off a little cove; we had the place to ourselves.

Teresa, I think out of confused deference to Monica, kept all of her bikini on. It was an electric pink, translucent affair that cost more per square inch than a Manhattan freehold and it made my libido groan. It increasingly took something special to get me going so much these days and she was undoubtedly something special. No matter how tired and hungover you know you should be, sunshine and lust will overcome. It's what I've been lacking, I mused. Monica produced pitta bread filled with cheese and salad for a snack and Sy hauled up a roped crate of beer which, his fridge being full, he'd lowered into the depths an hour before. After eating we each napped until Harris's barking announced the arrival of a powerboat in our bit of sea. Teresa offered "to race" me to the cove. She won, of course, for there was no way I was going to exhaust myself swimming hard. She cheered me ashore from her position on a long flat rock and I kissed her full, wet lips for a long time—ah, but this girl was dangerous, oh so dangerous. I ate her neck, her shoulders, her breasts, her stomach, her hipbones, and the cheeks of her bottom, down the back of her thighs, behind her knees and her glorious pussy. I tell you all this stuff about sperm swimming the equivalent of the Amazon to fertilize an egg is wrong; there is some sort of magnetism in the female that draws them up the Nile. All the sperm have to do is jump the cataract. She was miaowing and purring, licking my anus, then my balls, then my cock and it was only with a tremendous act of will that I was able to tell her to relax because I had a present for her. Having her pussy between my lips was wonderful and gently sucking it made her back arch. She opened like a flower. I liked her clitoris; as I licked then teased her, it became engorged. I sucked a little harder and then softer, only to increase the impetus again. Her nails were cutting into my scalp and her breathing became irregular gasps –"No - don't stop - yes - don't stop."I slowed but sucked harder then more softly. She was moaning—her noises becoming animal now. Look, this girl was bright, beautiful and very, very confident so she had to understand who was in charge at this moment of time and that this moment of time could be prolonged. But suddenly it couldn't and her scream must have carried back to the yacht. Then she sat up, nearly strangling me in her arms as she kissed my head again and again. She pulled me down with her and we made love—yes, we didn't fuck there on that flat rock; we made love and the stone accepted our bodies as if it were ducks' down.

I could actually hear the smirk in Monica's voice as it bounced across the sea through the loudhailer: "Is it safe for us to come ashore yet?" I clambered across the rocks to the cove's little spit of sand and waved them a come on. A few minutes later the peace was shattered by the Kriscraft's outboard as Sy and Monica, bless them, brought bottles of water with them.

Teresa was very quiet and feline. I'm afraid to have to admit that I was rather subdued myself,

"What's taken the wind out of your sails? Nautical pun ha, ha, geddit ?" Sy inquired brightly.

"Quiet fool," Monica was going girly-girly; I suppose from inhaling all, the pheromones or whatever it is screwing releases. She pulled at Sy's arm, leading him into the sea for a swim.

As I lay on the warm sand, Teresa traced my lips with her fingers and I asked "Feel good ?"

"You'll improve," she said and kissed me.

Well, well, sexually things have evened up, so there is a possibility of a relationship, I supposed. We'd press on to feelings next.

Our shipmates reappeared looking pleased with themselves an hour or so later—they'd discovered another cove.

Sy had heard from other rich sailors that there was an excellent fish restaurant at the back of a beach farther along the coast. As we were tugging the KrisKraft back into the sea, Harris began to bark frantically and we all saw a figure climb on to the *Casalinica*. Harris of course went for him.

"Get in," I yelled and started the outboard.

Sailboats are outside my repertoire but powerboats are not and we were there in twenty seconds. My mistake was to come round the yacht too fast. Figuring the intruder must have a craft moored on our far side I thought to cut off his escape route. I hadn't reckoned with the other craft being the 350-horsepower cigarette boat that had anchored near us earlier. It was taking off like a dragster on nitro and its bow wave threw the inflatable backward all but capsizing us. A guy in its stern was trying to prize Harris's jaws off the arm of a second. "Mine hund!" shrieked Monica.

Sy pushed both women over the side into the sea. "Radio! Radio!" he shouted at them, gesturing to the yacht.

Figuring on the baddies having fifty knots plus, I doubted we had twenty, but there seemed no alternative but to try. The other craft was swinging in an arc out to sea and I sought to cut across it—there was just a chance we'd get close. Were we able to, I'd no idea what we might then do, as if they chose they could slice through us easily; wild notions of fouling their propellers charged through my head. Hollywood superheroes would have managed that sort of thing, of course, but what two literally shagged-out guys, one of whom was past his prime could accomplish in real life was likely to be another matter entirely. Whoever those cunts were they didn't have much nerve because, seeing my naval tactics, they threw Harris into the sea and, of course, we raced to his rescue. That little wet hero was seriously pleased to see us; Sy pulled him aboard and, the intruders now far away, I turned back toward the yacht.

None of us had seen the name of the big powerboat and as it had kept heading out to sea—Monica had watched it until it was off the radar screen—we couldn't give the coast guard much in the way of clues. Nothing seemed to have been taken, probably thanks to Harris, and the others were inclined to put it down to a bungled opportunist attempt at theft. Sy said boat and boat equipment theft was big business in the Med and the Caribbean, and that out and out piracy could not be that far away in the future as the third world realized that a lifetime's local wages was left lying around on even relatively modest first-world pleasure boats. I kept my own counsel because intuition linked this event with that of the helicopter two days earlier. My experience has been that intuition, providing you can keep the ego silent for a moment, will not mislead.

It was dark, and finding the restaurant beach would have been difficult except that if something swam in the sea they grilled it in the open air. Our noses led us in to anchor amongst several other boats and, with Harris tight in Monica's arms, we ran ashore in the inflatable. I loved the place instantly: its style was distressed-ramshackle-make-do and the extended family that ran it severely disorganized as far as service went. The whole setup pretended nothing beyond the serving of simple fresh food. Our meals were something no PR'd celebrity chef in Paris, New York or London could ever achieve because that bickering extended family, perhaps originally fishermen, were at one with their beach, their sea, their bit of the island, their crude charcoal grill, their joke of a building and their ludicrous tables and chairs. They were of this very planet, its earth and its sea; their naturalness unencroached upon by labor-saving gadgets and thus they were also one with their cooking implements. Do you get what I mean? Their food tasted of love, not their love but the love of Mother Earth for her simplest children.

The kid in each of us was enchanted as genetic memories were satiated, sitting in the glow of candles eating that food; conversations were conducted at low volume. Wine came straight out of a barrel into crude earthenware jugs and nobody seemed drunk—just content in a special, subdued way. Even the dogs—those resident, ours and several from other boats—were aware of the naturalness of it all. Harris joined them easily, the odd growl and nip but no real arguments. They accepted each other, becoming an instant pack; eating the food thrown to them and patrolling the perimeter of the place with an air of contentment as if pleased to be doing real doggy stuff.

If I had found that beach before I'd found Teresa I might have built a house there and never left.

The following couple of days were idyllic and even the cupboard was tolerable with Teresa's body to play with each night. Things have a horrible habit of moving on though.

Later we tried to put into the port at Ibiza town again but, it being full, had to anchor outside. Isabelle had organized a dinner aboard her boat, but Teresa and I went over in the afternoon because she needed girlie stuff that was there.

Isabelle had a traveling domestic lady who hadn't returned from a day off and I pretended not to know the dinner was a not quite right reheat from Edi's. Monica, Sy, and Maximilian, an elderly bridge-playing German, were all too polite to comment and the wine was fabulous—you wouldn't get a case of it then for much less than three thousand dollars. Luxuriating in the knowledge that Paul could afford it, and believing I somehow deserved it, I poured too much down my throat. When Isabelle and Monica partnered against Sy and Max with the air-conditioning set to serious, I led Teresa out onto the stern well deck. On reflection I realize there was a tawdry proprietariness about the way I did this. No, I'm not beating myself up—I'm being objective. Believe it.

The night was more than balmy warm with some humidity. The parrot croaked a hello croak to which Theresa responded as we sank together into the soft-padded bench seating. "You know what I find extraordinary about you, Rick?" she asked. My antennae detected a slight edge, a sharpness wrapped in the silk of her voice.

"Well, most things I guess but specially my modesty." The best part of a bottle of that wine answered.

"Aside from that general wonderfulness—you know you've never asked me anything—what I do for a living or whether I'm married."

Ignoring an alarm bell, the inebriated, overconfident, thoughtless, yeah-I've-hit-the-jackpot-lad said, "Okay, so tell me what you do for a living and whether you're married."

"Yes I am, but you can relax. He won't be out for months yet."

"Out ?"

"Umm, yeah, out of jail. He was lucky really only getting three for manslaughter. Smart lawyer and a plea bargain." I was about dumbstruck and it must have showed. She went on "Him being a light-heavyweight pro, he had about everybody convinced he hadn't meant to kill those guys."

This needed time to digest emotionally, then time to think things through and maybe plan; right now, it was emotions that had me whirling and I struggled to tough it out saying "Sure, sure, I don't want the guy's life story, but what do you or did you do for a living ?"

Vaguely as if through a tunnel filled with glue made from rendered corpses I heard her say, "Oh, I did some modeling. Mostly my hands," slender arms stretched out toward me and wriggled slim and elegant fingers. "Then I met a somebody and we went down to Mexico bought some land on the coast together, built cabanas and rented them out. The business worked okay, but we didn't. I borrowed the money to buy him out and then let the whole thing to a couple of guys who run it. It doesn't bring in much, but the land value has increased a lot."

I wasn't really taking this in because now and only just now part of me was realizing the fact that I was in some sort of shock for I had very much stronger feelings than I'd supposed or admitted to myself about this woman. Love ? I pondered; who fucking knows, and it's blind just like the song says. No, the real problem or, I should say pain, was that I'd believed she had no small thing for me. Shit! But I really had stuff to re-evaluate and to figure out. A very deep part of me knew that whatever the situation, I wanted and was going to get this woman. Chatterers might say this was all sorts of wrongness and for all I cared that might be so, that however would not alter my wishes nor my actions. I experienced that strange inner absoluteness of grim resolve, you couldn't call it a thrill because a thrill is sort of transitory, almost girlie. No, this was the satisfaction of having made a decision and mentally committed oneself to a road that may or may not lead to victory. Mr Light - Heavyweight was going to go down and very out.

Know your opponent—know all about him and his relationships. "So how'd you meet the meat ?" I asked

"Sorry ?"

"Forgive me—how did your meet your husband?"

"Oh," she started to smile and then stopped herself. "He's Cuban, and I was in Florida sorting out a deal for the cabana site."

"Is that why you and your original partner split up?"

Uncapping a small Vittel, she drained the whole thing. "Ummm, I'm thirsty," she said as she stood. "It was complicated…I'll be back in a bit." She went off into the boat's interior, I assumed to use a bathroom.

Needing to walk off the tension, I got up from the seating; the parrot shuffled on its perch and started to croak. "Shut up bird—I need to think," I told it, but I just couldn't fulfill that need. I could emote but not think clearly and walked along the narrow decking at the side of the yacht's superstructure up onto the front bit—sailors call it the foredeck—and onto the prow where chrome railings angled forward to compliment and accentuate the boats sleek lines. Leaning forward onto that railing, I looked directly down into the harbor water. Oil slicked and dark, it was so completely in sympathy with the thoughts that arose in my mind.

How easily shadow land arrives; soft-footed and surreptitious, it slips in and lends support to our darkest thoughts for its plan is to facilitate, to ease the execution of the vilest intents. Then the cynic speaks from the rocky island that protrudes from those dark waters and tells me that if I don't like the idea of playing very serious hardball to win this woman, I can just forget her - it's only one woman, there are millions upon millions more so why bother it counsels.

My soul has turned away, whirling her cloak up and over, so that I cannot picture her; she is completely shrouded by that cloak and I sense she waits, her back to me, to judge how worthily or not I will act.

Heaven caresses my neck, fingernails scrape upward through my hair and then the palm moves softly downward across a cheek until the fingertips gently rest on my lips. A slight pressure turns my face toward hers and Teresa kisses my mouth; without reference to thoughts my anxious arms draw her to me and my traitorous body melds with hers. We ignore the sounds of engines and fishermen's calls out in the bay and for a brief moment I know paradise. Yeah right—it's just too simple. I roughly move her away from me. "Does your husband know you're unfaithful?" I'm utterly amazed at my Victorian turn of phrase. She does the stupidest thing—she laughs and for the first time in my life I hit a woman. Unthinkingly I smacked her face, not viciously, not to damage but to hurt and shock. I never saw the fist that uppercut into my jaw, which in turn jolted upward causing me to bite my tongue—fuck! fuck! fuck! The pain of that! I could not be furious because I could not not see humor in this ridiculousness bordering on the surreal—that this slim, beautiful heartwounding woman could have caused me such instant physical agony. Just as well that she'd moved back said my fury as it failed to block out pain. I think I actually jumped around for a bit there on the foredeck. Putting my forefinger in my mouth I felt around, the tongue still seemed whole and there was no blood on that finger. "Well I'll resped you for thad at leathst." I tried to look serious.

"And will you respect me for being a married slut?" She was looking very levelly at me.

Again my veins flooded with ice, even the pain is frozen. "No — for going to be a divorced slut."

"I'm afraid that's impossible Rick" she was really looking into me now.

"Oh yeah ? How's it impossible?"

121

Standing in the semidarkness diffused lighting from the shore left her face shadowed; she just stood and looked at me for what seemed like a long time and then walked over to stand immediately in front of me. Her face was visible now and I saw a slick of blood on her lower lip. "Because I've never been married, fool." Time stopped and my being was in shock. "I just wanted to see how you'd react."

It was quite an achievement not telling her how much she meant to me just then; what I managed was, "Well, I figured that!" lending an entire new dimensions of meaning to the word unconvincing.

Within my arms her body was molded to mine, we kissed and then she breathed into my ear, "I'll be right back." She stepped away, smiling and went off while I experienced a sort of euphoria. My phone's ring broke the atmosphere and Baa asked when I would be back; when I told him only when I needed to be I could almost hear his radar click on. "Aha, this somehow subdued yet chipper demeanor about you young Skywalker - what's her name?"

I knew he'd not let it go. "We are Mr Fucking Perceptive this evening, aren't we?" I replied.

"Ooooh!" I imagined his pursed lips and couldn't help laughing to myself.

I'd already told him I was standing on a serious boat belonging to Isabelle whose name he remembered but couldn't immediately place. "Isabelle's …" I began.

"Yeah, got her now—femme fatale type decorator woman—always fancied her actually. Some boat she's got."

"You mean her face or the yacht?" Baa doing old-London street cool, cockney rhyming slang for face as in boat-race/face. "I'd go carefully there if I were you: she's married to Paul the…"

"Ah, that Paul. She'd said something about a husband called Paul," he bullshitted.

"Well I guess because you were in such a hurry you didn't get to meet her sister…"

"Oh, the sister, yes of course, ugly tart—everybody's been there mate." He broke off awaiting my reaction. I didn't offer anything, so he continued, "Surprised at you, Rick," he paused. "You do know that she used to be a bloke, don't you? Chucked out the Merchant Navy for…"

"Yeah, I knew all that. It was in her advert."

"So what's her name?" he asked.

"Teresa."

"You poor, poor fuck – you uttered that. You uttered her name with that awful, soft, sighing, loaded with adoration and meaning tone that people use when they say the name of the person they're in love with." I heard him gulp something I supposed was wine. "And I mean IN LOVE. Oh well, what's she like?" he feigned a yawn.

I was not going to tell that currently she was my weakness and my strength, that when I looked at her I felt an overwhelming tenderness coupled with the urge to make love to her until I died smiling of exhaustion and that there were still many unexamined feelings pleasantly disturbing me.

"She's a woman" was what I did tell him.

"You're lost you poor sod—another here I think Miss," I heard him tell a waitress. He could be sentimental sometimes; I didn't know it, but there would be a smile in his eyes when he drank a toast to my having found what I'd suddenly accepted was love.

I appreciated his style and silently wished him only good things but said, "Listen, soft girl, I'd originally figured to leave here in a couple of days but if you keep me posted I'll cut it a little finer, okay ?"

"Sure I could, but things are moving, Rick—can you be here in four days?"

"Guaranteed. I'll see you then."

"See you." He hung up

Good fortune had brought Harris over with Monica and Sy to dinner and cards with Isabelle that night. Teresa and I were staying in her cabin, but when Sy and Monica and Harris went off in the inflatable to return to the *Casalinica*. It was gone. Anchored immediately outside the port amongst lots of other boats, it had been locked and secured, yet within four hours it had been removed and taken away into the night. Sy was furious and Monika was heartbroken; this wasn't a car that had been stolen, this was their home. Coastguards, the harbor master, and police were roused and the Spanish navy was informed.

• • •

No sleep that night. After officialdom had taken down details and left, Sy and I sat drinking coffee on the *Isabelle*'s bridge. Isabelle herself had insisted we take her boat out at dawn to do our own searching and we wanted to familiarize ourselves with the controls. It was all state of the art but there was a lot of engine to be managed. She'd actually gone off into the town to find some local guy who crewed for them so that he too could lend a hand.

Amongst the books in the main cabin was a large map of the Med and I laid it out on the bridge's chart table.

"Look, Sy, this boat's very fast but there's a lot of sea out there and we don't know how seriously the navy and what not are going to look."

"That's right—be fucking positive." He was really upset.

"Hey," I took his arm. "I'm on your side, you know. Now, just listen man."

"Yeah, sorry."

"Look, supposing your boat was taken immediately after we left her, which was around eight. Let's figure out how far she could get in ten hours, then twenty hours, and then thirty hours."

"The way the wind is coming up from Andalucia then swinging east she'd take days to reach the mainland, south would take forever so Gibraltar, Morocco, Algeria are out. She'll go north towards Majorca or maybe run east toward Sardinia."

"Okay, other islands or open seas north and east. Radio all the coast guards and offer a reward. That'll make them seriously look out for her. I'll hire a plane with a pilot and at first light we'll cover a lot of open sea."

Teresa came up the steps to the bridge with some coffee.

"Sweetheart, I'm going out to the airport to organize an air taxi to look for the boat."

"Good idea."

"Will you come? A bit of glam might oil wheels?"

"Of course."

Sy marked out the chart and Teresa and I left in the same cab that brought Isabelle and the sleepy local sailor to the boat. No local airtaxi was available but fate delivered a visiting pilot, Alvaro, and his ancient Piper. With the folded chart across my knees, we trundled into the sky shortly after dawn. Making radio contact, Isabelle told us Sy had offered 5,000 dollars as a reward to whoever found his boat. There were a lot of binoculars scanning the sea already. They could all have relaxed, for we found her within an hour. She was ten miles off the northeast coast of another island that I would learn was Formentera. Tied up to her was the very same blue and white powerboat we'd chased off a few days earlier.

Alvaro's adrenaline kicked in hard. He would have been a happier man in a fighter bomber, for as soon as I'd identified the yacht he flipped us into a dive that strained the rivets.

"No, up, Alvaro, up—*mas alto!*" I yelled, for we needed height to be sure of good radio contact. Height regained and some sort of fix given to Sy, we plummeted once more. Those bastards must have heard us on the first dive for they were bundling back aboard the powerboat. I swear our propeller passed less than a meter over their heads and by the time Alvaro had yanked his heap around, they were jetting off. Balearic or wherever blood aflame, he buzzed them to their probable and my certain terror.

"Look for something to drop on them," I shouted at Teresa. But of course there was only a fire extinguisher and I missed.

Alvaro calmed down a bit, told me I'd have to pay for the extinguisher, and flew wide circles above the powerboat as it roared off in the general direction of Mallorca. In passable English, he radioed Sy with their course, then repeated it in Spanish to the Mallorcan coast guard and on another channel, to any Spanish navy boats that might be around. The men on the powerboat were most likely listening in for they spun around and headed back the way they'd come. This made things harder, for the sea around Ibiza in August is a heavy traffic zone and the closer we got to the island the more our quarry was among other boats. Soon the only way we could track it was the fact that it was doing about forty knots, leaving a huge wake and dodging around the other boats. If it had slowed down we might easily have lost it.

The Piper's nose came up and we all but juddered to a halt in mid-air as Alvaro fought to avoid the huge gray helicopter that arose right in front of us from nowhere. Was I shocked? Yes. Was I surprised? No. I just knew it was our other old friend. In the movies this sort of thing is all good fun and thrilling; in real life it's gut wrenchingly terrifying and extremely disorientating. Squeals of horror came from the seat behind. "Darling, I don't want you to be nervous but I'm going to jump out and cling on to the helicopter, then force the pilot to land." I told an ashen Teresa. "I'll probably slap him around a bit first."

"Yeah, right, Arni." But she wasn't amused.

Alvaro had dropped us low to keep track of the powerboat, but the helicopter kept getting in front of us causing us to lose it.

"Okay, we go for cabron!" He meant the chopper.

"Ataboy." I patted his shoulder; I liked his balls. However, it was not to be. Not only would the thing piss all over us with its superior maneuverability, it could also outrun us and did so within twenty minutes. We returned to where we'd last seen the powerboat but it was nowhere to be seen. There were several dozen craft there now and we'd no idea where our quarry had gone.

Sy radioed that they had his boat in sight and we swung around for the airport.

There was something rather odd about the way the police and a couple of suits greeted us when we landed—nothing you could put your finger on exactly, just a distinct lack of warmth. They walked Alvaro away with some bland and dismissive reassurances to Teresa and I but subjected him to some heavy-duty yakking.

Alvaro extracted payment for the extinguisher from me, bade us a curt good-bye and disappeared into an airport building. Our adrenalin highs evaporated.

"What do you make of that?" I asked her.

"I'm going to be sick," she replied.

"No, you're not," I told her wrongly.

She got cleaned up in the airport john but still looked all in. Coffee refreshed but I couldn't reach either Isabelle's or Sy's mobile, nor could I gain access to a radio at the airport. Eventually I called Paul's office in London and had them send a fax over the satellite link to say we'd be finding a hotel and would meet them in the port that night or the next morning. I'd figured organizing the recovery of the boat would take them most of that day.

Back in town and tiring of hearing *nos estimos completes*, I sought out a berobed Edi who magicked up a room in Andre's pretty pastel pensione. "He is broadminded—but just be discreet my darlings"

Service like it I've never had anywhere else on this planet. Awaking in the dusk, I stumbled along a passageway to ask for tea, and barely fifteen minutes later, the lovely Andre's exquisitely manicured nails tapped on our door before passing in a tray bearing plates of smoked salmon, scrambled eggs and a huge pot of china tea. I was quite stunned and decided there and then if I ever went the other way he'd be mine.

Telling Teresa as much resulted only in her saying, "*Pad de rubirosa pled.*"

"Don't speak with your mouth full."

She swallowed "Please pass the *rubirosa*."

"The what ?"

"The pepper, peasant."

"I never heard it called a ribuwhatnot?" I handed her the fifteen-inch wooden grinder.

"Rubirosa. Years ago ladies in London gave it that name in honor of a charming Central American gentleman."

"Yeah, well eat your heart out kid," I told her.

We finished pigging the food, showered and lay back on the bed beneath an open window listening to early evening sounds, most of which were Fat Boy Slim.

Still exhausted, we slept off and on again, until Edi called for us the next morning. He took us for coffee by the market where he bought his seafood. Actually I simply trailed along behind him and Teresa; each aware that together they attracted the attention of more men. Sniggering a lot, each had an arm round the other's waist. "Look, I'm turning him," she called to me over her shoulder as we walked within the cool of the covered market.

"Pay attention children! Mama" Edi savored the word, "is going to show you" he gestured proprietarily at a huge array of seafood, "how to select fish." Reaching across the wet marble he picked out a largish example. "See, this is excellent—the tail sticks up, the eyes are bright an' the gills are nice an' red." He held it up and sniffed. "An' it does not smell. That, my dear, is exactly ho' I choose my fish."

"Bravo my darling!" said Teresa. "That is exactly how I choose my men."

"Slut! You cannot even be taken to a fish market!" Holding her arm, he flounced off toward another stall.

The *Isabella*'s berth still being empty and no sign of *Casalinica* and nobody on either boat being reachable on Teresa's mobile, we wandered along to the harbor master's office to contact them by radio. Those whose homes have been broken into say they feel like rape victims. Sy and Monica had not only suffered invasion but the theft, however short lived, of an entire home. You knew that in spirit *Casalinica* was their home rather than the house in France.

They needed support given in their own time and their need was greater because the boat had been ransacked. Although so far nothing appeared to have been stolen there was a phenomenal amount of mess.

"Sy 'as anchored 'is boat in a bay and I'm next to 'im. Say."

"Isabelle shall we come there tonight? Say."

"Zey are sleeping now—Jose," she was speaking to her crewman. "Where is zis place again? Okay. The east end of Formentera is where we are Rick, but look, I'm tired also. There's nothing you can do tonight—come in ze morning. Say."

It made sense so I agreed. The harbormaster showed me where the bay was on the map. I wrote it down, thanked him and we left.

It has to be some sort of universal constant, as the speed of light was supposed to be—a conspiracy of appallingness between weavers, designers, clothing manufacturers, fashion editors and retailers. It may have a benign purpose—any superior extraterrestrial civilizations would by definition have a better taste than the average human being and would therefore avoid all contact with, and the popularly supposed subsequent enslavement of, us Earthlings on grounds of taste. And we were only shopping for T-shirts and knickers.

Off the main drag, we found what we needed; our soiled clothes went into the shop's rubbish bin as we went into some of our purchases.

A pharmacy supplied toothbrushes and those tubes of overpriced glue or whatever it is that women find as essential as oxygen. Oh, but I did enjoy being with her—dangerously so. As we sat on Edi's terrace eating fillet mignon, I caught myself thinking my life had been all but a waste of time and effort before meeting her. Thoughts, terrifying for their normalcy, kept coming into my mind—some of them even bordered on the suburban. And my body was incredibly hot for her. Fuck me it's an early menopause, I thought giving up on the food. She knew exactly how it was and I could feel her changing gear—know what I mean, do you? That time when a woman decides she probably sees a child in a man's eyes. They're always scoping for it, of course. Do you think they look the way they do, with all those nice bits plus their femininity, just to cheer us up? Bollocks! That's all the reproductive and nurturing equipment arranged in a way to attract. Having attracted, they can then evaluate genetically. They're quite often barely aware they're doing so because it's a function of their bodies over which the conscious mind has little if any control, however much various magazine articles they read might delude them otherwise. Female skin can and does read male genetics by touch and that information is processed unconsciously and becomes an opinion. Men sometimes rant about illogical female behavior whilst never admitting the fact that female apparent lack of logic is often based on the most logical thing in human affairs— we each arrive on earth via a female. Women need a more inclusive logic than men do and that need can confuse both genders.

Having successfully avoided fatherhood I had no wish to now suddenly lose that battle but there was a compulsion about her that tore right into my solar plexus. Well, fuck it! If Nature was mounting such a serious assault, I was going to fight strategically and ruthlessly. I'm not quite a moron; I knew Nature would win so it would be a question of playing for post-conquest terms.

Our room at Chez Gay boasted bidet and shower and naturally we'd peed in the bidet but after we'd made love and she wanted to pee again, I got up and led her into the shower. Sliding a leg between hers I held her tight and kissed her mouth slowly. Her tongue was halfway down my throat, both her legs entwined around one of mine as her breasts ground the softness of paradise into my chest. I started to kiss her face and she breathed into my ear, "Baby, I have to pee."

One of my hands was on her buttocks and the other cupped a breast, forefinger stroking its erect nipple; I kissed her mouth again, sucking on her lower lip. Her arms loosened from my neck, slid down my back until her nails dug into the cheeks of my bum.

"Baby, baby, stop, I'll pee myself."

Holding her, I looked into her eyes in the half-light. "Do it."

A tiny involuntary tensing of her body: we held each other's eyes.

"Do you think you love me?" Her voice the breath of Aphrodite with the tiniest hint of mockery.

"No." I kissed her eyes, her nose, her chin, her neck. "I don't think I love you, Teresa." Our eyes locked again, her body was growing wooden as we tried to look into each other's souls. "I know I love you." She melted into me, her mouth found mine and I felt a warmth running down my leg. If you've not done this with the person you love, don't knock it. The first taboo we learn in this world is control of these bodily functions and when you break that discipline, that most fundamental acceptance of parental-worldly authority, then you have entrusted yourself to somebody. Like I said, this was love and a strategic matter.

After a while, I reached behind her and turned on the shower.

There was a strange innocence about our lovemaking for what remained of that night: we both knew it was all only real from now on. We were a bit like virgins who'd read the Karma Sutra.

Only care for Sy and Monica stopped me taking her away with me. The next morning I desperately wanted to, and she wanted it to happen, but we each felt they would need a bit of emotional backup.

To say that the *Casalinica* had been thoroughly searched would have been more than an understatement—the bastards had been ruthless. Bedding and clothes thrown out; mattresses slit; woodwork jemmied; and radio, radar and satnav ripped open—even the boats little engine pulled apart. Other yachties—the event was the talk of the local air-waves—turned up with stuff found floating including Harris's sleeping basket. Quite obviously they hadn't been looking for any old secreted valuables for they'd even found Sy's emergency hidey-hole. This six or so thousand dollars' worth of currency had been inside a strip of hollowed 2x2 screwed inside and under the top of the fixed cabin table as if it were an edge support. Its purpose was to be available should unforeseen circumstances arise and it was all still there only now strewn over the cabin floor.

"Anything I need to know about anything mate?" I was helping Sy retrieve papers that had been emptied out of box files.

"Rick, there's nothing. There's nothing of any serious value on this boat other than that dosh and boat itself. Monica's bits of jewelry are in a box at the marina and share certificates and papers are either with the brokers or with solicitors. My laptop's gone, but there was fuck all on it of use to anyone but me."

"Nothing from your China trading days that the inscrutables might not want you to have?"

He paused for a moment and thought and then said, "No nothing. When I sold the business to Histers, they got the contacts within the factories and trading companies there. It was all very straightforward." He looked really grim and pissed off. Teresa brought in a couple of bottles of welcome cold beer and then went back outside to Monica. I told Sy about Guy the Belgian's questions and his claiming to be in the importation business, "Yeah, I know," Sy said. "He said as much to me. He was just sniffing around Monica—Guy's just Lonely Guy."

The local fuzz and the coastguard were apparently as bemused as we were. Then some honcho from the mainland showed up and they suddenly got very interested. They asked Sy if the boat had been to Turkey (heroin), North.Africa (dope), West Africa (Columbian coke or diamonds), the Caribbean (coke and dope) and so on. But other than the odd day out or this trip, *Casalinica* had stayed around the marina on the Spanish mainland—all more or less verifiable. Sy drained his beer and, very decently I thought, said, "You'd be in the way here. Do your biz, and then come back and sail some more."

Sally lives in Chiswick, Inner West London in a house that had then appreciated in value by about 100 percent in a decade. Another decade on and it would have tripled from that and, despite thus becoming effortlessly capitalised free of UK taxes, she still works as a sort of free-lance secretary for me and one or two others. Each autumn, she gives a little drinks party, so we can all meet each other and ensure there is nothing any of us do that could conceivably put our Sally in a conflicting interests predicament. After calling Baa to say I was coming I reached her and within an hour she'd made travel bookings for me. Luckily I'd had my passport, phone and a credit card with me but my clothes had either been soaked or had disappeared during the ransacking, my grip had gone too. Isabelle loaned me pesetas and dollars, some of which were to go on another taxi to the airport for the next morning's early flight to London. It was a holiday charter plane - how does Sally manage these things?
Everybody was on the Isabella that evening and Teresa had bought me some fresh clothes. Dinner was out of the freezer and the going away blowjob was out of this world.

"Are you all right there, sir?" Not a question just part of a litany; he wore a name badge saying JULIAN.

"Yes, splendid thank you. I always fly Lilliput Airline." I proffered a folded twenty pound note. "Anywhere with a bit more room ?"

The charter plane sped down the runway then up into that morning's beautiful sky. He was back. "If you'd care to walk this way, sir." He led me toward the front of the one-class-squashes-all plane and indicated three empty seats.

"You noticed how I didn't wisecrack about walking this way?" I sat down.

"And I certainly appreciated it, sir."

The quality of morning light at thirty thousand feet was very special, contriving with the lingering scent of Teresa to intoxicate my spirit. Yes, she'd of course got her perfume on to my clothes so that she wouldn't be out of my mind. But oh, don't those touches of the primitive savage, that blatantly obvious wish to ensnare, excite? I suppose it was just knowing that I was desired, really desired, by that feminine darkness. That magic from deep inside woman reaches out and entraps our projections. All men are susceptible to this flattery—the trick is not to let them put the diapers back on you.

Sitting at an angle within the three seats gave a little more leg room, enabling me to doze for a bit, a reverie actually.

"You must have been at it!" Julian was proffering a tray bearing a cup.

"Shows, huh?" He still refused to accept the fifty.

"Don't worry, it's cool. Not quite every day I see a man sleep with smile. Coffee?"

It was surprisingly good coffee and I started to plan action and personal logistics for picking up clothes and money in London. I'd only been away a week but felt I hadn't seen my home for months. Having zero luggage sped me through LHR to where ancient sunlight stored in the dead material of another age rereleased inside a black cab's engine turned wheels that moved me along the M4 into the world's then second city. The meter priced this journey at a rate that would facilitate Frank the driver's chosen lifestyle. Long divorced, he lived more than half each year in a modest but comfortable village house near Nimes in southern France where his unpretentiousness had earned him an acceptance by his neighbors that was slowly metamorphasizing into respect as his French improved. His mind was on the two pear trees in his small southern garden and whether this night he would finish his sixteen-hour stint by sleeping inside the cab on the airport taxi rank. A hundred year old copy of Avebury's book on fruit cultivation lay next to his seat.

Just down the road, just along the river from Chelsea's multimillion-pound apartments and houses is the planet's second biggest financial center and, some might say, laundry. Are you sure it's the second? Remember this is Britain, the country that when at the zenith of imperial power balanced its books by growing opium in what is now called Pakistan and dealing it wholesale into China for payment in silver. Think real, my friend, when you think of Britain and perhaps remember that word *enantidromia*.

Today it seems that every bank in the world is represented there. Amazing, incredible might be the thought, perhaps the last thought, of an old age pensioner dying of malnutrition, general oldness and a hospital-acquired infection on a trolley in a crowded NHS hospital corridor. Well done you great British prime ministers and your governments. Well done that vast property company called the Church of England. Well done the unseen hands on the helm. And well done the Ministry of Education or whatever it's currently branded.

Depressing? Yes I know, but take comfort in the alchemy that results is Britain's Artlife; the future's shadow in which perhaps, just perhaps, some sort of salvation can be discerned. I had long ago somehow sensed it was all, and I mean all, bullshit, and I just wanted to buy myself space and time. I'd worked hard and I'd pulled a few fast ones and was not in the least bothered by gray areas but I'd not got into the deeply negative for it seemed self-evident that you lose when you win on that route.

Queuing to cash a check in the bank I make calls. Personal credit gets me an early morning diamond from a dealer in the Garden and over in Mayfair I'm owed a favor. Outside another of Baa's mincabs awaits, the driver brimming with a self-hatred that is exploited by smarter men who've decided the priesthood is better than working for a living. I express my genuine amazement that he, an undereducated inadequate, can believe he knows absolutely what God wants of him. He believes he knows because his heart has responded to the words of his priest, and it has not crossed his mind to suppose the priest has merely responded to the cravings of his complexes and his ability to pay a little money from time to time.

In counterpoint to the ugliness of his character, Old Bond Street yields a beautiful rhodium-coated platinum chain at a shop that will set the diamond that day and courier it that night. I walked, get this will you, with a spring in my step around to Berkley Square and then to a serious florist where I ordered a lot of flowers for delivery in Ibiza. Then at home, and as I fix coffee, there is a buzzing sound.

The video-entryphone reveals a small gang from a hi-how-r-u-we-can-do-style cleaning company Sally had booked to refresh chez moi. They'd wanted to send an adviser, but wary of that particular dance, she'd said "This is his credit card number charge it up to two max, wash and clean and touch up the paint in each room, put in four fresh towels and some plants so that by this evening he can eat off the floor. Extravagant? Not really when you recall that I'm expecting the woman I love to show up soon whilst I'm putting together a complex setup that might enable me to devote the remainder of my life to finding joint fulfillment for our souls. "Hi, good morning to you," gushes their leader. "I'm Androgyny Rogers. Call me Andri, everyone does." Not behind your back I thought

as the air kiss equivalent of shaking hands is managed whilst simultaneously scanning my living room. "But this house is so lovely. When are you
moving in?" Androgyny's gofer has already found my basement kitchen
to which she beckons two Philippino ladies.

"Painter ?" I ask.

"On the way."

"Gosh, Androgyny, I feel we're in a movie." She shines, "Here's my
mobile number." I pass a card stapled with two fifties as a tip. "I'm the
frontrunner for the entire Amsterdam office, which is relocating—get this
right and you'll get the account! When you've finished, all internal keys
in that drawer there, close the windows except the roof lights, and leave
all the extractor fans on—I don't want to smell any paint."

"You'll only smell heaven."

"Dave, a nice man but a musician, may show: I don't think I told him
you were coming today. If he does turn up and there's a problem, call me."

Baa's house is in that locality just northwest of Regents Park named
St. John's Wood after another group of knights from the times of the
Crusades. It is an area various pop singers, quite a few of Britain's surprisingly large population of ultra-quiet billionaires, and the merely wealthy
including our very own Baa have homes. That day its streets were, not unusually, full of armed police for members of the bloodline of the Imperial
Japanese throne sometimes reside in St. John's Wood. There's also an army
barracks in the middle of this incredibly expensive piece of real estate
that military chiefs' complaints of budget inadequacy and parliament's
attempts at defense expenditure cutbacks had until very recently ignored.

Baa's house is not small and rather like his mind has self-contained
offshoots. In one of these lives an ex-wife and in another, his aged mother
and her sister: other than the geographical proximity, he has little to do
with them. The main part of the building accommodates Baa and an
elderly Portuguese couple who look after the place. Two rooms have
been knocked into one to provide him an office, which contains three
identical tables placed end to end. Piles of papers proceed down one table
and then on to the next, where they are examined once a week by a person who comes in from an accountancy firm. Then, after being looked
at for a lot of pounds per hour all are micro-fiche'd, some are filed, and
the majority pushed further along on to the last the table to fall from its
end into a canvas hopper. The hopper feeds a shredder that is periodically operated then unloaded into an incinerator in the garden by the

Portuguese man. There are two totally separated computers in the room, one connected to the outside world, and the other not.

Pyotr is already there having flown in last night with Galena, who is busy investigating the facilities of Blake's Hotel. I catch Baa's eye, "I thought I'd treat these lovebirds. " he grins. "Soften them up a bit."

"And it is tempting me to delay finalizing our agreement," says Pyotr. "Baa's been explaining why you want us to do the manufacturing here in the UK."

"Better for Baa and me," I tell him. "But even better still for you, I think."

"It could be—but what about security here? You have all sorts of regulatory control bodies…"

"This is true," said Baa. "But the point about them is that their culture is reactive rather than proactive—by the time any of them got around to inspecting anything we could simply move on to different premises."

"They are really like that?" Pyotr was genuinely surprised. "But we always think of Britain as very organized." Baa and I exchange weary glances.

"That's part of the trick," explained Baa. "Britain's image is always civilization and sanity, but most of each occurs almost coincidentally to the making of money and indulging hypocrisy. On the one hand, it sucks in a lot of capital from the world's richest so those who own the planet have a vested interest in keeping it going. Then also, by whatever mechanism, there is a sort of alchemy of the world's needs that influences things." He struggled the first cigar of the day out of his case.

"And the secret police, your M15? They are not reactive from what I hear. They are very proactive!"

"They have their own very big and complicated games to play and I don't doubt their own agendas. Even assuming we were noticed, once they conclude we're not terrorists or a mafia with real or potential political influence, they'll have no interest. Coffee ?" Mrs. Portuguese, the housekeeper, came in with a tray.

"You know it might be an idea for them to have a cover, of some sort." I thought of Sy, and an idea came to me. "I know someone who sold out his business and went to live abroad."

"So do I," said Baa, figuring I meant Sy.

"Pyotr could buy a container of T-shirts from one of his old suppliers…" Baa began.

"And how would I know how to sell them on in a foreign country?" he asked

"Pyotr, anybody can sell about anything here if they give the buyer enough credit, and also perhaps you could sell some into Ukraine. Perhaps even subsidize the prices to get trade going. Rick could speak to our friend and get the supply organized for you."

Whilst we drank coffee, I told Pyotr about how sales revenue from the metal would go to an untouchable account in Zurich and be automatically moved to our individual accounts on preset percentages. He liked this idea, so Baa phoned Zurich and made an appointment for two days time. Separately each of us were to make mobile calls to airlines and buy regular tickets on different flights for the following day; Together we all, myself, Baa, Pyotr and Galena, Alexei and Ilya, would meet there and then visit the bank together. It would have certainly been more convenient and most probably have been cheaper to rent a private jet but that would have tied us in together. As the world becomes more complex, so the recording of people's actions and movements increases. One day we'll all be chipped in lieu of identity cards and passports just like Harris.

"But now we have to talk about selling the palladium." said Pyotr. Both Baa and I had traded precious metals for a number of years so commercial track records meant we would not attract any undue attention simply by dealing in physical palladium. However along with Alexei, we'd calculated that we could eventually be processing nearly seventy kilos per day, which at the summer of '99 prices was around fifteen million US dollars a month. That daily amount of palladium would fit in three briefcases and that sort of money was exciting, but seventy kilos a day was also around 12 percent of the palladium then being mined globally according to our calculations. After allowing for recycled material coming on to the market, we'd be handling around 11 percent of the entire global supply.

I told him, "This is seriously sexy."

"I hope it is not too sexy," Pytor said. "The world's largest stockpile of this metal is held inside Russia by Almazyuvelirexport and the quantity they hold is a Russian state secret."

"That could help things commercially—refiners and banks will assume it's coming out of Russia," I suggested.

"Well, Mr. James Bond, that's as maybe, but I figure more layering's needed," Baa said and stood up. "As is a pee, excuse me." He left the room.

"What do you suggest, Rick?" asked Pyotr.

I explained that silver bars stamped with assay marks might sound ideal because although the atomic structure of the metal was changed by processing, the overall appearance of the bar was not: visually the new palladium bar could pass perfectly as a silver bar. The problem was the weight—a kilo of silver is larger than a kilo of palladium. Any customs checks of shipments would instantly establish that the apparent one kilo silver bars weighed more than one kilo. I went on to say that impure bars, bars composed of a mixture of metals, could confuse matters and to some extent conceal their palladium content, but the whole matter was fraught with difficulty and so even medium term odds were not good for concealing our product.

Baa returned and sat at the room's external computer. He fiddled around with the mouse for long minutes then exclaimed an, "Aha," picked up a phone and dialed.

As Pyotr and I sat in silence, he got through to the owner of a casting business and discussed a large order for Zippo-style lighters with unpolished casings to be cast from silver he would supply. "No, I don't want plated. I want solid silver—you'd get it in grain form."

Baa's thinking was that we could buy grain, small silver granules, which would be delivered to the casting business.

There would be an eight-week lead time for the molds and then they would start churning out ten thousand lighter casing per month; we could have these hallmarked as silver, process them into palladium and ship them to Switzerland consigned to the order of the new Liechtenstein company, which would have then delivered straight into a Swiss refiner as scrap. It wasn't a foolproof plan, but it wasn't bad.

•   •   •

Theresa's phone wasn't answered for a while. "Buenos noches, senorita."

"Qui es?"

"It's me. I just got home." The suddenly school-aged boy in my heart explained.

"Who is this?"

"Who d'you think ?"

"Oh, I know the voice—you're the one who sent the flowers and stuff, but what was the name? No don't tell me—it's Prick or something like that."

"Big Prick actually."

"You wish."

"We both do, but you didn't complain"

"Not while you were here, but it just seems, as far as I can remember, not to have been that big. Well anyway, not until touched." Her voice lower, "Mmm, yes touching, I suppose…you know darling, to get it the way I want it, need it as a matter of fact." Fuck but she'd got me hard already. "Rick, I'm getting turned on. I want to touch you and touch myself the same time…darling, I know you're hard—touch yourself …"

"Baby, don't," I croaked. "Don't do this to me. I'm too old to jerk myself off."

"You're never too old. Do it for me please—please."

I'd really no idea why I was bothering to try and stay in control, and yet I said, "Baby don't be a pain."

"You've a pain? You want me to kiss you better?"

"Get a fucking plane, woman," I begged

"You get a plane hotshot," she shouted. "I miss you, you bastard. You didn't call for days and days—nearly a week you fucking shit! You think you can just send me a beautiful chain and then ignore me while you fuck around Mr. Prick? You don't know what you've got here…" I let her go on. Her anger wasn't as theatrical as she intended me to believe; it was just delicious to know that I mattered to this woman.

"Teresa, I love you. Please stop moaning and just get a plane, will you …please?"

"You'll just have to wait and see, won't you." She hung up.

•　•　•

There was a lot to do at the rented and sublet offshore, and then re-let four thousand square feet of industrial unit near Heathrow. The legalities were one thing, the practical considerations another. I explained to Pyotr and Alexei that as all our purchases were being paid for up front by bank draft, anybody we bought from need only have the name of the company—not our names. Bank drafts, unlike checks, did not carry our signatures. No written orders for equipment and materials were to be given out, suppliers orders should be verbal or on their headed paper and referenced only by the first name of the person making the order. That first name should always be false; however so we could identify it internally, it should begin with the first letter sound of the actual person's name. Pyotr would be Patrick or Pierre, Alexei would be Arturo or Andy, I would be Robert or Rauol, Baa would be Bertrand or Basil, Ilya would be Isaac or Ian, and Galena would be Geraldine or Greta. If there was a problem that seemed dangerous to any or all of us, or to our enterprise, the person aware of that problem would alert each of the others by direct speech, voicemail, e-mail, fax, and text stating < rumors US soyabeans overbought >. We would all separately check in to tourist hotels in the Russell Square area of London, acquire pay-as-you-go mobile phones and meet at 10:00 A.M. and/or noon and/or 4:00 P.M. in the British Museum forecourt or 8:00 P.M. at the Trocadero center at Piccadilly Circus to discuss the situation and swop phone numbers.

As we were ostensibly going into the T-shirt wholesaling business, we had contractors put in lots of shelving, partitioning and long benches. Printers produced invoices, letterheads and business cards. I managed to prevail in an argument with Baa who was lobbying for a photo shoot involving pretty girls.

XRF analysis equipment went into one of the two small office sections next to a heated foil- print system that could actually print on to T-shirts. Alexei explained that the central part of the production platform was very heavy and that he needed to dig into the concrete floor to check it for stability. The freeholder's office had willingly couriered over their building's construction plan with surveyors' notes, but Alexei wanted to physically check for himself. Glancing at Baa, I said "He da man."

"Agreed, we'll need a couple of electric hammer drills, ear mufflers and stuff. The hire company will need a credit card, so I'll rent them for delivery to St. John's Wood and bring them over by car tomorrow. While he used his laptop to find an inner London hire shop, I unwrapped the local yellow pages British Telecom had left when the phone lines were installed; we had six separate lines and put faxes on three of them. Alexei and Pyotr had e-mailed a metal fabricator for a partially constructed base, but the firm was quoting a five-week lead-in period before they would put the job into production and on top of this they wanted, we calculated, about 20 percent more than it should have cost. What we didn't want to do was shop around because although this welded part assembly was innocuous, it was also unusual. We sought to avoid any casual speculation amongst suppliers as far as possible. Going to other firms was therefore an option to be avoided. Using a landline and a bad South African accent, I got through to the managing director of the West Midlands firm and explained how totally up shit creek I was because this assembly hadn't been ordered months ago. He whined his commiserations and regrets that he couldn't guarantee to improve on the five week lead-in, so I delighted him by asking him to fax us a sales confirmation for the assembly against immediate payment of half his price by bank transfer. I then went on to say that his confirmation should categorically state that a second payment by bank transfer for 70 percent of his price would be paid once it was checked at his works and on the pallet ready to go to us within five working days. Thinking of the extra twenty percent clear profit on top of the twenty he'd already overquoted he said nothing as I counted a silent fifteen, and then added, "And because you'll have saved me my job, man, I'll be personally delivering two cases of very special South African wine as a personal thank you, and I promise our next order will give you the full lead-in time you want."

"You're a hard man to do business with," he lied as he thought of the next order.

"Come on, man, that's gonna be the best wine out of the Republic."

He said we had a deal and faxed a confirmation within the hour. I immediately TT'd money to their account.

A delivery of oxy-acetylene welding equipment with gas bottles arrived from our smelter. Two small diesel generators were delivered just as plumbers finished putting shower facilities, two domestic washer-dryers, double-sink unit and a dishwasher in partitioned off areas next to the toilets. They demonstrated that all was in working order and were paid in cash for which much show was made of asking for a receipt.

Alexei worked with Ilya using hand held equipment to take readings of the local magnetic field and chalk corresponding lines and numbers on the unit's floor; then they started to take electromagnetic readings, which were strong toward the front of the unit where power fed in from the mains. Lastly Alexei used a wooden divining rod to plot the course of some deep subterranean watercourse.

The next day, Baa was to go off with Ilya to an industrial plant dealer to acquire a large forklift ostensibly for unloading the pallets of T-shirts from containers but in fact to suspend the four-pronged forks of which there was no sign. "Are you bringing the assembly from Russia?" I'd asked Pytor, who tried to avoid giving a direct answer but when pushed explained to do so was not really practicable so Alexei would be building them here.

Having been there since 5:30 that morning, I took a shower and then realized we'd no towels on site; fortunately the weather was warm. Warm enough to put the hood down as I drove off at 6:00 p.m. into a stream of vehicles heading into London. Heathrow airport is huge, and I slipped up the A30 on its south side to link to the A4, the old Great West Road. Judging there was no point in trying to get on the M4 for the relatively short run into London, I wrestled through the A4's rush hour traffic until the roads converged and the naked underside of the M4's elevated section was a few meters over my head. I couldn't get Teresa out of my mind and desperately wanted to call her but, despite Italian traffic myths, there are few places on earth where the driving can get as ruthless as London during rush hour. Both hands were needed. On the North Circular Road roundabout, I hugged the inside lane and then accelerated hard up the slip road to join traffic leaving the M4 airport road. I forced my way into the center lane and then started to edge left again approaching traffic lights; my phone's tone told me the call was from T's mobile. I grabbed it. "You shouldn't answer the phone when you're driving," she purred

"Good guess sweetheart - how did you know?"

"I know everything about you." The traffic was halted at the lights and, with the phone in my right hand, I scratched at my left ear because something insectoid seemed to have blown in. "I can even tell when you're scratching your ear." I spun around in my seat looking at the nearby cars, her laugh and others cascaded out of the phone. I heard Paul's voice saying something uncomplimentary about my masculinity and the tinted window of the car next to me hissed down. Inside was Teresa radiating love. Isabelle doing sveltly knowing sat next to her and beyond her was a grinning Paul. Lights had changed and other cars hooted as we blocked two of the lanes that daily pour millions of tons of steel and aluminum into west London. Ignoring mounting chaos I got out of my car, leaned through the window and kissed Teresa. Oh, but she tasted and smelled and was so, so good. My arms were around her and I dragged her out through the window of that car into my embrace then turned and put her on the backseat of my car. All this was done with our mouths clamped together. By the time I got back into the driver's seat the light sequence was going to green again and I pulled away. She clambered into the front with me an arm went round my neck and, despite gear lever and hand brake, her body somehow melded into mine. Stopped in traffic before Hammersmith flyover the chauffeured car was alongside again and Isabelle tossed Teresa her handbag. Smiling broadly, Paul called across, "Yes, well it's nice to see you, too, Rick." All wits short-circuited I started to reply, but before I could, he continued, "It's all right. We're going to the Hyde Park Hotel—just follow on. We'll have a drink and a natter."

In the large car, Isabelle sighed, put a hand on Paul's shoulder and urging him back into the seat, almost shouted at him, "Zey don't want to be wiz us, English man!"

She was so very right. Their car followed us to my house where Eros had kept a parking space free. Their driver carried Teresa's suitcases in and carefully closed the door as he left. We didn't make the bedroom the first time; later we showered and I faxed an order to the home Room Service company who were laying the table within an hour and gone within two. "I missed you so much, you bastard," she admitted.

"Yeah, well you would, wouldn't you," I said with a nonchalance denied by my arms again clamped around her. I was having a lot of trouble not kissing her and even more letting go of her. Something utterly unconscious demanded I keep her very close—my skin needed to feel hers. "Epidermiatio," I thought, and she wriggled even closer. Sex was interspersed with brief periods of half-asleepness until physical exhaustion zapped us completely.

The next morning a shower partially woke me and I remembered to put on slacks and sweater before going out to get croissants. I made us coffee and then called Baa to say I wouldn't be showing up until noon. I started to explain to Teresa where everything was in the house, "Believe it or not I'll figure it out, you're not exactly over-furnished here you know."

"It's called minimalism, peasant. "

"No hon, it's called man alone," she said and grabbed my crotch through my slacks. "But you've nice things here apart from me." She sank to her knees as she unzipped me. 'She will kill you—you will die soon' I told myself, but this information failed to overly concern.

Whilst nearly all calls went through my currently switched off mobile phone there was a landline at the house, and the next morning whilst we laid in the bath in the top floor bedroom it rang and was picked up by the answering machine; Ellie's voice flooded out, "Hi, stud, your mobile's off—would you like to meet up later? Call me. Big kiss." As the machine clicked off the ball of Teresa's right foot settled and exerted a tiny but definite pressure on my testicles.

"Well, stud," she mimicked Ellie's voice. "Would you like to meet up later?"

"Be reasonable, darling. She's one of identical triplets new to city life. They look to me for guidance in matters urban." The pressure momentarily increased then the foot was removed from my scrotum and then her body from the bath. Suds dripped across the room to the discarded pair of five-inch Jimmy Choo heels; clever, clever girl, she wriggled her feet into these then still dipping water and suds stalked to the phone. She dialed 14713 to get back to Ellie.

"Triplet girl's name?" Steel within silk made vocal issued from a reality the image of which I would never ever forget. Yes, okay—I'm a very visual sort of person. It's not shallowness; it's just the way I am!

My throat had become constricted at the sight of her but I managed, "Not sure. Ellie, perhaps," I was enjoying feeling so special and might have enjoyed it more if T had used the phone on speaker, but she didn't.

I had to make do with only her part of the conversation "Hello, Ellie, this is Teresa." There was a quality of absoluteness in her voice that I hoped I wouldn't have to confront too often. "I'm with Rick, and we should meet this evening." There was a pause and looking at me she asked, "AZ at seven?" I nodded, "See you there." She hung up. Thrilled not just because she knew how to push my buttons but that she took the trouble to do so, I couldn't not smile to myself. Reading these thoughts she sat on the edge of the bath with one shod foot resting on my chest and the other in the water. "You may suppose all sorts of things, but the bitch's voice tells me she's a looker and that she's had you." She examined my face for clues. "And you've had her." That this was obviously worth a few hundred quids' worth of Jimmy's to her was no small boost either.

"And the other two triplets," I said pulling her back into the bath,

"Fuck off! This water's tepid."

Most of that afternoon was spent arranging a supply of cadmium to Sticky Stan, a one-man smelter and trader I'd done spasmodic business with over the years. I didn't want us to buy it direct but we needed to make sure it was high industrial standard purity. I'd asked Alexei if laboratory grade would work better, but he assured me it wasn't necessary. He also told me they'd previously imported it into Ukraine from a German company, so I got him to call them and order it for express shipping C.O.D. to Sticky; the German suppliers confirmed by fax but with a proforma invoice. Baa transferred a payment to the smelter's account. Intent on promoting his services, Sticky promised to van it over as soon as it arrived and went on to tell me that he was currently installing a new induction furnace to replace the one he had been using; he enthused about the new furnace and I told him I might have some business for him. "What are you doing with the old one?" I asked and learned he'd been offered so low a price from the suppliers of the new furnace that he'd decided to keep it and look to sell it on himself at some stage. Now I was familiar with the machine in question and knew it could melt up to 1,500 grams of platinum group metals at a time, but I asked him, "Will it handle small quantities of nickel?"

"Of course, if you cast your mind back—pun intended, ha ha—you'll remember it. You saw it working down here last year."

"Maybe it could be used to tidy up scrap—how much do you want for it ?"

"Rick, do you actually want it for yourself?"

"No man, but somebody who supplies me might and maybe I could send you some of the small bars he'd produce. Stan, I figure he'll pay cash at the right price."

We arranged he'd hold it, and I'd get up to him when I could to take a look at it. An induction furnace works by passing a current through a coil that surrounds a crucible containing metals. Its geometry causes the current to be induced into the crucible, where its energy converts to heat, causing the metals to melt. Coincidentally it conveniently tends to homogenize different metals to form molten alloys. I figured that as the palladium we'd be producing by transmutation was so close to 100 percent purity, it could be useful to be able alloy some with another metal and sell it as scrap through other refiners. It would of course reduce our gross take but if we needed camouflage at some stage that cost could be worthwhile. I also felt we could get the furnace at a good price and, even in a worse case scenario, the cost could be recouped.

That evening Teresa and I walked to Bar AZ with differing anticipations. I'd be lying if I didn't admit I was enjoying the sense of controlled deadly energy she exuded but, when we got there, Dave cleverly deflated a lot of the tension by calling out, "Hey, Rick, and Umm!" as we entered the gloom. He stood and holding Teresa's upper arms kissed her on both cheeks. I made the introductions. She and Ellie sized each other up like cats. For a while, they were within an aura where they communicated on matters that bore little or no relation to the words used. Instinctively both Dave and I recoiled from that dimension, becoming again like newborns afraid at finding themselves ejected into Nature's darker matter world. Teresa and Ellie settled the jungly business and then seemed to get on; I wasn't sensing antagonism between them and this was important to me for I loved one and the other, I suddenly understood, was the nearest I'd come to having a friend of the opposite sex. However nothing was certain for this was the world of women, where information of the size of a man's cock, his sexual ratings and the fullest details of his proclivities can travel at light speed. Just listen to their conversations and amuse yourself working out what their initial letter codes mean; the easiest to crack is probably the most oft used—CTQ. In real terms this is a woman's world which also happens to contain male entities.

Dave not only played but also wrote and arranged; the previous day he'd done a six-figure deal for something and wanted to treat us, but we'd arranged to meet up with Paul and Isabelle later. "No problem. Bring them too!"

"You sure?" I asked.

"Absolutely."

T shrugged a why not. Paul's mobile answered after a couple of rings, he muttered to Isabel and agreed to meet us at a then restaurant called Pharmacy in Notting Hill. By around 10:30, the others were talking about some event in Hoxton, but Teresa's eyes were drooping . She needed to sleep, as did I, so we left them and found a cab.

Paul phoned in the morning and asked us for lunch the following day, which was Saturday. "Happy to," I said while mentally running through anything he might have picked up about what I was doing with Baa. I concluded neither Ellie nor Dave knew anything and thus could have told him nothing. You wonder about such concerns? Well business is business and although Paul was, I believed, out of the metal business these days he knew his way around and Baa, Pyotr, Alexei and I were setting up a project that could make a serious amount of money. Perhaps I'd better tell you about Paul and how I'd known him for about five years. We'd done a little business together and we'd always got along okay—our relationship had been more personal than business. About a dozen years older than me, he was the sort of guy you could be pleased you knew on good terms. Four years or so back I'd been in the States and had about decided my marriage was going nowhere and would end. Luckier than most, my decision had occurred without accompanying rancor and my wife, who had in her own way been waiting for my logic to catch up with the situation, concurred. Without the need to split property other than disentangling some offshore stuff we'd set up principally to help her family, without children, with neither of us having fallen for another, the bitterness on both sides was minimal. We'd come apart fairly easily because we'd never been glued together by complementary shortcomings; in fact our relationship was based mostly on wide-eyed immature lust and loneliness.

"You know darling," she'd told me during our strange farewell night in the same bed. "We had a decent marriage, which is now being followed by a decent divorce—that makes us very lucky in terms of this world."

I'll maybe tell you another time about that marriage, but for now just explain that apart from her urge to reproduce, she'd never quite been able to leave her family. At some wiser level within this had seemed to be a contradictory situation, but I'd never been remotely close to my own family so didn't exactly trust my own judgment in these matters.

There's probably a planet-wide relationship quota—as mine and Vida's had finally ended, another had been starting. The voice bouncing off a mid-Atlantic satellite was definitely Isabelle's but qualitatively different— think suppressed thrilling happiness: she told me she'd met someone and in subsequent calls updated me on how the relationship was developing. I had other stuff on my mind and could have done without her blathering, but realizing she was in love, I was selfish enough to feel the sadness of a little loss and selfless enough to listen to her without offering opinions. A couple of days later and within an hour of putting the phone down after her fourth call, Paul rang from London to say he was Concording in and wanted to see me "as a mate."

In those days, it would never have occurred to him to ask if a visit was convenient, but all this phone attention had cheered me a little for the truth was that behind my front there'd been needs for human companionship I'd never admitted and now Vida was going. It was like the unfolding of a farce as, more agitated than I had ever seen him before, Paul paced up and down the rather theatrical loft I'd borrowed from some relative-by-the-now-ending-marriage. He was fifty at the time and quite seriously wealthy—he'd got there with his head and his balls as I'll explain later. Right now he had a problem his head couldn't help with; and his testes conspired in the confusion.

Reading between all the lines the man was in love and terrified.

Feelings of such intensity were an unknown world to Paul; it was a chaos his intellect dreaded. She'd told me the man was called Paul, and she'd spoken his name with that warm reverence women reserve for the name of the man they are in love with—the voice sort of echoes into another dimension. Now Paul was telling me the woman's name was Isabelle. It had to be that each was talking about the other.

I told him as much, he missed a beat or two and then said, "Did you and her…?" It was one of the times I've been really frightened; Paul is an extremely hard man who's been known to give his dark side free reign, and there was the absolute capacity for red-mist-alpha-male-murder about him at that moment. Poor bastard, he had it bad.

"Don't be such a cunt. I needed a friend not a lover," I'd answered and watched him relax back to super hyper extra tense mode.

"So, what do I do, Rick?'

"What's it like in bed together?" I applied camouflage paint.

"None of your fucking business." He was staring out of a window "Terrific."

"How old are you?"

"Fifty-five"

"Fuck me—fifty-five, eh!" I couldn't resist it. "A man of that age should be thinking about joining a bowls club mate or finding little place in the sun somewhere with a decent shed to potter about in—not chasing around after women. You could pull a muscle or something."

His grin was the wryest. "Truth is worse I'm actually fifty-five and a half, son."

"How do you feel when you're not with her?"

"How do you think I feel?" No way I was going to respond to that and after a moment he added, "I miss her."

"Miss her as in having her popping into your thoughts all the time?"

"Yeah."

"Look, I know some fabulous girls here—up for anything. Shall I make some calls?"

"No."

"Why not ?"

"Because I'm not bloody interested, that's why not. Can't you understand? I'm in a dilemma—that's why I'm here Do you know what flying fucking Concorde costs these days?"

"Do you know what fucking up in a fucking marriage costs these days?"

"I don't give a fuck what it costs!"

"I don't mean money, Paul."

I went and got a couple of beers from the fridge, but when I offered him a bottle he waved it away. "You mean sharing my life and all that?"

"Tell me why you have to marry her. Why not just live together and then, if your feelings change, you can part?"

"Because I'd feel...I." He fished words. "I'd feel more comfortable married to her."

"'Tell me, what would you do if she got fed up with waiting and dumped you for someone else?"

"Not sure...I can't quite think..." he sighed. "Rick, I've no idea because I've done a lot of things in my life, but they've about always been considered and now it's like I'm being run by something else." He picked up the bottle of beer he didn't want and took a sip.

"You're talking about emotion." I drained my beer unable to believe he was like some lovesick teenager.

"No it's not emotion...it's a bit like knowing a deal would be a good thing only more so but there's something in the equation I don't understand and can't see." He stood up and started pacing again. "To answer your question though...I just don't know what I'd do if she went off with somebody else...I might do anything."

"Like cry...or kill the guy?"

"Like I said, I just don't know." He looked tortured.

"Maybe you already know what you're going to do." I ventured and soon after he left.

I'd first met Paul in London years back. He'd been to cocktails at Nanina P's. Having been one herself for longer than anyone remembered or she would admit, Nanina adored colorful people. Mistress or wife of some of the twentieth century's characters in her earlier days, politicians, royalty, the mega rich and the merely glamorous were all in an average day to Ninina. She'd known everybody and upset many but was adored for while many can muster front, Nanina had panache; she carried things off like nobody else and perhaps some of the future's history books will include her name. She never wrote a book herself nor had one ghosted nor permitted a biographer because in knowing too much, she knew how things worked in the real world. A couple of days before Nanina had been flying, her complaints bitter and loud that first class was full of the wrong kind of people. She'd met the young Hong Kong-born mistress of some Frenchman. Maia was obediently traveling to await him at an apartment in London.

On arrival there she'd received a callous call, Monsieur Frog would not arrive for three days and she "Salop zat you are 'ad better behave," he'd instructed. Why do so many women like cruel men? Because in the forest his cruelty will ultimately improve the chance of survival for her and their offspring. Too simple? I think not. She phoned Nanina and the sisterhood clicked on. In competition they'll all but kill each other, out of it, they're united—does the feminine seek relationships at any cost?

Not unusually Nanina ensured there were a couple of unattached solvent males for cocktails that evening. Paul had left with Maia after she'd accepted his offer of dinner.

It was snowing outside when, with elegant German bisexual Zoe on one arm and Debbie, pretty Irish-West Indian straight on the other, I descended the wide stairway to the Polynesian-themed restaurant and bar. Both Zoe and I were trying to seduce Debbie into a ménage, but each on our own terms. I did fancy Zoe and was all but certain it was mutual, but neither of us was willing to concede any ground; it was surprise, surprise, a matter of who was going to be in control. Yes, you may well sneer for it is the sort of complex and ultimately pointless situation with which my personal life had been riddled. I was, however, feeling pretty full of myself as we checked our coats and headed off toward the bar. Mobiles were blocked and a couple of payphones were sited on a pillar. Paul was using one as we approached and Maia knelt down, unzipped him and started to suck his cock. Having from an early age endeavored to cultivate some sang froid, it's only to you that I'll confess I was a tad phased. This exotic-looking woman was fellating a guy openly in a public restaurant. True, the lights were not bright but the Oriental staff, part of the Polynesian theme, were traipsing past only five or so feet away. All either failed or affected failure to notice what Zoe, Debbie and I stood and watched. Paul stared right back. Maia knew her stuff and the inevitable happened. She swallowed it all and thoughtfully zipped him up again. "Happy Hour," he told us and we all laughed. Later after a meal together we went to Q Club and then split up. I'm hardly going to admit to you that I went with Maia to the bad frog's apartment for an hour or two.

Paul called two days later to ask if I would come over and rid his flat of Debbie, who was making let-me-nurture you noises. It seemed that after our separating at the club, Zoe had pulled an American blonde who, as Paul put it, did anything, and she'd taken them all to a large house in Belgravia that had a perpetual coke fest going on in its basement. Paul, not really into the drugs thing, took Debbie back to his flat. Her Catholic upbringing and his air of authority had somehow combined to convince her that he was the savior she'd needed whilst on the cesspit's slope, and she wouldn't go away. Telling him, I'd love to help but had to go abroad that very instant, I wished him luck and hung up. It was a response he appreciated and subsequently I made some commissions on deals with him. In due course, Debbie evaporated.

Paul was, according to his codes, an honorable man but you wouldn't want to be on the wrong side of this guy: when Ellie had first mentioned the Knights Templar it was a vague image of Paul that had crossed my mind.

Now you may have supposed that because at this stage I knew both Paul and Isabelle, they met through this mutual acquaintanceship. You'll have gathered that they didn't—they met later and utterly independently of me. It seems when people are to meet, life puts them together one way or another.

Paul and I had become loose pals, occasionally meeting for a drink or meal. Gradually I learnt he'd quit his job with a brokers back in the 1980s and got very rich very quickly due to Prime Minister Margaret Thatcher's grasp of strategy exceeding her knowledge of life on the street.

Pre-glasnost the Western world not only tolerated but actively supported any state that demonstrated they were anti-Soviet. The Republic of South Africa was such a place and one of its products were Krugerands, a twenty-two carat gold coin containing one troy ounce of pure gold—it was a way the South Africans' could promote and add value to the gold they mined. They marketed these coins as a convenient way for investors to hold gold.

Back then gold was subject to a value added tax, known as VAT in Britain and TVA in France. Vat is sales tax on goods and services but, in a gesture of support, Krugerands were specially exempted by a British government keen to show solidarity with the anti-communist Republic of South Africa. In case you don't know how VAT works, it is charged on about everything; it's on a packet of razor blades that you buy in the shop; the shop includes it in the prices charged. Along with your blades, you've brought some shaving foam and some soap and this costs you £8-05. The British government currently takes £1-05 out of that because the items only cost £7 and the rest is VAT. For whatever reasons, shops don't seem to want to show the tax as a separate item.

When a bank sold a Krugerand it did not charge any Vat on it; when one gold dealer sold a bar of gold to another gold dealer he charged Vat on it and that extra money he collected he then owed to the government. The British government department with the task of administering and collecting this value added tax then was Her Majesty's Customs & Excise Deperdment. Britain is a trading nation; there's a lot of extreme wealth in Britain and its laws protect the wealthy, which is why so many foreigners bring so much of their money to Britain. Part of this culture is the ease with which anybody can become a director of a British limited liability company—just call up a company formation agency and it'll sell you a ready-made but untraded company over the phone. Call HM Customs & Excise and they would happily register that company for Vat and issue it a Vat registration number. That company is then obliged to collect Vat for the government on the items it sells.

This is what Paul did. He then went into banks and bought Krugerrands on which no Vat was charged, took them to a jewelry manufacturer he knew, had them melted into a bar, took the bar to the London Assay Office and had it assayed and stamped and then sold it to a bullion dealer. Every day his company bought the equivalent of two hundred thousand dollars-worth of Krugers. By giving the dealer a photocopy of his Vat registration he was able to collect the value of the bar plus the Vat which was equivalent to thirty thousand dollars each day. From this he deducted the cost of the Krugerrands, the dealers 1 percent margin, the cost of the melting and the assaying charge. The rest of the money was his profit for he simply did not pay anything to HM C&E—he wasn't due to for three months. After three months trading the original company had ceased to trade and closed its bank account; in effect it had ceased to exist but there was another in its place. Paul didn't do this with one company at a time—he did it with hundreds at thirty thousand pounds per day per company gross profit. And he set up his own melting facility. He was far from alone in this defrauding; a whole spectrum of the demi-monde played the system. The norm for the serious players seemed to be to steal about 7 million British pounds and then get sentenced to three year's jail and be out after two with good behavior. Paul didn't get caught. He used different names to buy and become directors of the limited liability companies. When HM C&E, in their antifraud activities, started to check up on newly registering companies he'd fly in some foreign national for a week and install him or her in a rented office to make it look good. Registration achieved, the director would disappear back through Heathrow with an unrecorded payment in cash. Paul would also buy about any ceased-trading but still Vat registered company he was offered.

In an effort to stem the hemorrhage, for it must have been costing the exchequer hundreds of millions if not billions of pounds, the British government slapped Vat on to Krugerands. But by then, too many had got into the business and alternative sources of tax-free gold were found; tons of the metal were smuggled into the UK from countries that didn't charge Vat on gold or only charged one percent, particularly Belgium and Luxembourg. Paul once told me that virtually every lorry entering Britain on ferries through the Channel ports at that time carried a one kilo bar of gold and that a strike of Channel ferry crews caused a shortage on physical gold in the London market. Why only one kilo per truck? No driver was likely to risk serious punishment at the hands of the organizers for just one kilo. Literally tons of gold trundled into the UK via the Channel and North Sea ferry ports every week.

This stopped when HM C&E applied new regulations that prevented the dealers paying out Vat on gold to the registered sellers, but by then Paul had probably made in excess of 50 million plus British Pounds and big profits on the properties in London he'd been putting the money into: he owned a few blocks of apartments. Legally domiciled in two Central American countries he received his investment income via obscured offshore trust funds.

A few days before his marriage to Isabelle, I'd sat with Paul in the private wing of a hotel complex in Thailand. He'd flown two dozen of us down there for his last few days as a bachelor; wasted from partying, he insisted I heard confessions about yesteryear. I suppose even hard nuts sometimes need to talk.

The two burglars in the living room of his flat near London's Ladbrook Grove were clumsy, their noise woke Paul who slipped into the darkened room and smashed the nose and front teeth of one man with a wine bottle. The bottle didn't break and the second man cowered back as Paul switched on the lights. Glancing admiringly at the intact bottle he checked the label. "I must get some more of this," he told the second burglar.

Frightened, the man indicated his unconscious companion. "Stay away—I'll have the law on you!" he told Paul.

Remember folks this was Britain—catch a burglar, call the police and chances are they're too busy to come round or if they do come around they'll likely arrest you for roughing the burglar up. Paul saw this situation as just the polices' way of saying don't bother us, these criminals need the money to take care of their expenses so fuck off and don't call us ever, for anything. It was with this knowledge that he stepped forward, "Yeah, well you better take this, mate." He handed the wine bottle to the second burglar. As the man took it Paul's right knee slammed upward into the man's groin. He retrieved the bottle. When wide self-adhesive parcel tape secured each burglar around mouth, wrists, forearms, thighs and ankles he went into his kitchen and made some coffee then returned to the living room and dimmed the lights. The burglars seemed conscious now. "In a civilized society the police would take you to a court that would put you away from society to protect it," he told them. "However, unfortunately for you two shits, you're not in a civilized society. You're in a leaderless and decaying one." He sipped his coffee and then went on, "If I were to let you go..." Muffled yet distinctly affirmative grunts were heard from the burglars. "Yeah, I know girls, you'd fucking love me forever wouldn't you! So, it's nothing personal, but you're going to have to try to be better or at least quieter in your next lives."

Not inhumanely, he secured a plastic bag over each burglar's head and taped it airtight around the neck of each. Later their weighted corpses would sink to the bottom of the nearby Grand Union Canal to be passed over by an early narrow boat as it chugged back to Little Venice with groceries from the Grove's canal side Sainsbury's.

A year back and two streets away an elderly woman had died after challenging two burglars.

"They'd perhaps have done the same for you, but actually I didn't hear any of that," was all I could think to tell him and to lighten the mood said, "But word is that you were a naughty boy, a bit of a crook with the VAT."

"Crook!" He seemed genuinely surprised. "No boy, a crook is a dope dealer, a crook is a copper who conspires with the dope dealer, a crook is a surgeon who does unnecessary operations, a crook is the cunt who mind fucks the weak minded, a crook is a politician who takes payment for acting against his voters' interest: a crook is someone who damages people to make money. All I did was steal numbers off a government's electronic bullshit ledger." What he'd done financially didn't bother me; I was just teasing. He lit a cigar and puffed on it. "I'm just an investor." I said nothing and eventually he went on, "Do you know what made the British Empire?"

"Having a lot of front?"

Alcohol afforded him a second wind. "Firstly it was pirates de facto licensed by the British Crown to steal the gold the Spanish were stealing from the Americas. Do you think stolen wealth after a few generations of it becoming accepted and respectable alters the fact that it was stolen in the first place?" He pulled a silver money clip from a hip pocket removed an assortment of currencies and selected from these some new British twenties. "I'll only accept new ones of these from a bank and it can cause people to be suspicious because new notes aren't so usual," I shrugged. "Do you know why I'll only take new scores, Rick? No, you don't, so I'll tell you—perhaps you'll get fussy about them, too."

I stifled a yawn, "Why don't I just take any old notes you get and burn them for you?"

He sipped his drink. "The reason not to take used British twenties is there's a big chance—about thirty percent I figure—that used twenties have been up the arsehole of at least one con: mostly the twenties and also tens because prison drug suppliers aren't too keen on fifties yet." He sucked on his cigar "The world's still a theft-based economy."

"Well, gosh, thanks, I'm so thick."

He raised his eyes, sighed something inaudible and said, "I've always been a fan of Thomas Crapper, inventor of the flushing toilet, which became described as a crapper so that what goes into them came to be called crap. On some toilets, the crap drops directly into the water, you wipe your arse, throw in the tissue, flush the handle, and the shit's gone. Other toilet bowls are designed so that the shit falls onto a shaped ledge above the water level. You wipe your arse and drop the tissue in the water, but before you flush everything away you can examine your own shit: from it you get indications as to the health of your bodily functions. After learning from your own shit, you flush it away. You tell me, Rick, from which way do you gain more knowledge?" More drunk than I'd realized, he swayed over to a chair and flopped into it. "Before your time a British prime Minister called Wilson described politics as being the art of the possible, the cunt was believed by about everybody and, Thatcher aside, Britain never had a politician to lead it again, just slags practicing this art of the possible. Rick, if the governments do that don't expect simple businesspeople like me to play straight—what would be the point? The society's already doomed—make your dosh and fuck off, or do it massive and get a knighthood and stay." He glared at me, struggled up out of the chair and walked out of the open door to the wing's pool.

I joined him there and asked, "Didn't you steal enough to get a knighthood?" He laughed and two girls in Thai dress appeared from the shadows, hands placed together and heads bobbed in that beautiful gesture that indicates acquiescence to authority without being demeaned. "I'm not an evil man, Rick. Evil is—like nonces."

He'd touched on the evil most avoid thinking about: I agreed, "No question there, but we weren't talking about evil. We were talking about honest and dishonest and frankly I don't give a fuck how much you ripped off a government." Each of us was looking, really looking, into the others eyes; something passed between us. The girls stood a few feet away while, with sobriety now encroaching, I wondered if his marriage would last.

Now it was not only lasting but apparently working, each content and better for being with the other.

The Hyde Park Hotel suited Paul who was waiting at a table by the bar. "I asked the girls to give us half an hour if that's all right with you, Rick."

"I guess—is everything okay with you?"

"Never better." A waiter put down two martinis and left. "I'm in your debt for it, old son, I don't forget New York or Thailand."

I held his eyes. "All I recall about Thailand is being very drunk, nothing else whatsoever Paul."

He sipped his drink, "How's business, Rick?"

"Promising." I wondered if he'd any particular reason to ask and he got the vibe.

"Relax, I'm not ferreting. It's that I get a feeling you and Teresa aren't simply having a quickie and...well, you should know if you need any help, I'm around."

"Don't know what to say—it's appreciated, much appreciated." I tapped the rim of my glass on his. "Thanks." I was touched—the more because it was unexpected.

Merik came over to us, and I suddenly realized without understanding in any rational sense that Merik was the doorway to a new dimension of Paul. Suppositions cascaded through my mind but Merik had taken my hand in both of his and smiled—that guy's smile would warm an icecap in winter.

"Hello, Rick," he said. "It's good to see you again." Total sincerity, it came not only from never speaking idly or pointlessly but from a sort of heart. Extraordinarily I felt he reinforced something within myself.

We'd only met once before, just after the wedding when Isabelle and Paul had found and sort of adopted the strange young man. His looks were striking— blue green eyes, dark skin and that sort of Scandinavian white-blond hair. He looked ageless, perhaps early twenties, perhaps late forties and his regular features and slim body could have got him lots of women or men, but people said he was sexless; he struck me now as he had when I'd originally met him as a sort of archetypal monk. You sort of felt it would be crass to take him out with the boys; he wasn't effete, just differently colored-in than the next person.

Teresa and Isabelle appeared both looking sexy and both hugged Merik before either Paul or I received attention. "So it's him, is it?" It felt lame as I heard the words come out, but my mind was actually far away searching for something. T briefly pinched my cheek making there-there noises as to a child as we left the hotel, went around the corner and into Vang's.

Like the food, the service was superb, but it was impossible not to notice the special deference paid to Merik. We talked idly of the food, the synthesis of Vietnamese and French influences and moved on to France in general. I was surprised to learn that the nation of France was originally just the Ile de France, the island in the Seine around which Paris has grown. The country that the English fought so often was mostly just that and the northern part of present day France. "You know something," Isabelle was seducing Paul in a very smooth way —smart women never stop seducing their husbands. "I 'ad to get zis man for 'istorical reasons—it was my duty as a daughter of France," she camped and as Paul leaned over toward her chair to kiss her cheek, she leaned back, offering only her hand for his lips.

Teresa grimaced, "Straight from doing rep near Nimes, where her performances were acclaimed as shite," she said.

"Salop," her step-sister retorted.

"It's another alchemy—the love-hate relationship." Everybody stopped talking and looked at me. "English-French love-hate, I mean," I said, and they still just looked "Oh fuck you lot! History—I'm talking about history. What do you think, Merik?"

"Yes, there was always a kind of alchemy...toward something that would steer the world." He spoke with his mouth full.

Teresa said, "Would Joan d'Arc agree with that, Merik?"

"Maybe," he smiled. "The world needed the English language to evolve, to live, and become the lingua franca of the planet at this time now. If Joan had not acted, been possessed as she was, then the English may have succeeded in taking and occupying France."

"You're not making sense," Paul told him. "If the world needed English it would still have got it if the English had conquered France, only quicker."

"I absolutely disagree, Paul. In those days, French was a more accepted and developed language than English." We all knew he meant sophisticated but was too diplomatic to say so. "French would have continued to predominate amongst the rulers and submerged the then quite crude English language. That tongue could easily have degenerated into a dialect of the peasantry."

"But it did ma cher !" Isabelle told him with some emphasis.

Merik smiled and continued, "French would have become the language of America and been spoken in India and throughout Africa. The bigger picture prevailed—the English language was needed so the English had to lose the land of France."

"Well, I don't think you'd win friends at L'Institute Francais with that explanation. Why is English so needed?" Teresa's voice gave me a sudden feeling of immense pleasure.

"Because of its extraordinary qualities," Merik said this in a tone that supposed it was answer enough but seeing we were all looking at him with obvious need of explanation, he went on. "For example just look at the etymology—do you suppose there've been other languages that have a word like *live* that can have its spelling reversed to form its real antithesis? The devil, another real antithesis."

Recalling Ellie's views, I asked "The English leaving also resulted in the Catholic Church being able to dominate the continent for a while—was that such a good thing, Merik? Some people figure that church has been pretty diabolic"

"Whatever the cost of the Catholic Church, it saved a lot of children dying as human sacrifices," he laid a hand on Isabelle's arm. "I'm sorry I know you can't bear to hear about such stuff."

"Mais non Merik pas de tous—it absolutely thrills and opens ze appetite! Let's discuss it in complete detail now while we eat—but no, let's change our orders for rare meat! Sometimes you are..." she shrugged, "encroyable !"

He turned back to me. "But believe me, the old world was a horrendous place."

Isabelle, Merk and Paul were an odd trio.

In those days, just a door or two from Vang's, was one of London's niceties, a small cinema that on that very day was showing a Russian film made maybe twenty years earlier in Soviet times called *Solaris.* It's something of a cult for those who know, and they all wanted to watch it, so I went along too. Having seen it several times over the years, I sat in the dark with the others, but I was not watching the screen for I focused elsewhere.

For no particular reason I thinking about the original Knights Templar and was seeing their endeavors as a kind of alchemical parallel, instead of trying to make gold, they'd set off to recover some from where it lay buried in the ruins of an ancient temple on top of which another temple had been built. In doing this they, like alchemists, discovered other material that would change them. However where the alchemist might be supposed to be empowering himself through refinement and purification the Knights Templar were doing so by literally recovering gold and, if I'd understood the implications correctly, the acquisition of some egrogorial art. Because so many snake oil salesmen seemed to be involved in the religions business I'd avoided all involvement and thus used my own instincts to dertmine what was good and what was bad. I lived in a sort of psychological Eden. Now, sat in this darkened cinema, I sensed the inconvenience of serious adulthood looming through the future's mists and figured I had better start considering all sorts of things; a world of heavy responsibilities threatened. Naturally I'd have preferred to ignore all this but something, perhaps some blotted out wound in my childhood throbbed and worried at my ignorance of dark-side workings and led me to wonder. Thoughts coalesced.

Supposing that good and evil are fruits growing together and I, in the form of a hungry elephant, consume both then I wander around and every day I shit and within my shit are the undigested seeds of both good and evil fruits. Trodden into the ground with nurturing, partially digested products amongst my elephant-waste both will sprout and grow anew. But perhaps this Jesus person had figured that if the animal's dark side could be made to feel intimidated enough by the good fruit it would consume it and only it, in an attempt to destroy it. The effect of doing this would relatively deplete the regeneration chances of the bad fruit, whilst actually increasing that of the good. The result through time would be a diminution of the dark side.

Taking the general level of mentality that has to be reckoned with by any organization, it did seem to me, as Trim Woman had said and Baa had intimated that the genius of the RCC was the Mass, where the body of God's Son is eaten. God being consumed by the worshipers just about closes the door on the practice of blood sacrifice by worshippers trying to attract the gods' attentions and instead creating, in effect, a situation where humans eat a good god. That evening when Teresa and I lay in bed in each other's arms I'd thought to tell her my thoughts, but she suddenly started to tell me something of her background.

She and Isabelle were not true half-sisters, that is to say they didn't share blood just circumstances or, as she put it, destiny. Teresa's natural father had been an eccentric Englishman somewhere in rural Devon. He just about got by financially from letting caravans parked in a couple of fields to holiday makers. He otherwise filled his time by studying Celtic mythology and dabbling in alternative sciences. "A nice bloke but hopeless as a father" was the way she described him.

Her mother at eighteen was the youngest and prettiest member of a theater company that was touring the provinces. Prone to posturing, she was going through an intellectual phase when she met the bookish man and the eyes of love showed his introverted vagueness as aloof genius to the young actress. He also had a large penis. Their three-year relationship resulting in Teresa and a semi-detached with a frequently paid-late mortgage. It was a corner property and during one of the overcrowded British Isles' property booms became the object of lust by a local property developer, who saw it as a small block of apartments. Teresa's mother suggested to her father that it would be a good opportunity to sell, split the money and wave good-bye to each other. He thought she made sense—she usually did in matters concerning the world outside of himself—and readily concurred. They parted amicably; he with no more concern than if he was popping out on an errand.

Teresa and her mother moved to a tiny apartment in North London. Her mother did fairly well with bit parts in television plays, TV commercials, voiceovers and the odd film part. Isabelle's departed father, Carlossimo, "he was such a Charlie", came into her life when she was ten and it seems had more or less lived off her mother ever since. He sent birthday and Christmas cards to Isabelle when he remembered to and it was a twelve-year-old Teresa who'd accompanied him and her mother to France for Isabelle's first wedding. The gawky English girl had been intoxicated by her glamorous elder sort-of stepsister and written, phoned and occasionally met with her over the years of that horrible marriage. During that same time, she'd turned into a beautiful woman, left home, and opened a clothes shop with another girl. They sold it to a publicly owned corporation whose shares were then so overvalued the directors had acquisition binged. She wandered the world for a bit and wound up the proprietress of the beach cabanas in Mexico, which she'd sublet nearly a year ago now.

"But how come you weren't in New York for Isabelle and Paul's wedding?" Only Isabelle's mother had been present. An orphan, Paul had no family he knew or admitted to knowing of. I'd wondered if he'd sought and perhaps found any family members but had thought better than to ask him. He'd share such information if he wanted to: meantime it was none of my business.

Sentimentality is a persistent bastard and I found myself regretting Teresa hadn't been there because I was in love with her and feeling, as lovers do, that every moment of my past that had not been spent with her had been an a waste. That she hadn't been born until I was twelve years old didn't seem to count where I dwelt within the balloon of infatuation.

"It wasn't to be. I was away at the time." She gave me an odd look. "When I got back it had already happened, and my chance to be a brides-maid was gone."

"You mean you were away and nobody knew where to contact you?"

"Yes."

I could only love her more for that. Questionable theories about karma claim that before conception our souls choose our parents and hence our relatives, but those theories speak more of the fears of their proponents than objectivity. Even if correct, the whole point of a par-ticular choice might be to learn to escape the infectivity of those chosen? Who's to say quite what the soul's agenda is? But then again, who's to say my whole attitude to families isn't just a reaction resulting from my own experiences as a child?

•   •   •

Time passed and I was making a lot of money; I'd given a broker's investment department discretionary authority on the equivalent of half a million sterling and they were managing to lose some of it on dot-coms and bio stocks while increasing some other of it on different dot-coms and about any share that had the word communications in its name. The stock market was looking distinctly frothy. A lot of winners along with overseas investors were putting their money into a property market already surging due to banks making buy-to-let loans for property and flogging mortgages to all. Isabelle had a lot of connections with London estate agents from her interior decorating days and Teresa now used these to locate and arrange the purchase of a couple of long-lease apartments in what was known as Fitzrovia but was now being called NoHo as in North Soho. The value of these properties along with all others in London at that time was increasing daily. Many people were earning more on the value of their homes increasing than at their day jobs.

My time along with that of Baa, Pyotr, Alexei and Ilya was now spent almost entirely on processing and disposing of metal. Our gross take passed eighty million sterling ahead of any of our expectations in the first cold months of the new year, and we were actually transmuting about 15 percent more metal than we had anticipated. However as spring blossomed the really big boost to our take was the extraordinary price rise of palladium: from the previous summer's then reckoned to be high $9,000 per kilo it had more than doubled. We were now producing palladium which at current prices was grossing over $40 million per month plus around $400,000 per month of platinum and rhodium were occurring as by-products. Our silver, fabrication, shipping, power costs and rent costs were less than $150,000.

I sent a private jet with Teresa and a large bank draft to Monaco to buy an apartment and regularize herself as a resident there. Paul knew a local lawyer who dealt with the legals whilst Isabelle helped choosing an apartment. It took three trips spread over two weeks; it was done and watertight. As long as she conformed to travel dates quotas she was a resident of the Principality of Monaco and only liable for tiny amounts of tax on any money I paid or had paid to her.

Alexei designed and Ilya built a sort of Faraday cage at the unit: its sole purpose was that the five of us could climb into it and have discussions without any danger of electronic eavesdropping. This was not paranoia; questions were starting to be asked at all sorts of levels in all sorts of places. Broker chatter indicated that car manufacturers were starting to get concerned. These people had clout. Auto manufacturers had to buy a lot of palladium to coat the ceramic honeycombs of the catalytic converter every car has in its exhaust system. As you know the catalytic converter is there to reduce exhaust fume pollution to levels required by law. Given the now massive level of awareness among the population concerning pollution, no government was about to repeal or amend or suspend those laws just because the palladium cost per vehicle had gone up about sixty bucks.

Mobile phone and computer manufacturers easily absorbed the price increase because there was so little palladium in each of their units, and their products were selling about as fast as they could be produced.

"Okay, Baa, what are the problems if any that you see in the immediate future?" asked Alexei.

"As I've said before, it's possible the price of palladium will halve by next week but this has to be taken in conjunction with the possibility that it will double by next week. Nobody seems to know and the market here in London doesn't seem to have any one predominating view...today. That's not to say it won't have tomorrow. As far as I can gauge things, there seems to be a lack of information about supplies and demand. Again as I said three months back, I think we should sell as we produce, so that if the price falls we've locked in our profits. However I do now think we might usefully discuss speculating with say ten percent of the production."

"Speculate in what way?" the timbre of Pyotr's voice had changed over the months. It had become deeper and rounder as had his body; there remained very little trace of his original accent.

Baa looked at me so I explained that because the palladium price had been so strong and because, unlike for example the gold market, the actual volume of futures contracts in the metal was small, there were stiff requirements for speculators. Perhaps as much as an 80 percent deposit against a futures contract. A futures contract is simply a contract to either buy something or sell something at a future date and typically the price of that thing for delivery in twelve months' time would be its price today plus twelve months interest at about bank rate. So if the thing you we're selling had a value today of say $100 and the bank rate of interest was 10 percent per year somebody would agree to pay you $110 for it in twelve months' time: if the day's price of the thing doubles to $200, in a year's time the seller would honor his contract and the buyer would still get it for $110. If the price had halved to $50 in a year's time, the buyer would still have to honor his side of the contract and pay $110. Whatever happens to the price, both buyer and seller know what they've respectively bought and sold the thing for. "I'm sorry, guys," I told them. "I know you probably knew all this, but it's important that we're absolutely clear about what I'm going to suggest." I explained that there was no large traded options market for palladium futures contracts, meaning a market in options to buy and sell those futures contracts. I told them I figured that if we left some of our palladium unsold but effectively on deposit with the Zurich bank, we could then write options to sell contracts that the bank could guarantee on the basis that they were holding the metal.

"But, Rick, if there's not much of a market for such options who will buy them? Or do you suggest we start a market in them?" Ilya often vindicated Baa's initial appreciation of him.

"I'd really like to," I said. "But aside from the risk of raising our profile, I frankly don't think there's a broad enough demand. However, that doesn't mean we couldn't write some for the bank to push to the big users."

"Maybe speculators, too," said Baa "There's oceans of private dosh slopping around just now."

"What sort of money could we get for options do you think?" Pyotr wanted to know.

"If the palladium price keeps rising the buyers will want to cover some of their future requirements with contracts for physical delivery with mines. They'll look to buy a little on futures contracts as time passes if only to provide themselves with some time protection against price movements. But if they can buy our solid options via the bank, I don't see why we shouldn't collect a 10 percent plus premium over the delivery month's future contract price."

"And that's for just delaying the sale of metal we're going to sell anyway?"

"Yes and no; in the sense that we,ve sold the physical metal and blocked the money to cover more than the cost and downside risk of a future contract to back thje option we've just sold."

"So if the price increased more than 10 percent our option sales would be working against us. Is that correct?"

"No, it wouldn't. If we'd sold the metal in the first place, it would be gone anyway—if, and it is an *if*, we could sell options on what we already hold we'd just be adding value."

"Faster than the money would earn interest on deposit?" Alexei was chewing a pencil.

"So looking at a scenario where prices have kept increasing and have reached say $30,000 a kilo," Baa said. "A buyer might need to cover himself for a possible future requirement of a hundred kilos and so buy an option from us to get the metal at $33,000 per kilo. He would pay us an option fee of $3,000 per kilo?"

"Why would a buyer do that? If he needs a hundred kilos in the future, he could just buy a futures contract basis the days price of $30,000," Alexei was actually using the pencil to write on the back of an actual envelope.

"Sure, but suppose by the time he wants to turn his contract into metal the price has dropped back to $15,000 per kilo. He could just throw away his option-to-buy that cost him $3,000 per kilo and add that loss to the $15,000 he then actually buys the metal for, meaning it's cost him $18,000 per kilo. The alternative as against the $30,000 plus interest a futures contract would have committed him to: using an option has saved

164

him $12,000 plus per kilo, which is 1.2 million dollars on his hundred kilo requirement."

"For less than 15,000 automobiles," Alexei announced. "I believe we should try it."

We agreed I'd go to Zurich and see if a deal could be done. If it could, the others would need to go there physically to effectively vary the arrangements we already had in place with the bank. They'd arrive and leave within a few hours in separate private planes for we intended to continue avoiding any casual connections showing up on any radars. Also we were working fourteen-six to keep production up and at around a million pounds a day, and nobody wanted to lose time. The economics were simple—losing time by setting up options should become worthwhile as the quantity of options sold increased, but losing time flying commercial made no sense. Hiring staff was a complete no-no, and we'd long ago mutually agreed none of us knew or was related to anybody capable of working at the unit who we could sufficiently trust. The weakest link in our cover was actually the bank in Zurich.

Baa had told us that he believed Swiss banks were open to any requirements the Swiss secret service might have, but that the Swiss secret service would have no interest in our activities short of literally billions of dollars being involved; to them we were small fry conducting ourselves perfectly in accordance with Swiss law and in a business profitable to Swiss corporations. In those days it was then about treasonable for a Swiss bank employee to reveal account details without an extremely hard to get court order.

Baa said, "However guys, bear in mind that Zurich is or was the heroin capital of Europe. I heard that this occurred because a foreign intelligence service got frustrated at not being able to bypass Swiss banking secrecy laws, so they gave a lot of smack away there to create a market on the basis that sooner or later there'd be a few addicts hiding their habit whilst holding down jobs. I believe that one way or another this got them some account details. Not much an addict won't do when a fix is needed. I suggest that none of us give anybody there any information that is not absolutely necessary."

"I never heard anything about this, Baa," I said. "Are you sure?"

"I tell you that I had heard something similar — an epidemic came out of nowhere back in the 1980s," Pyotr explained. "I believe the KGB blamed the CIA, but that was to be expected. Rick, when will you leave?"

"If I can arrange an appointment with Stroeder for the morning, I'll leave early. I'd assume he can't make or wouldn't make a decision like this without reference to his board, so our timing will be in his hands. I'll go home soon and make arrangements—assume that I'm not here tomorrow, but I'll confirm to you later." We had evolved a system of communicating times, dates and places by coded double text messaging because just as we were producing around a million dollars' worth of metal a day, so we were having to move that same quantity of metal. I would use the same code to confirm the meeting in Zurich.

We all climbed out of the cage, Ilya and Alexei went back to setting up the next batch of silver for transmutation whilst Pyotr checked out a twenty-five-kilo rough bar of palladium to me to take into an airfreight agent at nearby Heathrow and a five-kilo bar to take home. Although that twenty-five kilo bar was worth around £300,000, it would be shipped to the Zurich bank associated commercial refinery as silver alloy with a declared and insured value of £2,650. As such, it would not attract the attention of the organized crime that some say skim a percent of all airfreight cargos. And what if it went missing? So we'd have lost less than £3,000 worth of silver and some time and effort, but our secret would be safe. And the thieves who stole our metal ? The dealer they sold some "silver alloy" to as worth a couple of thousand is, I think, hardly going to turn round and tell them it was really worth £300,000.

As I drove away, Baa was putting approximately six kilos in his glove compartment and thirty kilos into the specially created false spare wheel in his boot before driving to Hatton Garden, where it would be unloaded to a major dealer who would send it to their own refiners for credit to the Liechtenstein company's account. False spare wheel! Yes indeed, cars can get stolen. Within four days, the metal less charges would be credited to our Zurich bank's metal account with their own refiners. Metal accounts work just like monetary accounts and can even earn interest if you care to loan the metal out; to date, we'd always immediately sold ours.

Within hours, Sticky Stan's driver would call at Baa's home to collect the six kilos and then mine to collect the five; Sticky was delighted with this business and never realized there was any connection between these two conveniently timed London collections a couple of days each week. He stole less than 1 percent on "my" bars but a touch more on those from Baa, much to the latter's chagrin. Neither of us mentioned it for Sticky was very useful in that he credited the money to a fictitious overseas supplier he'd invented for himself years ago. So many years ago, in fact that this entirely fictitious entity now enjoyed excellent credit ratings on several data bases. From his fictitious client, the metal went to our banks anonymous joint metal account.

While all this was occurring, several of Ilya's relatives were becoming in-the-money T-shirt distributors across Ukraine and Russia; Pyotr actually had to buy another four containers of T-shirts to keep up with demand and had entered into a commercial relationship with a firm that printed logos on them. The printers delivered pre-specified batches at 8:00 each morning and collected a docket and plain T-shirts at the same time; the Royal Mail International Parcelforce van collected this merchandise from us at five every Wednesday and most Fridays. To the casual and even the-not-so-casual observer, our unit seemed to be in the business of distributing custom printed T-shirts.

I made a point of inquiring at the airfreight agent's office about cheaper rates, telling them margins on the silver alloy bars were getting tighter but backed off when they said they'd put their road freight people in contact. Then, hours earlier than usual, I drove to Chelsea where Teresa was very nice to me. What I mean is, she ran the shower for me and laid out fresh clothes whilst asking me what I wanted to eat that evening. "I thought we'd go out to eat, and it looks like it'll be nice this evening," I said for the afternoon was dry and warm.

"Whatever you want, my darling, and I do mean *whatever* you want," she could get away with stuff like that because of her voice. It got me going instantly even when she was playing: she knew it, and I rarely fought it.

"Don't uber vamp me, babe. I've got to make some calls."

"You work very hard," she advised as if I hadn't realised, that like the others, I was doing fourteen hours most days.

"While the money's there I'm going to get it—don't you want to live a life of ease and luxury?" My question was rhetorical but she responded.

"I want lots of things, darling, and believe me, I do appreciate the way you work. But I'm a woman and, like they say in the stories, I have needs." She came up behind where I sat at the table I used as a desk and kissed the top of my head making sure her breasts brushed gently against the nape of my neck. Then she left me to do my stuff. I called the aviation company to check availability then, as I clicked Send e-mailing an oblique message to the bank asking for a meeting the next morning,

I decided I'd ask T to come with me. She'd not had a lot of fun the last few months, and she'd never complained, been ultra-supportive and always honed beautifully that vague sense of guilt that lurks within every man. Stroeder texted within minutes offering me an 11:00 A.M. local time meeting which I accepted. I booked a plane to leave Northolt at 7:00 A.M. UK time and then went out on the patio to join Teresa.

"We're going somewhere tomorrow for twenty-four hours, unless you've got plans."

"Nothing I wouldn't cancel for the man," she exhaled the words. "Like a glass, darling?" She got up.

"Are you taking the piss?" I looked around as she went to the kitchen. "Or am I in the wrong house?"

"Relax, I'm taking the piss. Have a nice glass of champagne and tell me where we're going." She picked up her mobile and dialed a stored number to cancel a girlfriend. The grape was hitting the spot quite nicely when I noticed that what I'd taken to be a piece of junk mail laying on the patio table was in fact a custom-printed greeting card. It was from a couple in Scandinavia, and pictures of a baby covered half of the card; the other half announced the arrival of "their little prince" named Smorgasbord or something. The card went on to say how joyful they were now they'd become a proper "little family" with him in their "little town" also called something like Smorgasbord. "Oi, you, Mrs Woman!" I called out.

"Hold on sweetie," she covered the phone. "Yes. O Light of the World?"

"That's why you're doing it isn't it? These Smorgasbord things !"

"Things ?"

"Yes. Little this thing and little that thing! They've got you going with this bloody card." I held it up. "I'm going to write 'a hideous child' on it and mail it back."

She spoke again into the phone, "I'll have to call you back. The boy's mind is decaying." Taking the card from my hand, she announced, "It is a beautiful child."

"Beautiful child ? Don't be daft. It looks like every other child ..." I recalled the words of somebody and said, "It looks like Winston Churchill."

"Ours won't."

"Of course it will!" But I'll not ever let anybody say so though, I thought.

"It? Ha! It'll be they, lover !" She came and sat on my lap and kissed me in that slow way she had that actually let me feel my willpower draining away. The victims of vampires must experience similar.

"Teresa, do you have the slightest idea how much I love you, the slightest notion of the enormity and absoluteness of this whole thing?" My body systems were tuning up now. Unstoppable reactions were commencing.

Aware of this, she morphed into Doris Day, "Well, golly, gosh, Rick, I probably do. I'm going to get changed, so we can eat really early." She stood and went indoors. I sat enjoying the slight breeze that cooled nicely and tried to imagine not being in love with Teresa. Then I realized that physiologically I couldn't be in love anymore because that condition only lasts five weeks or so and that therefore I must now be besotted, enchanted, mad, or something new.

A voice in my head told me I'd better have another woman in order to regain some perspective on this odd sort of condition I found myself in; another voice asked why it was that I didn't trust myself to be happy. Yet another voice suggested I wouldn't actually want another woman anyway. The buzzer went and I handed Sticky's driver a sealed plastic envelope containing the bar in exchange for a prewritten receipt.

I went to the fridge for more champagne then my feet led me upstairs to where a showered Teresa sat naked in front of a mirror putting on a lot of eyeliner. In an effort to appear unconcerned, I went to the open french window with its squashed curvy-flat faux balcony I'd paid too much for and sucked grape. To the left of the back of the patio is the garden of a large house in another street. The optician had volunteered unbidden that a wealthy Greek ship-owner had recently bought that property and I was wondering what he might sell it for when I saw the breasts. Not ordinary breasts, these breasts were the sort Russ Mayer would have wet dreams about; attached to them was a leggy blonde in sunglasses and bikini bottom. I don't know if I'd gasped or let out some other exclamatory sound indicating programmed reaction, but of a sudden, the naked T was by my side and also gazing into the Greek's garden. Her vibe must have touched for Breasts Girl looked up toward us, Teresa waved down to her and she raised her glass and smiled back. "Do you like that?" Teresa asked.

I cleared my throat and said, "Not at all. I'm gay you know. Teresa, light of the long darkness of my life, of course I like that, you daft bitch. I'm programmed and conditioned to like that. I have no…" A forefinger pressed my lips together. She smiled and slipping some sort of shirt over her head went downstairs. I reluctantly followed with some idea of needing to make amends only to see the street door was open, and she'd gone. This was not like her, but I was certainly not going after her, so sat down on a sofa and had just got around to deciding I'd catch a TV news channel when Teresa returned. She ushered in Breast Girl, who was seriously beautiful to look at and now wore, above an endlessness of tanned legs, a sort of long cardigan, with large buttons down the front. "Rick, say hello to Paola." Apart from the cardigan Paola wore moccasins.

● ● ●

"Hello to Paola," I'd become Leslie Phillips in a fifties British movie and said as much to Teresa who advised, "No, dear, Benny Hill."

"Let me get you a drink, Paola "

"No sanks, Rick," smiled Paola who taller than T was about my height.

"Darling," said Teresa. "Paola's from wherever, loves London and thinks you're an attractive man. She's not surprised that you appreciate her breasts because people do and as a special favor she's going to let you have a closer look." She slowly undid the large buttons of the girl's cardigan and slipped the garment from her shoulders. Paola stood there, magnificent in her moccasins and the lower half of a bikini. She'd a pout on her full lips. Those incredible breasts were just there in front of me, defying the planet's gravitational pull and exerting their own. I think I said something like they're wonderful and involuntarily stepping forward my right hand rose to touch the gorgeousness my eyes beheld. "I forgive him," Teresa was saying. "But you know he is right. Your breasts are wonderful Paola. Would you...may I ?" Her hands also moved toward Paola's breasts. As our hands touched her, Paola's eyes closed and her head tilted back. A languorous sigh and her arms enfolded us. I'd gone to heaven. I watched the woman I loved, she woman who routinely turned me on more than I could have believed possible, lean forward and with pouting lips softly oh so softly kiss a nipple. I ached with a terrible, thrilling wonderful hunger that was already beginning to gently drown me. As a child did you like chocolate, did you like ice cream, did you like mint? Well it was all these things in the mouth at the same instant— ecstasy. I was drawn into a world of only sensation. Now you're grown up and an adult but what was your favorite food, drink, sweet? Imagine you've never had it and then suddenly it's there in abundance and you just immerse yourself in it—such imaginings do not even come close.

Teresa's fingers toyed with the two now very erect nipples and she husked, "I want to suck these." She did; she sucked on a nipple as Paola pulled T's head closer to her with one arm and mine with the other. "Suck me too—yes, suck me," she pleaded, and I did. Then Teresa's hand slid down over Paola's flat stomach while their mouths sought out each other. They both turned and kissed me, one of Teresa's hands undoing my trousers whilst the other slipped inside the bikini bottom to caress Paola. Then the three of us were on the sofa and T was feeding my dick into Paola's all-enclosing pussy. Oh, it felt so good. Using the flat of her hand, T slapped my buttocks hard. "She is beautiful, isn't she? You bastard, you want to fuck her! Fuck her darling, fuck her for me Rick!" I was gone, all but entirely lost, drowning in ecstasy as Teresa, robe discarded, straddled Paola's lovely face. Her smile was feline and her trembling lips parted as Paola's wet pink tongue lick teased into her, those full lips finding and sucking Teresa's clitoris. The beauty of a woman's high cheekbones brought into definition by the act of sucking is exquisite, one of the most stimulating sights I know and I was completely losing control.

Teresa's hands again caressed, and I do mean caressed, Paola's breasts until her nipples had swollen as if to explode. Slim elegant fingers fed one into her mouth. My mind just about coped, but my body did not, I came and came, and Teresa came and came, and Paola came and came. Repetition of the word *came*—so sue me, this was no time for erudition. Then we were off the sofa, and all together on a rug. Teresa's tongue was deep in the other woman's mouth and then licking down and across her body whilst her hand again played between Paola's legs. Warm Paolian fingers caressed my penis whilst guiding it toward her mouth. She and Teresa were fingering each other and licking and sucking my cock; then T kissed my anus, and her tongue was inside me while Paola sucked me, my climax was impossibly soon and impossible to delay. Again, I came and came and came, but now near exhaustion of energy and fluids lent piquancy to that orgasm. I was on the edge between ecstasy and pain. It felt as if I was ejaculating sand.

Unsteadily I served us champagne and suggested we go upstairs only because I needed to lay down for a couple of years. I got less than an hour, as Paola's stirring accent started to tell Teresa about Startrek "boldly going—captain, I canna hold it—beam me up— she's gonna blow—we come in peace etc. You like my English, Teresa?"

'We can eat early' was midnight sushi halfway up the Kings Road. Afterward I found a taxi and we dropped Paola home." Doesn't your boy mind you arriving home half naked in a cab?" I asked as I kissed her cheek and squeezed her butt.

Her reply was to return squeeze my cock through my slacks. "Knowing nothing for sure will excite him…" Then she leaned over and kissed Teresa full on the lips. "You are lucky, Rick, very lucky having this woman," she told me as she got out of the cab. She opened a gate to the house's foliage-filled garden and was gone.

"Where now?" asked the driver, and I looked at Teresa.

"Along the embankment, go to the Tower and then back please," I told him and Teresa folded herself into me as only she could.

"Would you say I'm a star Rick?"

"A galaxy." And I meant it as one hand grabbed her butt and the other a breast and my mouth hers. Her tongue exploded into my mouth, and I felt part of myself open to her as a flower would to the sun whilst quite impossibly my cock grew hard again. Sensing all of this, she swung herself around to straddle my lap, a leg either side of mine. "Mmm, mm you're going pussy on me—that's quite a turn on," she licked my eyelids. "I wonder what you'd look like in makeup."

"Keep wondering." I wrestled her across my knees, lifted the flimsiness of her dress and smacked her delicious arse. I felt the driver's eyes in the mirror: passing a note from my shirt pocket through the partition, I said, "It's okay, pal—celebration." He didn't look pleased but kept driving. Both Teresa and I burst out laughing and talked of how we each felt our nervous system humming with all the glandular activity the ménage had turned on, but our bodies failed to turn off. She also confessed to a vague feeling of something just the wrong side of where we should be.

"Is this what I've always feared—the approach of maturity?" she molded her body to mine again.

"I think it goes much deeper. Also I'm not sure I want Greek boy getting a hard on while she describes eating you."

We slept for under five hours, showered and black-cabbed out to Northolt. As the Hawker, leveled out five miles up, stewardess Veronica brought coffee, but I must have looked at her a nanosecond too long for T said loudly. "Well, well stud you want your gundog to fetch you that pigeon too ?"

"No, no, darling, please not now." I was sincere.

"Huh," she sneered. "You're all mouth and no trousers—as my granny used to say."

"You like it with women ?"

"Don't really know, last night was only the second time I tried it... would..." She leaned across and breathed words directly into my ear, "... would you like me to tell you about the first ?"

"Mmm," my mouth was full of coffee and pain chocolat, which eventually I swallowed. "Do..."

"Fuck off, slut boy!" She got up and went to the planes little bathroom, turned at the door, and said, "Don't bother, Rick—it's not that large in here." I heard the door lock from the inside and slumped back in my seat.

"What are you grinning at Veronica?"

"Sorry sir." She removed empty cups, grinning even more.

I catnapped for an hour; we arrived and sailed straight through Zurich customs and took a taxi to the Dolder hotel; T checked us in while I go on to the bank. The reception area, the lift, then Herr Stroeder is beaming greetings and I'm outlining an option proposition. I suggest Fat George's London brokerage can be involved.

"Do you mind if I bring in a colleague now or would you rather I speak with him when you've gone?" he asks.

"When I've left the building, please. I'm at the Dolder and I'd like you to have dinner with me there tonight. If there are any points to discuss that we can't cover now, we'll do so after dinner—if that's agreeable to you?"

"Yes, everything is clear," He reached for his diary. "What time this evening?"

We fixed on 7:30, and then went through the option idea in greater detail; he could see some snags I'd not anticipated but felt they could be gotten round, and he discussed what could be done with various of his colleagues before we met that evening.

I told him I wanted a quarter of a million sterling from my account to go into the new one for Teresa, and it to show on the statement and receipt slip he'd bring that evening; to do this, it was necessary for her to already have an account at the bank, so I arranged she'd come in and open one that afternoon with a one Swiss franc deposit. As this bank usually never looked at anybody with less than a million francs to open it required a couple of internal phone calls to sort this matter out. He said the option matter would keep him occupied most of the afternoon, so I phoned T and asked her to meet me at the bank; she arrived thirty minutes later. Because of the increasing legislation about money laundering, it took Stroeder's staff a further forty minutes to sort out her one-franc account by which time last evening's events and lack of sleep had caught up with us. We snacked in the room then went to bed and slept. "You know I've already got an account of sorts in Geneva at another bank. Why did you want me to open this one?" she'd asked before we slept.

"So your franc can grow quickly." I told her.

We woke bad tempered at around 5:00 P.M., got ourselves together and went out for a stroll that led to shoe shops where she found nothing for herself but bought me a pair of Tods. These must have cheered up my toes and then the rest of me for within half an hour, I was in better humor and Teresa suffered contagion.

A woman can accomplish so much; by the end of dinner I knew Stroeder, whose first name was Martin, was called Smarti by his wife and that they had two children in their teens. Also he'd actually made a couple of good jokes only one of which I'd previously heard. Sophie and Carmella are lunching somewhere for the super rich in Monte Carlo: having recently married the fabulously wealthy Mr Lipschitz, Sophie now wears a ring inset with one of the world's greatest stones: the famous Lipschitz diamond. Her lunch companion effusively compliments her on its magnificence. "Yes it is very beautiful," says Sophie Lipschitz wearily. "It's such a pity it's cursed."

"Cursed!" exclaims her friend. "What curse is that?"

"Lipschitz," she replies.

When he handed an envelope containing account details to Teresa, she showed no inclination to check the contents, so later when we went back to the room, I did. Everything was in order; in one account was one Swiss franc and in another the quarter of a million GBP "Keep those papers safe," I told her.

"Is my franc okay?"

"Yes, and it's made some friends already."

"Where ?"

"See for yourself." I handed back the envelope, and she went through the contents.

"Hmm, I see. Does this mean you want me to start doing weird stuff, mister?"

"Yep." I kissed her.

Stroeder had said he thought the options idea might work out providing the bank's lawyers okayed it after further checks. If they did he said his bank would give it their best shot once the other gentleman, he meant Baa, Pyotr, and Alexei had signed the necessary papers. These would take a week to prepare and check, and the bank would charge a five-thousand-franc administration fee and take 3 percent of the options sale price in commission plus a fee for legal indemnity. I told him that in view of the volume of business being done through him and the potential of the option business, his proposed administrative charge was an insult and the commission ridiculous. Stroeder made a stone face and said he thought he might be able to adjust these charges. I asked his indulgence while I made a mobile call. I phoned Baa and pointedly asked him for "the name of that guy at the other bank" and wrote down the apparent information. All very obvious, but Martin Stroeder dropped the idea of an administration charge and reduced his commission rate offer to 2.5 percent; we settled on two point one.

Within two weeks the deal had been okayed by the bank, and we'd signed the documents releasing 10 percent of our metal to the special options account; the net receipts from option sales would be credited to a new collective account for dispersal at a straight 25 percent each into our individual accounts.

Baa knew I'd bought a couple of apartments as an investment, and he gave me some auction catalogues for country properties—like I'd have time to go and look at them. It was a nice thought though. It turns out he'd bought a farm few months earlier. His stated reason was that he figured eventually the land would get re-zoned. If you are not familiar with the UK, you may think such speculation very long term or even unwise, so let me explain. Sixty million registered plus a lot of unregistered people live in a space half the size of France and many of those millions choose to produce lots of children. Barring cataclysmic events causing depopulation the entire British Isles will eventually get re-zoned for residential/commercial development. Even if it doesn't happen to your bit of land in your lifetime the perception that is going to happen eventually will have increased so it's difficult, although not impossible, to lose money. There is another aspect too - of more immediate importance concerning the situation. Farmers don't need Planning Permission for anything termed an agricultural building, nor do they suffer much in the way of controls or inspections providing they avoid livestock, a misnomer if ever there was.

The farm had been auctioned on the instructions of the late farmer's executors. What Baa knew about agriculture could be written on a very small piece of paper, but he told himself it made sense as an investment; his accountant told him that if he operated it, that is if he went through some farming motions, he'd be entitled to all sorts of tax breaks and subsidies that the accountant could then bill him for exploiting on his behalf. In truth none of these reasons had anything to do with his decision—his heart had told him to buy it and save his sanity; big deals and the huge amounts of money the transmutation was earning caused stress. The Babylons of London and Marbella were all very well but he needed to physically touch earth and he needed to be away from people. Baa was more introverted than he seemed; the polished exterior largely a mask. His cottage at Charmouth had been a step in the right direction but it was in the middle of a village that had street lighting and there was something he found a little unsettling about that part of the country— something to do with the coast. More than once he'd awoken there in the middle of the night quite convinced the land was moving about as if it were a liquid.

He was due a couple of days off and on a Sunday, ten days after completing the purchase, he'd choppered down to Wiltshire with a box of groceries and bits and pieces Mrs Portugese had insisted he'd need. She and her husband were oddly concerned with him being alone there. Knowing nothing of his exploits in Amazonia, they reasoned that alone in the middle of Wiltshire farmland was different to alone in a coastal village with streetlights, different to Marbella. The chopper had left and he'd slept like a log on the couch in the late farmer's living room. The property had been auctioned furnished. The next day he'd walked his fields and small wood, looked at his vast barn and thought of converting it into a dwelling. Later he'd feasted on Fortnum & Mason goodies, drunk getting on for two bottles of claret and staggered through the midsummer evening back toward the wood, at little more than an acre it was more of a copse, but it was ancient. Truly ancient. A stream ran through it and creatures unable to tolerate modern agricultural surroundings dwelt there in natural conditions. "Untroubled by consciousness mankind afflicts," he drunkenly told himself aloud.

"You're being too hard on yourself," said a tall figure who seemed to materialize from the gloom beneath the trees at the wood's edge.

Baa looked at a muscular form with horns growing from its head and cloven hooves on hairy legs. "Fuck me! Got to cut down—I'm losing it."

"On the contrary," said the tall being. "You've gained it, at least briefly."

"You're really there?" asked Baa, gingerly prodding the figure.

"Rather more than you're there. Shall I introduce myself?"

"No need," said a now much-sobered Baa. "You're the devil, aren't you?"

"No."

Baa looked around and everything looked normal in a rural sort of way. "Yeah, well, you would deny it wouldn't you?"

"Are you a church Christian?" the figure asked.

"No"

"Some other religion then?"

"Look," said Baa. "I may like a drink, but I'm not a moron. So if you're not the devil, who are you then?" More front than Blackpool our Baa. Some had said he'd get a peerage one day.

"I recognize you and, if you think about it, you'll know who I am—think back to when you were a child." Baa did, and he suddenly remembered his best friend, a boy called Edward and how they'd played in Hertfordshire woods that adjoined London's suburbs; he remembered the little brown people who lived in the woods that you never quite saw but knew were there. The people who'd forgiven Baa and Ed their bois- terousness, and sometimes even advised them on the building of dams on the rainwater streams that drained down through the sloping woodlands. These little brown figures were the subjects of an arboreal monarch, a god in fact, and his name was Pan. Baa made an involuntary and clumsy- with-drink bow. "Hmm," said Pan.

"Thanks for looking after us when we were kids," Baa heard himself saying. Then, suddenly ten–years–old again, he added proudly, "This is my wood, you know."

The figure regarded him for a moment. "No, I don't know that it's yours—you may own its title, but I assure you it's not yours." His words carried a terrible weight that, extraordinarily, Baa found enlightening.

"No, of course it's not mine. I meant to say I'd *bought* it."

"Quite," said Pan. "And what are you planning to do with it?"

"I don't know. I bought it because it seemed the right thing to do, and it will be a good investment," he finished lamely.

"You're no longer a child, Baa, and a wood is no small matter."

Pan walked Baa through the wood, stopping each of its many denizens as if frozen for a minute or so that Baa may be appraised of them and their natures,

When they reached the top end of the wood, they stood together where the stream that wound its way from the far hills entered. Pan tossed Baa a piece of wood shaped like a simple bowl and seemed to gesture to the stream. Baa knelt and filled it; standing he asked, "What about all the agri-chemicals and stuff in the ground."

"That's where they'll stay." Pan passed a hand over the bowl, and Baa sensed the water change. He drank and as it washed down into him he recalled the *secret* stream he and Ed had found all those years ago deep in the wooded hills; they'd struggled through bushes bending their young bodies double until eventually they'd entered a sunlit glade, where a secret stream emerged from underground to run over short water grass greener than either boy had ever seen. They'd looked at that water then and exchanging not a word each had jettisoned mothers' advices and cautioning to drink deep.

"May I offer you a drink?" Baa asked

"Certainly," replied Pan, and they strolled out into the fields that led down toward the farmhouse. "Have you hop, cereal, grape, or some other fruit"

"Only grape today—or rather tonight." It must have been around ten in the evening, but the high sky was still about light. "Do you care for wine?"

"Pan drinks all bounty with contentment." They entered directly into the living room via French windows that Baa had left opened. Uncorking a fresh bottle of Bordeaux, Baa noticed for the first time that Pan was actually naked except that from the area of the solar plexus downward to his hooves, he had a coat of hair or fur. Mrs Portuguese on perhaps some feminine intuition had packed two glasses and so it was with something of a flourish that Baa poured a handsomely large glass of wine for his guest. Pan drained it. "Aquitaine grape!" he exclaimed. "Soon they may grow here, Baa."

•　　•　　•

Sorted for LA, Ellie made her long-delayed departure that Autumn. Dave claimed he'd no problem, but I insisted he put his stuff from her flat in my top room and gave him keys. He had a house down in Brighton on England's south coast but seemed to not spend much time there. He lived with us about half of the time and sometimes brought friends over but there was no regular girlfriend. One day he rang from Paris, which was odd because Teresa and I had been playing backgammon the previous evening when he'd come in late, fixed himself a hot drink, and gone upstairs. Apparently he'd laid in bed pondering on the feminine and reading a book on La Jaconde, which in case you're as ignorant as me is the Mona Lisa. Around 3:00 A.M., Dave decided he better go and look at the painting which hung in the Louvre. He picked up his passport, walked through the cold night to Sloane Avenue, where his car was garaged, and drove to Dover. Getting to the museum well before lunchtime, he'd elbowed his way to the rail in front of the all but atomic bomb-proof fronted frame and looked at the world's most famous picture. The insight took about ten minutes to reach his consciousness after which he left the Louvre. Whilst having a beer farther along the Siene about level with the Ile Louise he phoned and left a voicemail saying he was away. In that part now known as Saint Paul Village was the Musee de la Curiosites et de la Magie on rue Saint Paul. Dave had some lunch nearby, wrote and posted a card, and spent part of the afternoon in that building.

Earlier that day at a meeting in the cage, Baa confirmed we had just passed the three hundred and seventy million dollar gross point, including the considerable profits from writing options. The palladium price remained stratospheric despite the odd spasm and although we were all still enthused, who wouldn't have been, we were also all very, very tired. Our problem was maintaining secrecy, we couldn't hire anybody even for menial work without taking an unacceptable level of risk and when you're making money at the level we were none of us wanted to take the slightest unnecessary risk with anything. If one took time off it directly increased the workload of everybody else—Alexei, Ilya and I were young enough to about cope, but Pyotr and particularly Baa were looking distinctly weary. Even Galena, who didn't really do anything other than administration, was looking stressed in an odd sort of way. Women often experimented with changes of appearance and Galena looked different—her hair had previously been short and dark but now it had got longer and it had that kind of violet-black color of East Asian hair: that the texture had apparently changed too I put down to the magic of modern hair products.

We discussed the difficulty, virtual impossibility, of maintaining production and deliveries if we took holidays in rotation, but only in general terms, as if unwilling to confront the obvious until Pyotr said, "The real point is we are all getting overtired and mistakes will occur because of this. If we, as you say push on regardless, we will become exhausted and then some sort of awful mistake will be made."

"He's absolutely right," Baa agreed. "And we could wind up losing more than we'd lose by closing down for a couple of weeks and taking a break. If we think prices might fall, we'll sell a couple of weeks' production forward."

During our operations at the unit, odd bits of material, including some T-shirts left in the wrong place and a couple of adventurous local rodents had suffered the same bizarre effects we'd witnessed in Russia, but there'd been no serious accident nor malfunctions. I thought this was down to the extreme level of devotion each of us maintained to the work in hand and said so adding, "The fact remains that we're using a process that could go horribly wrong if our concentration slips. I agree that we close down and take a decent break."

This was everybody's wish and the atmosphere lightened immediately, there was an end of school feel to our meeting. Not only to avoid any possibility of phone and internet traces to the unit but to ensure all the bookings were made correctly first time it was decided that Galena would go into central London that afternoon to a particularly exclusive travel agent. She booked something for us all. Baa suggested Punta del Este, where the southern midsummer was fast approaching. If we went soon we'd avoid the pre-Christmas build up.

"Where is this Putaless place?" Alexei wanted to know and, laughing, Baa explained it was called Punta del Este, and it was on the coast of Uruguay, where the Rio del Plata's massive 220 kilometer-wide estuary flows out into the south Atlantic. Full of enthusiasm Ilya exclaimed, "Concorde to New York and then we fly down there private—lot of cost, no jet lag!" Whichever way you looked at it, he was making sense; travelling the easy way would probably cost an extra 80,000 GBP, which was then about our net profit on every ninety minutes spent processing metals. Traveling in comfort would not only maximize the holiday's therapeutic value but save on travel recovery time on our return.

Galena left within the hour and four days later we occupied an entire wing of a hotel with its exclusively dedicated staff. Back in the UK, computer discs and hard drives had been stashed in safe deposit boxes or posted to ourselves by special delivery mail, so they would lay unclaimed in various sorting offices until we returned: the quadruple tuning fork had long been disguised—placed at the far end of the unit and wooden shelves stacked with cartons of T-shirts fastened onto it. We camouflaged it that way every Saturday afternoon and repositioned it over the processing base on Monday mornings. Our landlines were on divert to an office services company that fielded calls from suppliers and sales people.

Despite neighboring Argentina's then current economic situation, there seemed to be vast numbers of people from that country holidaying in Punta del Este. Throughout South America, men speaking with me pay tribute to the looks of Argentinean women and Ilya, bless his then twenty-six-year-old gonads, wasted no time. He disappeared inland with a gang of about fifteen people his own age in SUVs and only returned after five days. He was popular with the young men and fought over in a particularly Latin way by two of the girls. "Poor sap, it was always like that for me when I was younger you know," I told Teresa whose snort of derision caused her to choke on her juice. "Okay, you're right," I told her. "There were more women after me." A result of Ilya's becoming Mr. Popularity was an invitation to an extended family's party at a local holiday house.

Back from that party, a little before 4:00 A.M., I only dozed and awoke soon after dawn. Next to me Teresa slept deeply, her breasts moving slowly and regularly. For long quiet minutes I stared in wonder and appreciation at the woman I loved. Some sort of geometry, a magic code perhaps, manifested through her and a strange soft light bathed her form. Then these musings stilled - I was in a state of grace.

Our beach attendant was Juan-Carlos and that afternoon he put two cabana chairs next to where Alexei was seated alone on the surfline. We remained there in an easy contentment while the South Atlantic slowly rose over our toes. I snoozed until Teresa, indicating her magazine to Alexei, asked about the massive Cern project under construction near Geneva.

He was the right person to ask. "Everything, every atom, is made up of subatomic particles; they're tiny packets of energy. Each one of this countless number of packets apparently functions randomly yet out of that chaos comes constancy."

"Like what?" she asked.

"Everything you could think of; water boiling when you heat it, your gut digesting food, steel being hard, the sun being hot…everything." Leaning to the side he reached down to cup seawater into one large hand and splashed it on his face. "Scientists call constancy the rules of this and that but," a flock of gulls passed low overhead "because they can't predict what any individual energy packet or even small groups of packets might do, they're building Cern to investigate them, to look for new rules. Science likes predictability."

"But I like unpredictability !" she exclaimed. "Will Cern kill it ?"

He laughed out loud "Not while women exist, my dear Teresa." Just then a school of dolphins, in pursuit of flounders, leapt from the water no more than twenty yards offshore.

We all watched and Teresa said "You see, Alex, the ocean heard you."

"The ocean is an ocean behaving like an ocean but because it's big it doesn't seem so predictable…" the dolphins were driving the flounders toward the beach as he continued, "…and the cosmos is a cosmos behaving like a cosmos. Shall we have some tea? "

He called to Juan-Carlos who fetched a table and placed it above the high-tide line then our maid and his squeeze, Carmalita, laid it with tea, minute sandwiches and little cakes. We left the now ankle deep water and our chairs were taken to the table.

"This mag says Cern is an important investigation into the big bang. Is it?" she addressed me.

I shrugged "If everything started from a big bang you could say any investigation into any state of nature is an investigation into that big bang." I poured tea for us all. "Or, to put it another way, I don't know."

Alexei then immediately asked "Are you a creationist Rick? "

"As in a created universe or bigbanged-universe ? I don't see it as an either-or thing. I'd bet the odds and say both and."

"You never told me that." Teresa accused.

"You never asked and it's not a subject I'd lost sleep over." I had to raise my voice because of the raucous shrieks of the gulls now fighting over the floating debris of the dolphins' flounder hunt. "I think we left the water just in time."

"And you, Alexei, big bang or creation?" she asked

"Neither." He smiled and waited for one of us to ask for an explanation. Knowing this, neither of us did.

Teresa lifted the teapot, "More tea vicar?" she asked and I passed my cup and saucer to her.

Alexei smiled some more as he too proffered his cup and saucer. "Ok, if you don't want to know I shall not tell you. I may go for a swim."

"Water's not as warm as it looks." I gazed out at the South Atlantic, uninterrupted by land from our beach all the way to South Africa's Cape of Good Hope.

"If a shark ate him we'd never know," said Teresa "perhaps we should ask him now."

"Well my friends, "Alex did a neo-avuncular look of inclusion "there is actually nothing to tell."

Being seriously richer for having been involved with Alexei for eighteen or so months would predispose anyone toward paying him attention. It was beyond the millions I gained though; I had personal respect for the guy. No more oddball than any slightly introverted tech-head he was a self-disciplined, decent man. He was modest and he worked extremely hard. When Alexei spoke I paid attention with my brain in gear. "So tell us about nothing then."

He drained his cup before replying "There is no nothing, never was nothing and cannot ever be nothing. There was always, and always will be, something."

Silence, then. "That's it?" Teresa asked.

"Yes."

"Where does," she waved an arm to encompass the sky, the sea, the beach and our wing of the hotel beyond, "all this something come from?"

"Numbers." Neither T nor I said anything, he went on. "Positive and negative numbers !"

I leaned forward and asked "You mean matter is digital?"

"Not in the way you mean." Alexei too leaned forward. "Numbers are on both sides of the threshold between ideas and their concretion, ideas made material. Numbers are absolutes: they pre-date us."

"You mean before there was anything there was zero, right?" I asked.

"Wrong! There was never zero and there never can be zero." He poured himself some more tea. "Zero is only an idea, it's a device invented to make our mathematics and our accounting work efficiently on this side of the threshold. It is very useful but it does not exist."

"I think there's no zero in Roman numerals, "said Teresa.

"Really!" Alexei positively beamed at her." Perhaps they understood it could not be because it would be infinitely unstable."

"Hold it there, you just lost me completely." I told him.

He turned back to me "Look Rick, just for the sake of explanation, suppose zero did exist, it would instantly explode into plus and minus values; it is its nature to divide. Zero means nothing; nothing means no-thing and there cannot be no-thing. There is always some-thing. No-thing is a concept but only a concept. You have never experienced no-thing, nobody has, nobody could: it is utterly without reality and so must be utterly without stability."

I held up my empty teacup. "There's zero tea in this cup."

"Yes but zero tea is only relative, your cup is full of air." He sighed.

"Ok – what about outer-space? That's a vacuum."

"Maybe, but it's certainly full of energies" he said "as is the inner space of each atom."

"You mean there are energy packets, subatomic particle energies, in outer space?"

"I meant subtler energies that cause the formation of these so-called sub-atomics that, in turn, combine to form matter that combines to form you. You who has the thoughts that wonder about all of this."

"Alexei can you rewind and tell me what these plus and minus numbers, these values are of please? "Teresa asked.

"I already said, numbers," he replied.

I too was finding this difficult. "You are saying that zero is unstable and splits into, say, 1,2,3,4 minus 1,minus 2, minus 3, minus 4. Those minuses are negative numbers! How can they exist? They're only a concept like you've said zero is a concept!" I refilled my cup, "In fact numbers are only quantities – it's all very well to talk of say 2 or 3, but 2 or 3 what?" I asked.

Alexei's huge frame emitted a huge sigh and he looked up at the huge sky.

It was Teresa who answered "I get it darling, it doesn't matter what it's a quantity of – it could be particles, whales, planets or cups of tea – that's not the important bit. What's important is that whatever it happens to be its negative version is also there. That way everything will balance."

"Exactly, exactly !" Alexei again beamed at her and, apparently forgiving my confusion, said. "Rick, we are talking here about the threshold of everything – creation if you like – creation is not so much how everything came to be, it is why everything is. Everything has its opposite, positive and negative. I did not invent negative numbers nor did I invent negative electrical charges but both exist. Perhaps you should consider why every human story always has opposites—opposites struggling. Each opposite needs the other."

I figured he must have a point about electricity and as I knew that was a place where he'd would lose me, I let the details rest and asked, "How do negative and positive numbers or quantities pouring out of zero create anything?"

"Zero cannot exist so instantly explodes into positive and negative numbers and the tendency of those numbers is to recombine but +1 combines with - 4 to make - 3: +3 combines with -2 to make +1: +4 combines with –1 to make +3: +2 combines with –3 to make -1." Sweeping out from the shore another flock gulls flew a few meters above the sea to form a tight circle; they took it in turns to dive beneath the waves where the dolphins ruthlessly herded more flounders. "There are, of course, other combinations that just these few numbers can form."

"But Alexei that's a zero sum game, it creates nothing. When you put all these pluses and minuses back together they cancel each other out overall; you're back to zero so what's the point, what have the numbers created ? You've exploded zero which coalesces back to zero! Your creation is zero!"

"You're forgetting the most important thing."

"Which is?"

"Time! Whilst combining and recombining, time is occurring; the negative and positive numbers emit time as a by-product. Numbers don't directly create, Rick. Numbers facilitate creation by providing the basis for it to occur in time." His expression was oddly serene "Time, like life itself, can only exist when there is tension. That is why there is no zero. Zero would be an impossible harmony Rick – everything is always tension, everything is always movement. Stasis is insupportable. It is because zero is infinitely unstable that matter is. That matter exists."

"So it's as Shakespeare said" smiled Teresa, "it's Much Ado About Nothing. "

"How else could it be." said Alexei.

I'd heard the words and sort of got the idea but knew it would take a lot of digesting. "Alex, the more I get to hear about physics the more it seems less connected with actual touchable stuff than it is with idea – a kind of psychology of stuff; am I making sense?"

"Well, you're not not making sense." He refilled his and Teresa's cups from the glazed pot which I now noticed was decorated with Chinese characters.

Teresa stayed at the hotel that evening having stuff done to her nails and skin and hair.

I went out.

"There are more cows than people in Uruguay." Baa told Alexei and I whilst we consumed butter-soft steaks and some Chilean red in the town.

"Must have been difficult to count," I said "with them wandering about grazing all the time. How did you manage it?"

"While they were sleeping."

The meal and just a little too much wine more than contented me but they were for nightlife and I wasn't so returned to the hotel. Teresa was already asleep and wandering out on to our wing's terrace I found Galena and Pyotr. They'd eaten there and now sipped their coffees beneath the clear night sky. There was very little ground-light, the moon was only just starting to rise and the great star carpet of the Milky Way girdled the heavens like an immense shinning banner "It's very beautiful tonight," Galena remarked by way of a greeting. "join us Rick." I did and we chattered about what a good choice of hotel she'd made and how all of us were enjoying being able to relax for a couple of weeks. "Especially Ilya," her features softened "that young man is capturing hearts and some of those girls will pursue him back to London I think."

Pyotr, whose body mass looked to have added fifty percent over the last year, yawned and said "You suppose they're that serious? "

"Definitely. There's a competition going on and he is the prize." She advised as Juan-Rodrigo, our wing's butler and cousin of Juan-Carlos, delivered the espresso I'd signaled for along with water.

"Ilya will tell them he's going to Russia and they'll forget him before they can get visas." Pyotr said.

"He certainly compensates for his uncle, I've never seen Alexei take interest in any women." I prompted.

"I think Alexei is, if I have the correct word in English, asexual." Galena told me.

I'd wondered as much myself but told her "I've just left him down-town with Baa so that might change. Neither are exactly conventional thinkers." I focused, in as far as the wine allowed, on Pyotr, "Alexei was talking about negative numbers this afternoon."

"And how did you get on with that?"

"A bit surreal for me."

Pyotr didn't respond his attention seemed to drift off somewhere. The evening was balmy, warm air gently caressed as it wafted in from the ocean and my body enjoyed the sensation of my coffee. The great full moon was up now and gradually traversing the sky from our left. Pyotr looked up at it for a while then turned toward me saying "If Alexei has a fault it's assuming everybody can think as he does, to him numbers are really an arithmetic and geometry combined." I had not the faintest idea what he meant by that so remained silent; after a long minute Pyotr continued. "Our planet and that moon," he gestured at the huge glowing sphere, "result from twin planets colliding. What could that have looked like! Two planets orbiting around one another as together they orbit the sun then colliding, smashing and merging into each other. Think of the trillions upon trillions of tons of matter and the energy involved. Their collision resulted in the formation of this earth and that moon in geo-metric perfection."

"You mean about the moon exactly eclipsing the sun ? " I asked while wine inside and warm evening air outside persuaded me to see not violence but cosmic lovemaking.

"Yes. Did you never wonder how it formed two new spheres of sizes and distances from the sun that make a perfect eclipse possible?" I didn't answer "Algebra." He answered himself.

"You mean as in a mathematical equation?"

"The word algebra is from the Arabic al gebra which means the reforming!" He was talking at me rather than to me and I was tired so I finished my coffee and wished them goodnight.

Climbing into bed with a sleeping Teresa her beauty, that of her partially covered nakedness, struck me like a blow. It caused a never-experienced-before ache. I paused halfway on to the bed and regarded her for maybe five minutes while the ache persisted. "So this is what artist have to endure," I thought. "Poor bastards."

Then I too slept. Down, down I slipped until my body relaxed into unconscious physical freedom in front of emptiness. Two colored ed cards blossomed out of the nothingness and immediately drew other cards from it, and these, in turn, drew more. Each new blossoming caused a further blossoming, and each was larger and faster than the last. Each blossoming, after drawing more cards, then formed complex shapes. At first the smaller shapes, the ones that were among the earliest to form, seemed fluid and floppy and the later larger shapes seemed to be dealt as if in a game playing, or experimenting, with increasingly rigid and complex formations—some of these were stunningly beautiful. Then the constructs of cards flowed together to fit into one endless shape that self-adjusted toward an endless harmony: exactly as it achieved that harmony, it cancelled itself out. Each and every card contributing to that perfection vanished. Vanished and was instantly reborn, blossoming as before. Then the dream faded.

Perhaps Teresa's movements woke me, and I reached out to cuddle her, but she turned her back on me. My growing erection nestled against her bum and, not for the first time, notions beckoned. "Don't even think about it," she murmured turning back to face me.

"Did you ever?" I asked my lips touching hers.

"No." She kissed my eyelids, and the sweetest sophoria of enchantments beckoned. My dick like any other is unsubtle and urged its own brutish agenda.

"Did you ever think about it?"

"No." She kissed my eyes again as I fought against her opiate muskiness.

"Liar." I kissed her nose and then an ear as her hand took hold of me.

"My darling, do you really think I want this… " Oh but her fingers were so expert. "…shoved up my cute little bottom?"

"I think you probably do but just don't realize it. You could go for therapy or you could just trust me." Why did I have a lump in my throat?

"You really are Harold Smoothline aren't you?" Her head disappeared under the cover and she kissed my throbbing penis, my balls and then my anus; then her tongue was inside me and her fingers were back teasing my cock. Joining her under the cover, I found a long leg and kissed it behind the knee and then on the back of the thigh. She slid herself around so that my face was between her legs. I became a pool of ecstasy as her mouth did things to my anus. Desire to do the same to her all but overwhelmed me and I pressed my lips to her and kissed her there as passionately as I would have her mouth. She opened to my probing tongue just as I had to hers. Then a pretty finger was inside me as she took my cock into her mouth again. I felt myself about to come like an express train, but she smoothly extracted her finger and gently felt around my anus. "For somebody who claims never to have thought about stuff you seem to know something, or is it just instinct with you?" I panted as she drew away from me.

Smiling, she said, "Luckily for you apes, women talk to each other... about everything." She went off to the bathroom and I lay back on the pillow, my body in an impossible state. I could hear my heart thumping and called out that I'd have to do something to myself if she didn't come to bed. "You'd better come in here then," she called back.

Excepting heels, she was completely naked. It was a large bathroom, and she was leaning forward, her head turned to one side and the upper part of the front of her body pressed against the marble wall. There was a perfection within that image. Its symmetry intoxicated and stimulated simultaneously - its very transitoriness was part of its perfection. One shoed foot was on the floor, and the other on some sort of stool; her back was toward me and her beautiful bottom thrust provocatively outward. I bent down to kiss her there again—it had oil around it. I stood "Look, Rick, I don't have all day—if you can't handle it...ouch—bastard!" I'd slapped the cheeks of that glorious butt sharply to stimulate blood circulation and then started to insert myself. She kept her arse protruding and her upper body flattened against the marble; arms outstretched either side she arched backward to take more of me. Then as her muscles gripped an urge to just fill her with my being swept over me, and as I came, I told her she was a dirty fucking slut and shouting obscenities back she hammered the sides of slender fists against the wall.

We showered and I got a lot of attention back in bed, where she confided "You know in an odd way I really needed that." I rang for cafe completos and afterward told her I thought she was the greatest thing on earth and meant it.

That night we made love and in the passion of it all, her nails drew blood from my back. I couldn't get enough of her and then something moved. It was as if there was a sort of tremor in everything, and intuition advised we'd conceived. I'm serious—it was exactly like that.

She fell asleep in my arms and I in hers.

The dream came as dreams do. The room was large with a high ceiling and French doors leading to an ornate balcony beyond which I saw the trees of Battersea Park. It seemed to be an apartment that was several floors up and located to south side. The black-frocked priest and the man in the white lab coat bore familial similarities and were twins or cousins.

The one in white stood close to the window and gesturing through it toward the park's green expanse and spoke as if he were its proprietor. "In fifteen billion years we've gone from nothing to the whole of human civilization—its scientific achievements, art and culture. Mostly that's happened during the last few thousand of those years." He spoke a little too quickly in a slightly strained way and although he sought to move his arms in expansive gestures, he seemed to be restricted as if bound with invisible cords. He seemed tense, edgy and driven. I'd no time to speculate whether there was a yearning driving him toward something or a fear driving him away from something because the priest retorted.

"You talk of billions of years when creation occurred a few thousand years ago." He lifted a hand to silence his cousin. "Don't bother with radio-carbon dating, it's unverifiable. You are created and will be judged." The edginess in his tone was, like that of the first, yearning or fear. Perhaps an amalgam of both.

Each seemed agitated and about to continue speaking when Dave played a chord then continued scrapping a plectrum up and down over the strings; the amp volume was high and the physical shock of the sounds silenced the cousins. I turned to look at Dave; he was seated by another French door leading onto a balcony beyond which I saw the Jardins des Tuileries. Dave stopped strumming and as the sounds died away he leaned forward and addressed the two men, "You need to see in reverse. You should see your big bang in reverse and then you will learn the impossibility of not being."

"Hee hee," the priest squeaked.

Dave's finger pointed at him. "You might find God rather than other peoples' ideas of where God might be found - God is like a light that

shines in and out through your heart. You will have to know yourself."
He turned back toward the other "When you know the bits that don't
want to be known, your shadows will fear the light that disempowers
them! Then you may learn something of the All and Ever." Abruptly
Dave played an A chord and then he and the priest and the scientist
were gone.

I awoke.

Another week and we were back in a cold London, energized by the
southern sun and the first real break any of us had had for over a year. We
quickly got back into the swing of producing our fortunes. I suggested
to Teresa that whilst cells multiplied inside, she start looking at bigger
houses outside.

She looked up from a newspaper and said, "Darling, cells aren't mul-
tiplying inside. They're dividing inside an ovum inside me." The subtlety
that division and multiplication might be the same things depending on
whether they occur internally or externally escaped me at the time. T did
start looking at houses and she also got morning sickness; extraordinarily
the odor of it never bothered me once.

Dave's card posted nearly three weeks ago had arrived while we were
away and it told that the secret of La Jaconde was "overlapping chords."

It seems that I read this at about the same time as they were fishing
his body from the Seine downstream en route for the city of Rouen and
I was far too upset to deal with the missive.

•　　•　　•

The French authorities had been thorough and efficient, their investigation was meticulous; although Dave's car had disappeared completely.
The police said it was not murder and his voicemail to my phone had
seemed so cheerful and triumphal that I didn't for an instant suspect sui-
cide. Like the police I could only conclude it was an accident, and that
his car had been stolen.

When the formalities were completed and his body was en route
I phoned Ellie and then Sophie, the previous and long-term girlfriend
who'd left him. Neither Sophie nor I could locate one living relative
beyond an elderly man in New Zealand who expressed sorrow but was

not inclined to anything beyond that. I got undertakers to arrange receipt and preparation of his body and matters at Golders Green Crematorium; Sophie contacted mates of Dave from the music business and Ellie used her LA lover's personal jet to come over for the funeral. Only then did I actually take on board that Dave really was dead. I walked all the way from my house to St. John's Wood one cold night thinking about Dave; I guess I'd had some notion about going to Baa's, but as I got close had realized I didn't want to and circled to walk back to Chelsea.

It was January and bitterly cold; Sophie sang something melancholic about someone called George or Georgia or something to a backing track of Dave, and there was a bit of moist-eyed nose blowing before we mostly all went back to my house. Quiet caterers did things well and, when everybody except Ellie had left, I felt the acts of the day had given me what I believe is called a sense of closure. Not Ellie though, she stood there and looked at me and I knew something in her was hurting more than she'd ever suspected it would. "Yeah, when somebody's…you only know how much you miss them when they've gone," she blubbed, trying to explain her own feelings to herself. I hugged her and childlike she showed me a tightly rolled piece of paper—Dave's last note to her when she'd left for L.A. It said 'You dissolve me.' She wept anew now. "And you know what—all he wanted was to put his heart into sound and he would have done it too…"

She'd stood down her crew and booked herself into the Basil Street Hotel for the night; without thinking I protested that she could have stayed with us. That prompted even more tears. Teresa put an arm round her and led her down to the kitchen, and I realized my stupidity; if she stayed, she'd have been in Dave's room.

The cab I called delivered us through the thousand yards of cold dark late afternoon to the hotel to install Ellie. Teresa ensured the concierge organized some girl stuff she needed. I gave him money to get a few nice flowers for the room and then leaving the girls, walked along the street to Harrod's Food Hall and bought cold meats, truffles, frozen vodka, and some readymade salads. I figured opening packets and sharing their contents between ourselves would be more comforting than room service. By some unspoken understanding, we'd eaten sitting cross-legged on the floor and were mostly silent—banishing death's spector by consuming life's products. Ellie and I drank too much very cold vodka which gradually warmed within our stomachs to suddenly release too much alcohol into our bloodstreams. I'd switched on the TV but kept the volume low; as the pain dulled, I put the sound on and we watched *The Thirty-Nine Steps*, the movie that still grips.

Teresa was already metamorphasising, her body's orientation changing so that the fertilized busily dividing/multiplying egg she carried became the absolute priority for the miraculous internal systems that sustain the human body and thus our species. We left around ten.

At home in bed, with icy rain smacking the windows, I waited to see how Teresa would get around to asking me if I was still attracted to Ellie. I took her hand and gently kissed the palm. "Mmm, that's nice," she said softly and settled herself as if to sleep. I kept hold of her hand. "You're waiting to see if I'm going to make a fuss about you still fancying Ellie, aren't you?" That same hand now lay on my lips preventing me from responding. "But I'm not—she's quite pretty if you like the obvious and I'm sure that what she lacks in savoir faire she makes up for with yokelish enthusiasm."

"Oh, dear me," I laughed. "Her Highness Queen T intimidated by yokels. That'll never do—off with their heads!"

She sat up in bed. "Queen! What do you mean *queen*?" She was furious. I reached up, and taking her arm, feinted a movement to spin her down next to me and roughly kissed her lips while she fought. "Queen of my heart, of my soul, of my life, and of my being of forever and then," I explained and as she melted, I entered her world of deliciousness. She slept but I didn't, knowing little about physiology I started to wonder if making love would hurt the baby; these thoughts led me into realizing that things were all very real now and liberated society or not we'd better get married. "But what if she won't marry you?" a voice in my head demanded pricking the balloon of ego—women demand to be courted. Yeah, I know it's an old-fashioned word, but then women, in case you've not noticed, are pretty old fashioned about quite a lot of things. Yes, I would court her like she never dreamed of being courted and win her heart by making a situation that no woman could or would wish to resist. "Attaboy," said the voice. "But don't ever go soft on her—she'd loathe you for that."

At 2:40 A.M. my mobile rang, but I let it go to voicemail; then the landline rang and immediately went to answer mode. Teresa was also awake now. Baa's voice came from the machine, "Rick, it's me—pick up if you're there or ring back the moment you get this..."

I fumbled with the phone. "What's up?"

"Get your knickers on and meet me outside in five." He rang off.

I gulped some water from a bottle by the bed and struggled into clothes as Teresa got a coat for me. "Wear this—it'll be freezing." She ran downstairs and I heard her switch the kettle on. I opened the street door and waited for Baa. Teresa, bless her, ran out and handed me a thermos as Baa pulled up. "I love you, "she said.

He leaned across and opened the nearside door. "Insomnia is it?" I asked.

"Then some—the unit is about to get raided." I was half into the car but now got out. Teresa still stood in the street immediately outside our open door, "Don't talk, sweetheart, just get dressed and use a black cab to Victoria. Then get another one from the rank there and get yourself to where you met franc—call me when you're there. Understood?"

"Mmn—yeah, understood."

Baa went through Chelsea's silent back streets like a knife through butter, past South Kensington, then screeched up a mews and out on to the Cromwell Road where he slowed down to legal and caught all the lights on green. I poured coffee into the flask's cup and offered it to Baa. He waved it away, so I drank some. I pulled out my mobile to phone Ilya and Alexei, but Baa said he'd already called them and they were on their way.

Neither of us were aware that a driver, having missed the turning into the mews, now cursed aloud whilst waiting to turn at the Gloucester Road intersection. The lights were red and a police car was immediately in front of him.

As the coffee kicked in on top of the adrenaline I was considering that Pyotr would have been useful to have around but it had been his turn to go to Zurich to check all was in order with our accounts there. Since we'd started selling option contracts this took longer than it previously had. The road was all but empty and we were accelerating across the last lights before the M4, when Ilya's SUV went past us at about a hundred and twenty. "Oh fucking great. Ilya, you cretin—why not attract the law," Baa shouted.

I called his mobile "Da?"

"Ily for fuck's sake slow down." On the M4 proper now, I fancied I saw a glow of red brake lights through light mist a mile or so ahead.

"Okay, Rick. Slow now. I get Alexei and see you there."

"No, use the car park—you know where I mean?"

"Yeah, is understood, Rick, is multiunit..."

"Exactly." I interrupted and killed the connection. The car park was in the same road as our unit and belonged to a cash-and-carry warehouse that enjoyed such good business it had expanded to occupy five units all now joined together. We had an arrangement to pay two hundred a month to park on the management section of their property on the excuse that we didn't want to get our cars scraped and bumped by trucks delivering to us. Parking in Chelsea, being a pain I usually took the Piccadilly line tube or got picked up by Baa; his house had its own double garage. The real reason for our making this arrangement with the warehouse was that we didn't want private vehicles parked at the unit when we were working out of hours. Our business had bought two elderly vans for very little money, registered and had them certified roadworthy, painted the company name and logo on them, and kept them parked outside the unit; occasionally we'd shift their positions around by a few meters.

Baa turned off for the A30 and told me that when he'd got home after the funeral there was a message waiting for him from his sometime squeeze that she had some news for him. Nothing to indicate it was urgent or particularly important, so he'd consumed about a litre of caldo verde, the amazing cabbage soup that Mrs Portugese made, followed by fresh grilled sardines and boiled potatoes with a large glass of Dao wine. Then he'd dozed off whilst also watching *The Thirty-Nine Steps*, a movie that did not quite grip our Baa. He ignored the 1:00 A.M. phone call from his girlfriend, but when she rang again an hour later, he picked up. Antonia's news jerked him wide awake. She had been visited by Special Branch that evening and interviewed extensively about her dealings with Baa. "At first they were all butch and officious except for the one with the quite nice mouth and eyes, but I had made them some cheese on toast and tea, and they got a bit more human. It's amazing what a bit of mothering does to men isn't it, Baa dear?"

"Yes, I suspect it is," he said. "But what else did they ask?"

"Oh, how long I'd known you, had I ever been abroad with you, were you very wealthy—all that sort of stuff."

"What did you tell them?"

"What could I tell them? I just said I'd known you for a few years, you were a nice man, not unpleasant in any way and sometimes generous.

I did tell them I'd been to Spain with you in case they were trying to catch me out with things they already knew—they do that you know."

"You don't say," Baa's mind was searching for something that might explain Special Branch making inquiries about him.

"Oh, they made me sign a bit of paper and said I wasn't to say anything, but I signed it Marylyn Monroe, and they didn't notice. Then I heard the one with the nice mouth and eyes on the phone talking about there being no new information, so they'd go ahead with an airport raid."

"What! Say that last bit again, babe," he shouted, and she did. Already in his car, he'd rung Ilya and told him to get Alexei, and go to the unit. He'd immediately then rung me.

The Special Branch is a section of the British Police who operate in areas between the function of the regular police force and that of British internal intelligence service, MI5. What had actually provoked interest from the Special Branch in the first place was open to conjecture; it could have been any one of many small things, each insignificant and harmless in themselves, that had tripped some sort of wire.

My mind was now calculating; we had about three-quarters of a ton of silver bars worth about one hundred and ten thousand pounds sterling and nearly half a ton of transmuted metal worth eight million dollars at the current price of palladium; whilst this material was owned absolutely legally, it would be very difficult to explain away its origin. It could easily get impounded and require a lot of legal fees and time to regain it. Meantime information would be leaking and the price of palladium would plummet; we collectively had about thirty million dollars' worth of the metal in refineries and whist I didn't know about the others, I had a couple of million of my own money tied up in unhedged futures contracts. It wasn't simply that the actual material at the unit was worth a lot of money, it was what its discovery's potential effect on the value of metal worth a lot more could do. And that was without factoring in future processing profits. As a matter of course, news of the raid would be leaked to the press for money and if Special Branch were involved they might even leak the details officially to see what, if any, ripples of response occurred in the pond.

What the cheap and easy transmutation of certain metals might do to the world's economies was incalculable and there was the very real risk that vested interests in and out of governments might decide that it would be better for the world if we, that is, me, Baa, Pyotr, Alexei, Ilya,

Galena, and, I realized with a sudden sickness in my gut Teresa, were all to have unfortunate accidents and the process disappeared.

If you think I'm being overdramatic, just consider the world you're on. Pyotr and Alexei had never tried to patent the process and neither Baa nor I had even considered it. Suppose you are a ruthless power-mad bastard, i.e., a prime minister or a president running your first-world nation with a massive accumulated overdraft that we call a deficit and your powerbase is secured as much by business and banks as by your largely disinterested, as long as they've-got-enough-to-spend, electorate. Along come the bosses of a huge mining companies, pension fund chiefs who've big stakes in those companies and bankers who've extended a lot of loans to them and they say hello Mr Prime Minister / President we're about to lose x thousand jobs, and y billion pounds/dollars etc in pension fund investments, bank loans and shareholder value and you're going to lose z hundred million taxes and political donations just because half a dozen cunts have a process that will put us out of business: yeah I know, the math is frighteningly simple.

What had actually provoked official interest was open to conjecture; it could have been any one or more of many small things, each insignificant and harmless in themselves, that had tripped some sort of wire. It was unlikely to be a phone conversation because although about every phone call on the planet is monitored recorded and timelapse wiped unless a key word has occurred almost everybody knows this and is careful not to trigger anything.

"First things first," I told Ilya and Alexei when Baa and I climbed into their SUV in the warehouse car park. "We've got to move the palladium and the silver, and we've not enough boxes, so it'll have to go loose into this vehicle and Baa's, with some paper and T-shirts to cover it. The next priority will be to get the fork disguised as racking again. Are all the Vat ledgers in order and Vat paid?" I asked. Alexei was already ringing a sleepy Galena, who confirmed they were. "Okay, there's nothing they can touch us for legally—now let's move quickly." It was now 3:40 a.m. as Alexei and I hurried to the unit and, without switching on interior lights, opened the big sliding doors. I then phoned Baa. His car and the SUV drove in without lights, and we closed the doors behind them. Long ago, we'd taped black plastic bin liners to the inside of the window in the door, and now we put a few internal lights on and started to load seventy ten-kilo silver bars into the vehicles, plus a few smaller bars, mostly these went into Ilya's SUV. Five hundred kilos of palladium went into Baa's car, which sank low on its suspension; with the metals and Baa at the wheel, it would be carrying the equivalent of six large men—just about within its capacity. The SUV would have to carry the equivalent of a dozen men and its performance would, if nothing else, either verify or disprove its manufacturer's claims. Alexei would follow Baa down to the West Country, where they could avoid unloading immediately by driving both vehicles inside his barn.

"You know there's no cell phone coverage there," Baa told us. "And my fucking satphone's at home."

"Oh, that's great! Look, once you've stashed the vehicles, you'd better get to somewhere with coverage. If there's a fuck up, Alexei calls Galena and explains it in fast Russian slang—she calls Teresa and talks about a disastrous haircut. Teresa will get the news to me. Okay?"

"Clear."

We switched off the lights, opened the doors and the vehicles were gone. As I reclosed the doors, Ilya was already moving the forklift to reposition the actual forks in their weekend disguise mode. I ran about with boxes of T-shirts. By 5:30 A.M., we were drenched in sweat but finished and so pumped with adrenaline that the hot showers cleaned but did not relax. I invited Ilya for a fried breakfast at the early morning cafe down the road. "Rick, why do you think this happens?" He wiped yoke from the corner of his mouth.

"Because you're eating too quickly."

He grinned. "Of course—but you know what I mean."

"Absolutely, no idea, Ily. No idea at all, but I guess we'll find out soon enough."

"Do you think we should go back to the unit and wait for officials to come?" His question was exactly the one I'd been considering and whilst I was certain our activities had stayed within the law, the involvement of Special Branch bothered me as it had Baa. Those guys don't waste their time with small stuff; in fact, they were mostly concerned with activities that touched on or were political. I wondered if Alexei or Ilya or Pyotr supported any out-of-favor political party in Ukraine or Russia or here in the UK? Our business certainly didn't and what they did as individuals was nothing to do with me or my responsibility. Something to do with Baa's businesses? No, like me he was careful to stay within our homeland's laws. It shouldn't be any palladium mining company or group getting pissed off because we were spoiling the market with our big line of supply because we weren't: on the contrary the price of palladium was higher than it had ever been. Too many unknowns told me not to go storming in but to wait.

"I think that we've done enough for the moment and we should just go back into London and see what happens." We walked to the local tube station through the still dark morning on a circuitous route that took us past the end of our unit's road. All looked completely normal.

Riding into central London with commuters I told Ilya I thought we ought to be absolutely ready to start dumping the metal we had at refiners because if our activities were going to be revealed, the price of palladium and perhaps other metals would fall. "But we can only do the change with palladium and mercury," he told me. Whilst it was news to me about mercury it was hardly consequential as that mysterious substance's price was low due to more than adequate supply for the world's needs: market perceptions were a different matter. I didn't explain to Ilya that once a rumor got out that palladium could be formed cheaply by transmutation, markets would assume that the other metals in the group—including platinum, rhodium, iridium and ruthenium— could also be produced by the same process and their prices would crash. Considering this I felt an abyss of dire possibility open: markets would also seize on the assumption that gold could likewise be produced by cheap, efficient transmutation. The world's financial system appeared to move away from gold yet in the final analysis seems still tied to it. The U.S. Federal Reserve was encouraging all countries to sell their gold stockpiles and the central banks of Holland, Germany, and the United Kingdom were at that very time selling off tons of the metal, but the United States was certainly not decreasing its own holdings. Were gold to become all but worthless quickly there was a chance that economies would crash until the dollar could be backed by something else; beyond gold as an asset there is really only land. Country-sized lumps of land are only acquired by war and conquest—a new imperial age? It really didn't bear thinking about. We got out of the tube at South Kensington. Before Ilya went off toward his flat in Roland Gardens and I walked down to cross Fulham Road, I told him that we should talk later about disposing of the metal currently with refiners as soon as we heard from Baa and Alexei. He said that was exactly what he'd been thinking. I knew he'd not mentioned it himself because he was paid directly by his cousin Alexei out of his 50 percent. Beyond his reckless love of life there was deep inner reserve, a correctness, about Ilya that I increasingly respected and appreciated. The sky was light but overcast as we parted.

Yawning, I opened my front door but, before I could shut it, two largish men effectively blocked me from doing so. Flashing IDs, they introduced themselves as customs and excise investigation officers. Their IDs looked about genuine and I asked them what they wanted whilst inwardly breathing a sigh of relief. If this whole business was customs, it would be a Vat matter and there would be no problem. Galena had confirmed the Vat payments were up to date and in order. "Would it be possible to come inside?" Although now daylight, the temperature still felt close to freezing.

"It's not what you might call convenient," I told them, glancing round to see if I could detect Teresa still at home, but there was a note left on a low table so she must have left to get an early plane. "But if it takes up less of my time in the end you'd better come in."

They did and pocketing T's note, I asked them to sit down and if they would like coffee. They sat but both declined coffee so I said, "Relax and warm up while I fix myself one." Down in the kitchen her note advised she was taking the day's first Eurostar to Paris and would "go from there to see Frank." I kissed the note and put it into the waste disposal.

Although they'd refused my offer of coffee, they were obviously pleased that I'd made a cafetierre and brought extra cups for them. "So what's it about, gents?"

"You own a motor vehicle registration…" he flicked open a note-book and read out my car's number.

"Sure."

"Where is that vehicle now, sir ?"

"If the bastards haven't towed it away, it'll be outside somewhere." I thought as to where I'd last parked it. "In fact it should be farther along on this side of the street." I waved my arm in the general direction of Kings Road. "Is there some sort of problem with it ?"

"What exactly is your connection with H&HWholesale Company Limited ?"

"None."

"How about HarKnits Limited ?"

There was something familiar about the name, but I couldn't place it so said "I've no connection with it as far as I'm aware." I looked at my watch, it was still a good hour before anybody would be at the accountants or the lawyers, so I wouldn't be able to check if these were companies we'd bought off the shelf and not yet used. In any event, if they'd not been used they wouldn't have traded and thus would not be of interest to my visitors.

"In which case could you explain why your motor vehicle registration…" he again read the number from his note, "was parked at the premises of H&H Wholesale Ltd. on…" still looking at his notes he reeled of some dates.

A light-bulb illuminated within my head. "Tell me something, just where is this H&H place?" They glanced at each other and the talker then gave me the address of the warehouse along the road from our unit. This whole interview could be an elaborate ploy to get me to admit to a connection with our processing unit, but it would have made no sense. Anyone wanting to could prove my connection could do so with very little investigation as the connection was a matter of record.

"Gentlemen," I smiled. "You've had a wasted trip I think. I've a business involvement at unit number 19 in the same road and my company pays for car park space in the warehouse car park—they have a gatekeeper, vehicles are more secure there." I stood, the investigators did not.

"We will need to visit your premises there, sir."

"Of course, you're welcome to" I told them. "When would you like to do so ?"

"Now sir— if that's convenient to you." Meaning it had better be convenient now.

Looking down at them I sighed. "Well it's not, but if it gets me off your list so that I can get on with things, let's go right now and do it."

One rode with me while the other followed through the terrible morning traffic. "Want to tell me what your investigation is about?" I asked but my passenger didn't.

The end of the unit's road was blocked off by two police cars and uniformed police waved us away, IDs were flashed and we were allowed to park up on the pavement but not drive into the road. We ducked under police tapes and walked along to our unit. Farther down the road a small army of officialdom was giving a working over to the wholesalers and boxes were being loaded into police trucks. I opened up our unit and told the two men to "Help yourselves " then went back outside to call Teresa. Reg, the wholesaler's car park attendant, came over and excitedly told me, "It was like the Normandy invasion 'ere before—dozens an' dozens of 'em come out of vans an' runnin' dahn the street."

"Reg, I think Normandy was a touch bigger—thrilling as this is. Were the vans already here or did they come driving into our road here?"

"Ah they come screaming dahn the road from both ends an' smashed straight through me barriah !"

T answered on the second ring. "Look I'm sorry I couldn't get back to you first thing this morning, but it's all been a bit hectic here," I said.

"So it would seem."

"Well look, I'm sure we can move things on a bit as you're an old customer. There's really no need to speak to Frank. We'd like to keep all your business here."

"So, should I pass by later? " she asked.

"That might be good, but it's a bit early to say just yet. I'll check and get back to you later. Thanks. Bye." I cleared the line. "Never a dull moment is there, Reg? Come in here a moment, will you ?" I led him into the unit and introduced him to one of the customs men as being able to verify my explanation about parking at the warehouse. They wrote down his name and asked me where the books were kept so I took them into Galena's office and gave them our VAT ledger to look at; each entry had a document number next to it and I explained that the previous three months invoices would be on file each stamped with the document number. "And prior to the current three-month period they'll be with the accountants already," I told them. None of the metal transactions appeared in these ledgers because they were nothing to do with the T-shirt company.

"We'll need to take some of these garments—we'll give you a receipt," the other customs man said.

"You bet you will," I told him. "But what an earth do you want them for ?"

I wasn't to learn the answer to that immediately. My mobile rang and before he could talk, I told Baa of the customs visit and that we were now at the unit and how apparently they'd called on me because I'd used the wholesalers car- park and how the wholesalers was being emptied by the police and customs. "Sounds like drugs," he said and then went on to say he and Alexei were down in Bournemouth for the day and were considering whether to stay.

"Look mate, I can't gossip now. I've got vat guys here. I'll call you later." I turned back to the customs officers, "When will I get those back?

It's not that they're of any great value, but buyers get pissed off if a delivery is short and then they fuck you around taking ages to pay. You've probably realized this is a business we're trying to build and, frankly, it hasn't been that profitable yet."

"This not your principal business activity then ?" asked the officer who'd ridden in my car.

"I'm sure you know I'm registered for vat, I trade metals. Here I'm an investor…not the cleverest investment, but it's got potential."

I went on in witter mode until one of them said, "Look between you and me they probably won't be in much of a condition when they do come back to you—customs and excise will pay for them in due course providing you raise an invoice."

"Oh, that's just great, but I'll charge you full retail. Can I lock up now? I can't see work getting done here today."

"Yes, we've finished here." the officers, each carrying two boxes of T-shirts, and Reg went out of the small door from the offices and I followed locking it behind me.

"See you, Reg," I said walking back with the customs officers toward my car.

"If I've still got a bleeding job 'ere you will, otherwise you won't," he called.

As we reached the cars I said, "So for all practical purposes I shouldn't count on getting these boxes back from you guys? Are you going to wear them or something?"

While his companion loaded the two boxes into their car's boot, the other rested his own boxes on its roof, turned to me and said, "Look just between us, your neighbors have been importing knitwear from South America that's been soaked in a solution of dissolved class A. We don't think you're anything to do with it but your T-shirts will be very thoroughly tested—if you take my meaning."

"I see, I see. Tell me something, you never did think I was anything to do with all this, did you ?"

"I couldn't say," he replied.

"Well, I might see you again," I said. "Several other people from my unit also parked their cars in that same car park."

He looked at the other officer who sighed and asked me to get in their car, so I did. They also got in and one took papers from a briefcase. "Perhaps if I happened to read a list of names out loud, you might be predisposed to indicate, purely coincidentally of course, those names of people working at your unit." He glanced at his colleague who nodded enthusiastically. Baa's, Pyotr's and Ilya's names provoked comments from me for their connection to our unit would be a matter of record. The customs men looked pleased with themselves and wished me a good day. I left and drove back toward Chelsea through dense traffic.

You may have wondered why Alexei was collected by Ilya that night outside of London and not that far from the unit, so I'd better bring you up to speed.

Alexei was genuinely liked by all of us. Being the main man, he'd made well over a hundred million dollars net from our venture, and a lot of that had gone into overseas real estate. His entree into these exotic investments was facilitated by his relationship with Lin, who he'd met in England whilst our production line was in operation. More than merely an important meeting, it was rather as if two halves of one soul from another lifetime had re-conjoined. Alexei, you'll recall, was ever restrained, practical, and diligent; he was somewhat introverted and had an attractive modesty. He'd forgone the comfort of living in a central London to stay close to our Heathrow industrial unit. It was he who really handled the day-to-day production there; Pyotr, Baa., Ilya and I mucked in with the world's most profitable bit of manual labor, but Alexei was the only one who truly knew what we were doing. He was also smart enough never to tell any of us the whole thing. Months back he'd located a reasonable furnished flat over a Chinese restaurant in the area and moved there from the service apartment he'd had next door to Pyotr and Galena in Chelsea. "It is more convenient and more economical," he'd told us, and we'd all, exchanged glances. With the benefit of hindsight, we'd all been very trusting about his bizarre move: but then Alexei was Alexei and had this kind of aura about him. The flat he'd rented was owned by Lin Wei, a Hong Kong Chinese. Lin's father, Wing, had crossed illegally into the, as it was then, British colony from the Peoples Republic of China and worked in a sweatshop on the island making blue jeans. Unbeknown to any of us was the fact that pairs of jeans into which Wing had put the little metal studs that decorate and strengthen the pockets were in the first ever container load that Sy had bought when he'd started importing. Wing's hard work and disciplined frugality had not eased after he married Wendi; twenty years later he had been able to finance his son's move to the United Kingdom. Being family financed there was no snakehead to pay off and Lin was able to save much of what he earned from his work in the kitchens of various restaurants. Within a couple of years, Lin got work in the kitchen of a Chinese restaurant near Birmingham owned by a relative of another Hong Kong Chinese he'd met up with on Gerrard Street in the heart of London's Chinatown. There he fell in love with and married Beti, a niece of the boss and with the latter's help, got the tiny restaurant in west London organized. True, the rate of interest he paid his uncle-in-law was extortionate, but Lin, like so many immigrants before him, had learned that the a lot of people will eat and pay for just about anything put on a plate. Working a mere fifteen hours a day, seven days a week, he started to discern the after-debt horizon beyond which lay prosperity and sons.

Late each evening, after the hard drive was removed—it was never left anywhere, one of us always had it to hand - Alexei would scrupulously check that everything else at the unit was okay before returning to his little flat. He'd take a shower then go downstairs to his landlord's restaurant. Partly to help ensure his tenant was always fit and thus through work able to continue promptly paying his rent in cash Lin always saw to it that Alexei received good meals, the same food Lin and his wife ate. Lin found Alexei, with his large build, flattish face, and overall impression of fearlessness, a boon as a late evening customer. That this appearance belied a gentle nature was something the after-the pubs-close punters didn't realize and whilst Alexei tucked into his meal at the back table, neither Beti nor Lin ever got any trouble. When the restaurant closed its doors for the night Lin would sit at Alexei's table and converse with him in the Planet Earth's lingua franca of limited vocabulary English. Each man had an instinctive appreciation and liking for the other and each had the wit to understand that Lin's linguistic shortcomings precluded the level of communication each sought. So Alexei brought his chess set down to the restaurant and explained to Lin how the pieces moved. To say that the restaurateur became fascinated with the game would be an understatement: he became a fanatic. Alexei, always a keen player, was infected by his pupil's enthusiasm and improved his game immeasurably. It seemed to each that the gods who loved the game favored them in the day to day until, with sadness, Lin returned to Hong Kong for his father's funeral.

Spending a few days there after the ceremony he met for the first time his father's younger brother and sister. Each had remained in the

Peoples Republic after their sibling had left for HK. They told Lin of the, then in 2000, amazing economic changes taking place in China and how each had sons working together in the construction business in Shanghai. Following a hunch, Lin invested in a side trip to meet his cousins before returning to the United Kingdom. Shanghai blew his mind—whenever he took a quick meal, a new building seemed to have appeared by the time he'd finished. Chinese banks were eager to finance the construction of buildings and, in and around Shanghai, to also finance the purchase of land on which to erect those buildings. He extended his trip on the mainland for a further week and traveled around Guondong province. Meanwhile back in London Alexei continued making his end of our fortunes out of processing $150 kilos of silver into palladium which had continued to soar towards $30,000 per kilo. We were processing between 350 and 420 kilos most weeks; so much that our supply of the very pure silver we required needed to be safeguarded from the commercially curious and the possibility of bureaucratic nosiness. Baa had increased his existing investment in a private company that processed and refined scrap silver but the co-owner operator of the business had started to look his gift horse in the mouth and ask questions. We figured he'd try to set up a situation to squeeze a bit and so to teach him a lesson we switched to buying 10,000 troy ounce lots, a little over 311 kilos, openly from the London Silver Vaults off Chancery Lane for a few weeks. Compounding the inflexibility of this situation was the hard fact that neither Baa nor I had any sort of track record in dealing tens of millions of dollars of palladium at a time. We were placing over ten million dollars-worth per week at the current prices . Of altogether more weighty concern was that the then main mine supply of palladium was the Norilsk complex in Siberia and it could be assumed that there would be a degree of information sharing between them and the other major producers in South Africa and Canada. We did not wish to draw the attention of these people to ourselves. That Zurich might leak was a calculated risk the partial lock we had there being that Herr Stroeder had been led to suppose we were operating out of Russia with some sort of official approval. The Russian mafia existed in everybody's minds to the extent that an implied threat was sufficient to keep people from gossiping too much.

When Lin returned to London, his inadequate English adequately conveyed the nuts and bolts of the Chinese property scene to Alexei. This included the opportunities for construction outside Shanghai, where the margins could be higher than in the city. The chess players talked and talked; Lin told Alexei all about his cousin's labor-contracting business and the edge that family connections gave in matters. Alexei readily understood the further edge private capital could afford enterprises there. He wanted to do business with Lin in China but knew he couldn't ask us for time out. Ilya could manage things fairly well, but the process we were running was hardly something that came with an instruction manual. For obvious security reasons we were running a very tight operation and so there was no question of bringing in outside help. Alexei also knew he was bound to our arrangement for financial as well as familial reasons with Pyotr and contractual reasons with Baa and I. Alexei concluded the metal bird in the hand was worth a fortune and not to be risked for two building birds in the bush. Even if that bush was the world's most populous country with the world's most dynamically growing economy.

Each fortnight one of the four of us would go to Zurich to check that everything was in order—for the millions and millions we were making we didn't take anything for granted. We'd been doing this on a rota basis and I was due to go next so it was me Alexei asked to swop with. There was no reason not to accommodate him and so he left with Lin. They opened a joint account there into which Alexei put two million U.S. dollars of his own. In actuality that money was at Lin's disposal. It was a still stunned Lin who left his wife to take care of the restaurant whilst he returned to Shanghai, met with his cousins and then left for parts rural. Did he ever return to London? Six weeks later, he was back telling Alexei how the contractors had already started work on the first piece of land they, through Lin, owned. Lin had done a sharp deal with the developer that would leave them owning a big share in the building being developed and get their original purchase price of the land back with interest. Within a couple of months Lin had sublet his restaurant and was spending nearly all his time in the Peoples Republic buying land with loans guaranteed by his Zurich bank's joint account. Lin did some unbelievable deals and because of Chinese property laws at the time, these deals were always in his name. Alexei trusted him. Was Alexei crazy or foolhardy? Who could have said then?

Alexei was to become worth several billion U. S. and so was Lin. Both are big in businesses in China and elsewhere, but now they have big reputations and track records so can choose not to use their own monies. Banks seek their business but Alexei and Lin have long learned that banks essentially lend money they don't have—in the largely cashless world of big business it's only electronic ledger entries that count. Most people are not predisposed to really think about this but both Alexei and Lin were and would eventually and very discreetly own their very own bank. "Bankers sell a very special kind of oil that lubricates society" Alexei told Lin. They weren't to limit themselves to banking because the lure of industry beckoned seductively, but we'll hear of that later.

Stepping back to where we were, Alexei was well over a hundred very big one's ahead—no wives, no children, his extended family, who were pretty capable folk anyway, were already taken care of. So what was his motivation? He was not an obvious control freak and he was not overly concerned with creature comforts; he could have retired and investigated every diversion and every subject that caught his fancy but the guy just kept working. Did he want to be Bill Gates wealthy? Not really; what Alexei wanted was to be busy. The Chinese ethos to be productive and to honor the ancestors not only appealed but had been within him since his childhood. These goals fitted so perfectly with Alexei's needs that you might suppose his meeting with Lin was no coincidence.

For someone born under communism in the Ukraine, back when it was part of the USSR, Alexei had not had a bad start in life. His Ukrainian father was a supervising mechanical engineer for a regional government inspectorate and his Russian mother was a secondary school biology teacher. Both were people who cherished their children, both were determined to give them stable home lives, encourage their academic endeavors and keep Ukraine's great shadow from darkening the world of their children as it had darkened theirs. The Holomodor has been largely airbrushed from western perceptions but in the 1930's Stalin's monsters starved and murdered a million Ukrainians in order to establish a system of agricultural production called collective farming. His maternal grand-father had had some, never discussed, involvement with this slaughter; perhaps his mother's extraordinary level of dedication to her students an attempt at some kind of atonement.

Alexei was the youngest and the brightest of three, his conception an unplanned pleasant surprise to both parents and his birth a source of jealousy-free fascination to teenage siblings. That both parents were by then more secure in their positions and comfortable with themselves resulted in him receiving a good deal of mature attention. As he grew his predilection for things scientific and technical caused parental delight and elicited masses of informal tuition. By the age of nine, he was already assembling quite complicated, smuggled-in German made Fischer Technique kit models with only minimal guidance from his father and elder brother. Practical mechanics of machinery were counterpointed by the practical mechanics of biology as his mother devoted most spring and summer breaks to informal lessons in botany and the parallels between the two fields became obvious to the boy. By age twelve he'd already assumed, as had many others, that electronics and biotechnology were the future. In his reckoning, they would be the next great leap forward of technologies and thus the obvious choice for his career. Fate intervened.

The frowned upon but tolerated by communism Christian Bible was much quoted from by his paternal grandmother—his father had become an engineer as an escape route from her metaphysical propagandas and threats. Her cooking though was delicious, and despite sometime short-ages of some ingredients, she made dishes everyone adored. When Alexei visited her tiny apartment, he was fed religious tidbits with her meaty thick soup dishes in the winters and the thinner versions in summers. One Sunday fortified Georgian wine inside his father caused his wife and his mother to forbid him to drive his East German manufactured Wartburg home so Alexei and his parents remained at the grandmother's until late in the evening.

That same wine would not help his father's chess so, leaving him to doze, a bored Alexei took the Bible from his grandmother's bedside table and started to read. He didn't get past the first part of the Book of Genesis for, deeply shocked, he read it as the description of two separate creations. The first being a creation of people somewhere by something called God and another of biological robots created by those first people, presumably as slaves. Communism did not quite contradict this conclu-sion and Alexei's resilience enabled him to cope with it intellectually. Later, during early pubescence, he'd gone on to suppose that the people who'd created humans realized their creations had become self-aware and out of a sense of self-protection, and perhaps some moral decency, had shipped them elsewhere to live. He reasoned this could have hap-pened in ways subsequently paralleled by the developed nations' abolition and prohibition of human slaves. Then gradually he slipped into denial about the whole matter and into science ostensibly to avoid religions. Unconsciously, this was his way of gaining some area of control within the field of those he believed had created the human race. Heady stuff this and who can comment on the synchronicity of him buying that out-of-town house and of exploiting what he found there. Any conclusions about his partnership with Lin and the immense wealth and power he was acquiring might be premature.

He had a painting commissioned from a now rather famous artist of the domesticated gorillas Baa had told him about. It shows a simple domestic scene in ancient Egypt with a domesticated gorilla taking care of little children. It was a very positive thing. Illustrating not just a fact of life in a bygone world but Alexei's disinterring and confronting his own horror at possibly being a member of a race of self-replicating bio-robots. That fear had not dissipated.

My knowledge of chemistry being slight, I, as did the others, would always consult Alexei for answers on that subject. One day reading a textbook on physics—at 16 percent of a million pounds a day you try to stay up with what's delivering the dosh—I'd come across the terms *inorganic* and *organic* chemicals. It referred to something like a molecule of salt being an inorganic chemical compound of chlorine atoms combined with sodium atoms, whereas an organic chemical would be for example a molecule found in a plant and principally composed of atoms of carbon, hydrogen and oxygen. It was evening and a cursory look on the Web gave me no big picture so out of mental laziness I phoned Alexei and asked him to explain the difference. Unintentionally I upset his evening and his chess game. "The difference, Rick, is that we need to put things in a pigeon's hole," he meant pigeon hole "so that we can understand them. We do this because scientific knowledge is limited." I sensed an edge creeping into his voice, "If you puts lots of inorganic materials together, they may react chemically with each other, depending on what they are and whether they are heated or not. You know from experience, if you put acid on metal they react and make a metallic salt and hydrogen gas. Probably the hydrogen will ignite, taking oxygen from the air to form water and then you have a metallic salt that just lays there and dissolves in the water. So you have just rearranged the constituent atoms from hydrogen stuck to chlorine added to copper. They react together and make copper bonded with chlorine to make Copper Chloride plus separate hydrogen that then bonds with oxygen in the air to make water."

"Yeah, understood."

"When you put different organic chemicals together under many circumstances they will react continuously. They will absorb other chemicals from the environment, that is to say they will react with them, and they will release different chemicals back into the environment. The key is that they keep reacting, they do it continuously—they are doing primitive eating and shitting. People do not really consider this, Rick !" He was by now sounding irritated, so I thanked him for his time and hung up.

Beti got pregnant and converted from I know not what to the Russian Orthodox Church. She knew of Alexei's reckonings about Genesis and decided it was immaterial whether her ancestors had been made by God or by other creatures who had been made by God. "Whichever way, God is my first Ancestor," she told her husband. The wisdom of women shakes the earth, as do the light steps of their elegant feet.

Eventually the crawling traffic reached the Earls Court Road and I turned and cut through back streets. Pretty much exhausted by the time I got home again, I lay down to try and relax. Then I called Teresa back and said that before she left for London would she please "go shopping for whatever will give you pleasure."

"You're going to regret that," she said.

"*Je ne regret rien. Je t'aime.*"

"Wot a smashin' geezer you is, guv'nor." She cleared then rang a girlfriend in Paris to fix a date for lunch when she would learn the location of the retailer she needed. The shop would be that moment's essence of chic, the retailer of cutting-edge design. Sure enough, there she found a perfect rhodium-plated platinum ankle chain, and an ankle chain can be unforgiving, so it does need to be absolutely right. It was set with a polished piece of amethyst cleverly intertwining three of its links and for me she bought a platinum badge—you couldn't call it a broach—set with a complimenting amethyst. She congratulated herself on these purchases, jumped into a taxi for the Gare du Nord and a Eurostar to London. At Waterloo she queued thirty minutes for a taxi and, at 9.00 P.M., found Rick in bed sleeping the sleep of the dead. He didn't stir as she stroked his hair. Showered, she cuddled up to him enjoying the smell of man but then, exhausted herself, she plunged deep into a violet-colored balm. When she woke the cold sky outside was already light and he'd gone; next to their bed a note that said ' back v. late, x'. Just a little sick that morning, she bathed, dressed, then felt an immense unquestionable urge to go to a cafe on the Kings Road she'd never been into before and consume a bowl of minestrone soup. "Yes," she addressed the slight bulge in her midriff. "You really are your father's son." The soup was unspectacular in the extreme but not a drop remained in the bowl and the Czech boy who served her sensed that the café, the soup and the customer were dealing in some dark mechanisms of the female world.

Back at the house she put on the ankle chain and congratulated herself because it was absolutely right. Taking the gift-wrapped badge, she put it in her coat pocket, found Rick's car keys, and then located the car. He'd never actually forbidden her to visit the unit although he'd made it plain he didn't want her to go there; his car had no satnav, but she had the address, an A-Z guide for Greater London and what she herself realized was a creeping bovinity due to the pregnancy that excused her indulging her need to see him.

At precisely that moment Ellie was thinking about Teresa, who she'd decided she liked a lot and of Rick; she was looking at merchandise in the General Trading Company store by Sloane Square. They'd move to a bigger place for sure because of the baby but the arabesque wall mirror would work anywhere. It was very much a thing in its own right and was what counted in the world. Ellie had never been deterred by her own subjectivity.

Teresa inhaled the odors of the man she loved in his car and there were odors for it rarely, if ever, got cleaned; every so often he'd lower the hood and drive it very fast to "suck the dust out," as he put it.

The lights were red at the top of Sloane Avenue and she'd stopped behind a taxi the door of which opened to disgorge Ellie who crossed the road and went into Joseph. Teresa sat stunned until a car behind hooted. Half out of the car to follow Ellie into the clothing shop, she then thought better of it, sat back down and pulled away as the light turned red; more hooting, which she ignored. Her mind ran the video—Rick hugs Ellie who is crying after the funeral. Ellie arranges to stay one night in London. Rick arranges flowers to go to Ellie's hotel room. Rick's friend and business partner picks up Rick mysteriously in the middle of the same night. Rick dramatically sends her out of London for the day and is then asleep in bed when she returns. Rick is gone before she wakes in the morning. Ellie is still in London the day after she is supposed to have left! No question at all about going to that unit by the airport now; she wants to see if he's there and find out what's really going on. Some force clears a way through traffic and some spirit guides her to the unit without one wrong turning. The door is locked so she presses an entryphone and identifies herself to Galena's voice.

Inside, Rick, the still very-tired Baa and Alexei, along with Ilya and the just returned Pyotr, having sold thirty million pounds worth of physical metal over the phone are now determined to process at a faster rate than ever. They've each been rather more shaken by the previous day's events than any of them care to acknowledge. The unearthly sheen of the process is familiar to them now, but they all make conscious acts of will to prevent that familiarity breeding contempt for a science they still only barely understand.

Galena's quick embrace of Teresa lacked warmth. "I've come to see Rick if he's here yet."

"Yet ? He's here, but I'll have to buzz him—they're working and nobody's allowed in when they work." She picked up a phone and pressed a button but didn't get an immediate answer, then she tried again pressing a different button.

Annoyed, Baa picked up an internal wall-mounted phone "What?" he shouted.

"Teresa's here to see Rick," Galena told him.

"Is there an urgent problem?" Baa shouted and after Galena had replied that she didn't think so, he said, "Well tell her he'll be about half an hour." Baa hung up and turned back to the work in hand. They'd just run up the powering sequence and the suspended four-pronged fork was starting to glow with the pearlized sheen prior to loosing spatial definition.

Galena suggested that Teresa sit down explaining that "they'd said half an hour which can mean one hour." She turned back to the accounts software she was running on a laptop to reconcile emailed receipts arriving in their account from that day's earlier big metal sales.

"An hour?" Teresa thought. "He could get here from London in less than that and maybe enter through another door." She needed to get into the unit beyond the office but Galena had been strangely adamant that there was to be no entry yet.

"I'm so thirsty," she announced. "Do you have any water here, Galena?"

For reasons Galena didn't care to think about there was a rule about no foodstuffs or drinking liquids on the premises and that was why she kept bottles of mineral water and cans of cola outside in her and Pyotr's car. After the previous day's drama, they no longer used the still sealed-off warehouse's car park, so she slipped outside, huddling into her coat against the cold to fetch a bottle. As soon as Galena left the office, Teresa crossed the room and tried to open the inside door; it was locked from the other side. She went into what proved to be a toilet facility and there found another door. This one opened into a passage way with showers and it led into the unit proper. Immediately she was aware of a strange gray light and bone-jarring humming sound. She moved forward to where she could see Baa and Alexei doing something with what looked like an electronic control panel; then she saw me.

I looked up and saw Teresa smiling at me. She was there on the other side of the unit and coming toward me. Her mouth was moving; she was saying something I couldn't make out.

I ran toward her yelling, "Get out of here, get out of here right now!" I waved frantically at her, terrified that she was near running equipment and she was pregnant. Still she came toward me oblivious to what was going on a few meters from her. Alexei was desperately powering down the system and Baa had hurried to her side to shout above the noise that she should leave. She, poor darling, misunderstood; she was confused by events, disorientated by her condition, and had been worried sick I was into something with another woman, she interpreted Baa's shouts and mine only as rejection. She stopped, her hand went into her pocket and took out the platinum badge bought with so much love and care less that twenty-four hours ago and hurled it straight at me. Passing through the field, the platinum's close but off-key correspondence to the shift of ten kilos of silver into palladium caused some sort of arc in the flow of energy. This curled around on itself to form a pure white sphere close to where she now stood. Baa had put out a hand to grab Teresa but was now flung backward, losing his footing and falling awkwardly on the floor. I heard myself yell as I continued to run toward her; I managed to get a hold of a sleeve of her coat as she disappeared completely inside the sphere which had started to rotate. As if it were solid and had its own gravity, I was flattened against its surface. I felt myself losing consciousness as I saw Ilya run toward me and then be flung across the unit by some invisible force. With a sound like a massive bell being struck, the sphere was gone and with it Teresa. The whole four-pronged fork assembly collapsed because Alexei cut the power so quickly; Pyotr had fallen down. Baa and Ilya both had injuries, but I didn't care a jot for them or anything including myself.

I was distraught beyond any capacity of language to express—feelings of horror and desolation wracked me. Consumed by and within that horror, I loathed my entire being:the fight had all but gone out of me. From somewhere in deepest Harley Street a doctor arrived, gave me a sedative me and I suppose tended to the others. Days later Pyotr and a walking-wounded Baa took me out of the clinic and down to Wiltshire by helicopter. Pyotr looked at me in a very odd and disconcerting way and said, "Don't miss the wood for the trees."

He'd just left in the helicopter when Mr Portuguese arrived driving Baa's car filled with food: he unloaded the vehicle and Baa, his foot still in plaster and something wrong with a hand, dropped him off fifteen miles away at a railway station.

I felt less benumbed but remained uninterested in anything; a few times Baa started to tell me something about metals and our business, but I shushed him and remained submerged in awfulness. Late one night I heard him in conversation out in the garden and glancing out from the doorway fancied I saw a tall figure there cautioning him concerning Pyotr. "He tries to become what none may be."

The next evening PAN god of Nature's ruthless Being, it's beauty and brutality, directed Baa to prepare an infusion with the caution that it might kill me. I drank deep and fell through the bottom of everything. I came to in the same room with my desolation and sadness increased a million-fold. My body was inert, but my mind was in hyperdrive. I noticed that within the room I was also inside what looked like a huge transparent ovoid bubble; energies that had beneficent, malign, or neutral relationships to living things pulsed beyond the bubble. The energies seemed not able to pass through the skin of the ovoid. People were though—Baa and, eventually, others did and I noticed that the energies often reacted to them or interacted with them. They seemed unaware of this. Such interactions were only detectable by the smallest changes in their bodies—shoulder muscles would involuntarily tense, hairs would rise, the little colored glow I could now see around each person would change. I took all this in pretty much instantaneously as I did my inability to move.

Whilst I could not move myself consciously my autonomic system functioned—I breathed. But breathed incredibly slowly just as Baa and the others moved incredibly slowly; it seemed that half an hour would pass for Baa to take one step. The slowness of the day to day served to facilitate the emotional agony that grew greater as the awfulness of my loss endured and grew.

During what seemed like a century, I was transported in various vehicles and aircraft to a bland white hospital room. Always the transparent ovoid enclosed me and always my anguish grew. Eventually it reached a crescendo and, in as far as I could experience anything beyond the terrible aching of being, I felt fear. I felt a terrible fear for my sanity just as the ovoid burst and a great sheet of intense light flattened then carried me away.

I found myself in a strange blue place, but I was without substance—I was a hologram of myself, with my consciousness inside the hologram. The blueness glowed everywhere and within everything, the rocks, the carpets, the cushions, pieces of furniture, the ground. To my left what appeared to be a massive sideboard stood against the edge of a very still yet animated forest. I say animated because a sort of unstoppable life pulsed quietly within it. The quality of this place was life with a capital L and this quality was doubly curious because blue is most often rather a cold color yet here, wherever here was, blue seemed to hum with life- energies. The ground and the far off hills and the forest appeared to coalesce; in one sense all looked solid but I could not escape the sense that everything was shimmering energy liable to dissolve and reconfigure. There was a pattern or the illusion of a pattern vaguely like a curvy herringbone, not a color nor the hue of a color, more a textured pattern that ran through the sky and the trees and the ground and the river and the stream. The hologram that was I grew more solid, the blueness faded and I saw Teresa holding a male child whose eyes met mine and confirmed what my heart knew: he was our son. I ran over and embraced them both and, as I kept my arms around them, agony and ache drained away and calmness descended on me.

Eventually I asked her where we were. "Rick, my Rick—I don't know where here is. All I know is that it looks after us and it's somehow right for the time."

"Time ?" I was unsurprised at how unsurprised I was. "You were about five weeks pregnant and now our son looks a year old."

"He's more, but you my darling look about a hundred," pulling on my arm, she drew me down on to a rug and kissed my forehead. Our son looked on with that way the very young have of looking utterly directly: as if knowing nothing, they are able to see everything. My heart rejoiced, and I took him from her and sheltering him within my arms lay back upon a cushion and fell asleep. That our son was already born didn't seem strange; perhaps Alexei's ideas of the quality of time made all seem no more than it was.

Awakened by my son's movements, I instinctively reached out to hold him —he'd got out of my embrace and was toddling off to satiate some curiosity. Instinct made me lift him up and return him to the safety within my arms. Then just as I realized he probably knew more about this place than I did, he started to struggle. I felt, for the first time, my son pit his strength against me and so began to play wrestle. I encouraged him to kick out his tiny feet against my chest, and I made a great show of groaning in pretend pain and rolling away; he squealed with delight and I contrived to have him conquer me by sitting astride my chest. Teresa's touch to my cheek and look were familiar. "Can't make love in front of our son," I explained. "Already he feels he's the man—he's your champion. He mustn't feel usurped."

"What!" incredulity in her voice.

"Look," I held up our child. "This can conquer all, fulfill all that he's capable of, if he has a mother wise enough to encourage him without turning him into a pussy."

"What macho shit you talk—it's strange you'd never spoken like that before, darling."

"I've never been a father before, and it's not macho—quite the contrary. He must feel himself a victor now that he's vanquished the threat another man represents. Don't worry, later he'll know it was only play but by then he will believe in his capacities and trust in himself."

She sat quietly for a while then turned and said, "It makes sense." She got up and came over to where I now stood. "Rick, my darling, you know you can't stay here long—you will have to go back."

"Why?"

"Because here won't always be here. It's like a womb and nobody can stay in a womb forever—you'll see, I can't explain exactly how but I do know that," she announced as a simple matter of fact and I knew she was right. Tears were running down her face, I tasted them; salt is never sweet but it was then.

"What's true today isn't always true tomorrow because things can change. We're going to trust life and use our wits."

Her smile was sad and her kiss languorous as she said, "That's my guy."

Later and somehow knowing it was unnecessary I found a straightish piece of wood, used a stone to sharpen one end then holding my spear set off to explore this place, pausing by a stream to pocket some small pebbles. Even little stones are weapons. As intuition had advised, I needed neither stones nor spear. This place was like some strange hall of mirrors, I could walk forever in a direction and then turn about and instantly find myself at the start of that journey. Much to Teresa's amusement I did this several times. "It doesn't work that way here," she said. I spent a lot of effort trying to find three-dimensional sense to the surroundings but eventually concluded it was some sort of interactive place - we and it were not entirely separate.

With Teresa's head lent on my shoulder and our son in my lap I sat cross-legged on an intricate rug. It was a sort of kelim, blue-hued but otherwise incorporating the usual red, ochre, blue, green, off white but more intense than you would expect.

Later just as I was to ask about food, an elderly man appeared from out of the forest with a bag of vegetables and herbs, and a stick on which a couple of fish were impaled. He glanced at me in a not unkindly way but did not return my greeting; instead he assembled kindling and started a fire. My son concentrated on his every action. Then the man commenced preparing and cooking the food. The boy still watched him intently.

"He's learning something he'd never have learned from me," I told Teresa.

"Don't be silly! He's learning from one of his ancestors just as you could if you were interested to." As I heard these words, I knew she'd spoken a truth—the old man sensed my realization, paused to nod to me then went back to his activities with food and fire. We sat cross-legged, my son next to me in that amazing way that children sit with utterly straight backs, his mother next to him and the ancestor opposite. The ancestor did not put food in his mouth and realizing it didn't work that way for him anymore I went and got a broad leaf from a bush at the forest's edge and carefully arranged a piece of each of the different foods upon it. I showed it to him and then placed it in the embers of his fire where it slowly burned. The ancestor nodded to me again, then rose, and returned to the forest.

"He'll probably cheer up a bit when we get to know him better," I said and we both laughed. The young man in question laughed too—he was enjoying his family.

"Rick, I love you," her smile was slow "and I know you love me."

We made love whilst our son slept and, when that place's night had passed and the patterned sky grew light again, I woke from a dream where the ancestor had showed me lots and lots of carpets.

I drank from the stream then walked along its bank to bathe where it joined a river. Nothing was quite as it had been on the previous day, the colors had more contrast and there was an intermittent background noise—a hum not unlike far-away traffic. Intending to investigate I headed into the forest and must have gone less than a hundred paces when I came to a clearing in the middle of which was a dark pool. Although in bright daylight the pool was the darkest of dark blues and, as I looked at its surface, I was surprised to see that it reflected stars and large clouds of smoke. The more I looked into the pool the more stars I saw, there were hundreds perhaps thousands. How could it reflect smoke from a sky that was clear and reflect starlight in daytime? Taking a pebble from the ground and tossing it into the dark water I watched as it caused no ripples, it rapidly sank then disappeared. Adrenalin rushed through me as I stepped back from the edge of the pool that wasn't a pool; it was some sort of opening into space. I calmed my breathing and sought to ignore the, now increased, background hum. I closed my eyes for a moment. When I opened them the pool was still there but had grown about a meter wider. It was as if the ground I stood on was a photograph that had ripped to reveal a cosmos beneath, I was looking down toward a vast cloudy nebula through which stars were visible.

Shaken I turned and was back to where Teresa and our son sat eating some fruits. I sat down with them and related what I'd found. As I was doing so the noises stopped. Teresa seemed remarkably calm, then a tear appeared on a cheek and she spoke. "Each time the rip is larger and lasts longer. Each day more rips appear, my darling. It means here is breaking up—there'll be no here soon." My mind raced for I suddenly understood, with a terrible dread certainty that I could go back but they couldn't and they could go on but I could not.

The ancestor appeared and signed for us to follow him. He, Teresa and I walked slowly as our son resisted being carried. The child was now determined to walk, exhibiting that tirelessness children enjoy so utterly until, from one moment to the next, they become exhausted. You know what I mean—you had it once when time was only something adults lived in.

We eventually reached another clearing, this one was huge and cir-cular with very little topsoil; the ground was rocky but level with just the occasional tuft of grass or moss. It seemed to be a fairly precise circle.

The ancestor was pointing toward the center and, as the sun sank lower in the sky, the quality of light in the clearing changed and some sort of hazy movements in the air could be seen; it was as if complex thermal currents were becoming visible. These disturbances weren't thermals—they did not rise from the ground but just appeared at what I guessed to be about ten feet above the ground. Teresa's arm linked with mine and her body molded to my side, our son stood just in front of me. He was trying to speak, enthusiasm conveyed in the sounds he made. In retrospect, I was to realize I'd never felt so content in my life as I did just then; the woman was the missing half of my being, our son was the pur-pose our existence served and we were his foundation.

Later, in the night-time of the once blue place, Teresa was perfection — too sensual, too attentive, too much love for a mere man. "You won't be able to be here again, Rick." Her fingers touched my lips "No, let me speak first. That's what we saw earlier in the clearing—I'm not sure how I know, but I do know. I don't want you to kill yourself trying; that would be the cruelest, cruelest thing you could do to yourself and to me and to our son.

"You know words can't…" I began.

"Yes, I know and our son knows. It's because of your love for us and ours for you that you have to live your life. I know whatever I say you'll try to come back to us, but I know you won't be able to—not because you haven't tried enough or because you haven't found a way but because there will be no way. There can be no way back because we won't be here—here won't be here." She placed a hand on each of my upper arms and gripped me. "We'll be safe—somehow I know that, but we'll be safe in some other place…world…dimension…time…I don't know how to explain it." There was something of the absolute in her voice, my heart understood hers and a calmness enveloped me, sensing this, she contin-ued, "Don't be alone, you're not a man to be alone, and you're not a man to be in a crowd too much either." I'd not interrupted I'd listened and now I was going to speak, only I didn't because Teresa said "Sleep my darling." and kissed me and I instantly slept.

I awoke outside of myself to watch from a point several meters above the ground as Teresa tried to shake me awake. I was again a hologram and now so was she as was our son.

I shouted to them but as no sound came from me so panic came to me. I'd barely taken in that the boy seemed older than when I'd fallen asleep, when I saw that the place was fragmenting—great rents were appearing in the trees, the very ground, the stream and the river. The entire fabric of the place was being torn as if it were a flimsy curtain. My son called to his mother and she released my form to leap a new tear and grab hold of him. They were now clinging on to one of the rugs and separated from where my form lay. I could see the destruction of the blue place was accelerating. Whole sections were folding in on themselves and then draining off as if they were water, rivulets running off into different parts of the immensity of a nebula. The part where Teresa and the boy clung to each other started to enfold and a great energy of emotion deep within my essence got me back inside my form and I hurled myself after them even as the icy, dead certainty that they were gone swamped my being. Then I was no longer anywhere and confusion reigned. My point of perception was from within some psychic component that was more me than my ego had ever been. Somehow I was and wasn't corporeal, I wasn't me. I watched me as if I were another then, ceasing to observe as me, I became the other. I became him then not him.

I hung in a silent void of utter blackness.

Not blind - no, I felt I wasn't - there was simply nothing to be seen. I could move my limbs and felt resistance from a liquid that surrounded me - my skin told me the liquid was water yet I sensed an oily quality, a kind of latent viscosity about it.

It was a nanosecond after I suffered the terrible realization that the lack of sounds included those of heartbeat and breathing that the movement started.

Still without external references of which I was conscious, something told me I was moving in an arc at a tremendous velocity. This sensation continued and then the incidence of the arc was decreasing whist the velocity increased. Dimly and very far away a light appeared, then another and another. As the lights grew brighter I saw them as moving arcs - their tails fading as their heads preceded. The closer I drew the more apparent it became how distant from each other the lights were.

My trajectory seemed to be towards a point of intersection with the furthest arc: my fantastical speed decreased and that arc changed into an ovoid of light that rapidly expanded to fill my field of vision. As deceleration continued the ovoid shattered into countless fragments and the fluid around me darkened as I looked down upon a hundred billion stars.

The massive galaxy radiated out in spiral arms from its incandescent center. Had I breath it would surely have stilled at this magnificence spread out before and beneath me.

Again incredibly fast movement. The stars briefly coalesced then re-separated as I slowed. Still outside but now on the same plane as the galaxy I once more looked in towards the unimaginable brightness of its center. From its very heart a great vertical column of light poured out into space. Stirred by an unnamable knowledge Insight sent a tremor through Intuition to explode as an intensity of Joy within my Emotions. Joy mounted to a crescendo, overwhelmed me, permeated me, exceeded me, became more than Joy: it was Love.

Love remembered yet unknown and unknowable – possessing yet liberating, pervasive yet tolerant. It was Sublime.

Stars blurred briefly before I again looked down, this time upon the billions of suns that made up one of the galaxy's curving arms. I moved out along this carpet of stars then spiraled downward and stopped above one of them. Great spurts of plasma leapt a million miles out from it before arching back into the body of the massive sphere: spots of dark matter formed and swirled on its surface then disappeared beneath its mass. Also on that surface was a barely delineated perfect circle many millions of miles in diameter. Still I descended, closer and closer. Suddenly my movement became irregular jarring the very molecules which composed me. I felt panic as I jerked – I span, started to orbit the sun in the plane of its planets then away from it in a curve. Dread stirred within as my body became heavy. The liquid around me grew cold; as it froze it became opaque, I glimpsed solar-side hemispheres of the sun's planets before vision was lost – then came a rising cacophony of sound: a thousand different musics mixed with a billion agonies; endless physical buffeting – a hot wind shrieked past me then all was silence and blackness again.

I awoke somewhere amongst Dorset hills just before dawn; an unseasonable wind blew warmth from across the sea as tiny eyes stared at me. The eyes were those of a sparrow, those little brown birds then all but disappeared from England. I seemed to be half in a hedgerow, and perhaps my appearance there had disturbed the bird in its nest. As I watched, it toppled and fell down dead. I noticed the nearby tree neatly sliced as if by an especially precise bolt of lightning. Shocked by my transition, I ached dreadfully both physically and mentally for the loss of my wife and child. After a while I came to understand that I knew something in with my heart but not with my head. I arose, found a nearby lane and walked uphill away from the sounds and smell of the sea. Some mile or so later I came to a main road, at which I turned right for no reason other than that the lightening sky had said that way was east and so in the general direction of London. Within an hour, a car coming from behind stopped for my outstretched arm and raised thumb. The woman was in her forties, she smelled expensive from within a red cashmere dress. Violet-black hair, dark glasses and a huge jade bracelet inlaid with gold. She neither looked directly at me nor asked where I was going. The silence more than suited me.

I must have fallen asleep for quite a while because when I awoke we were a hundred miles away and driving past a preoccupied passport officer onto a ferry in Portsmouth Harbor. She took me to a cabin where I showered before she laid me on a bunk to instantly sleep again. Hours later, we drove off the ferry through a misty autumn Le Havre and sped along billiard-table smooth auto routes toward the City of Lights. I had no appetite whatsoever but when we stopped for fuel, I drank a lot of water and an espresso for which she paid. I did not find that or our journey or our complete lack of conversation at all extraordinary. In truth I simply didn't care about anything—only my loss was real. She drove with a relaxed ruthlessness that carved through the Paris evening traffic to the Ile Louis. Microwaves opened a pair of high metal gates to reveal a concealed ivy-bedecked courtyard in which the car stopped. I followed her through the house into a huge hall with flagstone floor and oak-paneled walls. Windows were set two meters higher than our heads and somewhere above them was an unseen ceiling. Not only would a tennis court fit into that room, but the game could be played there as well. A fireplace large enough to be a studio flat was full of flames and in the center of the room was a titanic table at which sat Pytor. I was not in the least bit surprised to see him. He regarded me with a sought of benign neutrality showing neither pity nor lack of it. He was now even larger, as if he'd put on another third of his earlier already increased mass and there emanated from him an immense sense of being—a sort of a silent, stern enthusiasm for existence. Existence without limitation. Believing he'd motioned me over, I went and sat on his left and saw the table was covered with bowls and dishes and jugs. There was every sort of food and drink imaginable from simple fruits through raw vinaigrette doused vegetables, dishes of rice, pots of sauces, tureens of meats, sauce covered herb-topped casseroles, fish, crustaceans, meat grills and roasts, and duck cooked into dozens of different meals. The subtlest sauces garlanded the choicest meats. Next to them, lidded containers of piri-piri'd fowl simmered within themselves. Pastries that could have won prizes. Wines and spirits and beers and juices and endless liqueurs. Curiously the plethora of aromas did not clash or overwhelm; each scent as if in its own little space simply seduced my senses. Suddenly all I was aware of was a ravishing, churning hunger that screamed upward from my stomach and permeated my being. It was with no small act of self-control that I turned away from the table to face Pytor. "My family ?" He gestured in a friendly way for me to eat. "My family ?" I repeated with great difficulty. His features perhaps momentarily softened a little and I came to an acceptance of my needing patience in order to understand that I was here and Teresa and our son were wherever it was they were, which wasn't here. I'd an inner certainty that they were safe and would be cared for, loved even. I'm not sure whether Pyotr himself was eating. I fancied he was, yet I can't recall seeing even one morsel pass his lips at that meeting. For me, I ate a little and sipped some pale pink wine that a silent servant poured for me.

"Pytor, I can't understand what's happened." He glanced at me as one might regard a goldfish in a bowl, yet not without sympathy. "I sort of alternate between total pain and numbness."

"Then sleep," he said, and I did. Later awakening in a bedroom, I showered and the servant came for me.

"Pyotr!" He glanced over to me but did not speak. "I have to get to my family." I fancied pity touched his features for a moment, "How did Teresa get there?" He was completely motionless as he stared right into me. I was being examined by an utter ruthlessness—not malice, just an utterly ruthless appraisal.

"All comes from that which cannot be. Know that and you know everything, yet that knowledge will not help you. However understand that, and much of this world is yours."

"Look, I can't deal with obliqueness, I need..." I began.

"Obliqueness ?" For the briefest moment, annoyance flickered in his eyes. "That is not obliqueness—that is a truth more than truth and more than great truth. That is truth that you've been told before but have not digested." He turned his attention back to the table. "It seems it will take time for truth to dawn upon you, and that dawn is terrible in its magnificence, yet that very terror can protect you." His tone softened. "Teresa was taken there perhaps by fate or perhaps the by the unknowable—sometimes human affairs..." He broke off to remove the stone from an apricot before putting the fruit into his mouth. He slowly chewed then swallowed. "You will not get back to where you were because where you were does not exist anymore—it was an aberration. But an aberration that saved her life, your child's life, and your heart. She and your child have gone on to somewhere inaccessible to you and anybody else from here. I regret there is nothing I can do that would make any difference. I am truly sorry, Rick."

I knew Pyotr spoke the truth and somehow it lightened my pain a touch. So extraordinary was that easing that I wondered if I was myself.

The silent manservant had glided into my field of vision and started to arrange meats and vegetables on a golden plate that must have been all of twenty inches in diameter. This he set down in front of Pyotr, who, utilizing gold cutlery, started to eat. Did this man ever not eat? Did he ever take a shit'? "Oh, yes," he answered my thoughts. Somehow I understood that all I could do was await him: after a few minutes he said, "I cannot rest—you've shown some curiosity about physics, take this." He handed me a piece of charcoal that had just appeared in his hand. He indicated the wall to his left, "Now go and draw what I tell you on the wall there. Draw a large spiral seen from an angled side view." I drew a sort of stylized spring narrowing at the bottom and widening at the top. "You might call this a split infinitive," he said and roared with laughter. "In itself the spiral is nothing—it's drawn simply to indicate a pathway. Now choose a point somewhere near midway along the spiral and put a little cross there." I did so, and he continued, "Do you remember our conversation at Baa's and then yours with Alexei in Uruguay when he spoke in terms of numbers?"

"Yes—what he said came down to the fact that there could be no zero because it would be so unstable it would instantly decompose into plus and minus values that would have occupied and thus created Time before they cancelled each other out."

"Well, you've remembered the words, and now I'm going to tell you of things in a more comprehensive way." Incredibly he'd cleared the massive plate of meat and vegetables and it had been replaced with an equally huge platter of cheeses and fruits. He'd also acquired a chalice into which the servant was pouring red wine from an old chipped earthenware jug. "Where you've put the cross is where zero might be were it able to exist—do you follow?"

"You mean it's a sort of notional point on the spiral?"

"Yes, except that the spiral doesn't exist yet...but it's about to."

"Okay, so the cross is there just because we've got to start somewhere?"

"Well the cross is there just because this explanation to you has got to start somewhere."

"Okay."

"Rick, do you know what is meant by the word *infinite*?"

"Sure—it means the absolute, the ultimate; it means farther than anything can be or go."

"Exactly. Everything exists in time, and nothing can not be in time. Yet here we are within time, so *no thing*, that which is referred to as nothing, splits into two self-canceling energies. Each of these self-canceling energies is curved movement. One energy is dark and curves one way whilst the other energy is light and curves the opposite way. The dark energy spins in ever decreasing circles down the spiral path toward an infinitely small point, and the light energy curves out in the opposite direction toward an infinitely large volume. Overall each energy exactly balances the other, so as they draw apart there is a sort of tension from one to the other. As they get farther apart, that energy, that connection gets stressed. This tension is what causes all existence of which you think you know and also that of which you don't know."

I was trying to follow what seemed very abstract to me. "You mean the tension is there because they are the same but being pulled apart—stretched like elastic?" I asked.

"You could put it that way, but it's a very incomplete explanation."

"May I?" I indicated a chair at the side of the great table.

His gesture invited me to sit down. I suddenly felt ravenously hungry again and just as suddenly the silent servant placed a dish of smoked salmon in front of me; black pepper and squeezed lemon were already on the fish, and a knife and fork were by my elbow. I cut and ate it as quickly as I could and gulped some metallic tasting rose wine.

"So that's how creation happens?" I asked, and it was as if Pyotr sighed without sighing.

Answering as if to a bothersome child, he said "That's just one take on one view of why material exists."

Having drunk some more of the rose and finding a delicious-looking piece of blue buffalo cheese and some quince, I spread both on a piece of seeded bread; my body momentarily rejoiced at the combination of tastes my tongue registered. "Where does our world, our universe, come into this?" I asked and pointed back to the charcoaled spiral on the wall while reaching for some fruit.

Was that a fleeting smile I saw cross his countenance? "The stresses between these two opposite energies are infinite, eternal, and omnipresent. As one energy spirals out as light to occupy infinite volume, it sheds, like raindrops, energies that spiral the other way—compressing toward an infinitely small volume of matter. All the while as the first energy spirals toward the infinitely large, the other energy spirals toward the infinitely small, and it, too, is shedding energies that seek to spiral outward to lighten and enlarge their volume. In each case, stresses exist between the original energies and their raindrop-like progeny. Those stresses cross, and they may be measured as a sort of field."

"All because the two energies curve in opposite directions ?"

He pointed back toward the wall. "Go and draw some waves." I did as he bid, quickly making a dozen parallel wavy lines as a child might draw a stylized sea. "Now put on two marks—place them randomly but not too far apart." I did this, placing one to the center and the other a few inches off to the left and an inch or so higher. "Now the two marks represent two temporary anomalies occurring. They will eventually cancel each other out, but there is a time difference and this causes what people call a universe to exist. Draw a circle enclosing some waves and including the two marks you've made." I did. "There, now you have your universe—all that is in the circle is all the universe you can perceive. All is a result of those two marked anomalies. A universe has bubbled into being."

"But this would mean there are lots of different universes."

"Why not?" His chalice refilled, he drank deeply. "True, it rather makes nonsense of calling a universe a universe—but that doesn't matter because languages eventually evolve to meet needs."

"I think I can understand how something occurs within the bubble, some-thing that can be termed a universe, but tell me, what actually happens within the circle to cause our universe as we experience it?"

"Ultimately nature doesn't waste anything material or informational." His tone indicated that this answer was sufficient, and that it explained everything I needed to know, but then he added, "Nature is within each universe and endlessly recycles energy, matter and experiences. In this one, in this universe at this time, quantum understanding of numbers and dimensional understanding of geometry, a temperature of absolute zero, and a speed of light are conceived but aren't generally reconciled just yet—that's why religious beliefs remain so undeveloped here."

"I was just wondering about that, Pyotr…"

"As well one might, as well one might…" Pyotr seemed to wondering himself but suddenly snapped his attention back to me. "If something gets infinitely large it will contain everything, and that everything will contain the something that became infinitely small."

I suddenly felt all but overcome with fatigue. "Go and sleep now," he said and already Jade Woman was leading me away. Asleep I saw our immense universe to be only a microcosm of something not just vast but actually infinite. Within this, now relatively, little speck of our universe I saw the anomalies in the field. They were actually mirror occurrences of the energies on the spiral, but here the energies were somehow more diverse. They were still fearsome but now less than absolute.

One energy expanded endlessly and was radiant light; the other spun ever tighter compacting itself into that state between energy and mass we call quarks, subatomic particles. Extraordinarily, as this was happening, each continually gave birth to its opposite. From the expanding light, drops of contracting new energy particles fell like rain and turned to wavy rivulets as they fell. From the contracting energies forming matter, new light sprang, radiating out in waves as it expanded and burst into fountains of droplets. I understood that particles and waves are the same thing—only their geometries are different.

Sub-atomics, the quarks and electrons, danced and danced forming atoms that grouped together; as each group of atoms grew in number they bonded with other elements to form molecules. Then molecules were interacting with each other and grew more and more complex and evolved from the inorganic to the organic. Great volumes of the radiant light that filled this universe started to coalesce around a double helix molecule and as I looked on all manner of creatures flew from it. So many different forms of life occurred that most hardly registered, but I saw androgynous worms, swarms of bees, lone reptiles and tribes of mammals. Then I stood outside the mouth of a cave and as I stepped inside I awoke.

I'd fallen asleep in my clothes. Rising, I peeled them off and walked naked into the bathroom that resembled my wet room in London in what seemed like another age. Now I was wherever I was and simultaneously fortified and horrified by an absolute certainty. Yet it was also sustaining me; I knew my family was completely gone but I also somehow knew they were safe. Reason wasn't comfortable with this knowledge but intuition was and I knew the only way to deal with events was to stay loose. Evidently when we start altering, you could say interfering, with the basis of day-to-day reality then the day-to-day is going to change. I spent a long while under the shower just letting water cascade over me and when I'd done showering and shitting and shaving, I found clothes along with a thermos jug of tea had been left in the bedroom. The contents inside me and some unrecognized clothes on the outside, I headed for the huge hall but got myself lost in passageways and other rooms I would never have supposed to be there. It was silent servant who appeared and led me to the hall and Pyotr.

He now wore a kimono-type robe and immediately before him on the vast table were a couple of dozen small plates and lidded dishes. In his right hand were chopsticks, and whilst the servant hovered removing and replacing the little lids on some of the dishes, Pyotr picked at various delicacies He looked at me with just the merest hint of humor in his eyes. It would have been the easiest of things to simply smile with him and to laugh as if at a joke that, whilst sensed, was not consciously known. Making no small effort, I told him, "I resist in order to persist, Pyotr. What I would like to know, to understand, is what the purpose of it all is, what is the intent of everything."

"A very western question." He gestured to a chair and I understood it as some sort of honor that a chair had been arranged for me a meter or so to Pyotr's left. I sat and ate some Chinese breakfast soup that was beyond delicious: it was made from vegetables. Then I found myself eating more solid fare from dishes the servant edged closer then farther from me in a system of gourmet prompts. Pyotr continued, "What is the intent is a question that arises because you suppose that causes precede effects and thus that any intention of creation somehow can precede creation. You've already understood that creation cannot be preceded—and no," he admonished with a hand. "Don't get into the Hindu breathing in and out of stuff. If the universe is being breathed in and out, it already exists. Such things could only occur within what already is."

I realized that what I was now eating were the exact same dishes as Pyotr, a delicacy known in the West as Peking duck. Traditionally it's forty or so different courses prepared from a duck's body. In rural China each village has or had ducks that traditionally lived on the village's pond eating insectorial creatures that thrive on the villagers' excrement. The dish, if properly prepared is sublime. Amazing and wonderful tastes produced from an origin composed from the lowest products. A sort of culinary equivalent of the Lotus. Don't be upset, the very body your consciousness is within right now is processed sunshine which got to be you via a lot of recycled matter. Know yourself and love yourself, like me you are not only an individual but also a part of bigger and bigger pictures.

Fortified by the food I said, "No, I didn't suppose an intent necessarily precedes creation, but I do suppose intent can be implicit within creation."

"Better perhaps to believe simply that what is, is." He sipped some rice wine.

"That will get me absolutely fucking nowhere!" I said.

He laughed, "Conjoined western and eastern ways of thinking might enable you to perceive that cause and effect are just different aspects of the same thing—just different faces of the same actuality."

"Is there a right way of thinking?"

"Once," he sighed. "An emperor of China sent seven of his generals with a large army to put down a provincial rebellion. The seven generals camped their army on the province's border and discussed how to conduct the battle against the rebels. The generals agreed there were actually only two ways to conduct the battle, but they could not agree on which option to pursue so decided to vote on the matter. Four generals chose battle plan A, the other three generals preferred battle plan B. Naturally they conducted the battle according to plan B because three is a more auspicious number than four in their way of thinking." His glance silenced my question and he continued. "The Western mind often strives to hide from what it knows. It professes a love affair with democracy and, blinded by that affair, would have been chosen plan A. Consider, which plan would be the most successful for the battle ?"

"I don't know."

"Exactly. Now let's see if your question can be answered with a question— what do you suppose an intent could be?"

In my mind's eye the eternal Absolutes spiraled away from each other and the pull between them caused a field of Absolute tension. From that sublime energy, universes bubbled into being and within each universe I saw all manner of galaxies forming. I fancied I looked into our own universe and eventually into our very own galaxy; then, out on one of its spiral arms, I saw our solar system. The giant gas planets attracted debris and comets and meteors so sheltering our own Earth on which myriad life forms fed off each other. Somehow I saw and was aware of everything simultaneously.

In an effort to come down from the vision, I concentrated on that part of the table immediately in front of where I sat; it was made of very old wood. After a while I said, "I suppose the intent could be to avoid the idea of nothingness, to always become a more complete entity." He did not reply, and it occurred to me that perhaps I'd understood what he wanted me to grasp or that at least I'd used the right words. I asked, "Where are humans in this whole food chain ?"

"A lot of places, Rick—but you should know it's not a food chain so much as a food complex."

Just then I noticed that what I'd taken to be a simple wooden stand on the table for one of the many dishes was actually a set of pipes, the sort Greek shepherds were supposed to use. "What's with the pipes?" I asked as I pointed to them.

"Music is a way of communicating," he spoke without looking up. The silent servant appeared and poured tea for me; I drank thirstily, surprised at how parched my throat was. Jade woman led me back to my room. I understood now that the blue place had drained my energies to a startlingly low level and so didn't try to resist sleep's balm.

Awakening I drank some water and, leaving the bedroom, took a couple of right turns and found myself in the house's courtyard where a massive bull now stood. If you could say a bull can glance, then that's exactly what it did—the slightest movement of the great head and its large eyes regarded me. Thankfully the look was without malice for the creature wasn't tethered. I crossed the yard warily and, as I suspected, found that the pad placed in the wall next to the main gate unlocked a small metal grilled door that led out into the street. There was a mist that obscured everything. I couldn't see a meter in front of my face and, meaning to move down toward the Seine's right bank, I turned to my left and then stopped. I could feel Dave's presence. He was there with me and his hand on my shoulder held me back. Very gingerly, I reached forward with a foot and felt nothing. Had I stepped close to a kerb ? No. I got down on my knees, reached forward over an edge with my hands and still couldn't feel anything. Was it a hole in the pavement I wondered, perhaps I should have brought a flashlight? Perhaps I should have owned a one. I moved carefully to my right, thinking to circum-navigate the gap. Again nothing. I turned nearly 360 degrees and could find absolutely nothing other than the pavement I had just walked across from the door within the gate. Carefully, oh, so carefully I made my way back to the courtyard's main gate and then the small door from which I had emerged. Now able to orientate myself, I decided to move the other way but a few paces in that new direction and again there was nothing. Retracing my steps to the main gate, I tried to set off directly across the road that ran past the building. Yet again nothing—there was no road there. I turned back and stepped to the side of the now closed grill door. I had no way of regaining access to the house without the large gates or door being opened from the inside. Next to the gate was an old fashioned bell pull. I gave it a couple of pulls but nothing happened. I was growing cold for this damp gray mist had no temperature to it, just a curious oily quality. I jiggled the ancient bell pull again a few times although somehow I knew it would elicit no response from the house. I sat down on the pavement and didn't so much fall asleep as drift back off into that earlier numbness. When I snapped into full awareness the mist had cleared and with it had gone Paris, the house behind me and the pavement I sat on. There was nothing other than myself. A dread so absolute as to be indescribable seized me. I was in a void and there was only void. I may have been falling through it; I may have been floating in it. It made no difference for there was no relative point to where I was. It seemed as if a long time passed, my mind scurrying hither and thither, trying to find something to latch onto to avoid the void. Trying to avoid comprehending that I was in a void. Trying to avoid under-standing that that there was a void, a void of no - thing. There's a saying that that nature abhors a vacuum and anybody who has tried to create a vacuum will understand this. Anybody who has used a vacuum cleaner understands that that is why the dirt gets sucked up—it's trying to fill the vacuum that the machine is trying to create inside itself. You could suppose the vacuum tries to fill itself. I suddenly realized there was no air, and I wasn't breathing—I was simply in this void. Or was I? Could I or anything else exist in a void? Could a void exist in itself? As this thought occurs, the evil arrived. I regret to say that I suspect it arose from within me. I suspect thoughts on the unconscious level went along the lines of there is no thing here, so there is nothing with which I can be constructive. Being no-thing there is no life; if there is no life, evil reigns supreme because evil is the antithesis of life. In English the very word is *live* reversed, spelt backwards. So evil was my companion, perhaps even my friend, for it was the only thing that was there for me and it expanded to encompass all possibilities.

Do something bad to prove to yourself that you exist was the bottom line of the fantastical thoughts that whirled through my brain. And then, then came light and I understood that light was coming because it had been attracted by an evil thought. Just as evil is the antithesis of life, so life is the antithesis of evil. Evil begot the good in that void. Suddenly light was all around me, it actually filled me, dazzled me. I could see nothing other than light entering my body, and I realized my eyes were actually closed. I opened them to find myself lying on the floor in the great hall while the silent servant tended to the seemingly eternal requirements of Pyotr. Jade woman helped me to my feet. "Rick! Rick look at this," she was holding her arm with the massive bracelet in front of my face. "Do you see the markings on the jade?"

"Yes," I croaked, working hard at focusing my mind.

"Well, those marks were formed in the jade by nature, but the jade is now in the form of a bracelet made by what?" Her voice was very insistent.

"Man."

"And what made man?"

"Nature."

"And what made nature?" I remained silent. "Why was nature made? What do you suppose is the intent of everything ?"

"I don't know now—I used to…" my mind span and I heard myself say. "I used to suppose we acted like little hard drives registering infor-mation of emotional interactions with the world, so that when we died those experiences could be downloaded." Jade Woman said nothing, so I continued. "I mean I supposed that in some way, we were just tiny parts of a greater entity."

"And free will ?"

I had to think about something I'd never considered before because I'd always taken it for granted. My mind was getting back in gear. "Largely an illusion I suppose…but there to a limited extent. In fact it could just be part of an emotional interaction equation."

For a while I felt truly miserable at this relativisation of my ego then Pyotr spoke, "The ego is a tool that occurred through nature but has to be learned about— like another of nature's tools" Now some delicious looking pastries were disappearing into him. "The human hand with its opposable thumbs and masses of nerves can be used to create great beauty," he said and indicated an extraordinarily elegant ceramic bowl I'd not noticed before on the massive table. "Or used to do great damage." I fancied I saw a fist that smashed through a pile of fifty of those bowls.

"Well, that's helped a lot, Pyotr. It's all about as clear as mud now."

"Good, so now you will think about important things and perhaps those thoughts will lead you somewhere. Whilst that is happening, you'd best go and speak with Baa. He's at the farm but don't try to phone him before you see him." It wasn't a suggestion or an order, but it was not something to be discussed or debated: it was what was.

I bid him farewell and went out into the courtyard with Jade Woman. I began to realize what you probably did long ago—Pyotr was no longer the Pyotr he had been. He was now something, and I do mean *something* as opposed to somebody. As if reading my thoughts, Jade Woman said, "He is now what he was always to be."

"And you were, are Galena," I said as the realization struck me.

"I've bought you some clothes." She opened the boot of a car and indicated some bags. "They should fit." Just this side of boring and not without elegance, the clothes were to fit perfectly. "I also got you a grip and some toilet things. Here's a phone, a passport and some cash." She handed me a an envelope containing euros and sterling. "Please change in your room and leave what you're now wearing in there. I will be waiting for you here."

I did as she asked and she drove northwards out of the Paris which again lay beyond the courtyard outer door. "Rick a radio can receive all broadcasts but is only tuned to one at a time; if it was tuned to more than one you would find the noise incomprehensible. It would drive you mad if you attempted to make sense of it." She drove fast and with great precision. "Existence is existence in the all and ever – but we only see the things we see in the piece of time that we are in." Within an hour she'd dropped me at Le Bourget from where a small plane flew through evening skies into a darkening Bournemouth Airport. Without a credit card or driver's license I was unable to rent a car so hired a taxi for the cross-country ride to the small city of Salisbury. Mindful of Pyotr's caution not to phone Baa, I thought it might be circumspect to break the journey so paid the driver off there and went into a crowded pub. A phone booth at the rear displayed a local taxi's number and I ordered a cab for the trip out to the farm which was eventually located after a few wrong turns. The isolated location, late hour and chill night conspired to make the driver nervous, and he was visibly relieved to be paid and able leave. As he drove away a light came on in the porch and Baa stood at the open doorway. "Had a feeling you'd come today, Rick. How are you ?"

"Not really sure, mate. Yourself?"

"Lots to tell you," he said as he led me into the farmhouse's kitchen which was untidy in an organized sort of way but still not very Baa. He caught my thoughts, "I haven't changed this place at all, and I've left Mr and Mrs Portugal in London looking after the house there. Foot's okay now, but the finger didn't grow back..." He held up his left hand and I saw the little finger and the outside part of the palm was missing. "Bit of a job explaining it away—went to Switzerland for the skin grafts. Do you want something to eat?" Beyond his rapid speech I could tell he was relieved to see me.

"Yeah."

He put steaks on the grill and got potato salad from a fridge. "Wine's through there; and bring some water will you," he said and indicated a door that lead into a broad passage with racks holding hundreds of bottles along one side. I found an Haut Medoc that felt right and farther on packs of Volvic. While I opened the wine he explained that, some little time after drinking the infusion, I'd collapsed on the floor. Pan had gone off and Pyotr had already left for London. Baa had got me onto a sofa and, thinking I was dying, started figuring out how to get me into his car to take me to a hospital. He'd driven through the fence into the garden and backed up to the French windows, but when he came into the house to try, with his broken foot and maimed hand, to manhandle me into the vehicle, he found I was becoming translucent and blue. Then I disappeared—only to reappear a few minutes later. "Did that shake you up ?" I asked.

"Of course not. I'm perfectly used to getting bones broken, bits sliced off me, lugging tons of metal in and out of cars and poisoning people who turn into blue glass then disappear!" Perhaps significantly, it was Volvic he drank deeply. "Of course it shook me up, you cunt!" He was looking pretty serious, so I said nothing for a couple of minutes.

"This skin graft, you sad tart—did they take it off your cock?"

He smiled. "Don't be daft—they didn't need that much. They took it off the side of my butt. I'll show you," he said and made to as if to undo his slacks.

"No, please, I'd rather you didn't—I'm going to eat soon. It's good to see you, Baa—well, what's left of you anyway." I handed him a glass of wine and raised my own.

Lifting his, he said, "There I was thinking I'd finally got rid of you and when I woke from my nap…" I'd raised an eyebrow. "Yes, I take a nap every afternoon now—a siesta in fact—anyway, I had this strong feeling you were on your way here." He forked the fillet steak on to plates and carried them to the old wooden table. "Nothing much surprises me anymore, Rick."

"If I need more of this infusion can you make it for me ?"

"Not willingly—it can kill you." He caught my look. "But, yeah, I wasn't that gone—I wrote down the recipe. But I don't think it will work." I hard eyed him for a long moment and he continued, "I don't understand the details, just the gist of the thing, which was some combination of the time, the planet's orientation, your emotions and some normal herbs enabled it to happen. Apparently the herbs were like an oil—the mechanism was an interaction of your emotions with the time." I remained silent, and he spoke again. "Emotions can kill. You can die of a broken heart."

We ate in silence as outside a night wind moaned through the trees and when he brought some cheese from a walk in larder, he said "You'll enjoy this, Rick, it's local and never been in a fridge."

"Why not ?"

"Because cheese isn't supposed to be kept in fridges…larders are what's needed, but people who build houses either don't know that or don't want to use the space."

"I'm pleased you've got that off your chest, Doris. Do you get out much these days?" I said. He went and fetched another bottle of wine. "There was a big guy here when you made the infusion for me, Baa—who was he?"

Baa gave me a long look and then said quietly, "He's of these parts and nothing to do with our business. He told me how to mix the ingredients for the tea and subsequently about the time and your emotions."

Now it was my turn to give the long look; I knew Baa well enough to know there was much he wasn't saying, but I was very tired; in fact tiredness was now rolling over me like ocean waves. "Baa, I'm starting to fall asleep. Sorry, but I'm not up to par yet." He picked up my grip and led me upstairs to what seemed to be a recently painted room.

"Bathroom's down the hall," he said pointing. "Sleep well, Rick." He was gone and I took off my outer clothes, slipped under the duvet and was asleep.

Sunshine pouring in through the room's small window woke me and something about the birdsong got me quickly from the bed. Looking outside, I marveled at the million different shades of the leaves on the trees and those that last night's wind had blown down. I gradually realized that it was autumn! I'd last been here in spring and had gone to the blue place, where time seemed a bit indefinite, but I reckoned I'd not been there more than a few days. Then perhaps a week, certainly no more than ten days, in Paris with a day or so for travel. And now it was autumn? Then another realization struck me—when Jade Woman's car had stopped for me down on the coast, it had been autumn. It simply hadn't registered because I'd been too shocked and desolated. I must have been away six months in the blue place .

I found the bathroom, showered and dressed. Downstairs there was a half full cafetiere in the kitchen and I helped myself. Baa was through a door in what I recalled was the living room where I'd drunk the infusion he'd made for me. He sat on a sofa working a laptop with his damaged hand and holding a coffee cup in the other. "Morning!"

"Morning—give us a second." He finished up his tapping and pushed the computer away. "You look like you slept well."

"Thanks, I did. I suddenly noticed it's autumn, Baa—I'd no idea I'd been away for as long as six months."

He spluttered into his coffee, wiped his chin with his hand, and announced "Rick, old son, you've been away two and a half years."

As he said it, I knew it was true but never the less, when he gestured, I went over to the laptop. He ran through several Web sites including the BBC's and dates confirmed what he'd said. "I was in Paris with Pyotr and Galena. You'd not recognize her now, but neither said anything about how long I'd been away." I emptied my cup. "Pyotr said I should come here and see you."

Baa sat silently sipping his coffee for a while, and then said, "Rick, I won't even try and pretend I know what's going on because I don't. I'll tell you what I know, and you'll tell me what you know. Then, maybe between us we'll figure things out."

"Agreed. Where do we start ?"

"With me if you like," he said. I sat down, and he started to tell me. After the events at the unit, the quadruple fork was useless, so Alexei and Ilya stayed to try and fix it. They rapidly concluded another would have to be built; after twenty-four hours Ilya started to get terrible headaches and X-rays at the Harley Street doctor's revealed a hairline skull fracture. The medic was concerned and, at Pyotr's suggestion, Alexei went with him to Lille in northern France and took him into the casualty department of a local hospital explaining he'd fallen down some steps whilst drunk the night before. The hospital routinely notified the police and, after shaving and binding his head, kept Ilya in for four days observation then discharged him. The police had confirmed that they had no interest in Ilya, so he and Alexei returned to England. Meanwhile most of the metal that had been brought to Baa's farm went to forwarding agents for transport to Switzerland and, after Baa's calls, a lot to Sticky Sid who thought Christmas had come around early.

After having spoken at great length by phone with Antonia, Baa finally determined that the officials who'd visited her before the customs raid on the neighbors were definitely not customs and definitely were spooks, either Special Branch as she'd originally said or something weightier . Now Baa was a guy with a lot of contacts, some of them very serious indeed, but he couldn't get any sort of handle on why the Special Branch would be concerned with him. He figured Stroeder, the banker, might know something, but despite the volume of business his bank had received from our little consortium, Stroeder would say nothing.

Baa also noticed something strange that he couldn't put down to coincidence—all the time we'd been processing silver into palladium the price of the latter had been rising toward a peak 800 percent above its mid-1990s level.

World consumption of the metal was rising and Moscow had been slow in signing export authorizations but, as far as could be determined, South African and Canadian mines were producing flat out and selling into the market. Added to that was the fact that, due to the incentive of very high price levels, recovery from scrap was increasing worldwide. Those continuing high prices could have just testified to a healthy demand from consumers except for the fact, and Baa felt this was too extraordinary to be coincidental, that just after our operation effectively finished, the price of palladium started to fall steeply. During the couple of years I'd been gone the price had fallen back down to less than 3,500 GBP a kilo although demand for it had continued unabated. Were others now transmuting it? No, it didn't seem so despite the chance a couple of governments had maybe figured out what we or somebody had done.

"Before you ask, Rick, your money's quite safe—Stroeder asked about you a couple of times, but we each told him you were busy and he accepted that. These days Alexei's such a big wheel no banker is going to upset him if it can be avoided."

"But you said you thought Stroeder knew something and wasn't saying— couldn't Alexei lean on him ?" The idea that I knew a multi-billionaire was slightly inflating.

"Alexei will die of old age one day. The world's banks won't because, as you well know, the game of government can't go on without an inces-tuous relationship with banks. No, Stroeder will do cartwheels for Alexei, I'm sure, but not if it meant giving what could be classified economic information."

"Okay, Baa, let's jump sideways a bit now—why do you suppose Pyotr told me not to phone you before I got here?"

"Let's take a stroll," Baa got up and fetched a sheepskin coat of his for me to wear and he put some sort of quilted thing on before leading me out into the bright autumn air. Nature's colors beyond beautiful and the season's smell of death and decay as the cycle progresses spoke to me only of Spring's rebirth drawing closer by the moment. We strolled down to a stream bridged by a couple of old railway sleepers and then we mounted a gentle slope that culminated in a tree-line about four hundred meters away. He brought me yet more up to date.

• • •

Baa had taken himself down to Wiltshire to quietly recuperate; too much had happened too quickly for him to deal with emotionally and intellectually. "And come to that, spiritually, too," he'd remarked aloud to himself one bright February morning whilst walking the field that sloped up to the wood. He reached his favorite seat, the tree that 100 years before had been struck by lightning and losing most of its trunk, had felt it prudent to grow almost at right angles for a meter or so before ascending again.

His feet dangled just off the ground, and his melancholy was exactly that; it lacked any hint of self-pity as he reflected on the events of the past one and a half years. These had apparently cost him his friend and business partner and that man's woman. It was now over a month since Rick had drunk Pan's infusion and become comatose, blue, transparent, and then, as Baa termed it to himself, *reopaqued*.

Then Paul and Isabelle had arrived unannounced. They apparently accepted what Baa told him, which was everything except the specifics of what they had been doing at the unit. Paul knew that pushing for the backstory wouldn't bring Rick out of his coma, and a conscious Rick was the only way to find out for sure what had happened to Teresa. Isabelle had sensed immediately that Baa was telling the truth and that he was in great distress, his physical wounds the least of his hurt. She and Paul stayed at the farmhouse for three nights; she cooked for them, and they discussed what to do.

Baa had put Rick on the best life-support equipment and regime that money could buy 1,500 kilometers away in a Swiss clinic. On the thirty-fifth day after drinking the infusion, connected to a bank of monitors and nursed twenty-four seven, Rick had vanished when that night's nurse, Paul, Isabelle, and Merck were all in the room. Baa's mindset had ensured the room was on CCTV and the tapes had been analyzed by the best electronics people he could find but to no avail. One moment Rick was in his cot all wired up and then he was not. Nobody noticed the monitors had continued function for a minute or two after he'd vanished.

The local police had to be brought in and their investigation was thorough: it led them to conclude that the missing man, who had apparently suffered only from being unconscious, had left of his own accord whilst not being watched and the clinic had either lost or altered the tapes to cover up their not having kept him under sufficient observation.

That the meticulous Swiss police had evidently not followed the case beyond that point was unheeded by any of them.

Separate experts hired by Baa and by Paul were to conclude the tape must have been digitally spliced yet could find not the slightest evidence of this; they were doing no more than producing a theory to fit the actuality. Baa had hired a lot of private detection, but Rick had disappeared as if by evaporation. Alexei checked the tapes but likewise found nothing. Pyotr suggested Rick was safe, but offered no evidence for that view. Baa, now newly traumatized, supposed Pyotr was just trying to offer some human comfort. Baa missed Rick more than he would have supposed. As to where Teresa, pregnant with Rick's unborn child, had gone, he had no news or intuition; he just hoped and somehow believed they were alive "or at least not dead" he mused not noticing how bizarre that thought was.

After the tragic events the unit had been effectively closed down and production had not been set up and restarted elsewhere. Once Baa was sufficiently physically recovered, Pyotr, Alexei, Ilya, and Galena had come down to the farm. Something immense hung in the atmosphere while they talked and they'd decided to stop transmuting for an indefinite period. Each felt they'd not do it again for each had felt the immensity lighten as soon as the decision to delay had been agreed. Pyotr and Galena had then apparently left England and he'd not heard from them. Ilya had stayed at the farm for a couple of weeks but when Baa's injuries improved he'd left and joined Alexei. Baa, Alexei and Ilya stayed in irregular contact. Anxious to attract as little attention as possible after Rick's disappearance, the three of them met and agreed that the unit should be emptied of all the processing equipment by Alexei and Ilya, the last T-shirts would be sent to Ukraine, due tax payments would be made by the accountants and the companies put into voluntary liquidation. They paid off the rent for the balance of the lease because one of Rick's businesses had been responsible for it and none of them wanted to load anything more on to the unconscious shoulders of this man who'd suffered such tragedy and was now missing. There was nothing left that should trigger a fiscal or material investigation.

As such thoughts and memories ran through his mind, four eyes watched Baa from a superbly constructed hide barely fifty paces away. The UK government lets its spooks contract active and retired SAS and SBS personnel for all sorts of tasks. This was the third day the two men had been observing Baa and his house from the edge of the wood. Each man only left the hide for minimal exercise and to bury small plastic bags of excreta in the dead of night, as did the second two-man team secreted by the track that led from the farmhouse to the public road. Neither team knew why the authorities were interested in this lone, seemingly peaceful, middle-aged man; they sent half-second bursts of digitally encoded reports every six hours detailing his doing nothing much. Their incoming messages had been restricted to acknowledgements of receipt of their reports.

Unbeknown to either team was the observance of them, in more guises than sanity would permit acceptance of, by Pan; the effect of his presence had been limited to the odd unexplainable shiver each man would suddenly experience or the hairs raising on the backs of necks. These men were dedicated within and highly trained without; they were equipped with some of the most sophisticated listening and viewing technology yet manufactured and each was armed with a Makarov pistol and a hunting knife. Late one chill afternoon while Baa dozed under Chateau blahblah's influence, they got orders to take him to a particular place; they were to use Baa's own vehicle to transport him there.

On the assumption that Baa must be somehow deadly—for what other reason would four experts be detailed to snatch him—they did it in the early evening's gloom and by the book. As two entered the farmhouse through upper windows, the others waited. They signaled the house was empty save their target, and then the other two rushed in and stuck a hypodermic in Baa before he'd properly woken up. Plunger depressed and he was sent straight back to lala. Even if not drugged, from his position on the floor in the back of his own car, he'd never have seen the herd of deer that suddenly appeared in the narrow farm track as the driver came around a bend at sixty. Its bonnet collapsed progressively just as it had been designed to do and a lot of its impact with several tons of protein was thus absorbed. Not wearing seatbelts, perhaps some oddness of fate ensured each of the four spooks were horribly impaled by antlers as the car slid on blood and mangled bodies into a ditch. Baa was pulled from the wreck by Pan and laid on the ground as the last vestiges of daylight finally faded from the sky.

No insect nor arachnid nor bird nor animal bothered as sleep started to heal Baa. Wakened by predawn coldness, he crawled a few yards away from the wreckage of death and Pan appeared with a cup of pungent-smelling liquid. Baa drank it, vomited and involuntarily evacuated his bowels. Pan handed him a second cup that was full of water which Baa, his back now resting against a tree, sipped. He felt a great surge of strength as dawn broke and unperturbed by his own and death's stench surveyed the scene. "They're all dead?" he asked indicating the human and animal bodies in and around the wrecked car.

"All have passed," Pan replied before striding off.

Finding his mobile phone was intact, Baa dialed a lawyer's mobile number before making a 999 call, thus initiating nearly three weeks of mental and physical abuse by an intelligence service, several interdepartmental shit storms in and around Whitehall including some feverish activity at the Foreign Office. Baa had gone into that situation smelling like a cesspit and emerged as bright spring water with a handsome if not extravagant compensation payment and a few heavy names that owed him favors.

At the approach of winter's depth he went to Spain intending to spend a couple of months at a newly purchased villa near the country's southern tip. Luxurious compared to the farmhouse its comforts failed to soothe him, but the ex-beauty queen's didn't. Although no longer young, her physical attributes remained as did her self-centeredness, and these combined with a pleasing lack of malice to make her attractively vague and undemanding. That setting suns backlit the coast of Africa just across the sea rapidly ceased to thrill him and, after ten days, Baa took them both back north.

She knew it was a mixture of his generosity and his need that would keep her at the farm for a while. She didn't know why she was not revolted by Baa's strange large friend and she didn't want to know why so much of her felt such an attraction toward him. This large one spoke to her in a curious old-mannered Spanish one day and told her she would leave in the spring and not for a second had it occurred to her that anything else could have been the case.

One evening several inches of snow fell and within the large living room old-fashioned radiators maintained the temperature while the open wood-fire Baa had insisted on lighting ate oxygen. She knew it pleased Baa to burn fallen wood this way although why he went around his land picking it up himself was beyond her comprehension. The man was clearly wealthy, she knew of wealth and men, and it showed in the way he carried himself; yet he chose to be here in the middle of nowhere passing hours outside in this cold countryside each day and in this old house each evening. They consumed excellent wine and, surprisingly, the simple foods he cooked tasted delicious, and his sexual requirements were not unpleasant.

Looking out on to the full moonlit land she sipped her wine "The snow has made everything so beautiful – what must the far, far north be like?"

Baa started to tell her about the Arctic and the Antarctic, neither of which he'd been to, and Pan sat on the far side of the room listening as Baa meandered from the factual towards the philosophical

"…the huskie pulling the mapmakers sledge knows of no purpose beyond holding its pack position and avoiding the whip" Baa told the beauty queen who'd drunk a lot less than he "…and a tick on that dog's body……" he tried pacing across the room for effect but tripping on a rug's edge over-corrected and collided with a chair. As his body fell to the floor he continued "…similarly our species – Ow!"

"Ai! Pobresito !" she exclaimed hastening to him "but you are so clever querido, you did not spill any wine." he discovered the glass, its stem still clasped between forefinger and thumb, was full.

Across the room Pan refilled his own glass.

When the snow was long gone and new leaves were preparing to burst out on the trees, Baa wrote a check and drove her to where a small jet waited at a small airport. A little over three hours later, and still girlishly thrilled at how handsome was his check, she again stood on the Iberian Peninsula.

•   •   •

"It's quite possible that Pyotr saying not to phone was more to protect him than any other reason," Baa said and stopped to look back toward the house.

"He has some sort of trouble?" I asked.

"Not with this world."

"Baa, I've been through stuff you can't imagine these last couple of …well years it would seem…I'd better put in my two pennies' worth now." I told him about the blue place and Paris as we walked through a couple of overgrown fields.

He gave no indication of doubting my sanity,

"When I saw the autumn leaves I was shocked, when you told me it was two and a half years I figured a lot of stuff needs rethinking. A bit trippy for you, Baa, but for me it's literally life and death."

He understood exactly what I was talking about, and being Baa, said, "Well fuck today's siesta. We've got to see if something can be done. I can't run around looking after business at my age and condition. You're needed here, old son." His bluster both saddened and yet somehow gave me heart.

I drove us over to the restaurant where I'd first been introduced to Pyotr, which it turned out Baa had owned 55 percent of at that time but had subsequently sold. Most of the staff had remained and now welcomed him warmly; the new owner had gone for more covers but by no stretch of the imagination could you have said we had to slum it with our two hundred quid lunch. Between courses I asked, "And what about Dave? Did anything ever come to light?"

"Nothing at all. Ellie said the French police had closed the file...she'd e-mailed me a couple of times asking about you and Teresa." He looked a bit uncomfortable.

"And...?"

"I fudged it...told her you'd had personal stuff to deal with and had gone away. She knew I wasn't being open, but she was too wise to push." Now he looked even less comfortable, and after a few moments he continued, "She's a friend of yours I know, and I feel she's not a bad person in herself but...but she seems to...," Baa made a wry grin. "She's a wet dream with a computer inside, it's like she's stood too close to something." I recalled Paul's comments. "She said she was in LA writing scripts but she didn't say if it was TV or movies; she sounded like she was okay."

I didn't know that over a year ago Ellie had married the then newly divorced Mr. LA. She had, she'd told herself, every reason to be happy: she was rich and doors were not only open to her but powerful occupants of the dominions beyond those doors beckoned and courted. Ellie was discovering that she had no great talent for acting but loved to write. Her screenplay outlines were good and attracting serious attention; she found though that her ideas worked only at their own speed and realized she'd never cope with the pressure of studio writing. She'd work alone. This didn't bother her for she was in an ideal situation but then one LA night the dream came. She stood halfway up a sloping suburban street and a gray dog, she took it to be an Alsatian, was walking up the hill from her left. It was on the other side of the road from where she stood, and it was on the pavement and leading a double line of young schoolchildren. There seemed to be no traffic on the roadway itself. She became aware that the dog was a large gray wolf; as it drew level she started to run across the road toward it. There was an excitement and a fear in her.

She awoke. "Well that's as weird as they come," she told herself and slipping from the bed went out on to the room's veranda where a realization struck her. "Weirder yet. Oh dear, Ellie, if you're going to do this, you will do it nicely." She stood for a long time as the sky grew light, a buzzer sounded and there was movement in the room behind. The bulk of her husband blocked her view of the Pacific. "Remember we've got money-guys tonight." She didn't reply with words. He said, "I know, I know—but that's serious money I seek to seduce my angel." Leaning forward he kissed her forehead. It was the kiss of a busy man in love in a busy man's way.

As Ellie passed her day getting polished by a variety of expensive processes in salons of Byzantine excesses she became ever more consciously aware that she was going to divorce her husband—leaving him might be kinder but would not serve her purposes. "His only real danger in this world is contracting rectal gingivitis—he'll survive," she assured herself. "But what's more important is that I do."

Not at all sure where these thoughts were coming from, Ellie was absolutely certain she would act on them. That afternoon she lunched without her usual half-bottle of champagne and siesta'd without her usual pre-nap joint.

The dream was startlingly vivid and Teresa, to her chagrin, looked quite incredible. Ellie followed her into a summer garden and sat down next to her on a cushioned bench. She felt Teresa's arm around her waist, and Teresa's hand flattened on her stomach. The touch was pleasant without being sexual, comforting without being motherly: it was a very female contact. Teresa said, "Look," and looking Ellie saw again the wolf leading the column of schoolchildren.

At her husband's party that evening Ellie was spectacular. No pair of eyes, regardless of sexual orientation or business agenda, was able to disguise their appreciation of her appearance. Already there as she entranced, and she did entrance rather than just enter, he strode forward to elabo-rately kiss her hand. "You are a jewel," he'd told her and meant it.

• • •

"Rick, do you want to reach Ellie?"

"I was just curious." In fact I'd not thought of her until a few min-utes earlier when the place's evidently loyal regulars Mr and Mrs Aged Rock Star were being shown to table. Albeit without the New Orleans girl whose name I couldn't remember they seemed quite sparky. Mr Aged wore a loose-fitting black suit printed all over with small white skulls and crossed bones and I wondered if that could that be homage to the Wasted Knights. "That logo there," I nodded toward the suit, "Is that band still going?"

"Don't think so. I believe one died and the band broke up, but that logo is a fashion thing with the kids for the moment—maybe something the band stirred up is surfacing again. A while back somebody said it reoc-curs in fashion periodically, but then it seems to me that most things do." He looked up from the menu. "I did have a thought about it though."

"And what was that thought?" I asked.

"Well, we always associate it with pirates and death but suppose that's not what it was intended to signify at all?" As he said this I felt a kind of echo. He went on. "Suppose it's a badge or a flag or a sign intended to indicate human beings." I began to raise a question but he went on. "Flags are used to differentiate groups—now if you had humans and nonhu-mans needing to identify themselves to their own and to differentiate themselves to each other, let's say in terms of territory then the skull and crossed bones is an ideal symbol."

"Tell me why." I'd forgotten my wine.

"If you used a human face, it would be too expressive—think smi-ley face or sad face. Too much would be conveyed and that could be as misleading or dangerous for the conveyor as to the viewer. What humans have is a skull and it's definitely a human skull, couldn't be anything else, so it indicates human beings yet it's expressionless."

"Do you mean as opposed to Neanderthals? Like a sort of sign our ancestors used to designate Homo sapiens territory or maybe extrater-restrials?" Something unidentified within stirred.

"Maybe something subtler, Rick. Suppose there was another dimension to our space and time and that we can't see its inhabitants clearly and they can't see us clearly. Suppose there have been people here seeking to function within that other dimension—suppose they felt they needed to clearly differentiate themselves from other creatures alien to that place."

On the drive over, I'd pulled into a garage for petrol and I noticed the price per liter was a lot higher than I recalled it being. Back on the road, I asked, "Oil price up or has the government had the auditors in and upped the tax?" Baa laughed. "No, they're still not bothered about balancing the books yet, but the Americans have occupied the Middle East and are fucking up Iraq."

"Recently ?"

"You went transparent springtime 2001, right?" I nodded and he continued "So I guess you don't know - airliners were flown into the World Trade Towers, killing nearly three thousand people."

"You mean in New York?"

"Exactly."

"Fuck—by whom?"

"Muslim extremists, say the Americans." he dead-panned. We'd been stopped at an intersection, waiting for a chance to cross a main road to where our country route continued southward on the far side, so I was able to look at him and raise an eyebrow. "Yeah, right but don't bother," he continued. "The world's awash with rumours and the only thing you can be sure of is that it's got spooks written all over it."

I accelerated across the main road and we were then on a pleasant lane again. On our right was a large mixed wood which seemed to exude a feeling of sanity that washed in through the open windows. "So these airliners were America's excuse for grabbing Iraq?"

"In as much," Baa was relighting his cigar. "But it's about China. They were saying to the Chinese 'Look, we're fucking serious hard ballers, so don't mess with us. They were also saying to their own people 'Democracy and the strict Rule of Law hasn't protected you so cut us some slack on accountability to the people.' They run covert prison camps all over these days."

"You think our wise rulers set up an attack on New York?"

"Count the beans—three thousand American dead to control the Middle East and another few thousand American dead each year to keep it is a fucking bargain if you're one of the power-mad cunts that run things. You know how the world works." he puffed so that the scent of Cuba mingled not unpleasantly with that of Dorset woodland. "Don't suppose it's far-fetched, Rick, when this little island," he gestured at the countryside, "used to run the planet, it did so under its monarchs who were blood relatives of other countries' monarchs but that didn't stop them having wars that killed millions. Power is power, and people like you and I wouldn't even qualify as junior players in that game. Just to keep the situation in total chaos, the U.S. president announced a crusade against his enemies."

Unsure I'd heard right, I had Baa repeat it then asked, "But why didn't he just tell the Arabs they'd either got the US army today and they'd take the oil at full market price or the Chinese army taking it tomorrow maybe at a price they'll fix?"

"Because the fundamentalists just might welcome the Chinese army. To the fundamentalists the price of oil would come a very long second. The Chinese in Iraq would not only get the region's oil, but they'd confirm the Kurds autonomy, which would destabilize eastern Turkey as its Kurds joined them. A country called Kurdistan would come into existence and might duly supply its oil to China. China in Iraq could put an end to the Saudi royals whose wealth distribution is a major support of those that run America. People might buy Renminbi Chinese bonds rather than US dollar T Bonds. China in Iraq could buy a whole Arab generation's goodwill simply by destroying Israel or giving the Arabs the weapons to do it themselves. If Israel is destroyed so is the underpinning of American Christian fundamentalist theology. The American fundamentalist Christians, and the millions of ordinary Christians, would say the Bible was not true. Their worldview would dissolve, their structure would buckle and there'd be mayhem. The states would disunite and become independent areas and the US would be no more. Then I suppose there'd be a sort of rerun of European history but hi-tech. Think about that, Rick. Millions of Americans take the Bible literally, and it says Israel exists by divine authority. If Israel were destroyed, millions of Americans would stop believing that the Bible is the Word of God— America would destabilize and fragment. The western politicians said Iraq was developing weapons of mass destruction, what they meant was that Iraq itself was becoming a weapon of mass destruction." He adjusted his position on the car-seat then continued. "China would have got itself about fifty clear years to dominate the planet and make itself impregnable. It would have replaced America as the destination for the world's material riches and would build itself into that new world's single super power."

There was a ring to what he was saying. If China went that route, unopposed by America, it would probably cost it less than a million lives—would a nation even blink at that price for owning the world?

Baa stuffed the cigar butt into the car's ashtray. "Think power, Rick. Those people will murder and sell their souls for it because it's what they do. They learned long ago that the more outrageous their actions the less likely Joe Public is to believe they've done what they've done. And even if they have to eat newborn babies to serve their ends, they'll do it for they can always tell themselves that if they don't some other fucker will."

I'd slowed down to avoid a pheasant brainlessly wandering near the middle of the narrow lane. I sensed rather than saw Baa peer intently at me; after a bit he said, "There's one other bit that's interesting—as the Americans began invading Iraq, the museum there was looted. It could have been done by all sorts of groups, but the stuff that went was most of the Mesopotamian stuff—very old civilization that. Could have been stolen to protect them or could have been done to hide them away."

"Stuff there that might undo accepted history ?" I asked.

"Perhaps that was another weapon of mass destruction."

Several hours later and with our lunches digesting I drove us back slowly north to Wiltshire. The sky darkened and Baa pretended not to be dozing in the seat next to me. It was a perfect opportunity to awaken and accuse him of extreme flatulence, but I didn't. My friend had aged a bit more than the two and a half years that had elapsed.

That night exhaustion mercifully overtook me again so that conscious thoughts of Teresa and my son were blotted out before they could tear into my heart. Sleep came quickly, and I saw my son and without thinking rushed to him; then somehow, it was as if I was him. It was as if I was still myself but somehow perceiving and feeling what he perceived and what he felt.

I was approaching what became gradually revealed as a symmetrical upright cross with numbers on each spoke, then I saw that there was writing, over the numbers, on each of its four spokes. On one was written Intuiting, on another, Sensing, on another, Thinking, and on the last, Feeling. As I finished reading these words, the cross moved into a horizontal position and started to bend; its center moved upward, as its arms moved downward, and then curved inward to touch each other. It had thus become a perfect spheroid with the original center now one pole and the ends of the four spokes joined as the opposite pole; the writing had become slightly distorted but was still clearly readable. The spheroid shape developed opaqueness and minor contortions occurred; parts of its surface swelled out and became extraverted whilst others contracted becoming introverted.

I became aware of light as I now noticed one side of the sphere was bathed in light and the other was in shadow. On the lightened hemisphere the sides of its protuberances and depressions were highlighted as their various sides received more or less light depending on their orientation. On the darkened hemisphere some of the irregularities of its structure seemed occasionally illuminated by a glow perhaps from within its interior. As soon as I became aware of this either I reversed very quickly or the sphere shrank—or it could have been that both of these things occurred simultaneously. That now tiny sphere was instantly joined by myriad others, and the memory of the atmosphere in the Paris house when Pyotr had had me draw in charcoal on the wall came to me. I recollected the moving spirals, one going inwards and down towards the infinitely small whilst the other went outwards and upwards towards the infinitely large. In front of me the now countless numbers of spheres were on an upward and outward spiral. Then I was myself again and stood next to my son, he smiled then was gone. I awoke and laying in quiet darkness felt contentment.

The next morning was overcast and looking out of the window I saw Baa giving directions to a couple of men who'd apparently arrived with an open lorry laden with plants; three or four others used a mini-excavator and a tractor.

Later I carried my coffee outside and seeing me he said, "Forgot all about this with the excitement of you showing up."

"Gardening or farming?" I gestured at the activity.

"Sort of both—I'm putting in a...what I mean is, a herb garden's being put in."

He seemed very hands-on with this project, so I told him I needed to see Alexei. Baa handed me an ordinary mobile saying, "In the names section, there are a lot for him, use AL main, it should find him wherever he is—although given your experiences perhaps we should qualify that a bit."

"Mobiles work here nowadays then?" I asked.

"Put my own booster aerial in years back."

The excavator was making a lot of noise, so I took Baa's phone into the house and made the call.

Within thirty-six hours, Alexei embraced me where Chile's Atacama Desert region met the Pacific. I was not jet-lagged for the second of his two personal airbuses had been leaving Moscow when he took my relayed call in the small hours of Chile's night. He had contacted the plane and had its over-the-pole flight plan re-filed to divert southwest and pick me up. Let me tell you, everything else being equal, living aboard such an aircraft all the time would not be much of a hardship. Alexei had eased up on the modest lifestyle thing.

That large plane was fitted out like a fair-sized apartment, including a gym and a twelve meter pool—alright so the pool ceiling was a bit low, and when there was turbulence all its water had to be pumped into a special tank to stop it slopping about, but it was a pool. Few people get to go swimming six miles up at mach 0.9.

At Santiago de Chile, Ilya waits at the bottom of the steps, hugs me tearfully, tells me he's so happy to see me again, and to know I'm alive. Then he proceeds to nearly kill both of us as he, now the proud possessor of some sort of license, flies a smaller jet out over the ocean, drops down to what feels like nine and a half inches above the Pacific, rollers, and screams southward to my meeting with Alexei. "What did the French do to your head," I asked, and he roared with laughter; my smile was for the gleam of exhilaration I could see in his eyes. Ilya, the eternal youth, and his sheer enthusiasm with being.

Nor did Alexei have entirely dry eyes, and I felt his feelings and barely got out "Russian pussy " before he did the hugging thing. Touched as I obviously was, in fact very touched if you want to know, by this, I didn't understand why Pyotr hadn't told them I was alive. Alexei explained that whilst they would occasionally hear from him, they'd no way of initiating contact, no addresses or phone numbers or even an e-mail address. "Be sure that I have considerable resources and can call on a lot of influence Rick—I have tried but failed to locate him or Galena! It is extraordinary, but then I find more and more that things are in this world."

We were now in a prefabricated site office three walls of which had architectural plans and aerial photographs all but covering them: the third wall was bare except for one single large black and white photo of a slim man standing in a roadway holding what looked like a white plastic shop-ping bag. As Alexei had been speaking my eyes had been drawn to this picture. In fact it was impossible not to look at it, and I felt a momentary dizziness. A glass of ice-cold water was put into my hand, and I sipped this and sat down on a large office chair.

The reason we were in the middle of nowhere was that, apart from property and banking, Alexei was now into industry and China's con-tinual easing of state controls meant he was positioning himself for a lot of vertical integration; raw materials from the desert shipped via a planned port across the Pacific ocean into his own processing plants and factories on the other side. We were to finish early that day and have a catered dinner at the prefabricated building Alexei occupied when there. "Big honor to you, Rick," Ilya advised. "Alexei never stops for anything these days."

Alexei was still in partnership with Wen, and it was some Nth cousin of the guy who oversaw the cooking of the best Chinese meal I'd tasted anywhere ever bar Pyotr's in Paris. When he came to ask how the food was I complimented him on his efforts and he told me it was a pleasure to cook here. He enthused about the continent of South America hav-ing the space and the facilities to grow everything organically "I hope that lasts for you" I said recalling the millions upon millions of acres being farmed in Brazil on the other side of the Andes mountains. Both Alexei and Ilya wanted to know where I'd disappeared to for the last few years and, thinking to tell the metallurgist-industrialist-banker -property billionaire and his of-this-earth relative my story as simply as possible, I related it to them in reverse order.

In Chile's Atacama it was springtime although nothing bloomed in that dessert of nitrates and outside a strong wind was getting up as I told the two Russians of how I'd only the other day learned from Baa of the length of time I'd been away. Then I detailed my meetings with Pyotr in Paris and how he and Galena had both changed so much. Each listened intently without interrupting as I explained that those meetings had all apparently occurred well within the last month.

"And the twenty-nine months before that, Rick ?" Ilya asked. "Baa had said you'd just disappeared from a clinic and we had the cctv tapes checked."

I said nothing then Alexei spoke, "We both thought there was more to it. But we trusted Baa, and he seemed very upset, so we concluded he genuinely didn't know where you had gone or what had happened to you."

"I'll tell you what happened to me as far as I know," I said. "But please understand, I'm not mad, I'm not fucking about and this whole situation is more than serious to me—it's absolutely vital." I had their complete attention "You may think that what I experienced is just some sort of psychological compensation for things but it's not. Please suspend any disbelief enough to consider what I tell you." I drained my glass of red wine. "You see, I desperately need any input you might be able to make." I didn't tell them about the infusion Baa had prepared but did tell them everything else about the blue place, it was late when Ilya showed me where I could sleep but I couldn't. Jetlag kept me awake through the desert night and I arose to a dawn filled with light and vegetable breakfast soup. I return to the bed and slept until late afternoon.

The multibillionaire had put a lot on hold that day and just the two of us sat in his office, within the prefabricated building, while I drank strong black coffee. What he told me answered Baa's puzzlement concerning palladium prices. The process, Alexei's process, you'll recall was a spin off from some 1930s Czech antigravity experiments that the Nazis had continued with out in Ukraine nearly a decade later during WWII. Gravity is generally thought to be a property of mass, but you might equally suppose mass is a property of gravity. The brilliant Alexei transmuted kilos of silver into palladium down in Ukraine, then at the pilot plant in Kaliningrad and then we transmuted many tons at our unit to the west of London under his direction. However, unbeknown to any of us, as fast as we turned silver into palladium with our process that very same process was causing other people's stockpiles of palladium to transmute into silver. There was confusion, accusations, lawsuits, and some lives were lost: the unforeseeable was occurring and the price rose 800 percent. What about supply and demand? Well, we weren't a mine that wrote contracts with users; we only sold directly or indirectly into the world market and there, as in all markets, are speculators. Buy today and sell in two days at a profit a couple of times and you encourage yourself to increase your rate of speculation. Speculators start to hold ever larger quantities. That means ever larger quantities are held off the market and thus the price rises. Our manipulation of matter indirectly ignited a lot of speculation in the very metal we were producing.

"It took me a long time to discover what had been happening Rick. I only knew for sure a year ago and I didn't tell anybody else, even Ilya." Alexei explained. "I calculated ignorance might protect."

"And you tell me now?" I said.

"Because of several things. It's partly my fault you're in the situation you're in, and I more than feel for you. Also I want to let you know that I believe what you've experienced most probably is objectively true. If I've learned anything from our...our venture as you might say, it's that very little is as it seems to be."

"That's what I'd call an understatement Alex—as for the blame, you should know I swallow an extraordinary amount of bitterness, but it's what's happened and nobody ever intended my loss. One way or another I have my family with me." I noticed my right hand touched my heart. "I just know that. Tell me, is there anyway what happened in the London unit could be run in reverse?"

"I have thought a lot about that, in fact I started thinking about it as soon as the disaster occurred. There's no way to reverse it, and actually there's no way to even repeat it." He looked right into my eyes. "Yes, Rick, it was tried, and a lot of damage was done."

"Rather more than just a lot of damage has been done to me, Alexei!"

"The whole rig was retried near Kaliningrad—you remember? Where you first saw the process?" I nodded, and he went on, "It didn't work. I rebuilt the equipment here, and again it didn't work. Eventually I understood why but not how. What I am trying to tell you is that it only worked at a certain time during some sort of conjunctions that have passed..."

"Conjunctions of what ?" I felt myself growing annoyed by how relaxed he was.

"I am sorry, very sorry, but I am trying to explain...I do not know what these conjunctions are of. In older times, it was supposed they were planetary conjunctions, but I think that is because in those times planetary conjunctions were the only things people could think to relate things to. Come, get up and come." He stood up and walked over to the door. I got up and joined him and he ushered me outside into the, now, cold night air. He called to Ilya in Russian and a few moments later the nearby lights were all switched off and our eyes started to adjust.

Overhead the absolutely clear dessert air and cloudless sky revealed billions of stars. "When you look up at all that it is not so difficult to understand why alchemists and herbalists put so much emphasis on conjunctions, is it?"

"No, but planetary conjunctions reoccur" I said.

"Of course, planetary conjunctions reoccur—ours is a relatively small solar system within one arm of a galaxy itself within a vast universe subject to physical laws we are only just beginning to glimpse. What we did, and I think others have done or tried to do, required some conjunctions far beyond those within our particular solar system." Alexei sighed and there was a weariness in that sigh, and weariness was something I'd never ever associated with Alexei.

A terrible certainty emerged from somewhere within and it was as if I understood with complete clarity what Pyotr had been explaining to me. Alexei put a large hand on my shoulder. "Rick, I promise you that other than the lives of myself and my family, I would do anything, give anything to do what you want—it's that it can't be done by design."

We went back inside and, lighting restored, drank some tea then Alexei got up again and walked over to the thickly glazed window to stare out across the nitrate dessert. "I've got a lot of interests, not just in China but Japan, Europe and the US; biotechnology and nanotech labs working on the most incredible possibilities! Just let your mind run free and suppose, think four-seater horses that consumed grass, ran at 200 kilometres per hour, self-repaired and self-replicated," he turned and faced me "Our species is going to have to learn to deal with vast amounts of amazing new information soon—it will destabilize a lot of people and societies. Sometimes I wonder if that's why there is such an upsurge in religious fundamentalism—comforting beliefs for the fearful to cling to perhaps. " He turned back to stare out of the window again. "Then I ask myself if the coming world is going to be any different from this, from the American world—lots of positive if blind progress whilst China races toward the top spot just like America a hundred years ago. Then an implosion as it stops progressing and becomes a glutton."

"Glutton ?"

"It's the right word—in the future students of American history will watch the Simpsons. Homer symbolizes it perfectly, and everything that flows from a society's need to keep all its Homers quiescent—much becomes pointless as the mind-fucking increases. "

Having been out of touch with so much I asked "China's free from religious madness isn't it ?"

"For the time being. Remember crusading communism is only just subsiding. I dare to hope that when China starts to become satiated with material wealth it will avoid the terrible mistakes of encouraging short-term attention spans and dis-education. I dare to hope that anaesthetic religions won't develop.

I was able to see something; it was subtle. Alexei's business had an omnipresent logo. It was on each building, each vehicle, the airbus and on the little jet Alexei had flown me in on and as well the other aircraft, a propeller plane and two helicopters that operated from the site. The logo was a stylized version of a man carrying a bag.

The next day Ilya flew us east across the desert and through mountain passes to another small airfield that also served a construction site. It was at the edge of a plateau that looked roughly circular and to be a couple of miles across. There were some simple wood-framed buildings, a generator and a dozen or so people grinding large stones; they ignored us. "Did you ever hear of the megalithic yard?" Alexei asked.

"No."

"It's a supposedly constant measurement used five thousand years ago in Britain, Ireland and continental Europe when megalithic structures were laid out. The builders had some understanding about the importance of the relative positioning and sizes of things in the solar system." He suddenly sounded passionate. "You know we live in a soup of energy which is there for free but we also live in ourselves and are programmed to seek control. To seek to control everything including the supply of energy. So instead of using what is freely available we extract oil and gas and play politics over energy and fight wars over energy - kill and maim children, destroy the environment and as usual, for our species, create an all but zero-sum game so that control can be exercised..." whilst he spoke we'd been walking out towards the middle of the plateau where there were a couple of four-wheel drive vehicles with low trailers attached. People, who mostly seemed to be Chinese, had apparently been siting finished stones. Their work done for that day, the only sounds had been those of the gentle breeze but suddenly the thunder of a massive twin rotor helicopter echoed across the plateau as it appeared from the far side with a huge rock slung beneath it. It lowered the rock, cables were unhooked and the aircraft moved off a hundred meters and landed. Some of the stoneworkers lined up and to go aboard, others made their way toward the buildings.

"I realized we live inside a massive machine…"Alexei knelt and smacked his huge palms down on the ground "… this weighs around six thousand billion, billion, billion tons, rotates at fifteen hundred kilometers per hour and is moving through space at thousands of kilometers per hour for an eternity and it doesn't have an engine! Don't you get it Rick? It is part of an engine; a massive perpetual motion machine. It's using more energy in a millisecond than our entire species needs in millennia. We don't want for energy, just the wits to organize ourselves to take it."

"And taking it has something to do with megalithic yards?" I asked.

"Absolutely, far back in our history people were able to understand that they were just a small part of creation and so sought to take a little energy from the solar system other than eating the plants that ate sunshine and the other animals that ate the plants. They watched the night sky and realized that, although there's a fraction over three hundred and sixty-five days of the sun rising and setting in a year, there is rising and setting of the stars at night. From this they worked out, for their intellectual capacity was just as developed as ours, that not only were we not the physical center of our solar system but that the sun was not the center of the galaxy. Using observations of the skies, they calculated a measurement we call the megalithic yard, which relates perfectly to those measurements of the sun, moon, and earth."

A memory of something hovered elusively, but try as I might, I couldn't bring it to consciousness. I asked, "But wouldn't any measurement do? You can measure things in feet or meters but it won't alter their actual size or their relative proportions."

"Yes, of course, but the megalithic yard did it in as close to whole numbers as those people back then could achieve, and because it was calculated from the positions of the heavens, it was transportable—a person anywhere could reproduce it. Think about that Rick! To safeguard our measurements today pieces of platinum cut to those measurements and stored at zero degrees Celsius in various places around the world just as references. We've only been able to measure time with much accuracy for a few hundred years but people, thousands of years ago, could measure it by the movements of the heavens related to a piece of wood that they'd just cut up and trimmed with an axe!"

A light bulb came on in my head. "And timing as well as size and positioning is crucial!"

A large hand patted my back, "You have it."

Up on that plateau near the Chilean border, Alexei was constructing an energy device. It would have no moving parts in the sense of movement relative to the ground on which it stood or to its various components, but it would move as all things do relative to the other bodies within our solar system, which in turn move relative to the rest of our galaxy, which moves relative to other galaxies. He was doing it not to sell any energy that he obtained, he was doing it to see what would happen. He was the child that is father of the man who looked down and smiled at his efforts.

Alexei was speaking. "You know Einstein's preoccupation—his last years of continually contemplating light's properties?"

"Yeah, he said thinking about it took all his time and interest."

"He was looking at it from the world of matter."

"So?"

"He was thinking light had properties that were anomalies because matter was normal."

"So?"

"It is matter that has anomalies—light is the normality. I think that's the correct English word. Light is light is light. It is matter—perhaps matters plural that are the odd things, the transitory time-bound things. Light and movement are the constants—the basis of everything. That's why the universe conspires in productiveness, perhaps conditionally." His eyes were looking far away but then refocused on Ilya and me. "However the greatest human constant seems to be hunger, so let's go and eat. We'll stay up here tonight. There is plenty of spare accommodation."

Fresh crab-meat had come up in our plane and, along with excellent Chilean wine, cheered those who toiled in the bleak surroundings. Something of a party atmosphere developed. Feeling very tired I excused myself and, climbing into bed in one of the prefabricated huts, I recalled Ellie telling me knowledge of measurement was one of those things crusaders brought back from Jerusalem. I fell into a pleasant sleep. Outside the temperature had plummeted as it does in deserts, but more so here because we were a couple of thousand feet up. I awoke in the dark at about 3:00 A.M. local time, pulled on an anorak, and went outside for no reason I knew of other than the impulse to do so. I walked toward the structure that was about a quarter of a mile distant from the hut; the air felt freezing. Overhead an ocean of stars shone light from unimaginable distances, and times.

A security guard ran up from somewhere on the left but recognizing my face, said something in Chinese and waved me on. Trudging forward, I started to understand something of what Alexei had been saying about relative positions. Here was I, a mass of protein formed into the most complex organic system of conjoined molecules we know of, walking toward an artificial structure built by my own kind that corresponded in some sort of proportions to the universe in which we were: I and the structure contained mixtures of atoms composed of the same energies as the entire universe that stretched off in every direction toward infinity. The proportions of the structure I was approaching mimicked the proportions of some of the universe and the structure of my body. Some inner promptings—intuition or anima or shadowy complex—was urging me into the structure. Why resist? Why not resist? I'd already lost what I cared for. For the first time in my life, although I'd not mentioned nor hinted of this to Baa or to Alexei, I was in despair about what I wanted do with myself. Inside me was desolation and I was at a loss. What I cared for, what motivated me, lay somewhere within my heart yet was as far away as anything could be; it was in another dimension. Knowing this, I could only feel sympathy for those whose loved ones had perished. How did they cope? They grieved and relied on Nature's program to BE to keep them living.

These thoughts ended as I reached the structure and entered between the polished standing stones. They were much larger than they'd appeared when I'd viewed them in daylight. There was something else that was strange but I couldn't put my finger on right away. Then it hit me—the temperature inside the structure was several degrees warmer than the temperature outside. This was remarkable because it was completely open to the elements. Or was I getting feverish? No, for I stepped outside again and the air was instantly cooler.

To the east the new day's sun was completely blocked by the mountains, so the highest part of the sky directly overhead became light whilst its visually low levels to the west became relatively darker. I shivered and re-entered the structure and imagined starlight ricocheted off the megalith's uprights. An intense white light glowed to my right and I believed I heard Teresa speak, the voice said, "Rick, dying won't bring us together. Talk to Ellie, then you'll understand." I snapped out of the paralysis the voice had induced and flung myself forward into the now flickering light but was instantly thrown backward and upward by an energy of unnerving massivity. Unconscious, I lay with broken ribs and arm on the ground fifty meters outside the structure.

My son was older; he looked to be about seven.

"Dad, that man Alexei is right. You have to see that light and its speed are what's normal and that the world of matter is only true in itself."

I, the father, must ask my own wise child, "You mean matter is an aberration?"

Laughing he said, "I don't know that word."

"Something unnatural."

"Well it can't be unnatural or it wouldn't be, but I think I know what you mean—it's right where it is but only where it is. It's like if you could get two things that don't like each other close enough, they will like each other but only when they're very, very close. If you put them a little way apart, they stop liking each other. They push each other away."

"Thanks kid," I told him.

"Pleasure, Dad." He ran off after a bird or something.

I regained consciousness envisaging myself flat on my back and glued to the surface of the massive rotating sphere. I was in bed and full of pain-killer. Outside a night wind went about its business whilst a half moon inched across the star-filled sky exerting its gravitational pull and moving the oceans. I sipped some water from a plastic bottle and slept again.

"I'm off for a bit." My son went into the forest.

"He's grown so much, Teresa. A moment ago he was about seven, now he looks nearer ten."

"There're no years here, my darling. I'm thrilled to say it's always spring—or at least it feels that way." She kissed my lips, and perhaps her clothes fell away taking my cares with them.

Later our son returned with the ancestor. Teresa prepared food, and we three ate whilst the ancestor seemed to doze. Unbidden my son said, "Dad, I know you didn't really understand about light. I know I don't have enough words yet, but I thought of another way of explaining it. Do you want me to tell you?"

I simultaneously felt humility in myself and pride in him. "I'm rather counting on it," I told him.

"If a beam of light is alone, it makes a pattern on things. But if a beam of light feels a friend nearby, it makes something just light up—it gives something to its friend."

I awoke, fuzzy headed from fading anesthetic, to find there was a dull ache from my broken ribs and now splinted arm. I let myself drift back toward my dream. My family was long gone, everything was now an ocean in which I swam and breathed. Then some great wave must have swept overhead for I was turned and tumbled and carried along quite quickly for a while until I came to rest by an opening shell. I peered inside and was confronted by a pearl that spoke; it said, "The oyster is my world."

Soon another current carried me away from this gem of Wildean presumption and, as I moved, either I grew smaller or my power of sight increased for I could see the microscopic world in clarity and detail. As I watched all manner of tiny creatures I became aware of amoebas and single-celled brainless things actually constructing bell-shaped dwellings from minute sand grains! What was the anesthetic that made me feel part of everything at once? I awoke again, this time cold and ravenously hungry.

Ilya flew me up to Santiago de Chile, where a doctor determined I needed to stay on a drip in a clinic. Within a couple of days I felt stronger and I checked out to dine with Alexei and Ilya next to a surprisingly morose looking Pacific Ocean. "Would you be able locate someone for me?" I asked Alexei.

"I would certainly try," he said and, with a theatrical grin, he took out some sort of electronic notebook. "What is the name and last known location?"

• • •

I arrived at LAX and, after having my plaster cast x-rayed and ultra-sounded then the Chilean clinic's bills verified, taxied to Santa Monica where I'd booked an adequate and pleasant service apartment. I'd certainly no financial concerns, but I needed to take things slowly and avoid pressure. I didn't want to be around people busily spending thousands and thousands of dollars for hotel suites. Having more money than I needed and more sadness than I could bear really cut through the shit for me.

I slept off and on for a bit before wandering out; I got a coffee in a bookshop then crossed a couple of roads to stroll through the strip of park-garden behind the beach. Bums and vagrants and who knows what hang around here, one of them sits on the grass emitting alcohol fumes and suggestions of oral sex to a passing steel-limbed sixty-something female jogger. "Fuck off and die," she advises without breaking stride.

Walking on I peer out over the Pacific toward Asia and not for the first time wonder if any of this world is truly real. Later, down on the sand, I remove my shoes to paddle in the ocean.

That evening I eat alone at Michael's, just around the corner from the apartment. I feel low-grade malevolence. Recently seated with wife and adult daughter, he is middle-aged, prosperous, inordinately pleased with himself and yet in some mysterious way discombobulated by a man, me, dining alone at a nearby table. Previously I would have been untroubled by this but, having grown sensitive of late, I am very aware of the hatred welling from within his deep discomfort with life. I discover I'm pitying the guy, seeing too much of things from what I suppose to be his stand-point, and this absolutely has to stop. His wife and daughter go to freshen up. "Hey, you," I say loud enough for him but not the waiters to hear. He looks in my direction and at the same volume, I tell him, "Fuck off and die."

The women return and shepherded by waiters, he and his family fucks off to another part of the restaurant. His daughter glares in my direction, but his wife does not appear to be entirely displeased. There is that slightest of twinkles in her eyes.

"That's a bit embarrassing," I confide afterward in my waiter. "I've had those people in long-term family therapy. I'd no idea they ate here."

"Oh, I see, doctor…" he starts warily.

"Professor." I correct him.

"I'm sorry Professor," he gushes. "I don't recognize those people. I guess they've not been here before."

Eventually I made a call to Alexei, and within a couple of days I'd had the plaster removed and I was ringing the intercom on the gatepost of a house behind Venice Beach. The woman who came to the gate and let me in seemed to know who I was and that I needed a cup of tea.

"Ellie only rented this house from me," she answered the question I'd not asked. "Her own place is up at Montecito, but I guess she's not ready for it yet."

"I'm sorry I don't quite follow," I said. "But you make very nice tea." This was true for her brew comforted as her conversation confused.

"I'm sorry, Rick. I'm sure you're pretty tired, so I won't bore you with tittle-tattle. Ellie's in Europe. She left a note for you." The woman opened a drawer and took out an envelope that she handed to me. It contained one sheet of white paper on which was written Hi Rick and then there was a mobile phone number with what I thought was the Italian international prefix. It ended with All love, Ellie.

"Is Ellie in Italy?" I asked.

"No idea."

For some unknown reason I didn't want to call the number just then; I stood up, "Well, thank you for the tea."

"You're more than welcome. Are you staying in LA? Do you need anything?"

"No thanks. You're very kind." She'd walked me across the little garden and opened the gate. Outside my driver sat with the engine running, windows closed, and air-conditioning on. "When did Ellie leave for Europe?"

"I guess three months ago. Via con Dios." The gate closed and the driver now stood holding open a car door.

As he took me airportward, I phoned Ellie's number. She was not in Italy but farther south on the island of Malta and there was no direct flight from LA. The charter jet booking person assured me they could have me on my way within three hours.

Just as you may be, I was wondering how Ellie had come to know I'd show up at the Venice Beach house. Well she was a smart one and, for all I knew, may have left notes all over for me. And, it suddenly occurred, for others too, although this last thought bothered me not at all.

As you may know the island of Malta is about the size of Washington DC and lies pretty much in the middle of the Mediterranean. A hundred centuries ago, it was connected with Sicily sixty miles to the north, and megalithic monuments on Malta, Sicily and the seabed between testify to human habitation in that time. Twenty plus centuries back, the Romans had it, appreciating its strategic position between their city and Carthage. Twelve hundred or so years later, crusader knights took the place over, and their descendants are still there today, along with the rest of an extraordinary polyglot population. Their language is as exotic as the ethnic mix having Latin, Turkish, Arabic and English roots it is written in European script: about everybody there speaks practical English. When Britain had its empire Malta, like Gibraltar to the west and the island of

Cyprus to the east, was a strategic colony facilitating naval domination of the Mediterranean and hence protection of sea routes to India and the Far East via the then Anglo-French owned Suez Canal.

I learned all this from an in-flight Internet connection I consulted between sleeping none too well, stretching my legs when we refueled somewhere in one of the Carolinas and the next day quickly buying some clothes in Madrid airport whilst we refueled again. It was perhaps indicative of my state of mind that I just binned my soiled clothing.

Ellie was awaiting me at the airport. "Private jet all the way—that's rather rich. I'd better fix my makeup." She'd hugged me briefly. "Didn't run to a proper bathroom though— let's get you home." Malta is small, some seventeen by nine miles and, although it was my first time there, everything seemed curiously familiar. That's not the best word to describe the feeling; what I mean is that Malta did not seem strange or unknown, just totally as expected despite my having had no conscious expectations or prior knowledge of the place beyond what I'd read during the flight.

I started to drift in and out of sleep as she drove through narrow streets and roads to a small town in the island's interior. We stopped in the courtyard of a white Arabic-style house. A late middle-aged woman appeared just too, too obviously sizing me up as potential wicked lover/ abusive husband material "This'll be your mum will it?" I asked.

Ellie grinned and put an arm round the woman. "I think she sometimes thinks she is. "Anuncia meet Mr. Rick." I held out my hand and the woman shook it with a mixture of surly deference and coyness overlaid with suspicion.

"I can see I'll have to keep an eye on you, Anuncia." I couldn't resist a wink as I handed her my grip.

"Rick I should explain there's only one bed here, if you can't bear that I'll get Anuncia's husband to get something put in for you." I said nothing because there was nothing to say; the last thing on my mind was sex with Ellie or anybody else; and both she and I knew this; we each also knew that simple physical closeness would not hurt me and was probably one of the things I needed. The difference at that moment was that Ellie knew this consciously and I did not.

After a long time in the shower and without drying I put on a bathrobe and, following the sound of voices, went down through empty rooms to a large kitchen. Anuncia's shortcomings were not in the soup-making department—it settled my stomach nicely before sleep beckoned and I nodded off where I sat. Each woman took an arm and led me upstairs to Ellie's bed.

Sunshine woke me still wearing the bathrobe, I stumbled into the bathroom to pee. "Out here," Ellie called. I found her on a flat roof that adjoined the bedroom, she sat on cushions scattered around a low brass table on which sat a coffee pot and a plate of little croissanty stuff. Above the sky was a beautiful clean blue and beyond the low white parapet of the roof the entire island sloped away in every direction toward the distant sea. Ellie stood up; she wore some sort of cotton caftan and seemingly nothing else; taking an arm she led me to face north. "There's Rome and Europa." She turned me to face in the opposite way. "There's Carthage and Africa." Now she turned me to my left. "In that direction, Babylon, Egypt, Jerusalem, and beyond them, India and China." She turned me again and took me around the outside of her bedroom's wall to another section of flat roof. "And that way lies Spain and the Americas—now have some coffee." She led me back to the low table.

"You left out Oz, you dumb sheila."

"You reckon, huh." She poured coffee.

"You seem pretty settled here," I said. She didn't reply but looked right at me; I looked right back at her and I realized I somehow knew her more than just knowing her, so I changed gear. "You all right, kid?"

"I guess time will tell."

"What happened in LA?"

"Growing up happened—in London I'd realized I wasn't Dave's mother and in LA I had a dream and knew that whatever I may be, my role is not that of Cesar's wife."

"And Cesar?"

"He's ex now, and yes, I do feel a bit of a shit about his first marriage— if it wasn't me he would have left her for somebody else though." She spoke evenly.

"When we first met, you seemed sort of in awe of him."

"He's very special but, ultimately, lost human being and I've a lot of respect for him." she spoke with no trace of bitterness.

"I'd figured it was a father-figure or power thing."

"Yes, yes, yes. Women get off on power, but dig down and sex is a lot about power—about who's in control of who. Sex without love is either simple lust, which is good if shallow, or it's a control game, which is fucking sad. It's about who's really got the power."

Not sure if she was posing a question I said, "I suppose that usually both think they have it but as long as neither really has a monopoly the game goes on…"

She interrupted "…and nature has won because there will never be stasis and so there will always be life? I not sure that's you Rick, my darling man. I think that's you trying to make it all sound like it might make some sense."

I said. "Perhaps it is me now…but you, so you won and just got bored?"

"No! I mean, yes. I won, and I got bored, but I'd have stayed. You know a deal is a deal, and I could have done my own thing there—given that we were married I about had carte blanche career-wise. Try these, they're delicious." She put a little cake in my mouth. It was a sugary affair with whole raspberries inside. "No, Rick, maybe I'm mad or deranged but there's something about people I can't take anymore. I'm sort of Buddhist—very tolerant. We all have to make money to eat and clothe and house ourselves and so on, that's sanity, but making money seems to have become the end in itself for so many people. The whole fucking world seems obsessed with not just having money but having more than the next person. What they really want is to be envied! To provoke jealousy! That makes no sense to me—it makes me ill." She poured some coffee into her cup and mine.

"Nowadays that really chimes with me, Ellie. I mean really." I gestured beyond the parapet and asked. "Are they so different here?"

"No, of course not, but, if you ignore a couple of tourist places, they're less intense about it. Maybe I *am* crazy, but I do feel it's gone past some quantum point, and that it's going to implode. Whether it does or not, I feel better away from the centers of it. Consumption has its moments but was never really my bag."

"I thought acting was, though—you seemed enthusiastic. Has that changed ?"

"Yeah, I guess. In truth, I've got the looks and figured it as an easy number, but it's not so simple. You know, Rick, I met big people and not only can they act, they have passion. Some of them were born to act to the camera. I discovered I wasn't born to and that I wasn't all that dedicated." Putting on a pair of sunglasses, she lay back on a large cushion: the years since I'd last seen her had made her more beautiful to look at; her face had more character and her figure seemed different. It came to me that she now wore her body as if she was more comfortable with it. There was a remarkably lack of traffic noise and we remained in silence for a while until she said, "Rick, I've got a motorboat. Come out on it with me ?"

"Only if you tell me about the note," I answered.

She stood and the daylight passed through the thin cotton of her caftan; she looked openly at me looking openly at her. She wasn't being sluttish; she was being something more. This was no bimbo—this was a very deep, clever, and reflective woman. Not for one moment did I doubt she had an agenda, and not for one moment did I doubt my trust in her. Going into her bedroom, she called back, "Give me ten to get ready. I'll tell you about the note later."

Later at the coast, we'd parked on the road and entered a dilapidated and apparently empty fisherman's house. She'd opened an internal door to steps that led down to another door. Beyond this was what looked to be a small but serious Sunseeker mounted on its launching trailer. Impressed I said, "Well this is a relief. I was a bit worried that your rant might mean we would be going on some old tub stinking of fish."

A servo motor opened the metal grill in front of the boathouse and an electric winch let the boat's trailer move smoothly down the slipway into the harbor beyond. Within twenty minutes we were powering out across gentle swell. The boat seemed as simple to drive as a car. Ellie handled it with confidence, and she looked very good doing so: I told her as much.

"Thanks, that was sweet of you," she said.

"It's the truth, girl."

"I know that stupid, but it was still sweet of you to tell me. Now be even sweeter and take the wheel for a moment please." I did, and she started fiddling about with the boat's electronics. Four hooded screens illuminated in front of me—one a depth sonar and compass heading, another a combined geo-sat positioning system and sat-nav, and the third was radar, and the fourth was what I was to learn was a Russian military sat-nav system as backup. "What's up? Are we expecting world war three?" I'd asked.

"Hope not. I can only get them all on together." I turned the boat to align it with second screen's direction indicator, settled back in the seat and enjoyed driving the beautiful, powerful boat. "Open her up if you want," Ellie said, and I did. As the boat rocketed forward it seemed to leap the waves and three decades fell away from me to leave a thrilled eleven-year-old boy breathing salt spray and producing just the right amount of adrenaline for life to be just one great, huge, splendid wonderful thing. After about forty miles the waves were growing larger causing the boat to shudder as it flew then crashed through them and Ellie to cling on to her seat so I throttled back.

Noise reduced we could speak and she said, "Your face was a picture, Rick. I've never seen you look so happy."

"This is a fabulous boat. She was doing fifty plus back there—when did you get her?" I didn't know why but I felt vaguely embarrassed that the younger me had been so visible.

"Around six months ago," she opened a small locker and pulled out a chart of Pantelleria. Whilst I drove the boat slowly and carefully toward the island, we talked.

It turned out that after buying the empty harbor-side house from Alexei, she discovered the boat in it. After a night of thinking about it, she emailed him to say it was there; a week later she got a call from a local lawyer asking her to come in and pick up the boat's ownership documents. Tucked among them was a faxed note from Alexei asking her to please accept and enjoy the craft as a gift. "Kind of impressive—was he hungry for your little butt…?" I asked.

"I wondered about that, so I rang him to ask. He's supposed to be asexual, you know, and although I don't fancy him in the least that sort of thing's a challenge for any woman."

I found I was not entirely unshockable. "Just watch out for a bloke called Baa," I cautioned. "But Ellie, you really rang Alexei and asked 'are you trying to shag me'?'"

"In about as many words, he laughed a lot and said he wouldn't know how, but perhaps in the next life. He said for some reason I made him feel very Russian and this made him prone to expansive gestures. Alexei's obviously incredibly rich, but he seems of a different order entirely from about everybody else. I really don't quite know where he's at—I only met him the once."

"Where was that?"

"In LA. Big fish including my then husband were courting mega money for investments, and Alexei is mega. We sort of gravitated to each other at a party, and somehow your name came into the conversation."

My ego perked up and I said, "Yeah, Alexei talks about me most days I shouldn't wonder…" Ellie gave me a look. "Okay, okay, so how did my name come up in a conversation between two strangers?"

"Via Dave. They'd met at your house." As she said this, I suddenly recalled an evening Teresa and I had Alexei to dinner when Dave was staying with us. "So ignoring all the big fish at this thing in LA, there was Alexei asking me if I understood synchronicity. I said sort of and gave him Jung's definition 'an act of creation in time.' I don't think he made any investments with my husband. He seemed to unnerve everybody, but we kept in touch through Emily." I must have looked blank for she sighed, "Emily! The lady with the house at Venice Beach that I rented. She's a world-class chess player, and she and Alexei play by e-mail!"

"Silly me, I should have realized that and possibly lots of other stuff, but how did you come to buy the fisherman house from a bloke you met once half a world away?"

"We were talking about the Mediterranean and I told him about my house here - where we stayed last night - and he said he'd this harbor house he wanted to sell because so many other Russians were buying here and he was concerned that they'd nose around his affairs once he got on their radar."

"Yeah, that's pretty much Alexei." I confirmed.

"Anyway he didn't do any favors on the price, but I figured it a good investment so bought it with some screenplay writing money I'd earned and royalty money that had been accumulating from Dave's will." I fancied I saw a shadow flit across her countenance.

"Dave had made a will?"

Her defensive look told me he'd still a place in her heart whatever she might claim. "You didn't know? You're in it too. Our beautiful easy-going Dave was surprisingly organized underneath—and more successful than I'd known. He left me a third of his royalties. I forget what he left you." She pointed to a narrow cove in the rocky cliffs topped with luxuriant green foliage. "This is Cossyra, daughter of the wind."

We anchored on a very short line and waded ashore, bought freshly sliced prosciutto and melon, and water at a mini-mercado. Then we hiked up a slope to picnic beneath trees beside the track.

I'd still questions to ask, but sea air awakens appetite, so I decided to put food in rather than let words out as we sat surrounded by nature's perfumes and birdsong. A piece of melon wrapped in a slice of prosciutto looked just right, but I found I couldn't swallow it. The throat wasn't constricted; the food in my mouth tasted perfectly good but whatever muscle sequence we use to swallow just would not function. After a moment I spat the food out into my hands and threw it away. Thinking I needed fluid, I tried to drink from a plastic bottle of mineral water but couldn't swallow that either so also spat it out. All the while Ellie sat watching with an extraordinary intensity. "Let it out, Rick. Let it all out," she said and I did. An ocean poured from my eyes as overpowering anguish wracked my entire body. Any sort of thought that might have been was drowned before its birth in that flood; only feeling existed in the world and the feeling was of hurt. Emotions came like an express train and smashed through my being. I was dimly aware of rolling on the ground, too hurt to be angry, too hurt to blame, too hurt to care who or what or where I was. Blackness came when that volcano of emotion had poured out the hurt and bitterness and pain. I slept. I slept in an Arcadian glade with arms about me and who knows what eyes of the night watching. I slept the sleep of a child, which is to sleep in the moment not as some transaction between consciousness and its limitations. I slept the sleep of a small freedom not that of brutish exhaustion.

I awoke with my head cradled in Ellie's arms and saw the moon and the first evening star beyond her head. "So he awakens," she said theatrically. "No, don't get up yet…" She used mineral water to clean dried snot from my beneath my nose. "Right, you look passable. Let's see if we can find a bed." We couldn't but did beg, for they were able to understand my Spanish, a couple of blankets and, wrapped in these and each other, slept on the beach until dawn woke us. The ancient woman whose son-in-law had lent us the blankets inched her way across the sunlit beach with a little pot of coffee and two cups. Before we left her husband appeared, in rumpled trousers and vest with several days beard on his face, and he favored us with what must have been his entire repertoire of coughing for what seemed like an hour before telling me the secret of life. His withered hand clutched my forearm. "Don't waste time with women, even a beauty like yours," he counseled. "A glass of wine and a good pair of shoes is what it's all about."

We circled Pantelleria to the harbor, where we refueled and Ellie confirmed what the old man had said to me in Italian. A little later eating pasta for lunch outside a restaurant I recalled us doing the same thing together a million years ago in London. I mentioned this to Ellie who affected not to remember but back on her boat she said. "So you bought me pasta in London did you, Mick?" She kissed my cheek. "Now let the big girl show you how to drive this baby!"

Asleep in the house in the middle of Malta, Ellie's arms were wrapped around my body, pinning my arms to my sides. From the depths of my sleep arose a sob so massive that I woke, lost in an inky darkness but such is the miracle of woman that her arms tightened their hold without her waking. Her arms had tightened as her body understood what my head could not and her's didn't need to. I went back to sleep comforted in a curiously impersonal way and woke up with an erection I didn't want and no Ellie. She was downstairs sorting out some sort of shopping list with Anuncia who today favored me with a kindlier glare than previously. On the kitchen table a change of my clothes lay washed and neatly folded. "Anuncia could you pick me up a couple of T-shirts..." I started to ask, but Ellie told her not to as she'd be getting them herself. In fact we all went off together to some tourist town on the coast and, whilst Anuncia bought food, Ellie got me trunks and other bits and pieces.

Back at the house we unloaded the car and I went up on the roof alone, lay down on a lounger and watched dozens of small birds flying high in the clear sky. Ellie came and lay next to me. "They migrate between Europe and Africa with the seasons," she told me. "On the south coast the locals build hides and gun them down as they come inland from across the sea—a source of protein for the islanders."

"I wouldn't have thought they needed little birds."

"Maybe they don't now, but they did once and maybe they will again. We live in strange times—gosh, Rick, I'm doing enigmatic."

"And so well it sounds almost oracular," I told her.

"There's no need to be obscene." Turning on her side, she raised herself on an elbow so that she looked down at my face and blocked out a lot of the sky. "You see for nature to work, we have to be divided, and those divisions ensure that we have the deepest most durable program. We have a prime drive to try and reunite, and it works amazingly on so many levels—sperm to egg keeps the gene pool healthy, light to dark keeps the psyche developing. Who knows, we just might end up knowing God's name...but that's not really your trip is it?"

I didn't reply because I couldn't connect what she'd said with the migrating birds. In truth Ellie was smarter and deeper than most. She got up and went away, returning with a couple of glasses and a bottle of champagne. "Would you?" she handed me the ice-cold bottle. I opened it and poured whilst she went over to sit on the cushions. Handing her a glass I remained standing and looked east from where the evening hours approached, bringing with them a sense of something downbeat as if especially for me.

"You know where so many get it wrong?" she said and I made no reply. "They think it's about the pursuit of happiness. Maybe a mistranslation from the French…you see, only children can be happy. What it's really about is the pursuit of contentment and you only get contentment from fulfillment."

"You think?"

"No, Rick, I know. I don't mean fulfillment of ambition I mean fulfillment of what each of us is in essence—we have to know we descend from something, something higher that we have to recognize, and then use our intelligence and feelings to develop it here in our individual lives. It's not about sweetness and light; it's about shit and light."

"No gain without pain, huh ?" Childishly, I wanted to be insensitive to hurt her.

"Maybe as long as you understand all the pain in the world could never guarantee any gain. It's about using what you were given to understand what gave it to you." Her voice was extraordinarily relaxed. I didn't reply, the approaching dusk was now accompanied by a melancholy, and time suspended. Then I found Ellie was by my side. "So science boy," she ruffled my nowadays thinning hair, and I didn't mind her doing it, in fact I rather liked her doing it. "These bits of atoms—what were they again?"

My mood improved as I sought refuge in the impersonal. "Electrons, protons and neutrons."

"Ah, yes—and you said all atoms have them except hydrogen, which only has..?"

"An electron and a proton." I stretched and luxuriated in the setting sun's warming of my back.

"And the sun turns hydrogen into helium by fusion." Back by the cushions she mixed orange juice with champagne, and I suddenly recalled that morning an eon ago on the *Isabellisima* with Isabelle and Teresa. That recollection was a knife that wounded and Ellie's expression told me my pain had shown. Ellie knows how to handle pain and said, "Look, stay focused here man—the sun turns hydrogen into helium by fusion, right?"

"Well, broadly, yes, I suppose."

"And helium has electrons and protons and neutrons?"

"Yes."

"So, it gets the electrons and protons from the hydrogen, but where do those neutrons come from, Rick?"

"Well, what you really have to grasp is that just because there's a name for something doesn't mean that that something is understood. All it means is that that something seems to exist, and it seems to exist because of the way other things, including us, react to it."

"Are you becoming a lawyer?"

I ignored that and continued, "It's complicated in the sense that all of these things are just energies that react with a background field—in a sense they're just sort of swirls in that field—you know how a wave's top in the sea sometimes foams."

"Look, I could deny you supper!"

"You should have said you were serious," I sighed. "I guess neutrons could be composed of neutrinos, three types of neutrinos seem to exist, and they seem to interchange with each other. I don't really know much about them."

"Rick do you think neutrinos could be thoughts?" Undeterred by my not immediately answering, she continued, "You know people worshipped the sun, in fact you could say that for human beings the sun was their first idea of god. And if the sun adds neutrons to hydrogen, and if neutrons are made up of neutrinos, and if neutrinos are thoughts, and the Creator thought this universe into being so that it could create…"

Like I said Ellie was a smart woman.

"Baby, that foam on the waves…" I started.

"Yes, and…?"

"Well maybe it's a possibility or maybe it's a probability…" I began but she interrupted me.

"Between those two maybes lies theology and physics and psychology and games of chance—do you suppose gamblers are trying for acts of creation?"

"You know, Ellie, you really are as stupid as you're boring," I kissed her forehead.

The following day we didn't leave the house and spent the afternoon on the double lounger I'd had delivered. That very morning I'd
struggled boxes up the stairs and assembled it, losing my temper with the
instructions and myself; also receiving a patronizing kiss, soothing comments and a nice lunch from Ellie.

The roof was not overlooked so we sunbathed naked on our backs;
looking a lot better than good, she prods me with an elegant foot. "Leave
me alone," I tell her. A hand on my thigh is used to lever herself slowly
upright.

"Rick?"

"Yes?" I close my eyes.

"Why is your penis getting hard?" She seems to be rearranging her
position.

"No idea—why don't you ask it?"

"Huh, you'll be lucky. Do my back please, would you?"

I discover myself to be sitting up with eyes open and hands squeezing
cream out of a tube. The moment I start putting it on her back, I know
and she knows. It's as if her body stretches like a cat, and she purrs. My
heart is beating fast, and she raises her pretty arse just enough to cause
the cheeks to open by some infinitesimal measurement that my entire
being registers and reacts to. I don't know what to do—I believe my
heart is still not and may never be mended but my body is on fire. I like
and appreciate this woman immensely, I respect her, and I desire her. I
certainly don't want to hurt her. I watch as my hands gently knead her
glorious arse which immediately raises again just enough more for my
hands to slip between her legs. My hands do not have a will of their own,
but they have become involved in some timeless ritual with her body—
her clitoris draws my fingers to it and, leaning across her back, I kiss the
nape of her neck as her orgasm shakes her.

She turns and her look tells me that she knows almost too much; her
lips press hard on mine and her fingers take my penis. That's all it takes.

My body tells me this was right for I am human and it seems the
heart concurs; I feel kilos lighter and my sperm is gluing Ellie's body
to mine. I start to say something, but she shushes me saying, "This is no
moment for smart-arse comments." She's right.

I don't recall us having any conversation but after a while we took
a shower together and made love again on her bed. It was very good; I
couldn't escape from a feeling bordering on certainty that we'd discovered

something. We dozed and then we made love again. Some time after she rested on one elbow and, looking down at my face, said "You look a whole lot better—do you feel good?"

"Good's not the word—I feel alive, I feel content, and I feel harmony," I said.

Ellie continued looking at me for a long time and then said, "Promise me you'll never delude yourself by striving for harmony—harmony is stasis, and therefore can't exist much. Just strive for balance, Rick. You used be in the metals business, right?" I nodded "Well even metal grows in the moonlight."

Ellie is Ellie. Back in another age when Baa had met her, he'd said that she was a wet dream with a computer inside, but I don't think it's a computer at all. "Yeah Beautiful, that might be all right for you, but for a dullard such as myself, working at harmony is my thing—perhaps my raison d'etre."

"Then you're doubly lucky to have me aren't you, shit-for-brains?"

"So, I have you, do I ?" She just looked at me and I looked right back at her "So I have you, Einstein?"

After a while she sighs and says, "Well actually you do seem to at the moment not quite shit-for-brains." She lowers her head to kiss me, and her left nipple touches my right. "I do believe you know what I mean—always balance because everything is always in motion, even when it seems not to be."

"You mean like the second law of thermo whats-its?" I want to tease her because, impossibly, my loins are what's termed stirring, again.

"You and those airport bookstalls! Like a lot of stuff treated as absolute facts the second law of thermodynamics is only absolute within certain parameters, and that means it is not absolute at all…but it is a partial illustration."

While she was showering, I went out on to the roof again. The sun was low in the sky now, and I watched an airliner climb across it. I felt her next to me, and each put an arm around the other's waist. "I'm not going to reproduce in this life." As she spoke the sinking sun touched the western horizon and a great wave of sadness struck me. It was strange for that sadness wasn't for me; Ellie not wanting children was if anything a relief to me, neither was it sadness for her because she was an extraordinary person and strong enough to make decisions that were completely her own.

I reflected on this sadness, trying to examine it, and felt it was a sadness of the soul for the spirit. I told her this while she still stood beside
me facing west. Turning she said "That's when I like you best, Rick, when
you speak from the heart. I love to hear the heart speak."

"Everything else is just function or shit right?" I prompted, unsure
whether she was being patronizing. Yes I know, you're right, she'd
unnerved me again.

"Or humor or play or construction or destruction or a thousand
things, and you know this so please don't insult my and your own intelligence." Her hand squeezed my backside. "Or I won't share my fabulous
treat with you." She brushed softly against me as she walked back into the
bedroom. My whole being smiled for knowing more and more of this
woman, I appreciate her apparent eccentricities for what they are—her
adaptedness to reality.

I lit a big candle in the earthenware bowl on the table and moved to
the new double lounger and lay back. Sure enough, Ellie emerges from
the bedroom with a plate of chocolate truffles.

•   •   •

The limo took me up the drive to the splendid if not vast house in
Montecino where Ellie waits at the open door. We hug and are aware
how we relax into each other's arms "This gravity that attracts us to each
other makes us—so does it make love or is it made by love?" she tells and
asks in the same breath. She often comes out with stuff like that, but I
always forgive her.

I kiss her. In this piece of time life feels good with a capital G and I
luxuriate in that feeling as we head for the bedroom. Meridinha taps on
the door and tells me a dour-faced man waits in the drive. He insists I
listen to a mobile phone after he has dialed a number. Alexei's recorded
voice says, "Be quick—you guys should leave right now. Remember the
old yard where we spoke?"

I hand the phone back to the Russian who returns to his car and
drives away.

"Who was that?" asks Ellie coming down our rather nice staircase.

"Nobody, sweetheart. But put some stuff and your passport in a bag. We should to leave very quickly. She turns on the stairs and goes back up; just how great is this woman who never asks pointless questions? In my heart I know this is as it should be for we're not in a real lalaland—we're here and now, and there are heavy matters on the horizon.

•   •   •

EPILOGUE:

Alexei, huge and indefatigable, stood just outside the great circle of new megaliths. He was pondering, as had many through the ages, that everything causes its opposite. That nothing causes all, that life causes death. It was almost as if another, a voice from somewhere inside, quietly told him"That's true in so far as it goes, but it's not quite that simple — there's a third component, a catalyst."

www.ingramcontent.com/pod-product-compliance
Lightning Source LLC
Chambersburg PA
CBHW070846250626
47159CB00003B/955